Few Are
CHOSEN

RALPH SORENSEN

To Bruce —
Thanks for dropping
by Table One — Sir
The best to you
From Paradise
Ralph Sorensen

Lucky Press

Copyright © 2000, Ralph Sorensen

Few Are Chosen is a work of fiction based on true-life episodes. Names have been changed, and the characters and events described are not intended to factually represent any specific person or event.

Published by:
Lucky Press
126 S. Maple St.
Lancaster, Ohio 43130
740-689-2950
www.indypub.com/fewarechosen
E-mail: info@indypub.com

PRINTED IN THE UNITED STATES OF AMERICA
BOOK PRODUCTION BY PHELPS & ASSOCIATES, LLC
COVER DESIGN BY KNOCKOUT DESIGN

Cataloging-in-Publication Data
(Provided by Quality Books, Inc.)

Sorensen, Ralph.
   Few are chosen / Ralph Sorensen. -- 1st ed.
   p. cm.
   LCCN: 99-96595
   ISBN: 0-9676050-1-6

   1. West Virginia--Fiction 2. Fathers and sons
--West Virginia--Fiction. 3. Fighter pilots--
Fiction. I. Title.

PS3569.O67585F49 2000   813'54
            QBI99-1649

ACKNOWLEDGMENTS

MANY AUTHORS EXPRESS THEIR UTMOST APPRECIATION FOR THE HELP AND consideration of their spouses during the difficult times of putting a book together. This author is no exception. Thank you, Deborah.

I'm also most grateful for the encouragement and praise given by Noreen, Mary Anne, and Roofer Ralph. All in the Fort Myers, Florida area.

Special recognition is given to "Table One" of the Mariner Inn located at Flamingo Beach, Costa Rica. The members — Gene, Donna and Nick Martin, Jimmy and Katie, Larry, Sonny, Dave, Dick, Ron, Doc, Jack, Dave H., Mark, Billy, Tim Barrow, Willy, and Onyx — all self-admitted nuts (and yes, thank you, I hope to be included) relaxed at Table One and provided the needed incentive to complete the manuscript. Their adventurous, international spirit made it possible to publish this book.

Muchas Gratias.

CHAPTER ONE

BURT HAD NEVER TRIED TO CROSS ON THE ICE. IT SOUNDED RISKY, AND HE didn't want to jeopardize his job … or his life. He needed both, especially the job. *But today is different. She may have the baby, and I should be there. She needs me.*

There has to be plenty of ice. I'll go for it.

When he left that morning at four o'clock, his wife, Rose, was not well. "Maybe it's time for the baby," she said. "I hope not … such a miserable day. But you have to go to work, sweetheart … I'll be all right. Now, don't you worry."

He did worry though, because he loved his wife, and he wanted her to be okay. And she was so young, only sixteen when they had married nine months ago. But he wasn't ready to be a father at eighteen. It was too much responsibility to have a child. It was scary. *It should have happened later,* he thought, *not now when it's tough to make a living. They told me I shouldn't marry a Catholic girl. No birth control, and damn, she became pregnant the night of the wedding.*

But she was right; he couldn't take off from work. It was 1932 and jobs were hard to find, and he had a good one. He delivered sliced bread and fruit pies to the grocery store.

IT WAS THE FIFTH HOUR OF LABOR FOR ROSE IN THE HOSPITAL, AND SHE WAS scared. It was her first child, and she wanted Burt, her husband, to be at her side. But she realized that he had to work because jobs were hard to find.

During the sixth hour of labor, the baby boy, the one she called Erik, was born. Before Rose had a good look at her new child, the nurse took Erik away for his cleanup and a check-in to the baby hotel, the nursery. His aunts and uncles saw the child and concluded that he was born with a banana head (at least a head shaped like one). Then they visited the new mother, and with tears in their eyes they said, "Don't worry Rose, he's going to be just fine. Yes … he's going to be a fine boy."

"Is he a beautiful baby?" she asked.

"He's a fine boy, Rose … a fine boy with blue eyes." And they all left in haste.

When Rose saw her new child, the one she named Erik, she knew why they were teary-eyed … and why they had departed in haste. She also cried.

Erik's head did resemble a banana, but the doctor said that it was probably a temporary situation, just some cosmetic damage due to the long labor. He ensured Rose that Erik would be a normal healthy son, that his head would reshape, someday … probably.

That was Erik's first day with his family.

THE SKY WAS DARKER, AND THE CROSSWIND MADE IT DIFFICULT TO KEEP THE TRUCK on the road. A two-ton Ford van painted white. *Damn, I'll never get home at this rate.* The nasty wind and icy roads made it impossible for Burt to make decent time. Then he remembered what the older drivers had told him about the shortcut. They said, "Burt, most winters you can cross the river on the ice … that's what we do. Saves an hour or so, cuts out the long run to the bridge."

He spotted an opening on the river bank and made a right turn to the edge of the frozen water. He shifted to low gear and gently eased the truck onto the ice. *All right. I think it's going to work.*

At a low speed, he forged across the half-mile icy span. A bit nervous at first, within minutes he was confident, perhaps smug. *Hell, anybody can do this … I can do this every day … well, every frozen day. It's no big deal. Another fifty yards, and I'll be on the road and make my last stop at old Cranky Anderson's. God, what an old bastard he is. My worst customer.*

Then he heard a strange sound. *The old truck is acting up,* he guessed. Then it sounded again … the sound … kind of a cracking sound. And then another. "Holy shit," he yelled to no one, "It's the ice!"

He yanked the door open, and hurled himself out of the cab. He landed flat on his stomach and skidded forward on the ice. The cracking noise became louder as he listened to the ice splinter behind him. With a quick glance over his shoulder, he saw his truck cling momentarily — as if making its final attempt to remain aloft — then disappear into the cold black water.

He remained flat on his belly, and he felt his heart pounding against the frigid ice. He realized that he could be the next one to fall into a perilous black hole. He lay there motionless on the barren ice, afraid to breathe. Burt still heard a cracking noise, but it was less audible. *I have to chance it,* he decided, and, with delicate breaststrokes, he eased himself forward until the cracking sound ceased. He continued the stroke until he felt the safety of thick ice. He sat up, turned, and stared at the dark ominous hole for several lonely moments. It was hard for him to believe that the old Wonder Bread truck was gone.

He began to grasp the seriousness of the incident. It was a significant loss, and the repercussions could be harsh. In spite of this, he had to grin — a grin of resignation.

This is not a good day. Cranky Anderson will be upset, and the boss will not take this casually.

Burt made the lonesome trek to the main road where he tried to hitch a ride. There was no traffic, so a cold, miserable Burt walked toward the nearest phone, which unfortunately was located at Anderson's store, some three miles down the road. He wasn't dressed for such a hike, and he noticed his fingers turning blue in color, and they were numb. He decided his feet belonged to someone else, not much feeling left. And without a hat, his head was wet, and the moisture tried to freeze. He was not a pretty sight when he finally arrived at Cranky Anderson's. As he fumbled at the door, it sprang open from the inside, and there stood Mr. Anderson. He didn't seem to recognize Burt, the forlorn hiker.

"Mr. Anderson, I'm Burt ... Burt Larson, your bread man, sir."

Mr. Anderson looked surprised. "Oh, yes, Christ, what a mess you are, and you're late. Where's my bread?"

"Sir, I'm sorry, I don't have the bread."

"What do you mean you don't have the bread?" Mr. Anderson looked out to search the area and said, "I don't see the truck."

"Well, your bread is in the river."

"In the river? What the hell are you talking about?"

"Yes sir, in the river, with the truck ... I lost my truck ... and your bread."

"You lost the bread ... My bread? You can't do that. I have people waiting for it," he yelled. "My customers depend on me. What the hell am I supposed to do?"

Burt started to tell him what to do, but thought better—it would not be polite, and he would be fired. Instead, he said, "I'm sorry about the bread, Mr. Anderson … and I must call my wife because she could be in labor. Can I use your phone, sir?"

"No, you can't use the phone. I have to call and find some bread. I knew you were no damn good when I met you. Some lousy kid trying to play grown-up while I struggle to make a living. Now, no bread … you get your ass down the road." He shook his head in exasperation and stomped off.

Burt was upset and cold as he trudged to the next phone. He had never been told that he was no damn good before. *What a bastard and what a day.* Near exhaustion, he made it to the gas station and used the phone.

First, he called his boss at the bakery. The boss was most sympathetic when Burt told him about his wife and possible labor … and the misplaced truck. The boss said he wished the wife well and hoped they had a fine baby.

Then he told Burt, "You're fired!"

After regaining some composure, Burt called his house. There was no answer. He then called the hospital, and the nurse told him that Rose was there, resting well with a newborn boy.

"May I talk with her?" he asked.

"That's impossible, because we don't have phones in the rooms. Your wife is resting, and the baby is a bit bruised, but we think he'll be just fine. It has to be a happy day for you and your wife."

"Well, thank you, it is," replied Burt, even though he wasn't that happy to be a father.

And he thought it inappropriate to tell the nurse he had just been fired.

That was Burt's first day as a father.

CHAPTER TWO

I T WAS A ROCKY TWO MONTHS UNTIL BURT WAS BLESSED WITH A NEW JOB AND Erik was blessed with a normal-shaped head. It was no longer shaped like a banana, even though his dad called him Banana Head on occasions, but never around Rose; she didn't like it.

Neither did Erik.

Burt found a job at a meat-packing plant, and, after training to be a meat cutter, he went on the road as a salesman … with a truck. He was a good salesman, and they eventually transferred the family (with a five-year-old Erik) to West Virginia to establish their products.

Erik's dad was on the road during the week while his mother stayed at home to care for their son. She was a gentlewoman, pretty, and always a lady. She loved God, her neighbors, and her family. But most of all, she loved her husband, Burt. He was the King, and no one in the family ever doubted it. No one.

The King was one of five children of Danish immigrants. His father, Lief, told him that he left Denmark because of the famine. However, rumors said he left to avoid the draft. Regardless, he was a hard worker and a stern, uncompromising disciplinarian.

A short stocky man with reddish hair and bull-like strength, he often bragged about the strict upbringing of his sons. He boasted about the frequent punishment he dispensed to all in his family — including his wife, if he thought she deserved it. With pride, he told his friends how he beat the boys if they got out of line.

He showed them the special paddle he had made for that purpose. He would split a three-foot coupling hose — the heavy air hose that connected railway cars — and then nail the two strips of hose to a hard oak handle.

"You leave some real marks on der asses with dis strap," he would say in broken English. "And dey needs dis a lot."

It wasn't cruel by his standards because he was a good family man who worked hard to provide a house, food and clothing. He didn't think he abused his wife because he only struck her on occasions when he deemed it necessary. It was the Christian and manly thing to do, concluded Lief.

His son, Burt, had learned well. He also believed in the Christian and manly thing. Rigid and unyielding, Burt was a tyrant in many ways. He didn't think his discipline was as cruel as his father's because he didn't use a coupling hose. He only used his hand or a belt, but he used them frequently.

Erik hated dinnertime with his father even though they always had meat when he was present. The quick, sharp smack from Burt's hand to Erik's face was a painful reality of family life. A sudden blow to his face would send him and his chair reeling to the floor. His mother winced, but knew to remain quiet. Erik struggled to hold back the tears. To cry would certainly bring another blow. Just a small blow to stop his crying.

Still, Erik loved his dad and wanted to be with him. He guessed that he must deserve the punishment, or his dad wouldn't think it was necessary to dole it out. Besides, Erik rationalized, he never saw him hit his mother. His dad did, however, make his mother cry during arguments, and they argued often, but he never hit her. *Mom was so proud of that fact.* "Your father has never hit me, " she said to Erik, "and I know other men hit their wives ... but your father would never do it."

Erik reasoned that Burt must be a pretty good guy because he didn't hit his wife.

ERIK SPENT HIS EARLY SCHOOL YEARS IN SAINT MATTHEW'S PARISH SCHOOL. IT was a typical Catholic school, with rigid, strict discipline that provided a good solid education. With the inquisitive mind of a bright youngster, Erik wanted to learn everything. He especially enjoyed the teachings of the Church, and he could recite his catechism word for word. It was a comfort to Erik, knowing that there was a God who knew and loved him. He spent many hours reflecting on this knowledge, and it made him feel warm and secure.

One afternoon, his fifth grade teacher, Sister Mary Elizabeth, announced, "Class, I'm appointing Erik as the blackboard writer because he has such beautiful penmanship, he's a good altar boy, and is devoted to the teachings of the Church." Erik was overwhelmed with such an honor. To write out assignments and other material on the blackboard was an award of distinction. He proudly told his dad, "Sister Mary appointed me as blackboard writer."

"Blackboard writer, what the hell is that ... some sissy-ass stuff?" his dad said, with no desire to entertain Erik's response.

It was morning recess, and all of the kids were doing their own thing, girls on one side, boys on the other. Erik stood outside of the boy group when the schoolyard bully, Gino, and three of his suck-up followers approached him. Gino Giuseppe was his full name. He was a domineering fat-ass who thought he was hot stuff because his father was rich. At least that's what Erik was told. "Hey, got a problem in there, you teacher's pet asshole?" he asked Erik.

"No, I don't have a problem, Gino."

"You sure as hell do ... big mouth ... who does the blackboard writing," Gino said as he gave Erik a little shove.

"No, Gino, I ... " Erik was worried ... scared. This is not going right, he thought.

"You little prick," Gino said as he grabbed Erik and pulled him up against him. Erik could smell the grease and garlic from his mouth and hair. Then Gino lifted him off his feet and slammed him into the solid ground. He stood over Erik with his fat face leering, and then turned and waddled off with his buddies ... all laughing at the "little prick."

Erik picked himself up. The slam to the playground had knocked his wind out, and he had to gasp for air. The small rocks had punctured his skin, and he hurt. And he was mad ... and scared ... scared mad. With tears in his eyes, he looked at Gino and the others with their backs toward him. *The cowboys do it in the movies ... why not?* And, with dread, he went directly over to Gino and touched him lightly on the shoulder. When Gino turned around, he had a look of puzzled disbelief. At that instant, Erik hit him one time, straight into the nose. Gino was shocked. He staggered back a foot or two, holding his nose with both hands. *Boy, I wish I hadn't done that. I know this is going to hurt ... Gino will probably kill me ... or come close to it.*

But the punch had been made, and Erik stood his ground. He waited for the fat-ass to hammer him, but it didn't happen. The blood spurted out from under

Gino's hands as he stood there. The tears found a way over his cheeks.

"You're going to get it, you little shit," Gino said, through his sobs and half gurgling sounds. Erik stood there, and the dumbfounded fans of Gino stood there. They waited for the next move. And Gino made the next move, a half-wailing departure into the school.

A minute or so later, Erik commenced breathing. And the air was good.

That afternoon, Erik was summoned to Mother Superior's office to discuss reasons why a little guy was always beating up the playground bully. It was a simple one-sided discussion ... and Mother Superior did all the one-sided part. "Erik, I'm told that you are a troublemaker," she said.

Erik was bewildered. "Mother Superior, I'm not a ... no ma'am ..."

"I'll talk to Father Donovan about my recommendation for dismissal. You belong in public school. That will be all," she said.

The next day in class, Sister Mary Elizabeth announced that she was appointing Gino as the new blackboard writer because he had good penmanship, was an altar boy, and was devoted to the teachings of the Church.

Erik was heartbroken, confused, and he told his mother the whole story that evening. "You are telling me the truth?" she asked. "This is the way it happened?"

"Yes, ma'am."

"Well, honey, you don't worry; I'll see Father Donovan tomorrow and get it straightened out."

Rose did see the good Father the next day, and she let him know that she was active in the Catholic Daughters and that she would fight to keep her son in the parish school. She let the good priest know that she would spread the word about the rich family's bully.

It must have worked, because Father Donovan decided that Erik should have another chance, because he was a good altar boy and believed in the teachings of the Church. It was a good lesson for Erik. Gino's family did have money, and it made a difference in determining right from wrong. And he was proud that his mother stood up for him. It was a first that he knew about.

But Sister Mary Elizabeth let Erik know she didn't appreciate the decision. She ignored him in class, and Erik suffered from the guilt and rejection. He wished that he could make things right, but each attempt to do so seemed to fail. He knew it would be a long school year.

Some weeks later, Sister Mary announced to the class that the Convent Home upstate, needed some trees for landscaping. She said they were looking for small evergreens, three to four feet tall, and they needed at least ten of them.

"Can any of you help us out?" she asked. Immediately, most of the hands in class reached for the sky, and Erik heard a clamor of responses. "Oh, I can, Sister ... I can ... I'll get 'em, Sister. I'll do it ... "

"Well, I hoped you would. I just knew this class would help the convent. God will bless you," she said while exposing one of her rare smiles. "And we need them in two weeks," she added, "for Christmas season."

Erik spent many hours on the mountain behind his house. He knew where to find the trees. He wasn't sure they wanted his trees, but thought it worth a try. For the next two weeks, he went out after school and dug up evergreens. He wrapped the roots in old flour sacks and watered them with attentive care.

It was Friday, the day the trees were to be turned in, and Erik had to go to school without them. His dad had said he would haul them over with the car if he was back in time — but he didn't make it back. Erik was terribly disappointed. *It could have worked.*

Sister Mary asked if the class brought in their trees and several raised their hands and replied, "Yes, we brought them, Sister."

She smiled and said, "Well, let's bring them up here ... see what we have."

Three students, Gino the bully, Little Susie, and Paul, went to the cloakroom and returned with their trees. They took them up front and piled them by Sister's desk. Erik couldn't believe it. Only four trees made up the pile, and they were the straggliest, God-awful looking trees he had ever seen. *I've hauled out used Christmas trees that looked better than those.* Sister Mary thanked them and told the class she had hoped for more, but she appreciated their efforts. The children responded with many different excuses and generally agreed they could do better next time. Erik raised his hand, and Sister Mary said, "Erik?"

"Yes, Sister. I have some trees, but they're at home."

"Well, why didn't you bring them on the bus?" she asked, showing visible agitation.

"No, Sister, I couldn't. I had too many ... Dad was going to help, but he didn't get back."

"Well, how many do you have, Erik?" she asked without smiling.

"I think twenty-five, Sister."

"Twenty-five!" she exclaimed, "You have twenty-five trees?"

"Yes ma'am, I mean, Sister, I think so." *Oh rats, I said ma'am, and now I will probably be whacked with the ole ruler. You don't call a Sister, ma'am.*

"Are you sure of that, Erik?"

"Yes ma'am. I mean, Sister." *Lord, did it again.*

Sister Mary immediately excused herself from class and left the room. She returned some minutes later with Freddy, the school's handyman.

"Erik, Mister Freddy can pick them up with our van ... Can you go with him?" she asked cheerfully.

"Yes, Sister, sure can."

They returned within the hour with the trees. Erik was apprehensive. *What if she doesn't like the trees? Lord knows what she will do ... probably put my desk out in the parking lot ... or something.* It was recess time when they pulled up to the playground and began unloading. The kids ganged around and watched. Suddenly, Sister Mary Elizabeth broke through the file and looked at the trees. Then Mother Superior appeared, and Erik wished he had never mentioned the trees. She stared at the trees with the look that only a Mother Superior could generate, and then said, "How many trees?"

"Twenty-five, ma'am ... I'm sorry, I mean, Mother Superior," Erik replied. *What a time to screw up.* Erik wished he was in Africa ... or someplace like it. All eyes were on the Mother, including Sister Mary's.

"Erik, those are the most ... beautiful blue spruces I've ever seen. So full and healthy. God will bless you for being such a fine young man," Mother Superior said. Sister Mary Elizabeth nodded in agreement.

"Thank you, ma'am," Erik replied, without noticing his verbal screw-up. He was too relieved; he was proud. It felt great to be accepted.

That afternoon, Sister Mary Elizabeth announced that Erik was re-designated as the blackboard writer because he had excellent penmanship, was an altar boy, and was devoted to the teachings of the Church.

CHAPTER THREE

THE SMALL LAKE WAS INVITING. IT DIDN'T HAVE AN OFFICIAL NAME THAT Erik had heard of, but the locals called it "the lake." Burt's brother, Bob, was on a visit from Ohio, and the family was in a festive mood when they decided to go to the lake for a Sunday picnic. It was an exciting day for Erik because of the fun things to do. Other children would be there, and he always enjoyed swinging from the tree into the water (They had a tire on a swing rope that you could loft out over the water, jump off of, and struggle back to shore).

Erik had been there once before with his family, and they had had a good time, even though he almost drowned when he stepped into a hole. In desperation, he promptly learned to dog paddle. *I'm a better swimmer now, certainly no Tarzan, but passable. Some day I want to swim like Dad does.* Erik envied him; he was good at everything, and Erik wanted to be just like him.

THEY ARRIVED AT A FAVORITE SPOT CLOSE TO THE LAKE. THE CLEAR SUNNY DAY provided unusual visibility, and the morning air had a special tang. *It was a fun day to be alive,* Erik thought, as he viewed the surrounding mountains and the mysterious fire tower that stood within a mile or two of the lake.

Fire towers were not unusual in the area, and Erik had seen many from a distance, but they always remained a forbidden mystery. *How much could you see from there,* he wondered, *and who lives there ... and how long, or does anybody? I will have to ask Dad.*

Erik joined a couple of kids that were hurling themselves into the lake from the tire swing. Erik took his turn, and it was fun, even better than before because on this event he could swim — almost.

The adults remained on the grass beach and were joined at times by another couple or two. It was a festive mood with a small fire burning, and Erik could hear and see them eat, drink, and tell their stories. Good stories that generated heavy laughter. *Particularly Dad and Uncle Bob. They always have fun times together.*

Although it was exciting on the swing, Erik felt that he couldn't miss out on the adult happenings, so he joined the group and quietly observed from the sidelines. *It's special with Uncle Bob here ... the first time he's been here in the mountains with Dad, and I can see they're good buddies.* And another thing Erik liked. Uncle Bob always seemed to have time to include him in the kidding and to bring him into his world with his WWII war stories. He was an infantry combat vet who won a silver star at the Battle of the Bulge. Someday, I'll be a vet and win a medal. "Hey, I've got an idea," Bob said, "Let's all go and climb the fire tower."

"Yea," said Burt, "sounds good to me."

The other adults responded with a polite decline. They said they had things to do, or something.

"How about you, Erik," Bob said, "Would you like that?"

"Wow, that's great, Uncle Bob. Okay with you, Dad?"

His dad nodded yes. Erik was surprised because it was always nice to be included with the grown-ups, and especially for something as exciting as a climb to the top of a fire tower.

His mom looked a bit disturbed, however, but said it would be fine with her, provided they were careful ... and no more heavy drinking. She said she would stay there with the other folks.

"Okay, let's take the car," Burt said, as he poured Bob and himself another sizable drink of Old Crow bourbon. "We'll be back before you can holler ..."

Burt, Uncle Bob, and an elated Erik made the trip to the tower in short time. There was a quarter inch chain at the entrance of the steps that led to the tower top. *Probably there to prevent unwanted sightseers.*

"Awe. This is nothing," Burt said, as he and Bob crawled over and then lifted Erik onto the second step.

The climb commenced, and Erik was mesmerized. *Boy, this is scary, but I wouldn't miss it for the world though.* Upwards they went, and, near the halfway point, Erik was more apprehensive, but he wanted to be like the big boys, so he forged ahead. Burt and Bob were joking between puffs of fresh air (they both smoked), and all were making good progress toward the top.

This must be taller than the Empire State Building, (Erik saw it in the movies, once), *and I'm not so sure I should be here with the grown-ups. It keeps going up.* But he followed closely, and they all arrived at the platform on top.

There was a small metal hut on the platform that housed the fire ranger when he was on duty (apparently he was off today). The hut was encircled by a catwalk with upright steel railings to prevent an accidental fall to the hard earth below.

Burt and Bob continued their bantering (and drinking) while pointing out familiar landmarks that were easy to see from such a height. Erik was spellbound. Perhaps terrified would be more appropriate. No, he was not terrified — it was a combination of fear and exhilaration. It was an incredible experience.

"Hey, Burt, how far you think we would fall?" Bob asked, half seriously.

"Hell, I don't know, Bob, maybe a mile or two," Burt said as he laughed. Erik didn't think it was quite so funny.

"What you think, Erik?" his Uncle Bob asked.

Erik didn't answer; he was too busy holding on to the railing. A gust of wind made the tower sway, and he tightened his grip. And, for the first time, he looked straight down at the ground below. It gave him the shivers. *God, it's a long drop. Maybe, I should've stayed to practice my dog paddling.*

"Bet you five bucks I could swing from this railing, Burt. What you think?" Bob said.

"Sure you could, Bob. Know I could. Hell, even Erik could do it." And then he reached over and grabbed Erik by the shoulders and lifted him off his feet. "Here Bob, take his feet, and we'll see."

Erik was stunned. He could not believe what was happening. Bob had grabbed his feet, and they lifted him out beyond the rail. Erik was afraid to struggle; they were too strong, and he didn't want to cause a slip from their grip.

"Hell, you can handle this, can't you Erik? Tough youngster like you … Lord, I used to do this as a kid with my dad," Burt said. Then he grabbed one of the legs that Bob was holding, and now Erik was hanging upside down. He stared at the ground below. *It is miles away...* Erik didn't know what to do. … He didn't scream, but he started to cry. He knew he was dead. And he was petrified.

Burt and Bob must have realized that the alcohol play had gone too far, or it wasn't as funny anymore, so they swung Erik back onto the platform. "You okay, Erik?" Uncle Bob said.

Erik couldn't hear him. He was nearly immobilized with fear. *Why did they do that? Are they going to do it again?* He was in a bewildered state of confusion ... and he was ashamed that he was crying. *You didn't cry around your dad. Maybe it was a dream, a nightmare that will go away. Dads don't do things like that, or maybe I should have been tougher and had fun hanging there.*

But Erik knew that he was still on a shaky platform and would have to make the God-awful trip down the steps. He heard his dad say it was time to go.

"Man, that was fun up there," Bob said when they were halfway down.

"Yea, Bob, haven't done that since we were kids," Burt said, "You okay, Erik?"

Erik had stopped crying, but he didn't answer. Maybe he nodded that he was okay.

"Well, I wouldn't tell your mother, Erik, it would just bother her," Burt said. "She wouldn't understand. Okay?"

Erik didn't understand either. He just wanted to get home.

Later that evening, Erik was alone with his mother. Bob and Burt were drinking somewhere. "Mom, do you know what they did today?"

"No, honey, who did what?"

"Dad and Uncle Bob. They hung me out over the fire tower. I was upside down, and I cried."

She was startled by the statement. She paled. "What do you mean, they hung you over the rail?"

"Yes ma'am, they hung me over. Dad had one leg and Uncle Bob had the other. I was scared, thought they were going to drop me." He began to cry again.

His mother looked as though she had been stabbed. "Now, honey, it's okay. I'm sure they didn't do all that ... they love you, and they wouldn't hurt you. Maybe you were a little mixed up."

She hugged Erik and said, "It'll be all right, honey. Now you have school tomorrow, so on to bed ... and it'll be all right."

Erik wasn't all right though; he didn't understand. *Is Dad ashamed of me ... 'cause I can't do anything? And why doesn't Mom believe me? And why does God let them do it? Am I that bad?*

CHAPTER FOUR

ERIK STILL DIDN'T UNDERSTAND THE FIRE TOWER INCIDENT. HE HAD MIXED emotions, but, in some strange way, it increased his desire to win acceptance from his father. *Maybe in the new town...* His mom had told him that they were being transferred.

By the end of the month, they moved to Scantsville, West Virginia, and Erik wasn't happy about it. He had been accepted and comfortable at the Catholic school, but now he had to attend public school.

It was different in public school. The teachers didn't call you stupid like the nuns did at times, and they were not nearly as strict as the nuns, but they did gear their pace to the slowest student in class, which in most cases turned out to be a notch or two above "brain dead."

Erik's class had twenty-seven kids in it. One of them was good ole Junior Jackson, who had spent a great portion of his life in that grade — three years. He sat in the back of the room, slept or read comic books, or both, and the teacher would say, "Now, we do hope Junior is keeping up with us today, don't we class?"

It was a good day, the day Junior left the sixth grade and joined the United States Marine Corps.

School became a boring experience for Erik. He lost all enthusiasm to excel. It had become a matter of showing up and making a passing grade. He couldn't understand why they had to put time and effort into worthless classes such as West Virginia history and Mrs. Edmonson's music appreciation class. They would spend a class each day learning the history of West Virginia, which Erik decided could have all been summed up in a matter of minutes. *Like, who really gives a rat's ass about a mister what's his name starting another poor town in a poor state.*

And the music class, what a joke that was. Poor Mrs. Edmonson, looking a hundred years old, would shuffle over to wind up the record player, a 78 RPM of the same vintage as she, and would crank ten minutes to obtain a tight spring. Then she turned the switch on. Somewhere between the scratches you could hear musical notes, but Erik could never decipher a tune because the speed of the record varied. Since it wouldn't stay at a constant speed, each selection had a weird tempo. And, when the spring lost its tension, the class would have to tell Mrs. Edmonson, who was half deaf, that the record quit turning and the music had ceased. She would always seem to be surprised, but soon recovered and shuffled back to the Victrola to repeat the process.

Erik wanted to be something special, and school was not the answer. He believed all of the boys were bigger, faster, and better looking than he was. He was lonely (even though he had lost his banana head), and he searched for acceptance. He thought he found it in the Boy Scouts. He had joined the Scouts when he turned eleven, and he was a good Scout. He earned many merit badges and moved up rapidly. He was a proud youngster when he was promoted to Life Scout, and he thought that his dad would be pleased. It was only a short jump to Eagle. That would have been an honor, but, unfortunately, it didn't turn out that way ... and his dad was not pleased.

Erik was a member of Troop 127, a Methodist church troop. He wanted to be in a troop from his own church, but they didn't have one. One night, Troop 127 was in a camporee with another troop when a small rock-throwing incident occurred. Unfortunately, one of the kids from the other troop took a hit, and, after a stitch or two, made a formal complaint. Erik and three others from Troop 127 were called into the church council of wise men, and they decided that Erik was the one who made the direct hit. How they came to that determination was a mystery to Erik, but perhaps they concluded that a Catholic boy threw a rock more accurately than the Methodist boys. So, Erik was drummed out of the troop; his young Scout career was terminated. The good ole church boys were allowed to remain. The council of wise men decided it would be unwise to throw out a son of a tithing church member.

It was a serious setback for Erik, another lesson in the world of grown-ups. Someday, I'm going to be something or somebody special, he pledged. *Maybe a cowboy. Everybody respects cowboys, or at least they do in the movies.* But his real dream was to be a fighter pilot. A tall handsome fighter pilot, who would be free to look death in the eye and shoot down the bad guys. *Everybody would like me, even the girls. The bad guys wouldn't like me though, but that would be okay. I would be somebody. A fighter pilot like the Red Baron ... only I would be on the good side.*

ERIK'S DAD, BURT, WAS NOT AN EDUCATED MAN, HAVING DROPPED OUT OF SCHOOL IN the eighth grade. He seemed to replace this deficiency, however, with his quick wit and knowledge of current events. Tall and good looking with a contagious, robust laugh, he was well liked and always welcomed center stage. He was a hard worker and believed that true success was the direct result of a man's hard work.

"Erik," he said, "a man isn't worth a damn if he's not working. Remember that kid." He never called Erik "son." And Erik believed him; it made sense.

Then, Burt told him a story about his own childhood:

"Me and my brothers worked for Lief, your grandfather, on the road gang of Mid-Union Railroad. It seems that Dad was moving a steel drum in icy below-zero weather, when he cut off his big finger. Yea, his right hand finger, somewhere around the second joint.

"You know, he was stronger than a damn bull. That barrel had to be two or three hundred pounds. But, apparently the drum slipped as he was putting it down, and it caught his glove on the bottom rim. He tried to jerk his hand out, but was unable to free it all the way. Freed most of it though, but not all of the fingers. One stayed in the glove. Unfortunately, he was too proud to let anyone know that he had screwed up. Maybe, if we weren't working with him, it would have been different. But he didn't tell anyone, and he continued work until the end of the shift, some two hours later. God, what a tough old bastard!

"We thought that he had hurt himself, but hell, we didn't know how serious it was. We could see he didn't use his right hand, just let the arm hang by his side. And we didn't know there was a pool of blood in the glove.

"It was close to the end of the shift when we noticed the boss talking to Dad. Guess the boss saw the bloody hand and sent him to the railroad doctor. We heard later that Doc removed the glove, threw away Lief's finger, and stitched up the stub on his right hand.

"When the Doc found out that Dad had worked with a cutoff finger for a couple of hours, he told him that he should have bled to death. But he said it was his guess that the glove acted as a compress, and, with the freezing temperatures, the two probably combined to help restrict the flow of blood. It saved his life.

"The Doc told Dad that it was a stupid thing to do. But Dad would rather take the chance of dying than lose face with us, his boys ... and the rest of the crew, I guess."

Erik was amazed. "Holy cow, Grandpa did that? ... Cut if off and didn't say a thing?"

"That's what he did. Your grandpa didn't have time for any nonsense. He was a proud bastard ... and he wasn't easy."

Erik wasn't sure of the full meaning of the story, or at least how it applied to him. *Maybe I have to do that when I'm a dad ... or, if I cut my finger off tomorrow, I'm supposed to go to school before getting help, but only if it's wintertime.*

That was amusing to Erik, but he liked his dad's story. It reinforced Erik's desire to be a hard worker. And it certainly reinforced his opinion that all dads are tough.

CHAPTER FIVE

ERIK HAD FAILED TO IMPRESS HIS FATHER BEFORE. BUT THIS TIME HE WAS going to do it. *This time I will for sure. I'll be good in sports and … be somebody.*

Burt had told Erik that he had been a "star halfback" when he had played at school. "Won many letters and awards when we went to the state championships," he said. It all made sense to Erik. After all, he would have expected such because his father could do anything. And he was good at it. There was a slight problem, however, because his mother told Erik that he had quit school in the eighth grade. At times, Erik wondered where his dad had played such fine football. But dads don't lie, he surmised.

In junior high, grade seven — despite his size — Erik was allowed to try out for the junior high football team. He was excited. *Yes, I'll be a football star, and Dad will be proud of me.*

Practice began early Saturday morning. A hot Saturday morning in Scantsville, West Virginia. The air was still, and it looked dirty. Dirty, like the town itself, settled in the hollow among coal mines. It was poor country with magnificent mountains providing a rich contrast to the tired buildings and the poor people. Not hungry poor, just things poor.

Like many towns in the South, Scantsville had two schools for each grade level. One school for the blacks, and a better school for the whites. That's the way it was. Erik's school, Scantsville Junior High, was a better school. Erik stood around the school grounds with the rest of the tryouts from the seventh, eighth, and ninth grades. Some twenty or thirty wannabe stars. He recognized a few of them, but many of them he didn't know, and they all looked bigger and faster than he was. *Maybe this wasn't such a good idea.* But just then Coach Barns stormed over and took charge. He was not what Erik had expected. He had pictured the coach as a tall man with a movie star tan and an educated way with words. Instead, he was a short, overweight no-neck with a high blood pressure tan. He did have a way with words, however, but they were more profane than profound.

"What the hell are you clowns milling around for? Get your dumb asses over here and line up," he yelled.

All of the "dumb-asses" scrambled to get in line, and Coach Barns immediately began to reposition them. Veterans from the year before were put in the front of the line, followed by the unknown big kids and the smaller ones who looked speedy. At the end were the pint-sized, skinny kids who looked like they would be slow. Erik started his sports career at the end of the line.

"You dumb-asses follow me," the coach growled as he set off toward the school basement.

The colorless, mismatched line of devoted athletes responded obediently.

"In here, you will draw your equipment. Some new, some not so new. Norman, the equipment manager, will issue what you need. Stay in line, get your gear, get a locker, and meet me on the practice field in one hour, that's ten o'clock. Everybody got that?" And twenty-seven would-be athletes nodded that they "got that."

The veterans were receiving their shiny new practice gear. Silver satin pants, bright orange jerseys, white waxed helmets, black leather cleats, many different pads, and one pair of athletic socks were all stacked in their arms as they departed to find a locker.

What beautiful colors. I can't wait to put them on.

When the big, speedy newcomers got to the head of the line, Erik noticed, with some alarm, a change. The pants were no longer new and shiny, the jerseys looked tired and faded, the cleats had seen a season or two, and some sizes were not available. Erik wondered what he'd get when he faced Norman, the equipment manager.

Norman sized him up, then handed Erik his gear. There was no helmet, not even a dull beat-up one. The cleats looked to be at least three sizes too large. Worse yet, one of the shoes had its sole secured with layered wrappings of electrical tape. It took courage for Erik to say to Norman, "I don't have a helmet, and the cleats are size twelve or thirteen."

"The helmets are gone, and the shoes will have to do," replied Norman. Then, seeing Erik's disappointment, he leaned over the counter and said, "Wait a minute, kid. Let me give you a ball cap until we get a helmet … you know … someone will quit and turn one in." He returned with a used orange baseball cap.

Erik put the cap on; it covered his head and most of his ears. *A little large, but no big deal ... my head may grow into it. At least it's part of a uniform.*

He heard the banging of the lockers where the vets were suiting up, and he headed in that direction. He felt the lingering dampness from the leaky shower room as he made his way down the dimly lit corridor. The aroma of dirty socks and jock straps permeated the locker room. Erik had been told that the players never washed them because it was unlucky to do so. He breathed deeply and thought what a fun place it was to be. He felt the spirit of competition in the air, and it was exhilarating.

He put his gear in a locker and took a seat on the bench. He was surrounded by the tryouts, all in various stages of dress, some naked, and others in full uniform as they departed for the field. It was unusually quiet, no talking, just the banging of lockers and the crisp grating sound of cleats on the concrete floor. *It's good to be here. I'm part of a team.*

He glanced at one of the bigger boys, who was putting on his jock strap. Erik tried to look the other way, but couldn't. *Damn, look at the size of his dick. God, it actually fills the jock strap, and he has hair on his body, and pubic hair … a damn bush of it.*

Erik knew that he couldn't fill a jock strap because he didn't have a bush, just some fuzz. It was awful. He wanted to be somewhere else. *I'll never be that big. What a dick ... how in the world am I going to dress without showing mine?*

Erik said a little prayer. He had to convince himself that his day would come. But he wasn't sure that he believed it.

The locker room was almost empty. Just a few of the little guys were suiting up. He noticed with satisfaction that they didn't have big dicks, and no hair on their body. He quickly donned his practice gear and anxiously departed for the field. In the corridor, he caught sight of his image in a full length mirror. He was startled. The shoulder pads, sized for a two hundred-pounder, were enormous when placed on his one hundred and ten-pound frame. His small, ball-capped head was dwarfed by the uniform. He could hardly see his mouth, and certainly not his chin, but had to assume it was there, behind the pads somewhere. The pants, that were supposed to be knee length, hung down to his shins, and the knee pads flopped about as he moved. *And that's not the worst,* thought Erik. His chicken legs were deformed by the oversize cleats, one wrapped in electrical tape. It was depressing, but he smiled with resignation. *Coach Barns called it right. Maybe I am a dumb-ass clown. He turned and headed for the field. From a star halfback to a clown, and all before ten o'clock in the morning.*

He was the last to arrive and immediately ran out onto the yellow-orange field of clay that was sparsely covered with mowed weeds. It didn't look like the football field he had seen over at the high school. The lack of bleachers, the faded lime yardage markers, and the tired, rusting goal posts did little to instill inspiration. A few wooden benches were placed to mark the sidelines of the field, and all of them were in need of substantial repair.

In the center of the field, Coach Barns was surrounded by the tryouts in their mismatched uniforms. Erik hustled over to the group and was surprised that no one appeared to notice him in his ridiculous outfit. They were giving all their attention to the coach, who was addressing the "plan of action" and the "ground rules." *I must have missed most of it...* The coach barked, "All you dumb-asses give me ten laps and be back here at two o'clock this afternoon, ready to go. Now move out!"

They all peeled out double-time to the edge of the field and commenced the first lap. The vets set a fast pace, and the team was strung out half the length of the field. Erik struggled to pass the kid in front of him. He knew he had to pass him because Coach Barns was watching, and Erik presumed he would never make the team if he was last. As he closed the gap, the kid in front picked up the pace, and Erik fell back into his trailing position. The kid obviously had the same thoughts about being last.

By the third lap, Erik found it difficult to breathe. The hot moist air resisted Erik's attempt to inhale it. He was wet with sweat. His skin was clammy and blotted with various shades of pink and red. *Laps are not fun.* Then it got worse. The oversize cleats were beginning to chafe and the electrical tape was separating. The right sole was beginning to flap. The knee pads banged against his shin bones. The shoulder pads bounced into his jaw and chin. All of this took place with each stride, and only seven laps to go. And the coach was still watching.

Barns had long gone when Erik completed the tenth and final lap. Limping off the field with his flapping noise (the sole was almost off), he noticed only one other kid going into the school basement. *That must be the kid that I was trying to pass. He doesn't look that tough ... I should have taken him.* And then, he realized that he was hurting, not just mentally because he finished last, but physically as well. The showers will feel good, regardless of the embarrassment.

As Erik stripped in the locker room, the damage to his body became more apparent. The knee pads had damaged both shins. They were bruised and marked by small cuts. The shoulder pads left their mark in the form of red blemishes on his jaw and chin. Worst of all, he had three blisters, two on one foot and a big one on the foot that received the flapping. And this was just the result of running laps, no body contact. *This afternoon will be better,* he assured himself.

The afternoon arrived, as did all the tryouts, including Erik and the other scrubs. He had repaired his shoe as best he could with spanky new tape. He had alcoholed his shins, band-aided the blisters, and covered them with a fresh pair of athletic socks from home. Then came the pads, pants, and cleats. No helmet, of course. *Not too bad, not bad at all. I can make it through the day.*

As he departed for the field, he noticed himself in the mirror, the same one that startled him earlier, and, unfortunately, it startled him again. He still resembled a clown. More cuts and bruises, but still a clown.

Arriving on the field, he joined the others who were again mobbed around Coach Barns and giving him the best of their attention. Coach outlined the practice procedure and selected his vets — by name — and the other big, speedy boys to participate in pattern drills. The patterns consisted of running twenty yards down the field, cutting to the left or right, as designated, and blocking their man to the ground. Their man was a dummy made of cotton pads wrapped around a vertical steel pipe that was welded to a base plate.

Two of these dummies were placed downfield, one on the left, the other on the right. Then, two of the selectees would sprint the distance, cut right or left, and hurl themselves through the pipe and padding. Executed properly, this would lay out the opponent, in this case the dummy.

The vets and the big speedy boys made several patterns, and then Coach Barns allowed the scrubs, including Erik, to lay out a dummy. Erik got his chance. With all the speed and strength he could muster, he sprinted down field, cut, and hurled himself through the air, smashing into the dummy with a clean professional blow. Slightly stunned, Erik picked himself up from the clay and noticed that the dummy had won; it was still upright. Somewhat humbled, he returned, flapping as he double-timed (the spanky new tape was unraveling) back to the line of departure, where the mob was.

Coach observed most of the patterns while he stood or sat on a sideline bench. He occasionally yelled out, "Hustle girls!" Hustle!" or "Hit-em, goddammit … get your dumb asses into it!"

When the scrubs finished their shot at the dummies, he blew his whistle. He grunted out a few "attaboys" and slapped a few shoulders and butts of those who had impressed him, mainly the vets and the big speedy boys. He then pointed to Erik and one other scrub and motioned them over. For a fleeting moment, Erik thought that, perhaps, he would get an "attaboy" or a slap on the rear. But reality set in when Coach Barns told the two of them to go out on the field and become the dummies. He then said to his vets, "It's better to work against live dummies than the steel pipe dummies." Erik wasn't really happy to be chosen for the honor, but he did appreciate the recognition and was confident that he would do a good job. So, he flapped his way out to his designated spot.

In position, Erik saw the first set of vets sprint off the line and make their cuts. He became a bit apprehensive as his man, bigger and faster than he had realized, was rapidly approaching the point of launch to wipe out the dummy. Upon reaching it, he launched and hurled himself through the air … crashing through Erik, the dummy, with the force of a truck. A big truck, Erik concluded.

The vet must have realized that he overdid it, and, as he picked up Erik, he apologized and asked if he was okay. Erik didn't respond as he tried to regain consciousness, but finally assured the big speedy guy that he would be all right … soon … he thought.

With that assurance, the vet scampered back to his "attaboy" and pat on the rear.

Erik's head began to clear, and his vision returned to normal. He clearly saw the next set of vets make their cut and head toward the dummies. The vet closing in on Erik was even bigger than the one that just wiped him out. *No way...* As the vet hurled himself through the air, Erik feinted to the left, then quickly side-stepped to the right. The vet, with a look of astonishment, remained airborne for an unusual length of time before he crashed into the hard clay turf with a resounding thud of body and gear. He didn't get up. Erik suspected that there would be no "attaboy" on this one. He was correct.

Coach Barns sprinted over and assisted his star warrior back to health. Apparently there was a problem with the shoulder, dislocated or jammed perhaps, but Erik wasn't provided with the on-field diagnosis because Coach Barns was too busy yelling at him.

"What the goddamn hell did you do to him?" he howled. "Who told you to do that? Jesus Christ, can't you follow orders, boy?" He finally ran out of words, and, with a look of complete disgust, ordered Erik to the showers.

Erik shuffled back to the distant locker room, alone and teary-eyed, confused and defeated. It was a long walk with a flapping shoe.

CHAPTER SIX

WITH RELUCTANCE, ERIK FINALLY TOLD HIS FATHER HE HAD QUIT football, and Erik was surprised at the lack of reaction. Burt had little to say, other than, "Damn, don't know why you didn't stick it out." Erik found out later that his dad had quit his job and, obviously, had more important matters to think about. He didn't know why Burt quit his job, but thought it had something to do with a promotion going to another man.

Jobs weren't that easy to find in 1946. The big war (WWII) was over and returning veterans needed work. Burt was not a veteran (claimed he was 4F-medically unfit), so he was fortunate to find work selling mining equipment for a local distributor. He was happy with his new job. He learned quickly and made adequate money. It was no surprise to Erik, as his dad always worked hard and provided for the family.

Erik was surprised, however, when his dad told him that he had passed the test for his mining superintendent's license. He also told him that he had leased a small coal mine. Erik couldn't hide his excitement, "You have a coal mine?"

"Yes, a small one over on the state line. It's just a pony mine, " Burt replied.

"Wow, a mine ... are you going to work in it?"

"Hell yes, I'm going to work it," his dad said.

"Wow! ... Can I work in it?"

"Well, maybe. We'll have to see how it goes."

This was great news for Erik. He wasn't sure what a pony mine was, but he knew he wanted to work in it. He had been to some of the slope mines with his dad, and he always found them fascinating. He had never been inside one, but he could see the entrances — the mouths of the mines — and they were always mysterious. Miners would ride into the mine in empty loading cars. Later, these cars would return with full loads of coal and dump their contents into the tipple.

Erik was always intrigued with mine operations and with the miners. He was puzzled because they all seemed to have the same characteristics. They were slim, sinewy, dirty, and tired — a tough, hardworking group that never seemed to smile.

It was an anxious week for Erik. Summer vacation had started, and he knew if he was going to work the mine, he had to start soon. He couldn't get an answer from his father. Time was running out. Then, the night before Burt was to depart for the mine, Erik heard his mother and father talking. They were discussing his request to work the mine.

"I know he is young, Burt," she said, "and I'm worried about the dangers of the mine, but it would mean so much to me if the two of you could be closer. I know that times have been tough on you, but he tries also … so let him go with you, and work together." Erik didn't hear his father reply. Perhaps they moved to the other room, he guessed.

Erik couldn't sleep; he was too excited; he felt that he had a chance, now that his mother was on his side. Later on his dad came into the bedroom and said, "I'm putting you on as a coal loader at half-pay … by the ton, like the rest of the loaders. No favors … not going to have the miners bitch about favors to the boss's son."

"That's great, Dad, thank you, sir!"

"We'll leave at four in the morning." Erik got little sleep. The anticipation was almost too much for a fourteen-year-old, soon to be coal loader. He thought that it would be an exciting, fun time.

They departed on the three-hour trip on schedule. Soon they would be at the mine, the pony mine. Erik asked many questions. Burt told him that they would be working a small slope mine with about thirty employees. They would haul the coal out with ponies and dump it into a bin. Then they would truck the coal three miles to a big mine and use their tipple. The big mine was run by a friend of his, a superintendent named Jason.

"It's tough work, kid, only forty-two-inch coal, but we're only running two shifts now." He continued, "Don't have the ponies to run three."

Erik was trying to imagine forty-two-inch coal. "How do you measure the coal?" he asked.

"That's the seam of coal. The seam is between layers of slate, or shale. All the big seams have pretty much run out, or are about to. No more six to ten foot seams like the exhibition mine we drove the car through."

Holy cow, only forty-two inches! That's not much more than a yardstick.

"You really have to bend over to work, don't you?" responded Erik.

"Sure do," his dad said, "On your knees, the whole time, with your shovel."

"But the mines we saw ... you know the ones you took me to on the job ... looked a lot bigger than forty-two inches."

"That's just the entrance; they make them bigger with timbers. That's not the seam; it lowers after you get in there. Maybe down to forty inches or so."

"But the ponies, how do they get in there?" Erik asked.

"Because they're damn small ponies. How else would you think?"

"Don't know, but I didn't think they would be that small," Erik replied. *God, they must be the size of dogs,* he thought, as they were coming into a small town.

"This is it ... just a few miles outside, and we're there," Burt said, "We'll be staying at Alma's boarding house, just outside the mining camp of the big mine."

Erik could see the camp off to the left. He had visited several, and this one looked the same. They were filthy, drab, and smelled of coal dust. The wooden houses were identical, painted white at one time, but the years of weather had colored them gray, an ugly, hopeless gray. Some had indoor plumbing or at least running water. Then he saw the house on the hill. That's always the superintendent's house, he had been told. It was always white, a clean white, and it had a washing machine with hot water. And it always had a toilet, indoors. They pulled into Alma's long driveway; and a middle-aged lady came out to meet them. Nice looking lady, matronly, with an apron, and a neat bun of hair.

"That you, Burt?" she called out as she approached.

"Sure is, sweetheart," Dad answered with a big smile.

"Oh ... so good to see ya again, Burt," she said, as she hugged him, "You been a bad boy ... or stay-un out of trouble?"

"You know me, Alma," he replied in mock surprise, "And how are you ... still hitting the shine?"

"Oh, you rascal, you know I don't touch that lightning. That's devil's stuff. Well, I declare, is this your boy?" as she looked at Erik.

"Yep, that's my kid, Erik."

"Well, I'm plumb delighted, son ... you have to be a good'un if you come from Burt," she replied, while giving Erik a warm hug.

"You git in the house, and I'll fix you up some breakfast. You both look a mite skinny to me."

They went into the house, and Erik realized how he envied his father. *Hell, everybody likes him, everyone he meets. They all laugh and have a good time. I wish I could be like that, someday.*

They arrived at the mine before ten that morning. It was raining, not hard rain, just a drizzle. The mine was not what Erik had expected. It was bleak, colorless, similar to an old war movie scene after the bombing. He could see the mine entrance going into the side of the mountain. There was a flat clearing in front of the entrance, maybe a half acre or so. On the clearing, Erik could see a couple of equipment sheds and some low-slung mining cars. There was a small, wooden structure that displayed a small, weathered sign that read "Office."

There was no hustle or bustle, just one miner who shuffled toward an old, wooden coal bin that was lower down the mountain, thirty or forty feet below the clearing. Erik saw a lone set of tracks going into the mouth of the mine. Straight into the side of the mountain. Just like all slope mines do … kind of eerie and awesome. He was a little disappointed, though, at the lack of activity, but the mystery of the mine was still there. He was anxious to get started.

Burt took Erik over to one of the metal sheds. "I put some equipment away for you last week. Knee pads, miner's hard hat, and a pair of boots. They're steel-toed boots. Don't know the size. But they should work until you get your own. You got your lunch pail?"

"Yes, sir, Alma made up the lunch," Erik replied.

"Good, you're all set. You can pick up a shovel from that shed," his dad said, as he pointed to the one a few yards away. "And you can get with the shift boss as soon as he comes out. You go in with him on the next run, okay?"

"Yes sir, I think so," said Erik. It was all happening so quickly. *That's the extent of my training, that's it?* Then it hit him. Reality set in. Erik felt weak when he realized that he would soon be in that dark, black hole, shoveling "God knows what." *This is a little scary.*

Erik did his best to remain calm, and he reminded himself that it was his idea, his desire that put him here. He went into the shed and selected his gear. He strapped on the knee pads over his jeans. Then he put the boots and his miner's hat on. The boots were two sizes too large and he had to wear his ball cap under the miner's hard hat to keep it above his eyes. *Haven't I been through this before,* he thought with a nervous smile? *Damn, doesn't anything ever fit? Maybe it's the banana head.* He was embarrassed, all 110 pounds of him, but he tried to assure himself that it would all work out.

He stood outside in the drizzle, with shovel in hand, when he heard noises coming from the mine. His attention was focused on the entrance when the ponies burst out with loaded cars of coal. A miner in the first car drove the ponies, five of them in line. He hit one or two with his long stick as he yelled and cussed, "Come on ya' bastards ... ya' no good, lazy sonabitches ... git on out there!"

The sight and sounds stunned Erik. He had never seen anything like it. The ponies were the size of large dogs; he couldn't believe they were that small. When they stopped at the bin to unload, he had a closer view. He was appalled. They were in terrible condition. He saw the steam from their labored breath, and he smelled the wet manes and hides. The ponies were skinny, scruffy, and listless; they looked like they all suffered from malnutrition. He saw blood on two of them. They all had fresh sores and others that were in the process of healing.

Erik went over to them; it was sad. He reached out to pet the brown and white mare, and she jerked back in alarm. Erik could sense her fear and, with a calming voice, he tried to reassure the animal. Again he reached out to pet her. She countered with a sudden, solid bite to Erik's hand. Erik flinched with the pain. He could see the blood flow. Angry, he wanted to retaliate, and he started to kick the pony, but held back when he looked at the animal. *I can't do that; the poor thing is in worse shape than I am.* Erik tried to stop his tears. *Don't blame her for biting. I would do the same.*

Erik shoved his hand into his jacket pocket and squeezed the material. *That should stop the bleeding. The bite is not that bad, and no way am I going to let Dad know I screwed up.*

"You must be Burt's boy," an older man said as he approached. He was soft-spoken and slight of build, perhaps 5' 9".

"Yes, sir, I am," replied Erik.

"I'm Gabe, kind of crew boss here ... helping Mister Burt get started."

"I'm Erik, sir."

"Saw you and the ponies. Kinda sad, ain't it?" Gabe said, "You should of seen 'em before Mister Burt got here. A goddamn mess they were ... looking almost good now."

Erik nodded in half agreement; he couldn't believe they had been in worse shape.

Gabe apparently noticed Erik's concern, "Well, it's the damn night crew ... they beat hell out of 'em ... think some get their rocks off."

Erik nodded.

"Mister Burt said you're in on the next run. Asked me to get you set up," Gabe said. "You been before?"

"No, sir, not really."

"Well, no problem, I'll work with you a bit, then you're set to make some money ... earn your keep," Gabe said, as he grinned.

It was the first time Erik saw a miner smile. The whiteness of his teeth leaped from his coal blackened face. His eyes were not as pronounced, but Erik could see they were pale blue ... and tired. He sensed he could trust them.

"Let's git your lamp on, and we'll git on in," Gabe said as he took Erik's lamp from his hard hat.

"This here's a carbide lamp," he said as he unscrewed the lower half, and spit onto the small pieces of carbide. Erik smelled the carbide gas immediately; it burnt his nose and eyes. Gabe closed the lamp and lit it with a kitchen match. He adjusted the flame. "This should do it," he said as he handed it to Erik. "Don't have the battery lamps for this little mine, too expensive."

They went over to the cars, and Gabe told Erik, "You sit facing forward, down on your knees, and be sure to keep your hard hat on. You can look, but keep your head low, and keep your back down. Don't need any more cuts."

Erik thought of his cut hand. *Gabe must have seen it.*

Gabe and Erik were in the first car with the driver, while six other miners were in the cars behind them. They entered the black hole, the entrance, and the cars gained speed. The driver yelled and cussed at the ponies, and Erik didn't understand why it had to be like that. They were well into the mountain, perhaps a half mile, and Erik was captivated, almost spellbound. The shadows from their carbide lamps danced about as strange forms of life. Perhaps from the past. The slate roof raced by just inches above. The temperature was warm and pleasant. It was another world, exactly as he had been told.

They rode another ten or fifteen minutes, and Erik lost track of time. It was eerie and wondrous. The cars came to a slow stop, and a miner crawled out, detached two cars, and moved them onto a side track for loading. Gabe and Erik moved on while the driver yelled and cussed at the ponies. At intervals, he would club them with his stick, and they would momentarily gain speed.

Erik was concerned about the animals, so he rose to get a better look, and he hit the roof. Instantly, he felt the sharp, stabbing pain down his back. "Damn ... that hurt!" he exclaimed. He wanted to cry, but realized that coal loaders don't do that. *What a stupid move that was, Erik.* Gabe saw what had happened. "Keep your back down, Erik, that damn roof will tear your spine off!"

They stopped a few minutes later, climbed out onto their knees, and detached two cars. Gabe put them on a side track for loading. *What a strange feeling. I'm actually walking on my knees ... in a black hole with a shovel.*

"This is your room, Erik; the drillers were here last night and knocked out coal ... I see we've got some water in here."

The room was maybe twenty feet across, maybe less, but Erik could see the water.

"Do we pump it out, Gabe?"

"Well, we do over in the big mine ... but here we just shovel it into the car and dump it with the coal. Takes a little time, but you git used to it."

Erik entered the room on his knees. It sloped off, and suddenly he was up to his hips in cold water. *This is not good. This is more than "a little water."* He became even more apprehensive because he didn't know if he would drop out of sight or just be eaten by a snake, or something. Gabe reassured him, "It's okay, Erik, you're doing fine. It doesn't drop off. Deep as it's gonna git."

Erik began shoveling the water into one of the cars that Gabe had spotted for him. He could reach it with the shovel.

"I'll be back shortly, Erik. Have to go off-load the rest of the crew," said Gabe as he disappeared into the blackness.

Erik shoveled water for what seemed like hours, and he finally got down to the coal. His spirits picked up in spite of the pain as he shoveled real coal into the other car. Every muscle and joint, including the cuts, screamed out to Erik. But he was determined to fill a car with coal. He forced himself to continue until Gabe came back to check on him. He had no idea how long Gabe had been gone, but he was glad he was back.

"Good work, Erik. You have a load. Let's quit for now, we'll catch the next run out, and you can hit her again tomorrow," Gabe said as he pushed the cars out for hookup.

Erik didn't hear the driver cuss the ponies. He was too wet and too cold and too tired to hear. They arrived back outside into the drizzle and the remaining daylight. Gabe said he would take care of the unloading and that Erik should go over to the fire and warm up. Erik crawled out of the car and dropped to his knees. He moved a step forward before he realized that he could stand up and walk. *I hope no one saw that, but I really don't care if they did.*

He made it to the fire, and it felt good. He pulled his gloves off, and he noticed that his hands were waterlogged from working in the water. *They look like prunes.* Then he pictured himself as a prune, a one hundred and ten-pound prune with knee pads on, and big boots. *That would be a sight,* he thought as he smiled.

Burt must have noticed Erik at the fire. He walked over and asked, "You okay?"

"Yes sir, just a little tired," he said as he tried to look like he could stand up straight.

"We'll be leaving soon, and you can get some rest," Burt said. "Big day tomorrow."

I can hardly wait.

It was early the next day. Erik managed to make it to the mine on time … with the encouragement of his father. He didn't remember the night; he had slept it through. He was stiff and sore throughout his body and the cuts on his back and hand declared, "Yes, we're still here." *But no one said it would be easy.* He was ready for his shift.

He was putting his knee pads on when Gabe appeared.

"Morning, Erik, you be ready for loadin'?"

"Yes sir … ready to load," replied Erik.

"Well, here's your tags. Forgot about 'em yesterday."

Gabe handed Erik some round metal tags about the size of a silver dollar. Each tag had a small hole near the edge, and each had a number stamped into the middle of the tag.

"You hang one of the tags on the side of your car when you finish loading it," Gabe said. "That ways you gits credit for your load, and you can draw your pay at the end of the shift … if you've a mind to."

"My tags have number twenty-nine on them," Erik said.

"That's right … the tag man, who's the bookkeeper, pulls 'em off the car when the loads come out and marks down number twenty-nine, and yor tonnage … then he hangs 'em on the tag board. Then you know how much you made that day."

"Wow, that's neat," Erik said, "you mean I can get my money right away?"

"Sure can, but it's scrip," Gabe said. "Not real money, perten near though. You spend it down at the Company store. Buy yourself a beer, or something."

Erik had seen scrip before, in Scantsville. Some of his classmates told him you could spend it at certain stores, but it was only worth fifty or sixty cents on the dollar. "You get the whole dollar's worth, Gabe?" he asked.

"Yea, you do, down at the Company store," replied Gabe, "But you don't have to take scrip. You can wait till the end of the month and get a check that turns into green money."

"I like scrip," Erik said, "Can't wait to hang some tags."

"Most all miners I know take scrip … well, you git a loaden and hang some tags, ole number twenty-nine," Gabe said as he grinned.

Erik was on his way to his loading room, the same one he worked the first day. *I hope it's dry,* he thought as the driver cussed and yelled at the ponies.

Erik was more comfortable, but not completely at ease. He'd been told of many mining tragedies close to his home. There were numerous mines in the area, and sometimes you could hear the mine whistles. Long blasts for shift changes and a series of short blasts for an emergency. One by one they would all sound their short blasts announcing their terrible accidents. Gas was the main culprit, and all slope mines had gas, lots of natural gas. The mountains were full of it. Gas leaked into the mines, and the first spark or flame produced a deadly explosion. Erik remembered the stories of the miners taking a canary in with them. Canaries are sensitive to gas, and, if one became sick or died, the miners would have little time to evacuate before the explosion. They also watched for rats. It was known that rats would scamper for fresh air at the first indication of gas. A wise miner would quickly follow.

Erik heard that it was risky in the mines, and it became even more of a risk if you were equipped with an open flame lamp such as the one he had on. He tried not to dwell on the risks. Upon arrival at the room, Erik's spirit fell rapidly; there was water, more damn, cold-ass, miserable water. He had prayed it would be dry. Must have seeped in during the night, he reckoned.

He spotted his car and entered on his knees — and a pleasant surprise — it was only half as deep as yesterday. Erik shoveled out the water, and within an hour or so he loaded coal. He finished his first car, and with lots of pride, hung his first tag, "ole number twenty-nine."

Erik hung two more tags that shift. Wet and cold, bone tired and ready to drop, "twenty-nine" had had a great day.

The next morning Erik was on his way to his assigned room, and he convinced himself it was almost routine as he listened to the driver yell and cuss at the ponies. He was confident he would have a good load day. He was a little disappointed though, when his tags from yesterday were not on the board this morning. He saw others, but not his. *Maybe it takes some time...*

The day went well for Erik, less water and more coal. He had three tags that shift. He was pleased with the results in spite of the pain. Your body is supposed to hurt, he reasoned. Besides, it will hurt less when I draw my scrip. At the end of his shift Erik, went to the shed to draw his scrip. "Sir, I'd like to draw scrip," Erik said to the tag man behind the counter.

"What's your number?" he said without looking up.

"Number twenty-nine," Erik said with pride.

"Ain't got no twenty-nines," he replied without looking up.

Erik was irritated, upset. "You have to have twenty-nines!" he said, "six or seven of them!"

"Nope ... no twenty-nines," he said, again without looking up.

Erik couldn't believe what he had heard. *This is wrong. I'll get Dad. He can make it right.* He found him working on the bin. "Dad, they just told me I didn't make any scrip. ... Can you believe that?"

"Well, did you?" he asked.

"You know I did. I turned in seven of my tags."

"No, I don't know that you did. ... Do they have your tags on the board?" he asked.

"No, sir, they're not there."

"Well, let me tell you, Erik, if you can't keep track of your tags, then maybe you're not old enough to work for tags. Understand that?"

"No, sir ... I mean, yes, sir."

Erik did not understand, and he wished he was home. *I'll quit. Damn bunch of miners. Let the bastards keep my money. No, that's crap. It's my pay; I earned it, and Dad doesn't even care. No one cares.* It was a long night for Erik.

The next morning at the mine, Erik found Gabe. "Do you know they can't find any of my tags, Gabe?" Erik said.

"None of 'em?" Gabe asked. He looked surprised. "Did you hang 'em like I showed you?"

"Yes sir, just like you showed."

"Well, you make your shift, and I'll check around. How many you have?"

"Had seven, sir."

"Okay ... ain't saying I can do much ... but you go in and get more today."

The shift changed, and Erik hopped a car to his assigned room. As usual, the driver yelled and cussed at the ponies. At routine intervals, he smacked the shit out of them with his stick. They responded with more speed. *God, I wish he would stop that. Poor little bastards.*

He arrived at the room, and, as always, there was water. *This is absolute bullshit. I work my balls off for nothing. Not a damn cent. And Burt doesn't give a shit.*

Erik loaded three cars during his shift. That's all the coal that could be loaded. It was time for the drillers and blasters. *Not bad, for a kid with no pay.*

He caught the next run out, and immediately headed for the tag board. He arrived at the board and looked for number twenty-nine. He didn't see his tags; he guessed they wouldn't be there. He was disgusted and hurt. He turned to leave. *No, look again ... be sure.* He gave the board another check, a closer look this time ... and there it was, number twenty-nine. "Yes!" he yelled as he saw his tags hanging on the pin. What a beautiful surprise. He didn't know how many were hanging, but they were stamped twenty-nine, and there were a bunch. *Wonder how they got there? Oh well, mining is not that bad.* He headed over to the fire and waited for Burt.

On the way to the boardinghouse, Burt said, "You find your tags, Erik?"

"Yes sir, sure did. Thanks, Dad."

"Hell, I didn't do anything ... but glad you found them."

Erik made his shift the next morning. It was Friday, and he was told that he could have Sunday off. *A couple more days of work and a day to sleep ... and heal ... that will be nice.*

The driver yelled and cussed the ponies as Erik headed for a new room. *That will be a nice change, a different room.* He felt rather cocky because he did the work of a miner, maybe not as much, but close. He shifted his body and raised slightly. Smack! His back met the ceiling and the pain raced through the spine. "Damn," Erik called out, "Jesus, that smarts."

The collision ripped off the scab from his first encounter with the top of the seam, the roof. He tried to hold back the tears. *Why can't I learn to stay down? … What a dumb-ass.* He off-loaded at the new room and was happy to see that it was almost dry. He wasn't sure he could work the dirty water with his bleeding back. He knew it would be painful, but he decided to get a load out and then get patched up. He filled the car within a couple of hours and headed out with the load. He arrived at the entrance, off-loaded, and made his way to the warmth of the fire. Gabe noticed that Erik was out early, so he decided he better check on him.

"You okay, Erik?" he asked with concern.

"Yes sir … just scraped my back, no big deal. Hardly even hurts," he said, hoping Gabe wouldn't notice his blood and tears. The tears that left streaks of white through the coal dust on a loader's face.

"Well, let's take a look, son … hell, it took me months to quit scraping the top."

Erik took his jacket off and Gabe lifted the back of his bloody shirt. He had taken a good lick and his spine had a six-inch gash on it. The bleeding had almost stopped and Gabe could see that the wound was not that deep. It wouldn't have to be stitched.

"Not so bad, Erik, nice solid whack though," Gabe said, "You'll wear a scab for a long time, like the rest of us dumb shits."

Gabe poured iodine on it, and Erik damn near passed our from the hurt. He struggled to stay on his feet. Gabe taped a compress on and said, "Tell you what, Erik, why don't we go on down to the Company store. You look like you could use a break. We'll grab a couple of beers."

"Oh, I'm too young for that, Gabe. They wouldn't serve me."

"Don't know why not, you're a coal loader, ain't you? Same age I was." Gabe said. "You go get some scrip if you need, and we'll git on down to the store."

Erik went over to the tag man and asked for some scrip.

"What's your number?" the tag man asked without looking up.

"Twenty-nine," Erik replied.

The tag man looked up and said, "Twenty-nine? Oh, you're Burt's boy, I'm Roy ... How much you want?"

"How much do I have coming, Roy?"

"Well, Mister Burt said you get half-pay. Comes to three or four dollars a tag; you got twelve tags ... that's forty or fifty dollars, I guess."

That's a lot of money. "I'll take ten," he said, trying to sound professional.

"Ten it'll be," Roy said as he counted out a five and five ones in funny looking scrip.

"Thank you, sir," Erik said as he stuffed the money in his jeans. He wanted to look at the scrip more carefully, but he'd wait until no one was watching.

When they arrived at the Company store, Erik saw it was large and loaded with merchandise. Hardware, clothes, food ... you could buy almost anything in this store, he guessed. "God, they have a bunch of stuff," he said to Gabe.

"Sure do, Erik, you can buy what you want ... but they charge the shit out of you."

Erik noticed the store was fairly busy, mostly men. They were obviously miners, probably just off a shift. He noted that many wore coal dust and grease, and filthy jeans. *Hell, I must look about the same as they do,* he thought, for a scary moment.

They didn't smile, and they looked tired. And for the first time Erik realized why. "Let's git out to the bar," Gabe said.

They made it to a small bar attached to the outside of the store. Erik was surprised. He thought it would be filled, but they were the only customers. They grabbed a couple of empty stools and claimed a spot at the bar. It was another first for Erik, and he was nervous.

"Hey, Gabe," the bartender said, "Off early?"

"Naw, just takin' a break. Luke, give us a couple of PBR's," Gabe said, "Me and my buddy needs a lift."

"Tough day, huh?" Luke said as he set up two bottled Pabst Blue Ribbon beers and looked at Erik, "Haven't seen you 'fore."

"This here's Erik ... Mister Burt's boy," Gabe said. "Makin a loader of him, a damn good'un."

"Oh yea, Burt's boy," Luke said as he nodded to Erik. "Been tryin' to git out of these goddamn mines for years, and you're comin' in ... ya must be a fuckin' idiot ... anyways, good to have you here."

"Well, thank you, Luke," Erik replied, somewhat shocked by the idiot remark. Erik took a swig of beer. *Not bad.* It wasn't his first taste, but it was his first at a bar.

"I want to thank you, Gabe, for finding my tags."

"Hell, didn't find 'em, Erik, it was yor dad. Mister Burt raised so much shit, thought he was goin' to fire the whole goddamn shift. Holy Jesus, he was mad."

"He said he didn't do a thing," Erik responded in surprise.

"Bullshit," Gabe said as he laughed, "I helped, but it weren't me."

"How did you find them?" asked Erik.

"One of the loaders comes up and said it might be Basil, an asshole that no one liked. We checked his tags, and no way did he load that many. He was pulling yor tags and slipping his tags on yor load."

"Holy shit," said Erik. He thought it appropriate to say shit, now that he was a loader and drinking beer.

"You don't worry, Erik, Mister Burt fired his ass on the spot. I was there … God, it was funny. Mister Burt said if he ever caught him around the mine, he would shoot his goddamn nuts off. Bet that fucker is out of the county."

Erik was shocked. "My dad said that?"

"Hell yes, he says that. … Your dad is one tough son-of-a-bitch, the crews love him, and they know he will do it."

"Holy shit, Dad would do that?" *And, I thought he didn't give a damn.*

"I know two or three that got shot stealing tags," Gabe said, "Hell, the bastards are stealing yor money, they should be shot … goddamn nuts and all. Fuck 'em … dirty bastards!"

Erik agreed. It all sounded good to him.

Gabe talked about the mines and his family. "My pa and his pa worked the mines," he said, "They both died from the mines … died before reachin' forty." He paused as his eyes gazed at the floor.

"Wow, that's too young Gabe, what the hell happened?"

"Lung disease," Gabe said, "Goddamn black lung got 'em. It's bad shit, Erik, gets most miners."

Erik was surprised. He hadn't thought about lung disease; he thought you would die of an explosion or a cave-in, not from disease, and certainly not so young.

"Why don't miners get another job, Gabe?" Erik asked.

"Don't rightly know, Erik ... but most miners don't know nothing else and can't read or write. I wish to hell I knew, maybe I coulda gotten out. I think it's mostly the Company though, they gotcha by the balls. You draw scrip first time, cause it's easy and quick. Then ain't no pay check, so you start each month broke, so you draw scrip again. Never no check. And the rent's free, so you stay. Live off scrip."

"Then they got you other ways," Gabe continued, "This goddamn company store makes a fortune. Their prices double some in town."

"And you can't buy in town?" asked Erik.

"Sure ya can, but yor scrip ain't worth but half. Makes a difference on the store and the coal company. They don't even take some companies' scrip ... ain't no good they say, going broke."

"Jeeze, Gabe, I didn't know any of this stuff. How long you been putting' up with this ... you know ... working the mines?"

"Hell, twenty years, Erik, started at fourteen, like you." Erik could not believe it; he was stunned. That made Gabe thirty-four, and Erik thought him to be around sixty. He was embarrassed, and he felt sorry for Gabe ... and all of the poor bastards. *No wonder they don't smile, and no wonder they kick the shit out of the ponies. They probably think they're worse off than the animals.*

"But the union is changin' things, Erik. Ole John L. is kicking ass," Gabe continued, "Getting us more pay, getting a lot of things ... already got us bathtubs."

Erik had seen the bathtubs; it was depressing. Most were sitting on the side porches, filled with coal. Made a nice, big coal bucket, he was told.

"John L. is the union man?" Erik asked.

"Yes, John L. Lewis ... he's the man, hell, if it weren't for him, we'd all be dead. Says he gonna clean up the air ... ya know, in the mines. Gonna be lots safer."

"Well, I hope so ... was kind of thinking about mining ... you know, after I finish school," Erik said.

"Not less you can't do nothing else, Erik. Don't never get caught in the goddamn mine trap," said Gabe, "cause you don't never get your ass out of it ... not till you're dead anyways."

The conversation was discouraging. They finished their beers and returned to the mine. Erik had a lot to think about. *Thirty-four years old and he looks sixty, or older ... poor bastard ... just like his father and granddad. He'll be lucky to make forty.*

Erik worked for the next ten days, but he saw little of his father, who was over at the big mine most of the time. His dad had sold them several pieces of equipment, and he was helping out with the maintenance. But Erik made his shifts and loaded coal. He was tired and the glamour of the mines had disappeared; he was ready to start school. It was his last week, and he was anxious to get home. *Just a few more shifts,* he thought, as he walked to the mine.

When he arrived, he noticed things were not normal. Parts of the crew were standing around the fire, and ponies were tied to a line. Then he realized that no one was working the mine. He sensed something was wrong, and he decided to find Gabe, or his dad. He found his dad down at the bin. He was just standing there looking out at the big camp. Erik could see that he was troubled.

"What's wrong, Dad?"

"We had a small cave-in last night," he said. "Thank God, we didn't lose anybody, at least not dead. Sure screwed up Gabe, though. May lose his leg. He's over at the hospital in Bluefield. It's a good one, I hear."

Erik was stunned. He didn't know what to say. *Not Gabe ... what a good guy. And now he's all screwed up. What a way for him to get out of the mines. It's terrible.*

"How did it happen, Dad?"

"A section of the top came down last night," he said, "caught Gabe and two of the ponies. Gabe was luckier than the ponies; he's going to make it. They didn't.

Erik was totally confused, and he had to sort it out. He hadn't thought much about the dangers, except the black-lung that he and Gabe had talked about.

"And another thing," his dad said, "the damn crews went on strike ... Local union says they can't work under such conditions. Unsafe, they say. Now the big mine is thinking of doing the same thing. Hell, I don't know. Goddamn wildcat strikes." He looked off onto the horizon, as though talking to it.

"Can't do a damn thing. Our men want to work, I think, but we can't; the goddamn driller ran off with the bits ... afraid we would work, I guess."

"Can't we find drill bits?" Erik asked with some concern.

"No, they won't sell them to us. Wouldn't make much difference though, they'd find a way to stop us," Burt said as he turned and looked at the bin. "All this damn coal in here, and I can't get a red cent for it. Can't even truck it."

"Jeeze, I'm sorry, Dad … about the strike, and really sorry about Gabe, and the ponies. What happened anyway? An explosion?"

"No, not an explosion. At least we don't think so. Sounds like we didn't have enough timbers up for support. Don't know for sure, but anyway, we lost some of the slab. Could have been much worse … thank God, it wasn't," he said as though talking to himself.

Erik had never seen his dad look so helpless and pale. Thoughts of the cave-in raced through Erik's mind. *It could have been me with Gabe, or Dad. No, it couldn't happen like that; dads are indestructible.* He wanted to help, but he didn't know what to do or say. The silence was disturbing, then, Erik was the first to speak, "I don't understand, I saw the crew putting up timbers … thought that everything was okay. It's the foreman's job, isn't it … to make sure it's done right?"

"Well, yes and no. It's really the superintendent's responsibility."

"The superintendent?" Erik said, "That's you, Dad." Almost instantly, he realized what he had said to his father.

"I'm sorry, Dad, I didn't mean it like that, I …"

Burt looked at Erik for the first time in the conversation. There was a long pause, and it became intense. "I think you better go," Burt said, in a determined voice, "and call your mother before you bus on home … and before she hears of the accident."

Erik started to say something, but it would have been useless, he thought.

Why did I have to open my mouth and say that to Dad? What a dumb-ass I am.

Erik went over to the ponies. They didn't try to bite him. *Maybe they sensed something unusual.* "Goodbye, you poor little bastards, I wish there was something I could do." He knew they didn't have a chance.

ERIK WAS HOME A WEEK BEFORE HIS FATHER ARRIVED. BURT LOOKED TIRED AND drawn. Erik knew it had been rough on him. His dad told Rose that Gabe was going to be all right, maybe a limp or two … but the strike was still on. No idea when it would end.

"Had to let the crews go," he said. "Hated to do that … but no money. Jason at the big mine said he would cover what we owed in the payroll. We're fortunate most had drawn scrip … said he would take the coal in the bin to cover it. Erik, you won't get paid though, neither will I."

"That's okay, Dad, I don't need the money," Erik answered. "I just hope you can get it going again, and I'm glad to hear that Gabe is okay. Well, going to be. And the ponies … what about the ponies?"

"Found a farmer with grassland; he took them," said Burt. "They'll be okay. But the mine is gone. I rolled the cars into the mine … and blew her up."

Erik was taken aback, confused, "You mean you blew the mine up?"

"Yes, the mine. Blew her up," Burt said. "Had to … can't leave an open mine with kids and such around. Not much choice with no money. … I'll find something else to do."

Holy shit, it's gone! The whole damn thing is gone. It's difficult to believe … that fast and it's all finished. But thank God, Gabe is going to make it … and the ponies are better off (most of them … those that escaped the cave-in).

CHAPTER SEVEN

ERIK'S LIFE TOOK A SUDDEN TURN THAT FALL — UPWARD. HE HEARD THAT A Civil Air Patrol (CAP) Squadron was forming. This exciting news activated a dream that had lain dormant since he was nine years of age, the same year the Japanese had hit Pearl Harbor. Everyone was patriotic that year. If you were unable to join the military, you helped the war effort the best you could. People bought war bonds and stamps, collected scrap metal, and saved on gasoline. Boys anxiously awaited the day they would be old enough to wear the uniform.

Erik had created mock battles with miniature ships, tanks, and slogging foot soldiers. He built model aircraft to provide air superiority and had many aerial dogfights with handheld machines of tissue, balsa, and Testor's glue. He spent hours immersed in Walter Mitty fantasies. He would bank, dip, and roll his toy fighter planes into the pursuit curve that set up the fatal shot. His imagination ran wild as he engaged the enemy high above the clouds. *You've had it, Red Baron, I'm on your six o'clock.*

Erik joined the CAP Squadron as soon as he could and found it to be exhilarating. He learned principles of flight and other subjects needed to complete preflight ground school, a requirement for taking the first flight. He studied hard, and his efforts rewarded him with a sound basic knowledge of flying. He was now qualified for the real thing ... to become a student pilot.

He went to the local airport to meet the flight instructor, Harry Hawkins, the only flight instructor within thirty miles. Harry was a cantankerous old ex-Navy jock who was trying to eke out a living by selling airplane rides, both sightseeing and flight lessons.

His standard fee for a one-hour lesson was seven dollars and fifty cents. When Erik complained that he couldn't come up with that kind of money, Harry growled, "Look, kid, I'll give you lessons for five bucks each, and that's special ... take it or leave it." Erik took it.

The first flight was scheduled at daylight on Tuesday, the first week of December. Harry told Erik that the best time to fly in mountainous terrain was early morning or late evening, when the wind was down and turbulence was at a minimum. So the sunrise special, as Harry called it, would allow a smoother flight and get Erik to his school classes on time. Harry did, however, caution Erik that he had a tendency to oversleep, so if he was not up and about, Erik should bang on the trailer door to wake him up.

It was dark and clear that cold morning. You could see your breath rush out and struggle to hang around before fading away. Where does it go, he wondered as he crunched through the crusty snow toward his first flight lesson? But he was soon engrossed in the forthcoming flight, his first at the controls.

"What if I don't do well?" he said aloud. Then all of his old demons of failure emerged, and it took concerted effort to force them out. He would not allow them to ruin his dream. It wasn't just the fear of losing his dream. It was the fear of failing again that tortured him. I will make this work, he pledged.

The small airport was surrounded by mountains and coal mines. The runway of crushed shale was too short to accommodate large airliners, but was adequate for smaller aircraft.

In the predawn gloom, Erik could just make out a plane, a tin hangar, a windsock that needed wind, and a small travel trailer on cinder blocks that served as Harry's home. In front of and adjoining the hangar was a concrete parking ramp — an apron some fifty by one hundred feet — that provided tie downs for the one lonely looking airplane, a Piper Cub. He crossed the ramp, not slowing to look at the Cub.

He had been told that Harry had a problem with the bottle, and he wasn't always pleasant to be around. As he feared, the trailer was dark. It appeared deserted, and the silence was heavy. Erik was nervous as he stepped up to the door and tapped it lightly. "Harry, are you in there?" Erik asked in a low voice. No response from within. *Damn, I was afraid of that, now what do I do?*

He stepped closer and banged on the door with gusto. He listened. Still no response. He banged again, louder. *I know people can hear me for miles.* As he was about to give up, he heard sounds within the trailer. Then, "Who in the hell is out there?"

"Sir, it's Erik … time to fly, Harry!"

"Erik … Erik who? Get the hell out of here. It's too goddamn early to fly!"

"No sir, you told me to get you up, Harry! You told me."

There was no answer. Erik waited. He thought he heard movement inside. At last, Harry spoke again. "All right, goddammit, just knock off the noise. I'll be out."

Five minutes passed, then the trailer door opened slowly revealing Harry in flight gear. He half stumbled out into the cold, windless, almost night. Snorting and wheezing, with an odor of used booze, he stomped around as he tried to generate some circulation. Eventually, he caught a glimpse of the confused Erik and appeared to soften. He turned toward him and muttered, "No one but a dumb-ass would fly this early … and I'm one of them."

With coffee in one hand, a lit cigarette in the other, he wore a tired leather jacket … a jacket that resembled his face. They both displayed more years of wear than they should. They bore scars of multiple carrier landings, combat, and booze. Even his white silk scarf and his cloth helmet exposed wear. Erik looked at Harry and wondered if this could be the same man that flew off carrier decks and attacked the Japs and their Zeroes.

He must have been a proud man. And now he flies the sunrise special with a skinny kid.

It was nearly light when they both turned and headed toward the ramp where the J-3 Cub rested. As they approached the aircraft, Erik realized how small and fragile it looked. The skin of yellow canvas, stretched over a frame of small tubing and powered by a sixty-five horsepower engine, was not that impressive. The Cub had a good reputation though; it was a proven, tough airplane. A true champion in its class.

Harry climbed aboard and settled into the back seat, then strapped himself in. Erik untied the aircraft and waited for Harry to give the word to start the engine.

"Clear! Contact!" Harry called — meaning the switch is on and hot — and Erik was cleared to turn the propeller by hand. There were no mechanical starters on these aircraft, so all were started by hand, a dangerous process. Dangerous because the starter person could slip and fall forward into the turning prop. Erik was aware of this and had practiced the procedure many times while hanging around the airport.

He replied with a "contact" and pulled the prop through; the engine came to life with a smoking cough and bad breath. *Not unlike Harry.*

Erik strapped himself into the front seat and quickly scanned the instrument panel. The only instrument showing life was the tachometer. It was trying to settle down on a specific RPM, but the engine was running rough. Erik guessed that it would smooth out when it warmed up to the proper operating temp. The other instruments, airspeed, altimeter, needle-ball, and compass, were lifeless, as they should be because they were on the ground and the Cub was not moving. He was somewhat surprised at the simplicity, that is, the lack of fancy gauges and switches. No radio, no intercom, just a throttle, stick, and rudder pedals.

As the engine warmed, it smoothed out, and Erik knew things would begin to happen. Nervously excited, he awaited instructions from Harry. He would have to listen closely because of the loud noise from the engine. He heard Harry yell out, "Follow me on the controls" as the aircraft began to move. Erik grabbed the stick and throttle, placed his feet on the rudder pedals, and experienced the sensation of his first taxi.

Harry was controlling the aircraft, and Erik felt the controls move as they made a series of gentle "S" turns to the other end of the field. Because the aircraft was designed with a tail wheel, it was difficult to see in front of it — or over the cowling — when on the ground. The "S" turns enabled the pilot to see ahead and ensure a clear path.

About halfway there, Harry said, "You have it," meaning that Erik was to take control of the aircraft. With some anxiety, he took control and attempted to continue the taxi in the smooth manner that Harry did. But he was too tight on his first "S" turn, and the plane almost stopped. Erik gunned the throttle to keep it moving, and it spun around in a full tight circle, almost tipping over on the wing — ground looping. Evidently Harry came to life because he spilled his coffee. Erik felt the throttle yanked from his grip as Harry jerked it back to idle. His voice was loud and clear over the engine noise. For two minutes he shouted words of encouragement such as dumb shit, asshole, and Christ, where did you learn that? Erik was devastated; it happened so quickly.

They sat there, Harry ranting and Erik trying to gain the strength and composure to quit, or to go on. *I have to settle down.*

Then, incredibly, Harry softened his voice and said, "Hey, these things happen. No big deal. You'll get the hang of it." Harry put the aircraft back on path and guided Erik through the taxi process.

As Erik taxied to the run-up position, he began to feel confident. The aircraft responded to his demands, and he thought that perhaps he had made a good choice. *God, it feels good.*

The run-up procedure consisted of locking the brakes and running the engine up to full power in order to check its performance. In addition to the power check, Erik moved all of the controls — stick and rudder pedals — to their limits, while he visually checked the elevator, ailerons, and rudder to determine whether they were free of obstructions and operated properly. With these checks completed, Erik taxied into position and added full power for takeoff.

While Harry monitored every move, Erik released the brakes, and the aircraft moved slowly over the rough and uneven shale that made up the runway. Slowly accelerating to takeoff speed, the craft began to ease over the bumpy terrain as it acquired more lift. Erik could hear Harry yelling, "That's good ... don't let her swerve, keep her in the center ... you're doing a good job. Lift her off now ... good. We're airborne."

Erik had never felt such exhilaration. His senses were alive; he was airborne and felt unattached. The earth below was ghostly with its leafless winter clothing. The mountains were awesome as they provided a jagged and formidable horizon. Erik knew that he made the right choice.

Harry took the craft and demonstrated some of the basic maneuvers he wanted Erik to practice and attain proficiency in. He showed Erik how to climb and turn and dive and soar as a bird. He handled the craft with professional tenderness. He was in his element, and it showed. Erik turned around to catch a glimpse of Harry in action and caught the expression on his face — an expression of serenity, confidence and, perhaps, a longing for days past.

Erik was a natural in the air and progressed rapidly under the skillful handling of Harry. He had a genuine respect for Harry and flew some ten or twelve hops with him over a two-month period. He would have flown more if he'd had the money.

He spent all of his free time at the field, hustling pilots to wash their aircraft for an occasional free ride, and, if lucky, some stick time. One of these pilots, Stew Chambers, was a member of the CAP, and he had taught Erik some of the ground school classes. Despite an age difference of ten or so years, they became good friends and spent many hours together discussing aviation — and the art of growing into manhood.

Stew was an ex-Army Air Corps pilot. He didn't see combat action, nor did he fly a front-line fighter, but he had earned his gold lieutenant bars and his wings of silver. This qualified him as a hero in Erik's eyes. He was a personable, good-looking guy with a shock of white hair that projected from an abundance of jet black. With a boyish grin, he recounted his greatest war experience. "There I was," he said, "with the big boys at the O'Club fighter bar, sporting shiny new wings and acting out an aerial dog fight with my hands. Damn if I didn't lose my balance and fall off the bar stool. The fall tore up my knee, and, ninety days later, I was released from the Army. My career as a future war hero, terminated."

Stew went out to the field each week and rented the Cub for an hour's flight. Occasionally, when he was alone, he invited Erik to join him, and Erik was delighted to go with him at every opportunity. Free flight time was not easy to find. So, when Stew gave Erik instruction and let him fly the plane, it was fun as well as rewarding.

One late afternoon, they were taxiing for takeoff when they came abreast of the old billboard at the edge of the field. Stew said that he often stopped the plane and slipped behind the billboard to relieve his bladder. A "nervous pee," he called it. He stopped the craft, pulled the engine back to idle, and walked toward the sign. He took ten steps or so, turned toward Erik, and said, "If the wind comes up, you know it may upset the aircraft ... put you and the bird in danger. Just remember that you can handle it ... even if you have to become airborne!" He then disappeared behind the sign. *Did I hear correctly? Is Stew giving me the go ahead for solo? Certainly, he knows it is illegal, and it may cost him his license. But Stew had never taken a "nervous pee" before, and there is little time to make a decision.*

Without further hesitation, Erik determined that the wind was up and threatening. He turned the bird into the wind and added full throttle. The plane gained speed as it bumped down the old field, and Erik gently lifted the nose to become airborne. They were flying, and it was his first time alone.

It was thrilling. He was stealing an aircraft and making his solo escape. He felt the aircraft break her earthly bonds and climb up and away from the field; Erik yelled out to the world with uninhibited, unrestrained elation. His dream had become reality. He knew he had to calm himself, for there was much to do. He had to land the plane, and he wanted to look good. There could be no errors, or Stew's — and Erik's — flying days would come to a halt.

From force of habit, he looked around at the back seat. No Harry, no Stew, just one cavernous hole, and he became aware that he was alone. It was difficult to control his breathing. Hyperventilation set in as he turned downwind into the pattern at eight-hundred feet above ground level. He set up his 180-degree abeam position at the proper distance and lowered the nose slightly. He reduced power and started his turn into final, and then intercepted the landing glideslope. *It looked good, really good.* But then more apprehension. *What if I've forgotten something important?* He mentally raced through the check list. Carburetor heat … *damn … forgot the carb heat switch. Not good thinking, Erik.* He pulled the switch out to the "on" position.

The touchdown point rapidly approached, and there was little time for mind games. *This was the real thing. Control your breathing; act like a professional.* And he did, with a smooth touch down and roll out. When the aircraft slowed to a safe speed, he turned it toward the billboard. He saw Stew scurry from behind it.

Erik tried to be Joe Cool as he taxied toward him, but a moment of panic set in when he realized that Stew may not have intended for him to solo. These doubts were removed when he saw Stew with his broad, personable smile. Erik pulled the throttle back to idle and opened the cockpit door for Stew, who beamed with the pride of a new father. He shook hands with Erik, and, over the engine noise, he yelled, "congratulations, Erik, the wind came up and you handled it like a pro. That was one hell of a flight!" Then he climbed into the back seat and calmly said, "Now take us back to the hangar, Ace." And Ace took them back.

CHAPTER EIGHT

THE SOLO HAD TAKEN PLACE, BUT, BECAUSE STEW WAS NOT A FLIGHT instructor, it was not official. Stew asked Harry if he would certify the solo, and Harry replied in his usual charming manner, "Hell no!" Actually, in fairness to Harry, he could have lost his instructor's certificate if he had given the go ahead. He later explained to Stew that he would fly a couple of hops with Erik, and, if they went all right, he would officially sign him off for solo when he was sixteen.

Official or not, the impact of the solo was significant to Erik. It had to be rated as the most important day of his young life. He was fully captivated by flying, and he considered his solo as one of the big three events he had experienced, and it was guilt-free. The other two events — his first orgasm and almost getting laid by a real, live girl — were big, but not without guilt, and therefore, not as special.

Erik was puzzled, however, because he finally did something special — he soloed — and when he told his parents, his father said little or nothing. No congrats, no attaboys, no nothing. He just nodded as though it was another day.

Erik resented his dad's lack of interest and support. It was a big disappointment. *Could it mean so little to him? Was it because I finally did something that he didn't, or couldn't? Jealousy, maybe?* Erik was quick to dismiss such thoughts because he knew that dads didn't do that. Not his dad anyway.

The CAP Unit became more active, and Erik became more involved. They promoted him to Cadet Corporal, and he sported a proud uniform on the nights of the weekly meetings. For the first time, Erik sensed that a career in aviation could become a reality.

Individual CAP Units were sponsored by the Army Air Corps, and this sponsorship allowed the units to acquire a surplus aircraft of their own. Erik's local unit eventually received one of the surplus airplanes, a light observation aircraft. It was to be utilized for search and rescue and for downed or overdue aircraft in the area. To assist the unit with the burden of paperwork and other logistical matters associated with the plane, the Air Corps designated a liaison officer for Erik's unit. He was an active duty pilot, a major, who resided in and worked out of the Southern states. He would routinely visit the unit, flying into town in his T-6 Texan advanced trainer. It was not a P-51 Mustang, but in the eyes of a young student pilot, such as Erik, it was an awesome, impressive bird. Equally impressive was the man who piloted it, Major Belford. In his early thirties, trim, tall, and the personification of a fighter pilot, Major Charles A. Belford became Erik's new liaison officer ... and mentor.

As an academy graduate, Major Belford had an enviable record that included several fighter kills and a tour as a test pilot. This provided him with an unlimited number of war stories that he related to his receptive audience. His seven rows of ribbons — topped by his silver command wings all set on an immaculate uniform — were an awe-inspiring sight for young CAP cadets. His presence assured a full house for a "command performance," and, like most of the cadets, Erik never missed a session. He told Stew that he wanted to be just like Major Belford, and Stew agreed that it was an admirable goal.

A few months passed with regular visits, and the Major and Erik appeared to establish a sincere instructor–student relationship. Erik asked his parents if he could invite Major Belford to dinner, and they agreed. Erik made the invitation, and, somewhat to his surprise, the Major accepted without hesitation. He told Erik that he would be back in the area in a couple of weeks, and they could get together at that time if it was okay with his parents.

The two weeks passed, and Major Belford called Erik at home and said that he would fly in during the next day at 1600 (4:00 P.M.) and wondered if Erik would meet him. Erik gave him an elated, "That's a wilco, sir."

The next day, Friday, at 1530, Erik was at the ramp awaiting the arrival of the Major. He was excited, proud, and nervous. Nervous because it was important that all went well. It was his first time he invited an adult to join his family at dinner, and he thought that the outcome would hinge on the reaction of his father. His dad could be very charming, but Erik had seen him otherwise, a bit unpolished, he thought.

It was almost 1600 when Erik heard an aircraft some distance east of the field. He spotted the aircraft coming over the horizon and recognized it as a T-6. The engine noise increased in strength, and Erik guessed that it was wide open; all 450 horsepower strained to acquire maximum speed out of the bird. It had no more than thirty feet of altitude when it made a high speed pass down the runway, just in front of Erik, at a speed of three-hundred miles per hour. Erik couldn't recognize the blurred face of the pilot as he pulled the aircraft up into a steep climbing turn and entered the landing pattern. For Erik, it was an awesome display of sound and speed. The noise from the changing pitch of the propeller would not go unnoticed by the surrounding locals. It was an impressive entrance, and Erik could only dream that he would have his day, the day that he could make such a high speed pass announcing his arrival.

The T-6 taxied up to the ramp, and Erik could recognize the pilot as Major Belford, who sat tall in the front cockpit. The canopy was open, and the Major's white silk scarf flowed along the port side of the fuselage. The waxed, silver aircraft was most imposing with its guttural sounds that only a radial engine can produce. In the eyes of a youngster, who had only flown a Piper Cub, it was a striking, powerful piece of equipment.

As the aircraft reached the ramp parking area, Major Belford swung it around into position and shut her down. He climbed out of the cockpit as Erik strode up to greet him. Showing a generous smile, he waved to Erik as he climbed down the side of the aircraft.

On ground, Major Belford removed his starched tan flight suit, exposing a full uniform with all the colorful ribbons and insignia. *This is real class, how could anyone be so lucky?*

A few airport people and some sightseers began to gather around, asking Major Belford about the flight and his aircraft. He was most gracious with the new guests, and Erik felt their respect for him. He was proud when the Major told them he had flown in to have dinner with his new cadet friend, Erik. It was Erik's first experience in the limelight, and, even though it was a small part, he enjoyed the basking.

The group began to thin, and Major Belford announced that he and his young friend had to leave, as they could not be late for dinner. With that announcement Erik escorted the Major to the taxicab, and they rode home to meet the parents.

Dad and Mom were awaiting their arrival, and Erik was pleased with the response of all. His dad was congenial, and, as always, his mother was a lady and a charming hostess.

The dinner of fried chicken with mashed potatoes was heartily welcomed, and all appeared to enjoy the evening. Major Belford said it was time to leave, and during the process of thanking each other for a warm, pleasant evening, he mentioned to Burt that he was attending a CAP conference in the northern part of the state. He said he would be glad to take Erik with him in the T-6 if it was all right with the parents. They thought this was a great idea and thanked him for his generous offer. Erik was overwhelmed with such an invitation and his parents' response. It was difficult to restrain himself from becoming a giddy teenager.

It was time to end the visit, and Burt drove the Major to the local hotel. And Erik awaited the big day.

TWO WEEKS LATER, THE BIG DAY ARRIVED. ERIK, DRESSED IN HIS FRESHLY STARCHED cadet's uniform, was at the airport early awaiting the arrival of Major Belford and his T-6.

Hearing the sound of an engine from the east, he searched the horizon and as before spotted an aircraft coming in at a low altitude. *I hope he is going to make another high speed pass.* And he did, even better than the first one, and Erik could never tire of it.

The aircraft taxied up to the ramp; the white silk scarf streamed from the open cockpit as the Major kept the engine running at idle. He motioned to Erik to climb aboard and strap into the aft cockpit. Erik was so excited that he had trouble sorting out the straps that secured him into the parachute. And these were tangled with the helmet and the dangling cords of the lip mike. Finally, the Major turned around from the front cockpit and pointed out the different connections and gave Erik a "thumbs up" when all were joined properly. He then added power for taxi.

It all happened so quickly, Erik was afraid he would miss some of the flight. He wanted to see everything that was done. He wanted to feel it, to be a part of it.

As they taxied, he looked around the cockpit. It was huge when compared to the Cub, and it had many instruments and switches. It also had a full set of flight controls in his cockpit, and he dared to think that he would be allowed some stick time once airborne and leveled out.

As they arrived at the runway, they swung out into takeoff position and, without stopping for run-up and release, the Major kept her rolling while adding full throttle. As the engine gained RPM, the noise level climbed, and Erik was mesmerized with the apparent power of such an engine. He smelled the heavy fumes released at the higher RPM, fumes of burnt fuel and oil.

The aircraft raced down the runway and literally jumped into the air, and, as the gear came up, she gained speed rapidly. Erik felt and heard some reduction of power. He knew that Major Belford had pulled the throttle back to climb power and was resetting the pitch of the propeller. Erik had learned this was proper procedure; stay in takeoff power only until safely airborne. High power settings destroy the life of the engine.

The climb-out over the mountains was always impressive. It never ceased to be a humbling experience. The mountains were majestic, threatening, and endless. At ten thousand feet, Major Belford leveled her out and set up cruise power of seventy-five percent and reduced RPM by increasing prop pitch — the increased bite of the propeller for more efficiency — and Erik settled back to enjoy the second most significant flight of his life.

It was an exciting experience with the radios and headset active, navigational instruments moving, and the Major talking to the flight control center. Erik had some doubts that he could ever learn the complexities of such a craft, but he could not allow himself to dwell on these doubts. He knew it took dedicated training, and he already had proved that he could be trained. Ten minutes after level-out, Major Belford came over the intercom, "How are we doing, Erik?"

"Doing great, sir. Never had such a thrill."

"All right, son ... you take the controls, hold 219 degrees and ten thousand five hundred feet."

Without hesitation, Erik took the controls and, for the first time, encountered a relationship with the aircraft. He heard stories from the older pilots that an aircraft should be a part of you. It was not a part of him as yet, but, more important, he knew that it would be in the near future. This was comforting to Erik, as he had never been more at peace with himself, or with his God.

They arrived at their destination where Major Belford attended two short meetings. Erik dutifully sat on the sidelines and patiently awaited for takeoff time and the thrill of becoming airborne. At 1500, Major Belford said to Erik,

"Let's get out of here, my friend." And they did. The takeoff and climb out above the mountains repeated the same thrilling experiences for Erik.

Once at altitude, he was allowed to handle the aircraft; he did a good job. And he knew it.

Sometime after 1700, they landed at home field, and it was almost dark. The Major said that he was going to stay over in Scantsville and would fly out early in the morning. He asked Erik to ride into town with him. He said he could drop him off anyplace convenient. Erik agreed that the hotel would be a decent drop-off point because it was close to the corner drugstore, and he may get to see a buddy or two. Erik wanted a chance to brag about his flight.

They boarded the rental car and drove into town, some ten minutes en route. They talked about the flight, and the Major explained some of the procedures he used. Erik was fascinated with the discussion. "Sir, it has been one fantastic day," he said to Major Belford, "and I don't know how I can thank you."

"I'm glad we could do it, Erik. I like to help out youngsters, and I'm sure we'll do it again."

They arrived at the hotel and pulled into the parking lot. Before they got out, Major Belford said that he would change clothes, then have dinner.

"You think you can join me, Erik?" he asked, "It would be a nice way to end the day."

"I would love to, Major, but I have to check with my parents." *The chance to brag will have to wait.*

"Good, that will be fine, Erik, you come up to the room. I'll change clothes, and you can call the folks. Then we'll decide where to eat."

They got out of the car and walked the short distance to the hotel entrance. Erik realized he had never been inside a hotel. How strange, I've been here all these years and have never paid any attention to the only hotel in town. He had been told it was a seven-storied beauty in its time, around the turn of the century. The old timers used words such as "regal" and "stately" when they talked about it. But Erik could see nothing regal or stately about the structure. *"Rundown and weather-beaten" would be more appropriate. Time has not been good to this hotel.* He smiled when he saw the red neon sign. It was supposed to flash "Scantsville Hotel" but obviously some of the letters were dead because the sign flashed "Sca t   le."

They entered the lobby, and Erik's first impression was stale air and the aroma of old carpet. Through the obscured light, he saw a large, crystal chandelier dangling from the center of the high ceiling. Erik guessed that the crystal had given up its attempt to sparkle, but perhaps in the past it was splendid. He couldn't imagine, though, that the old carpet with its faded flower designs was ever splendid.

The Major's room was on the fifth floor, and they used the elevator. It acted as though it were making its last trip … slow and creaky. Erik was not at ease. Nothing he could identify. Perhaps he was tired or anxious to tell someone about the day. And after experiencing the spacious beauty of the flight, it was difficult to be cramped up in a hotel, particularly an old, musty hotel.

They arrived at the room, some fifty feet down a half-lit corridor, and entered. It was little better than the rest of the hotel. It was small and colorless and smelled of old paint and dank carpet. There was a sink exposed in the corner and a bathtub half hidden behind the closet. An old dresser with five drawers and a wood finish with cigarette burns sat at the head of the bed. The bed was too small to qualify as a double.

Major Belford tossed his case on the bed, opened it, removed some clothes — and a pint of bourbon. He opened the bottle, grabbed a glass off the dresser, and poured himself a shot.

Turning toward Erik, he asked, "Care to join me in a drink, my friend?"

"No, sir, I don't drink," Erik responded without thinking. *What a jerk I am, lying to the Major. Of course I've had a drink. Never had whiskey with an adult, but certainly, I've had a drink.*

"Oh, go ahead and have one," he said, "I won't tell your folks. It will make you feel good … feel relaxed."

"I feel relaxed already, sir."

"No, I mean really relaxed, Erik."

"All right, sir, maybe just a small one."

The Major poured Erik a small shot and handed it to him saying, "A little eye-opener will never hurt you, son."

Erik thanked him and with a nervous smile took a sip of the bourbon. It was hot going down the throat, and he hoped he wouldn't get sick. Actually, Erik had had only two or three drinks of hard whisky in his lifetime, and one of those times was a disaster. He had thrown up, and he was embarrassed because that was not the manly thing to do. But it appeared that the whisky was going to stay down this time. He was relieved, thankful.

Major Belford downed his drink with one swift gulp and without delay poured another. He set it on the dresser and began to remove his flight suit. Erik, who was near the center of the room, was uneasy standing that close to an important man who was undressing. It was an awkward situation, and he wished that he had gone directly home. It disturbed him that the Major didn't look nearly as impressive standing in his baggy skivvies and tank top undershirt. *He's not very tall. And without his uniform, not nearly so tan and handsome. Almost frail and ... pallid white. Almost disgusting.*

Then, Major Belford took the drink from the dresser and broke the silence, "Did you enjoy the flight, Erik?"

"Yes, sir, I did. It was one of the best days of my life and ... I can't thank you enough, sir."

"No, I mean did you really enjoy the flight, Erik?"

And with that question, he downed his drink as before. He poured himself another before Erik had a chance to answer, "You know I did, sir, it's all I can think or talk about."

"Well, I don't think you have shown any appreciation, Erik."

Erik was jolted by that statement. He set the remainder of his drink down. He thought it best not to drink it. He was confused. The conversation was not going well, and he couldn't pinpoint the reason, but he knew he was uncomfortable.

"I don't understand, sir, I don't understand at all ... I have thanked you many times, Major."

"Well, what I mean, Erik, is that you haven't shown me any ... real appreciation."

Erik couldn't grasp what was going on. Such a beautiful day, and it was not so pretty now. It was tense.

"Sir, I'm sorry, I guess I'm just a dummy. Real appreciation ... I just don't know what you're talking about, and ... maybe I better go."

"No, wait, Erik, don't leave; it's okay. You haven't done anything wrong."

Erik turned, and Major Belford came over and put his hand on his shoulder. For a moment, Erik thought things were all right, and he was relieved. Perhaps he had misunderstood, but he wished that the Major would explain things, then all would be as before.

Without speaking, the Major placed his empty glass on the dresser, then stepped closer to Erik. In a low tone of voice, he said, "This is what I mean by showing appreciation, Erik," and he suddenly reached out with both arms and pulled him up against his body.

Erik tried to jerk away, but Major Belford held tightly. He tried to force his mouth against Erik's cheek. *This cannot be happening, but it is.* Erik thought he would vomit.

The Major grappled Erik's head down onto his chest and shoulder. He was pinned, and the pungent smell of the Major's underarm was sickening. He could see the hair extending out from the arm pits; he could see the pale, almost clammy white skin of his half-naked frame; he felt the sting and disgust of the day-old whiskers. This was all new, and he became more frightened. His mind continued its race. He had never been embraced by a man. Men didn't do that; his father didn't do that, and he was terrified. He felt the pain of panic. He was not afraid for his life. He was afraid because he didn't want to believe what was taking place. His dreams of flying, his idol, his fighter pilot was no more than a common queer, like the one who volunteered to drive the basketball team … an old fat fuck, soft and pasty white. He saw him once, but all the kids knew.

He had to break away, to break loose. He couldn't imagine hitting Major Belford, his ideal, his mentor. Major Belford kept pleading, "Please show me, Erik … show me some appreciation!"

He struggled to kiss Erik on the lips. Erik felt the pain of the Major's fingernails as they dug into the back of his neck. He thought he would pass out, not from the physical pain, but from the shock and nausea that rushed through his body. The pathetic cries of "Please show me, Erik … real appreciation" kept ringing in his mind. Erik felt dirty, ashamed, and helpless. He wanted forgiveness, and his body cried out for someone, something to correct the wrong.

Then, a flash of sanity, and, in an instant, it was clear. He could break the hold; he could get out of the room. He forced his arms inside of the Major's, and, with all of the strength he could generate, slammed them into his chest. The force of the blow freed Erik and hurled Major Belford against the wall. He saw the surprised, pathetic look on the Major's face. He looked so helpless and for an instant Erik felt sorry for his hero.

But the gravity of the incident alerted his senses, and Erik tore out of the room, down the many staircases, and out into the fresh clean air of the night. He didn't look back. He ran.

He ran away from the musty odors and the bourbon breath. Away from the pallid white skin, and the crystals that lost their sparkle. Away from the bygone days of splendor — that had been evicted by dank carpet and day-old whiskers.

That night — the shame, the shock, the anger — it all engulfed him. He felt alone, dirty, and dazed. He cried, and he cursed. He cursed his hero and perhaps himself; he couldn't understand. *Was I a part of it ... did I cause the problem? ... It has to be me ... it couldn't be the Major. He's too much of a man, too damn good to be like that. He's a fighter pilot for Christ's sake. Maybe, I exaggerated, maybe, it was my fault. Does that mean Stew is like that? ... and my Dad? Do they hug and kiss men ... and boys? Is this what I'm expected to do ... now and when I grow up?*

He couldn't understand, and he couldn't tell his dad because he had heard him say, "All queers should be shot." Erik had always wondered why he said that.

Confused and defeated, he took a long night's walk. "Why ... why did it happen?" he pleaded, "Am I just another one? ... Did I enjoy it? ... Should I?" It was all too distorted for Erik to grasp. All he could do was curse Major Belford ... and the world that shattered his dreams.

I'm just another goddamn failure. I'll never fly again, and I'll never be like Major Belford ... never.

CHAPTER NINE

BURT ALWAYS WANTED TO BE IN BUSINESS FOR HIMSELF. THE OPPORTUNITY came about, and he was able to open a small wholesale meat company. He didn't own it outright, just half of it. His partner, Mr. Beasley, whom he had met through the parish priest, Father Harris, put up the money, $9,000. It was agreed that Mr. Beasley would not participate in the business, and that Burt would run it. He was a proud man the day they deposited the money into the Larsen's Wholesale Meat bank account.

The next day he leased an old, one-story, brick building that adjoined the railroad tracks. The building was as colorless and glum as the surrounding area. It was fifty feet by a hundred feet with wooden floors that sagged. "It's suitable for the purpose," Burt said, "and affordable ... cheap."

Not a busy location, one train a day, but the train was capable of dropping off a boxcar on the siding. The site depressed Erik because it was so rundown, but his dad had confidence that it could be a success. "Hard work will do it, kid," he said, and Erik became his first employee.

Within a week, Burt found a surplus walk-in meat cooler from a recently closed army camp. He also found a truck, a one-ton step-in van. It had one seat, at the steering wheel. It was an old truck and orange colored. Larsen's Wholesale Meat was in business.

Erik spent most of his free time working there. Free time, meaning time not in school, tenth grade. He learned the basics of meat cutting, which, for the most part, meant trimming the final scraps of meat off the bones. Boning, it was called. It was a boring job, even though Erik cut himself quite often, not seriously, just often. But boning was necessary, he was told, because you could not afford to waste the meat, the meat that turned into hamburger, and profit. At times, he thought he would never get out of boning and get the chance to cut "real meat," but the day came when Burt said that Erik was ready to be a meat-cutter. Then Erik began his second phase of training, and it ceased to be boring.

Burt was not a patient man, but he took pride, and time in teaching Erik to be a professional meat-cutter. "You are not a butcher," he said, "you are a meat-cutter; butchers work in packing houses where they kill cows and pigs; they don't cut the beautiful steak … and cutting steak is an art." So Erik avoided the term butcher and strived to become an artist.

Burt spent most of his day and night selling, cutting and delivering meat. Then he bought more and repeated the cycle. He was a tireless worker, but it was obvious to Erik that he could use some help. So the timing was right when he asked if he could get his driver's license before he was sixteen, the age required by law. He explained to his dad that he could do most of the deliveries after school and would still be available for meat-cutting. To his surprise, Burt concurred, and they both told the state that he was of age. Just a little lie, rationalized Erik, less than a year.

With his license, the work became even more interesting, for he was the delivery man, driving a real truck, doing things that real working adults do. And he didn't know any of his schoolmates who drove a truck, and that made it even better. The hours were long, and he still had to bone, but deliveries took priority, so most of his work time was on the road. At least for three months it was on the road.

In the third month, a state trooper stopped Erik and his truck. It was nearly dark when the uniformed trooper sauntered up to the truck and looked it over in detail. Erik was wide-eyed and nervous.

Damn, why do I always have to screw up? … Dad is going to stomp all over me. It seemed like minutes passed before the trooper spoke. "You have a driver's license?"

"Yes, sir."

"Hand me your license, please."

Erik handed the trooper his driver's license, shaking. The trooper studied it in detail. Finally, he looked up and handed Erik the license. Erik was having difficulty with his breathing.

"Kind of highballing it, weren't you, son?"

"Yessir, guess I was … anxious to get back to the plant, sir."

"Well, I tell you what, son, you tell your dad … that's Burt isn't it?"

"Yessir."

"Well, you tell Burt to bring over your birth certificate and your driver's license to the station."

"Yessir."

"Now, I want you to take it easy on the road. You will do that, won't you?"

"Yes sir."

It was a long ride home for Erik. He wasn't sure how Dad was going to react. And how did the trooper know that Burt was his dad? And another thing Erik wondered ... how did he know he was too young to have a driver's license?

Burt took the news of the "highballing" experience much better than Erik expected. Actually, he was quite calm that next morning when Erik told him.

"Did you hit anything with the truck?" Burt asked.

"No, sir, I didn't ... just speeding."

"Didn't I tell you to watch your speed?"

"Yes sir."

"Then why in the hell did you do it?"

"Don't know, sir."

It was later that morning when Erik heard his dad on the phone. "Well, Carl, it's my fault ... I could use the help, and I thought it much better for him, you know, keeping him off the streets and working. So I made the decision ... yes, sixteen this fall ... I agree ..."

The phone hung up, and Burt called to Erik, "I'm taking your license until your birthday. When is it?"

"It's in October, sir. The twelfth."

"Well, that's what I thought ... Okay, put it on my desk."

And Erik put it on the desk, where it remained for two months until his birthday.

The grounded time was good training time for Erik. He learned much about meat-cutting. He learned how to use the proper, or improper, chemicals that would keep the meat red and fresh for a longer period. They were called sodium nitrite and sodium nitrate. He also learned that one was really a form of formaldehyde. The slang term was "dynamite." Cube steaks (bucket or minute steaks), chops, roasts, hamburger, just about all cuts, were dipped in one or both of the chemicals, and he could see that they worked.

He also discovered that you could add flour to the hamburger, and the flour would hold water, about five pounds of water to one pound of flour. The name of the flour was Bull-Meal. He learned that you weighed all retail cuts with the paper or wrappings on, for the extra weight would pay for the materials. He learned that, if the meat didn't stink excessively, you could probably sell it after you wash it with some dynamite.

It was interesting work, and the shop was busy. Salesmen and other people would be in and out of the plant, and Erik heard many grown-up stories about the meat business.

One of his dad's favorite stories was the time he was a youngster working in a meat market. He worked behind the meat counter, and he learned many things from Mr. Katzman, the owner-boss.

Burt's boss demanded that his employees add a few ounces to any and everything put on a scale. You added this weight by use of the finger — discreetly of course — or, if it was a whole chicken, you would slip a lead plug up the chicken's ass before it was weighed. Naturally, you had to pull it out before it was wrapped.

One afternoon, Burt was caught pulling the plug by a little ole irate lady who reported him to his boss. Mr. Katzman was visibly upset, and he thanked her profusely for bringing it to his attention. He told her he would fire the youngster, even though he knew the kid desperately needed a job because of his sick mother ... and a father out of work. Then he stomped back to the counter, pointed at Burt and said, in a voice to be heard throughout the market, "After all I've done for you and your sick mother, you cheat Mrs. Golen. You embarrass me ... You are fired!"

And Burt slowly took off his apron, hung his head in sorrow, and started for the front door. The market was silent, and as he approached the door, he turned, and with stage performance, pleaded, "Sir, I'm sorry, I was only trying to help ... I knew you could use the extra profit ... you've done so much for me and my family ... if I could just have another chance?"

"I said you're fired. We don't have people in this store that will cheat Mrs. Golen. You're fired and that's final ... now get the hell out!"

"Oh, Mr. Katzman, I didn't mean for you to be that hard on him," Mrs. Golen said.

"I'm sorry for the language, Mrs. Golen, but we just can't have that kind of behavior."

Then, with a tear, if he could develop one, Burt turned, and looked into Mrs. Golen's half-shocked face and, in a low, almost inaudible voice, said, "I'm sorry, ma'am … I'm really sorry." And he left the store.

Then, he went for a cup of coffee and returned later through the back door of the market. Mr. Katzman met him, chewed him out for getting caught, and then patted him on the back for keeping up the good work — bringing in the extra money. Cheating.

The next time Mrs. Golen came to the store she was relieved to see that young Burt had been rehired, given another chance … just as she had recommended. She thanked Mr. Katzman, and he replied, "Well, Mrs. Golen, I reconsidered … a sick mother and all … he's just a kid. And your wishes Mrs. Golen, you are a kind and gentle woman. God wanted me to forgive him."

Erik liked the story, but it was confusing. *Does this mean that I'm supposed to cheat the customers?"* No, I won't do that … *I'm not going to confession and say, "Yes, Father, I put a lead plug up a chicken's ass, so that Dad could make more money.* He had to laugh at that, even though it was serious.

CHAPTER TEN

ERIK WAS OFFICIALLY SIXTEEN WITH A LEGITIMATE DRIVER'S LICENSE. BURT put him back on the delivery route with a new refrigerated three-ton International truck. He enjoyed driving the new truck, and it was always a pleasant benefit to be away from the scrutiny of Burt. *I always seem to screw up a lot when he's around,* Erik thought.

One night, close to ten, Erik was returning from a full day of deliveries down in Pine County. He was slowly making his way up a narrow mountainous road in a steady, cold rain. There was little or no traffic, and, in the surrounding darkness, he spotted a flicker of light ahead, just off the roadside. Visibility was poor, and he was apprehensive because he had heard stories of truck-jacking in the mountains, and he didn't carry a weapon like many of the truckers did. As he approached, he recognized that it was a person signaling with a flashlight. Erik continued with caution toward the light, then he noticed two other figures with him. All three of them hovered under a piece of tarp they held above their heads in a feeble attempt to gain relief from the rain. Erik suspected some sort of emergency, so he stopped the truck to offer assistance.

The man with the flashlight yelled over the drone of the engine, "Hey buddy, these here are my kinfolk, Clare and Cecil. They can't start their car and they got to git in town ... You help 'em out?"

"Well ... not supposed to ... well, all right, climb on in."

It's a yucky night, and I'm sure Dad would go along with it.

Clare got in first, and Cecil squeezed in with some difficulty. He was unable to get the door latched, and, as Erik reached over to help, he realized why they had trouble starting their car. The both reeked of alcohol (he had smelled it before), and the truck cab immediately filled with the foul odor of wet clothing and used booze. He regretted that he had stopped to help out. But the decision had been made, and he decided it would not be wise to tell them to get back out into the dark rain. *Besides, Cecil is most likely a coal miner, and you just don't tell miners to do things like that. Not unless you want to bleed all over.*

It was crowded in the dark cab, but, with little trouble, Erik shifted into a lower gear and began the slow climb up the mountain. They both thanked Erik several times for helping them out, and Cecil continued to talk. He never stopped. He told Erik he worked in the mines, he was married to Clare, he was forty, that Clare was thirty-five, what a great guy Erik was, and on and on.

The three of them were on the road perhaps fifteen minutes when Erik began to feel more at ease. Cecil was still talking, but he wasn't loud, and Erik decided he wasn't that offensive. The hum of the geared-down engine was relaxing, and the rain began to slack. He drifted into his own thoughts when he was startled by the touch of something on his thigh. A quick glance identified the "something" as a hand ... and it was resting on his thigh. He didn't know who's hand, but assumed it must be Clare's. Then a scary thought rushed through Erik. *My god, it could be Cecil's....* But another look confirmed it to be Clare's.

He regained his composure; he was glad the hand was there. It felt good. Then, without warning, the hand started to move; it was no longer resting, and Erik tensed. It continued its move, right into his crotch area and proceeded to unzip his fly. Within seconds it touched and held his penis — which turned hard almost immediately. Erik breathed with difficulty. He had fantasized such a setting, but not in a truck cab with a husband at arm's length. *This is not a good situation. In fact, it's crazy, and most of all, it's damn dangerous.* Clare didn't stop caressing, and Cecil didn't stop talking ... and Erik didn't stop breathing. He decided that the pleasure – ecstasy – was worth the threat of injury. He truly wished that the trip would take longer than it should. It was a first for him, and all he could think of was, *I'm actually being fondled by a woman.*

Within an hour they arrived in town, just before midnight. The weather remained dark and chilly, but no rain. The windows of the darkened cab were trying to steam, and Clare was still holding onto Erik's penis when they arrived at the couple's house. Cecil thanked Erik again and said to his wife, "Clare, thank this young man, and let's git on to bed."

"Okay ... you get on in ... I'll be there shortly."

"No, you come on now ... he's got to git the truck back."

"Well, I'm comin', Cecil, I just wanna thank him ... that's all ... I'll be in."

"Come on, Clare," he half pleaded as he opened the cab door and stepped out.

"I'll be there, Cecil ... just wanna thank him."

"Well, okay then, but don't be long," he said as he went on into the house.

Erik was definitely confused. He couldn't believe that she actually talked her husband into letting her stay in the truck. He was afraid to say or do anything. It was all so bizarre, and no one would believe him. She took her hand out of his trousers and leaned forward in the cab and began pulling her panties off. "I'm gonna thank you ... really thank you," she said.

Erik was spellbound, entranced, frightened. He was overwhelmed by desire. He wanted to screw, and he wanted to screw her, but he didn't want to die either — or at the least, incur serious bodily harm.

She finally worked her panties off and began to work her naked rear into position on Erik's lap. Erik couldn't take his eyes off of that white ass ... it was beautiful, even in the dim light. It was soft, smooth, and looked delicious ... and God, the best part, so accessible. It was right there, and he decided that it was worth the chance of dying ... well, almost, he reasoned.

She found her position, and he could feel the head of his penis touching her vagina. He was electrified with desire. He couldn't wait. *What the hell,* he rationalized, *it can't be that dangerous ... besides you have to die sometime. And he penetrated her to the limit.*

He had never felt anything quite like it, pure heaven, and he heard Clare react with a gasp ... a wild groan ... and a trembling, "Oh God!" Then she shuddered, lunged forward ... and puked! She puked with her total body, loud gushing sounds and spray, not unlike the opened fireplug Erik played in as a kid during the hot summer days. She managed to spray most of the cab, and Erik, with her gift from the stomach of old booze, pizza, and God knows what else.

The screwing and the gushing ceased before the third stroke was completed. Confused in a tense situation, Erik hurriedly zipped up his fly. He opened the passenger door – a wet stinking door – from the inside. Clare promptly rolled out and fell to the grass. Erik leaped out from the driver's side and scurried around the front of the truck to help her up. She lay there with her dress up about her hips, and unfortunately, without her panties.

His heart raced, and his body was nearly immobilized with fear. Then he heard it. He heard the front door of the house open, and he heard heavy footsteps on the porch. Cecil's footsteps, all 6' 4" of him, was on his way to find out just what the hell was going on. Erik leaped to the grounded Clare and with one movement pulled the dress below her knees. He spun around toward the husband and made a special attempt to regain composure before speaking.

"Cecil, I think your wife is sick ... I was trying to help."

Cecil stood there, looked at Erik and at his vomit-covered trousers, then at the reclining Clare ... then again at Erik. There was a long silence, and Erik realized that he could be in trouble, big trouble. *My fly ... it's open.* Then he realized he had zipped it shut ... *thank God.* You just don't screw around with a miner's wife. Erik knew that. He had heard the horror stories from his classmates.

Cecil, face drawn and tight, walked over to Erik, looked down at him and said, "Thanks ... she's been drinkin' ... I'm gonna take care of her, and I think you better git on down the road."

"Yessir," he said, and Erik proceeded to "git" on down the road.

A relieved and thankful Erik was gone. He took the mess, the stench, the vomit with him. It was an exciting night, he thought, and it isn't over yet. Maybe Cecil was too tired or drunk — or both — to notice Clare's bare ass. *Man, I hope so. How could I have been so damn stupid?*

Then he realized that the truck – and himself – had to be cleaned before his dad arrived. Dad had a habit of working early and alone in the mornings. The timing could be close.

He hosed his trousers off, then the cab; he prayed that the truck would keep its "new truck smell." And then he saw the panties lodged half under the seat. He smiled when he thought about his luck. *They could have been in Cecil's front yard ... greeting the sunrise.*

He carefully picked them up between two fingers, and looked around to ensure that he was alone. Cautiously, he went over to the trash barrel and released the panties into the security of darkness. *That should do it,* he thought, as he smiled. He was feeling better, then ... *Damn, here comes Dad. This is not good.*

The car pulled up, and Burt came over to the truck. "You're running kind of late. Any trouble?" he said.

"No, sir," Erik said, "just cleaning up a bit."

"Cleaning up what? Have you been drinking?"

"Oh, no sir, you know I don't do that, Dad."

"Well, it smells kind of strong ... what's going on?" Burt asked. Erik could sense the growing agitation.

"Well, Dad, I was hoping you wouldn't find out, but I got kind of sick, and heaved ... I'm sorry about the truck, sir."

"Well, you should have called ... you okay now?"

"Yes, sir, I'm fine."

Burt looked at Erik and the truck, then said, "Well, you get some sleep ... we have a big day today."

Somewhat numb, Erik left immediately. He couldn't believe he had lied to his father. That was the first time (except for a white lie or so) that he could remember, and it was not pleasant.

On the way home, however, he had to smile. *Jeeze what a night. Talk about close calls ... Cecil, then Dad. Yes, I am one lucky guy. It was a close one, Erik.*

But I got laid ... I think.

CHAPTER ELEVEN

BURT LEASED A SMALL PACKING HOUSE THAT HAD FAILED TO SURVIVE THE business world. It was good news for Erik. Packing houses have a kill-floor (slaughter room), and he had heard that kill-floors were exciting. *Now I can become a butcher ... not just a meat-cutter.* There was also a sausage prep room — a kitchen — and he could learn how to make the different lunch meats, hot dogs, and sausages. He wanted to work in all areas. Erik knew that he worked hard, but he didn't know if he was a good employee because his dad never told him so. But Erik worked for half price, and that had to help make him a "good employee" in the eyes of Burt. He was sure that Burt was happier about the wage scale than he was.

It was a big day for Erik when he was assigned to the floor. He was anxious to be part of the action. School was out for the summer, and vacation provided him with sufficient time to learn the process. He met Cliff, the chief skinner and "kill-man," his new boss. He was a short, wiry, half Italian who looked ornery in a friendly way. Cliff spoke softly and was a bit of a mystery to Erik. He fascinated Erik because he had heard about kill-men from Burt. *It must take a different type of man to come into work and kill animals all day.*

Erik arrived at 5:30 that morning, his first morning on the floor. Cliff told him it would be cow-killing day, and Erik tingled with excitement.

He had his new work uniform on, a clean white, heavy cotton uniform consisting of shirt, trousers, and a full-length apron. All starched, pressed, and clean smelling. Shoes were replaced with knee-high, black rubber boots, and his head was covered with a white, ball-cap-style hat.

He felt good that morning, almost professional, as he strapped on his belt that embraced the tools that were sheaved to hang from his side. The sheaf contained a skinning knife, an eight-inch boning knife, and a sharpening steel. Erik felt like a man.

The livestock to be slaughtered were put in holding pens the day before. These pens were connected to the kill-floor entrance by narrow wooden fences that formed a path or a "shoot." You could drive one or more animals through this shoot onto the kill-floor, or you could hold them at different points in the shoot until you were ready for them.

Erik was impressed with the room used for killing. It was mainly concrete, with a poured slab floor and block walls that were whitewashed. The room was sizeable, some fifty-feet long and thirty-five feet wide with high ceilings, maybe twenty-feet high. It allowed sound to produce a hint of an echo. The windows were set close to the ceiling, and they were too high to allow a normal view of the landscape. The windows did, however, allow daylight to enter. A steel track hung from the ceiling with two chain hoists on rollers that made it possible to move the shackled animals to different locations.

At the other end of the kill floor, opposite of the shoot entrance, there was a large walk-in meat cooler for storage. The cleaned carcasses were pushed directly into this cooler on the overhead rails.

He was surprised how clean the slaughter room was, and it even smelled clean with no odors of dead meat, or blood, or urine, or guts. He noticed that the floor was smooth, wet, and rather slippery. There was a thin layer of water that ran across the floor and into one of the drains in the middle. A steady stream of water trickled from the hose that was neatly coiled on the block wall. The same hose that Cliff used for the morning wash-down.

"Erik, always keep your room clean," Cliff said as he hosed everything down. Erik had wondered why they wore rubber boots, and now he understood.

"Well, Erik, are we ready to start the day?"

"Yessir, Cliff, I'm ready to learn to be a kill-man," Erik replied. His grin exposed his excitement.

"Then let's do it, son. I'll make you a damn good one!"

Erik followed Cliff out through the narrow shoot entrance, and they opened and closed several gates before arriving at the pen that held fifteen head of cattle. The cattle appeared nervous. *Perhaps it's just the strange surroundings ... they couldn't know what's in store for them.*

Cliff selected one of them and calmly cut it away from the others by using his arms and body motions to herd it out of the pen and down the shoot. He didn't use a stick or an electric prodder. He didn't raise his voice; he simply separated a cow from the security of her kind and moved her into the narrow shoot.

"You come out of the pen now, Erik. Close the gate, and stand behind her while I climb out and slip a line on her."

Erik was a little apprehensive, but did as he was told. He watched Cliff scramble up the side of the six-foot-high fence and move forward to the cow's head. Leaning over the side, he spoke calmly and slipped a rope around her neck. Erik was impressed with the apparent gentleness of the entire procedure. Yelling and screaming at a terrified animal was not part of the scene.

"That's the way you do it, Erik," and Cliff climbed back into the shoot and led the animal to the kill room.

"Erik, don't try to do the same thing with the bulls," he said, "They'll knock you on your ass. ... I mean right on your ass."

At the entrance to the room, Erik sensed a change in the peaceful atmosphere. The cow began to struggle against the lead, and he saw Cliff tighten the line and force her to follow him into the room. When she stepped onto the smooth concrete floor, her hooves slipped, and it was difficult for her to keep her footing. Erik saw the tension mount within her body. The strange place frightened her, and she struggled to return to her kind. Without hesitation, Cliff pulled her near the center of the room and quickly slipped the lead line through a steel ring attached to the floor. He secured the line, and then she must have sensed the real danger because she increased her struggle to remain alive. Perhaps she could smell the old blood of her kind.

Erik saw the fear in her eyes. They were large and rolling. Her breath was labored, and she snorted ... and her nostrils drained. Erik thought he could smell the fear, and he was not at ease when Cliff tightened the line and pulled her head down, down to within a foot of the floor.

She urinated, and the splash produced a heavy smell of ammonia mixed with other unpleasant, mysterious odors. He felt the warmth it generated in the coolness of the room. He was aware of his own tenseness and ... fear. *This is terrible...* Then Cliff said, "You ever seen one of these killed, Erik?"

"No, not really Cliff ... I mean I saw it once on the farm when Grandpa shot one. But no, I haven't," he replied.

"Well, let me show ya how it's done," and with that statement he picked up a short, heavy, sledge hammer. "You just take this hammer and hit her between the eyes, or here, on top, just behind the horns," he said while pointing out the two spots.

"Give her a good solid rap, don't want her to suffer." And then he smacked her right between the eyes, and she immediately dropped to the floor … straight down to the floor with a heavy thud … all eight or nine hundred pounds of her. She didn't move, and Erik didn't move. This was a first for Erik, and he felt weak. It was quick. A matter of seconds, one short smack into the head and she was down. It all took place a few inches in front of him. He sensed he would be the next one to drop if he didn't regain his composure.

He tried to say something intelligent, but all that came out was, "Wow … that's a … that's something, Cliff." He wanted to say "scary" or "terrifying," but that would tell Cliff that he wasn't ready for the kill-floor.

Without delay, Cliff straddled over her head. He had his curved seven-inch skinning knife in his right hand, and, with his left, he twisted her head around to expose the long neck and throat.

"This is how it's done, Erik," and cliff made a long incision the length of the throat to open the jugular vein. The blood pumped out profusely onto the concrete floor. It was a large stream of blood, all red and warm smelling, and it sought its personal passage to the center drain … where it developed a fragile whirlpool, then reluctantly, disappeared. Erik realized why kill floors had drains. And fresh running water.

"Cliff, I have to take a leak, be right back," Erik said as he sprinted to the small men's room in the corner. His pale face reflected in the grungy mirror. Desperate, Erik felt his pulse increase. *I have to pull myself together. I have to be a man.*

Erik didn't urinate, and he didn't throw up; he splashed lots of cold water on his face. Good, cleansing, cold water. He did it twice, maybe more.

He returned to the kill-floor, and he hoped that Cliff wouldn't notice his pallor and embarrassment. Cliff looked at Erik and said, "Everything come out all right, son?"

"Yessir … when you have to go, you have to go." *What a stupid answer that was, now he really knows.*

But Cliff didn't let on that he knew. He continued, "Here's what we do now, Erik," and he picked up a shackle and put it on her left hind leg. He hooked the shackle to the hoist on the overhead rail and lifted the lifeless cow until it cleared the floor. Erik noticed that she appeared to have some life, or at least he thought so because there was some movement in her stomach. Perhaps it was muscle contraction, but he was sure Cliff would tell him later.

Without hesitation, Cliff took his skinning knife and promptly made an incision down the full length of the carcass. He cut from the anus, into the udder, and down through the stomach area to the throat. As he did so, a mass of guts and body fluids rushed from the animal. Erik was not prepared for the scene. The odors that released were not pleasant. A warm, indiscernible stench was all that Erik could relate to.

And the colors, shades of oranges, browns, and purples, were unexpected. He never anticipated that there would be color. He was mesmerized as this heaping glob of mass plopped out, with authority, onto the concrete floor. Erik could feel the heat and smell the intestines. Fluid ran out of the cavity. Erik couldn't identify the liquid. He realized it was not just blood, but looked and smelled more like a combination of urine, water, and perhaps milk. It was not a pleasant sight or smell, but Erik couldn't turn away.

He was captivated by the events. As he stared into the strange mass, he recognized certain organs and parts, such as the heart, liver, and stomach. Then, he saw movement within this mass. A definite, non-patterned movement. It was eerie, mysterious.

Erik could feel the tension within his body; he was afraid he would have to excuse himself for another run to the men's room. He heard Cliff say, "Erik, as soon as the guts drop, we go to the stomach and find the uterus," and he went to that area with his hands. From underneath he pulled up a fleshy, sack-like mass. A large mass moved, and, at that instant, Erik remembered that cows were pregnant most of the time (he had been told), and the sack could hold an unborn calf.

Don't panic, don't run, he thought as Cliff made a clean shallow incision the length of the sack, and out fell a live, kicking, miniature cow — an unborn calf with closed eyes. It was attached to an umbilical cord that Cliff cut without fuss. The tiny cow stopped moving, and Erik felt sick again. He turned to leave the kill-floor, but stopped when Cliff said, "Okay, Erik, you take this little fellow and put him in the bone barrel. We don't grind them into our hamburger like some packers do. And we don't try to skin them for their little unborn hides."

Almost mechanically, Erik turned and faced Cliff, who handed him the small, messy package. Without a word, Erik crossed the floor and put the package into the bone barrel. He stood there for a moment … perhaps more. He stared into the barrel and at the "little fellow." *I'm not ready for this … really not ready. Maybe I can't be a butcher … and as usual, Dad will be disgusted with me.*

And with those thoughts, he joined Cliff, who was in the process of skinning the cow. He saw the long smooth strokes of the razor-edge skinning knife. He watched Cliff, with his powerful forearms, knife the hide from the meaty carcass. Cliff stopped skinning the half naked cow. He looked at Erik and said, "I know it's rough, son … I did the same thing when I started, and it's still tough. You're doing just fine. You take a little break … Burt will never know."

And Erik took a little break — the rest of the day.

CHAPTER TWELVE

WITHIN TWO WEEKS, ERIK FELT MORE COMFORTABLE ON THE KILL-FLOOR He gained experience and, in so doing, increased his speed and confidence. He still didn't enjoy the actual act of killing the animals. And he hadn't become a good "skinner" because he cut more than three holes in the hide. A hide with more than three holes dropped to grade B, and the price paid for grade B hides was much lower than grade A. His dad noted the increased number of B hides and decided that his son should apply his talents in other areas — before they all went broke. But Erik stuck with it and learned all he could. It was important that he pleased his father.

Burt hired a couple of new employees. They were local boys in their late twenties who were recommended by Cliff. They were named Billy Bob and Jesse, and they referred to themselves as "just good ole country boys." Carefree and easy going, they kept their sense of humor and included Erik in all of the kidding. Also, they were good workers, especially when Cliff was there watching, which was most of the time. Erik tried to fit in; he wanted to be one of the boys, one of the crew. But it was difficult to be an adult and take all in stride, as he suspected adults did.

One day at work, the crew was cleaning up after cow-killing day. Erik was pulling a carcass into the chill room, and he yelled to the crew, "Hey guys, did you hear our new slogan?"

"Nope, haven't heard that," they yelled.

"Well, I gave it to Burt the other day, but don't think he liked it."

"Now we have to hear it … Hell, he's just the boss–owner, what's he know?" Billy Bob said while grinning at the others.

"Okay, here goes, our new slogan," Erik said. "YOU MAY BEAT OUR PRICES … BUT YOU CAN'T BEAT OUR MEAT … LARSEN PACKING."

The good ole boys howled, and Cliff laughed. They thought it was a great slogan. And Erik felt good; he sensed he was now accepted as one of the crew.

It was early morning, and all of them, Erik, Cliff, Billy Bob, and Jesse, were out at the holding pens to look over the stock for the day's kill. Erik was always intrigued with the animals, even though he knew their fate, and this morning was no exception.

There was a large bull in the group of thirty or so cattle, and he caused all kinds of commotion. He was mounting — or trying to mount — every animal in the pen, and that included the steers (they're castrated bulls, Erik had learned). Cliff and the rest of the crew leaned over the shoot fence and observed all of the activity. "Get her, goddammit," Billy Bob hooted.

"Yea ... look at the size of that dick," Jesse replied as they slapped each other on their backs.

And then Billy Bob said, "Hey, Erik, bet you would like to have a dick like that. God, the girls would hang on your ass day and night. What a stud!" And they all laughed.

Erik was embarrassed, not because of the laughter, but because he was so fascinated with the bull that was trying to screw everything in sight. Erik wanted to be adult, cool, but it was too much for a sixteen-year-old kill-man. Yes, it was the biggest dick he had ever seen, and he was mesmerized. *God, it must be three feet long and several inches in diameter at the thick part.*

And, out of its sheath looking formidable, it was stiff-hard, red, and pointed at the end. He had never imagined such a dick, and there it was, attached to this excited, horrendous bull that attempted to stick it in any available orifice. Erik fantasized about having such a dick, and he could feel his excitement grow. He became aroused, and he hoped that the crew didn't notice his own erection, which was as hard as the bull's, but unfortunately not as impressive in length.

"Get her ... get her, big boy!" Billy Bob called out to the bull.

"Yea, she'll love it when you gets her," Jesse yelled, "Sock it to her, big boy, get her in the ass!"

Then, Erik heard Cliff say in a low voice, "That bastard ... he's tearing up the beef, bruising the rounds."

Erik continued to stare at them, the bull and the cow, as they passed in front of him. She was frantic as the bull made a desperate attempt to stay mounted. It was a struggle with his big dick, stiff and waving in the air, as it tried to find a target.

Erik felt the heat of their bodies and smelled the pungent odors. He heard the guttural tones and the short gasping sounds of air that rushed in and out of their nostrils. Then Erik, in the corner of his left eye, saw a flash — a flash of glistening steel that streaked out toward the bull. Then it was gone. The flash was gone, the glistening was gone — and the dick was gone. Erik saw the blood gush from the bull. The animal stood silently, apparently in shock.

"Holy shit!" Billy Bob yelled, "Have you ever seen anything like that?"

"Cut his dick right off … Jesus, that had to smart," Jesse replied. And the two of them laughed and slapped each other on their backs.

Erik was stunned. He couldn't grasp what had happened. In an instant, it was gone. Then he heard Cliff say, "That should take care of that."

Erik turned, and it became clear what had happened. Cliff was wiping the blood off his skinning knife and, without comment, holstered it into the sheath that hung on his belt. Erik could not believe that Cliff was so composed — and so cruel. And why?

Cliff could see that Erik wasn't joking around with the good ole boys.

"Erik, you know why I had to do that?"

"No, sir," Erik replied.

"Well, he was tearing up the meat … they do a lot of damage."

Erik nodded in response, but he didn't understand.

"You see, Erik, when the bull gets that excited and mounts them all, he bruises the hindquarters, and I showed you what we had to do with bruises … didn't I?"

"Yessir, we had to cut them out. Some were deep," Erik replied.

"That's right, and we had to throw away the meat … good steak meat, the expensive stuff, into the ole bone barrel."

"Yessir, we did, we had a lot of waste," Erik said.

"And waste is money," Cliff said, "and I'm here to make your dad a profit. And lord knows there ain't much profit in the meat business."

Erik nodded in agreement, and Cliff looked at him with some concern, "Are you okay, Erik?"

"Yessir, I feel better."

"That's good, son … now let's get our butts to work."

Cliff and Erik turned and headed for the slaughterhouse. Billy Bob and Jesse followed.

With a trace of a grin, Cliff put his hand on Erik's shoulder and said, "Erik, we have to kill the bull first ... you know, the one without the dick? Don't want him to bleed to death ... out there anyways."

CHAPTER THIRTEEN

CLIFF AND ERIK SUITED UP FOR WORK THE FOLLOWING MORNING.
"It's a good day, Erik, it's hog-killing day."

"But, I didn't see any hogs, Cliff."

"Oh, they're coming. The truck called ... be here in a half-hour. Gives us time to set up."

Erik followed Cliff out to the holding pens. They checked the gates for security and made a few minor adjustments. The pens were ready for the new, but temporary residents.

It was Erik's first hog-kill day, and he didn't know what to expect. He was excited though when he saw the big tractor-trailer coming down the steep dirt road. The road was pot-holed, and Erik heard the hogs squeal each time the truck jarred over the mini-craters. The driver pulled up in front and waved to Cliff. He then backed the big stake-body trailer into the off-loading ramp. Erik was impressed with the skillful handling, but he was more impressed with the number of hogs he could see ... and smell.

"Must be a hundred, Cliff," he yelled over the increasing noise.

"Yea, I think it's supposed to be a hundred twenty-five or so, Erik."

The driver and Cliff opened the trailer doors and made their way through the hogs to the front of the rig. He and Cliff began to yell, "Sooie, sooie ... git on out." Those that didn't respond were encouraged by a shot of the electric prodder. One jolt from the prodder made them leap to the front of the pack and scamper down the ramp.

They squealed and raised hell. They were angry — and frightened. Erik was surprised how little time it took — just minutes and the truck was gone. *What a stinking mess ... and the noise.*

They fought, snorted, and jockeyed for their own space. Despite the unpleasantness, Erik enjoyed the commotion. He was fascinated by the number of animals. He had never seen so many together. Most weighed around two-hundred pounds, and they were called shoats — kill hogs. But he noticed five or six larger hogs. They were the boars. And they were twice the size of the shoats and much more active. They thrashed about as they tried to mount the shoats — and each other. *Oh no ... not another case of cutting a dick off!*

He glanced at Cliff and felt more at ease because Cliff showed little concern about the mountings. Apparently they didn't bruise the meat like the bulls did when they mounted the cows and steers. *What a break for the boars ... and for me.*

"Erik, we'll separate the boars, kill them first, then get the others."

With skill and patience, Cliff separated them into the shoot. They snapped at anything that moved, and some things that didn't move. *Nasty fellows, big and ornery ... and yet, it's somewhat sad ... their time is almost over.*

Billy Bob and Jesse had the kill-floor prepared for the hogs. Unlike the beef that were skinned, the hogs were de-haired. They were shackled on their hind leg, then hooked to a hoist and lifted several feet above the floor. The kill-man would stick the hog's jugular vein with a knife to kill the animal and ensure proper bleeding.

After they bled, they were lowered into scalding water and then placed on the de-haring machine. It was a large contraption with heavy rubber flippers that were tipped with steel fingers or plates. The drum rotated at a constant speed and flailed the fingers against the hog's hide. This action removed most of their coarse hair. The remaining hair was scraped off with knives, by hand.

It was a messy, wet job. And the smell was unpleasant, not unlike the breath of a booze hangover, only mixed with steam and sopping hog hair — and bladder waste. Today would be worse because they would kill the boars. It was always more difficult to process the boars because they were much larger and tougher to handle. Also, the boars were not killed the same way as the shoats that were shackled and stuck with a knife. The boars were generally shot with a rifle.

There was a big difference in the meat though; the boars had a strong odor, almost rank. So strong that Cliff would mix it with the shoats at a low ratio — maybe one pound of boar to nine or ten pounds of shoat.

Erik was on the kill-floor when he heard Cliff, "Look alive ... he's coming in!"

Billy Bob had the rifle ready, and, in moments, the boar appeared from the shoot and onto the concrete floor. Erik was surprised that the hog looked so docile. He expected it to be confused and aggressive.

The boar stood silently for a few seconds. Billy Bob fired. The boar dropped straight to the floor almost before Erik heard the crack of the rifle. Cliff went over to the animal and cut the jugular. Jesse shackled the hog and hooked it to the overhead hoist. Erik was impressed and couldn't understand the fuss made about killing boars. It looked quite simple to him, much simpler than killing bulls.

"Erik, you want to take a shot at the next one?" Cliff asked.

Billy Bob and Jesse chimed in with encouragement, "Yea, Erik, you can do that … just knock him on his ass … it's a ball!"

"Well, hell yes, Cliff … if you think I'm ready?" Erik replied. Erik wasn't so sure that he was ready.

"You're ready … nothing to it," Cliff said, "Jesse, you run a hog in here for Erik."

"Okay boss, be right back," Jesse said as he headed for the shoot.

"Get the big one, Jesse," hollered Billy Bob, "Our boy can handle his ass. Right, Erik?"

"Sure can, Billy Bob, they don't make 'em that tough."

Erik had the rifle ready when he heard the commotion in the shoot. The boar, all 395 pounds of him, came through the shoot door and stopped momentarily. He appeared more aggressive than the other. Perhaps he smelled the blood. Erik wished he had watched another kill before taking on the real thing.

The boar was agitated; his head jerked side to side, and Erik sensed that he was ready to come at him — to charge. *I better get this over with, like soon … better drop him now.*

The rifle cracked, and the bullet was on its way. Unfortunately, it didn't find the mark. The boar moved just before impact, and the bullet didn't find the center of the skull. It hit him above the eye, and all hell broke loose. He squealed like a banshee and made a full head-on charge at Erik. *Oh shit! This is going to be bad,* he thought, as he leaped for the scraping table. The flashing tusks passed inches below his legs.

Erik could see the blood flow from the boar's head and nostrils. It drained into his mouth, and he became more aggressive. He charged everything on the floor. He was in a frenzy, and Erik was concerned about the guys. He was relieved when he saw Cliff perched safely on the de-haring machine. Then he spotted Jesse on the Maytag washer against the wall. He didn't see Billy Bob in the room; Erik assumed he had made it out the shoot door.

The boar, still at full speed, turned sharply and headed for Jesse and the Maytag. He hit with such force that the machine and Jesse became airborne and flipped to the concrete floor. The boar skidded as he attempted to make a quick turn on the wet surface. It gave Jesse a moment to scramble to his feet and make a leap for the scraping table. It was a good leap; the tusks missed Jesse.

"Holy shit!" Jesse cried out, "Look at that son-of-a-bitch go!"

"You all right, Jesse?" yelled Erik.

"Hell, yes ... never had so much fun."

"Man, you sure pissed him off," Cliff yelled over the clamor.

"You sure did, Erik ... he's after your ass, son," Jesse said. He and Cliff laughed. Erik was embarrassed. He had never seen such chaos, and he recognized that he was the cause of it.

The boar suddenly wheeled and headed for the big steel doors that separated the kill-floor from the rest of the building. They were heavy swinging doors that could be bolted shut. Apparently they were not bolted because his charge popped them open like the old saloon doors.

"We're in trouble now," Cliff hollered as he leaped to the floor and took off after the hog. Erik followed immediately, but he wasn't sure why he followed, and what, if anything, he could do if he caught them.

As he ran across the shipping room, he saw the boar ... and Cliff ... heading down the corridor toward the open front office. Cliff yelled, "Loose hog! Heads up! He's coming at ya!"

The boar was squealing, but Erik heard another squeal. It was a different squeal; it was the office girl's. It was Paula's, and she jumped on her desk, as the hog — and Cliff — dashed through her area and headed straight into Burt's office. When Erik reached her office, he saw his dad, Cliff, and another man – a salesman — and the hog, all sprinting toward him. It was a funny sight, but Erik had little time to enjoy the humor as he turned and, in a dead-run, led the entire silly-looking entourage back to the kill-floor.

With the hog gaining, they all scampered through the swinging steel doors, and the men scrambled aboard the skinning table.

The boar stopped abruptly and wheeled around in the center of the floor. He stared at the wide-eyed group who had vaulted to safety. He was now bleeding profusely and spewed blood with each labored breath. He was tired.

Cliff raised the rifle and fired into the boar's skull. The animal shook his head. He did not fall. Cliff fired another shot, and Erik could hear the bullet impact the skull. Still, the animal did not fall. Three more times Cliff fired into the skull. Finally, the boar dropped to the floor — dead.

"What a tough son-of-a-bitch," Cliff said.

"Holy shit," Jesse said, "that was one helluva show, Erik."

They all climbed down from the table and cautiously walked over to the hog. The boar didn't move, so Cliff stuck him with a knife to drain the remaining blood.

"If you don't get him with the first shot using a .22, you're in trouble," Cliff said, "If it misses a bit, it makes him mad. Pisses him off. Makes the adrenaline run."

"You're damn right about that, Cliff," Burt said, "I've seen ten or twelve shots into the skull; the bullets flatten out, won't penetrate. Have to use a 30-30 sometimes."

"Well, he's dead now, Burt, hope he didn't tear up too much ... I should have made sure the doors were bolted."

Burt laughed, "Sure scared the shit out of Paula in the front office."

"I'll bet so," Cliff said.

"Scared the shit out of me too," Erik said. They all laughed. Then he realized be had said "shit" in front of his dad. Erik was embarrassed.

"Well, no harm, Cliff, it was good exercise. Hell, I've done it before ... several times," Burt said.

"Well, I should have taken better aim, Burt, don't know why I missed him, just fucked up," Cliff said.

Burt laughed, "You didn't fuck up, Cliff, the hog did."

They all smiled and nodded in agreement, all except Erik; he was not smiling. He turned toward Burt and said, "Dad, I'm the one who missed the shot ... not Cliff."

"You missed?" Burt said, "I thought you were a better shot than that. Hell, I couldn't miss when I was eight years old."

"Yes, sir, I know."

Burt and his salesman buddy returned to the office. The crew started to clean up the place. Erik was troubled. He had screwed up. And he was angry at himself … and his father. *That bastard didn't shoot boars at eight or any other age. And he didn't have to say that in front of Cliff and the others. What an ass-hole!*

CHAPTER FOURTEEN

SOMETHING IS WRONG WITH THAT HAYSTACK, ERIK THOUGHT AS HE ARRIVED for work around daylight. The stack, located by the holding pens, was constructed to provide food for the livestock that were held longer than a day. If the animals weren't killed promptly, they lost weight, and weight was money.

It was different today because Erik noticed a cow, or bull, feeding at the stack. Erik walked toward the stack, and he saw a large pair of gonads. Yes, it was a bull, he decided. And the animal had practically buried itself into the stack. The bull was on his feet; his head and shoulders disappeared into the stack. Erik heard him eat, and he saw his stomach move as it received the food. His huge set of balls lingered below and between his powerful hindquarters. They swung in slow motion. *God, that's impressive.* Erik smiled as he fantasized.

He started to scare the bull out of the stack, then he realized that it was probably the farmer's bull that had been destroying the fences. Most likely he was trying to join, fight, or mount the unlucky ones in the holding pens.

Burt had complained several times to the neighboring farm owner, but he apparently did nothing to restrict his bull from visiting. Erik heard his dad tell Cliff, "I'm going to get that son-of-a-bitch one of these days!"

Erik didn't know if he meant "get the bull" or "get the farmer."

He saw that his dad was at work, so he hustled in to let him know the situation.

"Dad, I think we have your bull."

"You mean the bastard that tears up the fences?"

"Yessir, that's the one … I think."

"Where is he?"

"Eating in the haystack … almost buried in it. Can't see his head."

Burt grinned and said, "That's great, kid ... you go tell Cliff to come up here. Tell him we have some work to do."

Erik departed to find Cliff. When they returned, they noticed Burt rummaging through a desk drawer. "Here we go," he said as he pulled out an old carbide miner's lamp. "This should do it."

Erik and Cliff looked at each other and then followed Burt out to the haystack. The bull was still there, perhaps deeper into the hay.

Without comment, Burt unscrewed the bottom of the miners' carbide lamp and spit into it. Erik had done this many times when he worked at the pony mine. The spit (a substitute for water) activated the carbide, and it generated an explosive gas that you could light. He then reassembled the lamp and rolled the flint wheel to ignite the flame.

"Damn, he's not going to light the haystack?" Erik whispered to Cliff.

"Beats the shit out of me," Cliff replied.

Burt adjusted the flame. A long thin flame, some six inches in length. It was a dirty flame that put out considerable soot.

Burt was apparently satisfied because he stopped adjusting and went over to the stack and quietly kneeled down behind the bull. He took the lamp and put the tip of the flame on the bull's sack (scrotum) and balls. Then he moved the flame up and down the balls in slow, short, positive strokes. Erik was shocked, "Holy shit!" he said. Cliff shook his head and then grinned at Erik.

The bull didn't move, and Burt continued the process until the bag and balls were turning black from the soot.

Erik saw them begin to smoke. *This is unbelievable, it can't be ... he has to feel the pain. God, his balls are black!* Burt continued, another five, ten seconds or so. Then it happened. A deep thunderous roar came from within the haystack. And the bull went straight forward through the entire stack. No wavering ... just a straight charge through the mound. Hay flew in all directions as the bull made a full speed dash toward home — his home on the next farm. He went through two barbed wire fences as if they were made of string.

"Look at that son-of-a-bitch run," Burt said as he shut off the carbide. He had a big grin on his face.

"Not sure he'll ever stop," Cliff said, "He's sure hauling some ass."

They watched the bull disappear over the hill. They could still hear him bawling.

"That had to hurt ... really smart," Erik said, "Dad, you kept the flame on him for a couple of minutes. He didn't even move!"

"Naw, he'll be all right ... just a little sore," Burt said.

"Yea, just a little sore," Cliff said. "Bet it's three years before he even thinks of fucking."

They all laughed as they walked to the plant. The mood was good.

Erik doubted that the bull would ever return. *Damn if I would* — as he caressed his own balls through his jean pockets.

CHAPTER FIFTEEN

WITH VACATION OVER, ERIK WAS BACK IN SCHOOL. HE WAS NOT AVAILABLE for the kill-floor, so Burt assigned him the job of shipping clerk. A job that started in the early mornings and allowed Erik full-time work. He returned to cut meat at two in the afternoon. Erik completed his last day on the floor and was taking a break out on the shipping docks. Cliff, Billy Bob, and Jesse came over.

"Burt told me this was your last day, Erik," Cliff said, "and I thank you for doing me a good job … am gonna miss you. All of us will." The other two nodded in agreement.

"Well, thank you, Cliff, for putting up with me … I'm sure going to miss working with you guys. Lots of fun."

"Well, we have a little present for you. We made it specially for you," Cliff said as he handed him an object that looked like a polished stick.

"Thank you, Cliff … now what the hell is it?"

"It's a bull-dick cane, Erik; we thought you'd like it," Cliff said as Billy Bob and Jesse grinned at each other.

"A bull-dick cane!" Erik exclaimed, "I never thought they were for real."

"Yep, for real all right. I cut this one off myself, let it dry for a month, and the boys shellacked and polished her," Cliff said, "Ain't she a beauty?"

"God yes, Cliff, sure is a beauty," Erik said as he held it out and stabbed it in the air.

The cane was a burgundy color with a high polish, close to three or three-and-a-half-feet long and maybe two or three inches around at the big end; then it tapered down to an inch. They had capped the bigger end with a shiny, silver ball.

"Must have been a big bull, Cliff; this one's bigger than the one you cut off out at the pen," Erik said, and then half seriously, "It's not the same one is it?"

They all laughed, and Billy Bob said, "No way. This one wasn't cut off; it's the whole thing, clear from his ass to the tip of the dick ... course the tip falls off when it dries for a month or so."

"Yea," Jesse said, "Four or five inches falls off."

"I wouldn't want four or five inches to fall off my dick," Billy Bob said as he was laughing. "How 'bout you Erik, you wouldn't like that, would ya?"

"Lord, no. Hey guys, I'm not sure I've got four or five inches ... I mean the whole thing," Erik said. He hoped they thought he was kidding. They had a good laugh and shook hands. The crew departed, and Erik took his new present home.

Two weeks of school passed, and Erik decided the time was right to take in the bull-dick cane. It was an immediate success with the guys. Somehow the word spread rapidly, and, between classes, they would come up to Erik to get their first look at the bull-dick. "This for real, Erik?" they asked while holding the cane.

"Sure is, guys ... made it at the packing house."

"Goddamn, look at the size of this dick ... boy, I could sock it to ole Betty Lou with this mother."

"Yea," another would say, "Man, with a dick like this we could fuck 'em all."

Erik never had such attention. He was never that popular in school. He had one or two friends, but he mostly remained a loner. Work took up the majority of his time. He liked the attention, he decided. It made him feel good that he may be accepted as one of the guys.

He was a little embarrassed, however, when several of the girls came up to see the new cane. They were the pretty ones who seemed to avoid Erik. But their curiosity was insistent. They were intoxicated, and they had to see the cane.

"Erik, is that really what the boys say it is ... you know, a thing?" Amy Jo said. She was one of the prettier ones. *But they're all gorgeous.*

"Sure is, Amy Jo. It's the real thing, right from the bull. Yep, it's real."

And they kind of giggled. Erik noticed that they were hesitant about staring at it, but the fascination must have been too great. "Can I touch it ... I mean hold it?" Connie asked.

"Sure," Erik replied, feeling more at ease. He handed the cane to Connie, who, in turn, let the others feel it.

"I ... I just never thought anything could be this big," she said. The others nodded as they devoted their attention to the bull-dick.

"And so hard," one of them said.

"Wow," said another. And, they looked at each other as if they all held secrets they shared. Then the bell rang announcing the start of class, and off they went with chatter and giggles. Erik wished he could hear what they were saying ... and thinking.

Erik was in his last class of the day. It was social studies, and it was not his favorite class. He found it painfully boring. And the teacher, what a dip ... old Mrs. Gerber. She lost her husband years ago ... probably ran him off. An old prune who thought she belonged with aristocracy. "Queen Dork," the guys called her, behind her back of course.

Erik was at his seat with the bull-dick cane lying beneath on the floor. Mrs. Gerber came over to Erik. "What is that?" she asked in a stern voice, pointing at the cane with a finger that looked half-wrinkled.

"Ma'am, that's a cane ... you know, just a stick," Erik replied.

"What kind of a stick?" she asked in her sharp tone.

"Well, you know ma'am ... just a cane stick. They gave it to me at the packing house."

"I've heard what it is, Mr. Smarty, now you take that ... that thing ... that disgusting thing down to the principal's office. Mr. Wilson is expecting you. I will never have anything like this again. Do you understand?"

"Yes ma'am."

Well, there goes the old "C" in that class, Erik thought, as he headed for the office. The big "F" is a shoo-in. He entered the principal's office, and Mr. Wilson was expecting Erik. "Just stand in front of the desk, Mr. Larsen. Do you know why you're here?"

"No, sir, I don't."

"Because you disrupted Mrs. Gerber and this school."

"I'm sorry, sir, I didn't mean to disrupt anyone."

"That thing, you carry," Mr. Wilson said, "that penis ... or God knows what, is a shameful act of defiance. It's immoral and sinful. But you probably wouldn't know about that."

"Yessir, I know about that. It was all just in fun, sir," Erik replied.

"Well, it certainly isn't funny to me. I'm suspending you one day of school. And I'm calling your mother. We'll see how funny she thinks it is.

Now get out of here, Mr. Larsen."

Erik's mother called Burt and told him about the call from Mr. Wilson. "Burt, you cannot believe what your son did at school today."

"What kink of trouble this time?" he asked.

"The principal, Mr. Wilson, said that Erik … said he was showing his penis, or something. My God, Burt, do you think that's true? What are we going to do?"

"Showing his what? What the hell are you talking about, Rose?"

"Said he was a disgrace or something. I was so upset. I'm not sure I heard it all. Carrying or showing his penis … I've been almost in tears."

"Well, you settle down. I'll find out when he gets here for work. If it's true, I'll kick his ass from here to Boone County!"

Erik arrived on schedule to find his dad waiting impatiently. "You have some trouble at school?" his dad asked.

"Yessir, I did."

"Your mother is all upset, says you were running around school with your dick out … or penis she called it. What the goddamn hell is she talking about?"

Erik was stunned with that one, "Sir, I don't know anything about my penis hanging out … no, sir, I don't do things like that."

"Well, dammit, you better tell me what's going on. Your mother is crying, and I want to know why."

"I wish I could explain, Dad, but I don't know what they're talking about." Then it dawned on him, became so clear. "Oh, I know … I bet it has something to do with the bull-dick cane. I took it to school, Dad … has to be."

Burt looked puzzled. "You took a bull-dick cane to school?"

"Yessir, you know the one the crew gave me?"

"I'll be damned. That's the penis that was hanging out ... out of you?"

"I guess so, I sure didn't have my dick out, Dad." Then he realized he said "dick" in front of his Dad. "I'm sorry, Dad, didn't mean that … meant to say 'thing out.' "

"You call your mother and apologize," Burt said, "Get it cleared up." And he added with a trace of a grin. "Don't take that damn bull-dick to school. Jesus Christ, where do we get such idiot teachers. And you … you should know better. You're supposed to be there to learn so you can get a job. Not to wave dicks around."

Man, that wasn't so bad. Maybe he is a good guy.

CHAPTER SIXTEEN

A S SHIPPING CLERK, ERIK HAD TO BE AT WORK BY FOUR IN THE MORNING. It was cold work in the winter because the big sliding doors were opened to allow the trucks to back up to the loading docks. Erik called out the items on the customers' orders, and two or three men would scurry to the different locations to find the items. They would return with them — weigh, package, and mark if needed — then place them on the truck. It was a fast pace, and he enjoyed working with the new crew. Unfortunately, the hours were terrible. Erik started so early that he had little time to hang out at the corner drug and watch the girls.

Most nights, Erik was in bed by nine or ten, but last night was an exception. He hung out too long and overstayed his limit. It was late when he arrived home, near midnight, and he knew he had to be up and ready for work in three hours. *No big deal, I can handle it. I'm really tough … need very little sleep.*

It must have been close to three when he heard his mother at the foot of the stairs, "Erik, honey, it's time to get up … you're going to be late." Then she repeated it, and Erik said, "Okay, Mom, I'm getting up. I didn't hear my alarm."

The room was nice and dark and warm. Erik dozed off, back to sleep, and he heard her again, "Erik, you better get moving … you know how upset your father can be if you're late."

"Oh, to hell with the old man, I've been working too hard … tell him I quit," Erik replied, still half asleep. Then he suddenly realized what he had said to his mother. *Damn, how could I be that stupid?*

Then within a minute, he heard it, the sound of heavy footsteps. Heavy footsteps coming up the stairs to his attic bedroom. In an instant it was clear. *Holy shit, it can't be … oh fuck, it's Dad, and he's coming fast.*

Erik was terrified as he leaped out of bed and landed on the floor. At that very instant, Burt reached out for him. Erik guessed that his dad was not on a social visit. No sir, this was not going to be a father-son talk.

Burt clenched Erik around the throat with his left hand, and lifted him up until he couldn't reach the floor with his feet. He spun Erik's half naked body around and slammed him up against the wall.

"You don't talk to your mother in those tones ... who in the hell do you think you are?" he said, as his hand slammed into Erik's face. Erik didn't fall; he couldn't. He was still pinned to the wall.

"No son of mine will ever ... ever ... talk to his mother like that!" And for a fleeting second, Erik saw the fist coming at his face; it looked huge and it moved fast. *Oh, God, this is it,* but by the grace of the Good Lord or somebody, the fist opened, and the hand imparted a deafening blow over his left ear. A blow that sent him reeling down the staircase located in the middle of the room. Erik hit all of the steps, all seventeen of them. *God, what a ride, I'm fucking dead ... or soon will be.* He lay there at the bottom for a second or two and then realized he was conscious and breathing. He looked up and saw Burt coming down the stairs. *Oh shit, not again,* he pleaded to himself. Burt reached the bottom and stepped over Erik. He turned toward him, and said, "You okay, Erik? I forgot about the steps."

"Yes, I'm fine, Dad ... I think," he replied, as he tried to get up.

Without hesitating, Burt turned to leave and said, "Well, you get to work ... and don't sass you mother."

Erik scrambled to work, bruised and sore, but nothing broken. *Never should have said that to Mom, no siree, at least not with the old man at home. But, thank God he opened his fist. If he had hit me with that fist, I'd be passing my own teeth during bowel movement.* He had to grin at that one, a slight grin of course, his face was too sore for a full-fledged grin.

CHAPTER SEVENTEEN

BURT BELIEVED HE COULD SAVE MONEY BY SETTING UP HIS OWN POULTRY house. The decision was made, and Erik was offered the job of running the new venture. He could work before and after school hours, so Erik accepted the offer, and thus began his career as a "chicken-man" at fifty cents an hour.

They leased a building to be the new home of Larsen Poultry Company. The building had recently been used as an auto repair shop, and the location was convenient, four miles from the packing house. The rent was cheap because it was in the part of town called Mucky Hollow. It was also referred to as colored-town or nigger-town, depending on who was doing the referring and their degree of prejudice. It was usually called nigger-town.

It was a dilapidated old brick structure sitting across the road from the main — and only — business district of Mucky Hollow. This district was made up of three businesses: a barbershop, a small grocery store, and a gas station. Most of the area's activity involved one of these places. The store provided the beer and staples, the gas station provided the moonshine, and the barbershop provided the hangout.

Looking over his new plant, Erik lost some of his enthusiasm. The concrete floor was covered with a permanent stain of grease. There was a small bathroom that contained a toilet and a broken sink. A small potbellied stove provided the heat, and the open garage door provided air conditioning. *It certainly fits in well with the district,* he thought as he smiled.

He was not so concerned with the building, however, but with how he would be accepted by the colored folk. He had heard that he would be the only white man (boy) in the area, and he didn't know how they would respond. He knew the job would be more pleasant if they were for, and not against, the chicken plant with a white boss.

It wouldn't take long to get a response though because Erik could see three of the locals gathered on the dirt parking lot adjoining the building. One tall, one short, the other in-between, and all dressed in mismatched fashion. Old suit coats that had long lost their companion trousers and shoes that were well ventilated by wear and tear appeared to be in style.

It was a cold nasty day, all gray and dreary, not unusual for West Virginia, so they were all involved in the task at hand, building a small fire in a steel drum. That made sense to Erik as he watched them huddle around the barrel to grab some heat from the steady flame.

The three locals watched Erik as he left the building, and he decided the time was right to meet them. He was uneasy, and, with some reluctance, he sauntered over to the fire.

"Hi," Erik said to the huddle.

"Hey," responded the tallest one.

Apparently the other two were more interested in the fire than meeting Erik. They never looked up.

"Cold day … nice fire," Erik said as he found a position at the barrel.

"Uh," replied the short one. There was silence as the huddle continuously adjusted their positions at the fire; turning back side when their front was too hot, then turning front side when their back was too hot. Erik had to smile … *it takes practice to make the right adjustment … and they have had practice.*

"You be the owner?" the tall one asked.

"No, my dad is the owner. I'll be the boss, and my name is Erik … Erik Larsen," and he extended his hand to shake with the tall one.

The tall one didn't return the handshake; he couldn't, at least not with the right hand; he didn't have one. Then Erik realized that the arm was missing also, or most of it. The shoulder was there, but no arm. "I'm sorry … I didn't notice," Erik said.

"It don't bother me none. Been like this long time … my name is James … James Roosevelt Jones. They call me Willy … Long Willy Washington," he said, sporting a giant size grin.

"Long Willy Washington?" Erik said in surprise, "That's an unusual name … why don't they call you Jimmy or Rosey Jones?"

"Don't know … but it be Long Willy Washington."

"Well, pleased to meet you, Long Willy Washington."

"What you gonna put in the building?" he asked.

"We're putting in a chicken plant, Willy. Going to kill and clean them, then sell 'em to the stores."

The other two perked up immediately when Erik made that statement. They must not have known what the building was going to be used for.

"You be sellin' chickens to us?" asked the short one.

"Well, I think so," Erik said. He couldn't say for sure because he hadn't cleared it with his dad.

"That be good," the short one replied, "You give us a good deal?"

Without waiting for Erik's response, Long Willy, apparently the leader, introduced the other two.

"Mr. Erik, this here, Shake," as he pointed to the short one, "And this here, Turner," pointing to the other. *I'm not going to ask about the name Shake ... or Turner.*

"Good to know you, Shake and Turner. You men work around here?"

Long Willy answered for them, "We all do odd jobs ... work full-time is hard to find ... but we wants to. You be doin' some hirin', Mr. Erik?"

"Well, I sure think so, Willy. Don't know who yet, or how many, but I'm sure we'll be hiring."

"That be great, I tell you, that be great. I make you a good worker, Mr. Erik, a real good one," Long Willy replied. "And I would always be on time, 'cause I just live over yonder, behinds the barber shop," as he pointed in that direction.

"Well, I'm sure you would, Willy, but you know, I don't know what we are going to pay ... or any of that stuff yet." Actually, Erik did know, because he had been briefed by his dad, and he knew pretty well what he could offer, but he didn't know what he could do with a one-armed man. Erik sensed that he and Long Willy would get along, but he wasn't sure how to handle the one-arm situation, and he was somewhat embarrassed. Long Willy must have noted the awkwardness and continued with his enthusiasm.

"Don't you worry about this one arm, Mr. Erik, I can do the work of two ... no, I do better un two." Shake and Turner nodded in agreement as Willy continued. "You see, I have a fake arm I put on with straps. Have other hands too ... a hook, and a pincher. And on Sundays I wear the good one, a hand ... well, kinda looks like a hand. They carved it for me. Ain't good for nothing though, just for looks when I puts my suit on and goes to church. But the straps break sometimes ... makes no difference. I fix'em anyways."

"Yea," added Shake, "He don't need no arm. His good un is strong … stronger un two. Ain't it so, Turner?"

Turner looked up from the fire and nodded in agreement. Shake took that as full support and continued on, "Yea, Long Willy's a worker, harder un any I seen."

The conversation took a break as Turner threw more wood on the fire, and all repositioned themselves to the new hotter flame. Erik realized Turner hadn't said a word since his arrival, so he commented to him, "You don't talk much, do you, Turner?"

Turner looked up from the fire and shook his head no, and Long Willy added, "No, he don't." And Shake nodded in agreement.

They all continued to stare at the fire, and Erik realized that it would be good to have a man like Willy. He could make his start in the area much smoother. Erik said, "Willy, I can put you on, full time, fifty-cents an hour."

Willy grinned and, without hesitation, replied, "Thank you, Mr. Erik, I do you right," and extended his good arm to shake hands. They shook hands, and Erik said, "Start tomorrow, I'll meet you here at eight."

As Erik departed, Shake called out, "You pays on Fridays, don't you?" Erik said he did, and then Turner looked up from the fire and said, "That be cash?" And Erik nodded, that be cash.

Erik saw his dad that evening, and told him that he had hired his first man. "We'll get started early in the morning, Dad."

Burt appeared a bit surprised when Erik told him. Perhaps he thought Erik should have cleared it with him.

"Who did you hire?" he asked.

"A colored man, named Long Willy."

"A colored man?" his dad repeated.

"Yes, sir, a colored man about forty, named Long Willy."

"Long Willy?" his dad said in a bewildered tone.

"Yes, sir, a one-armed colored man named Long Willy Washington."

"One-armed?" he asked in a more concerned, irritated voice.

"Yes, sir, one-armed."

Erik was uneasy. He had seen his dad angry many times, and it could be nasty. There was no immediate response from his dad. He just stared at Erik, a long discomforting stare. He finally said, "What are you paying him?"

"Fifty-cents, sir … same thing I get."

Burt nodded as if approving. "You watch him," he said as he got up and left the room. Erik could just make out the faint voice from some distance, "Jesus, a forty-year-old, one-armed nigger named Long Willy Washington."

The next morning, a nervous Erik drove to the new plant. The full impact of yesterday settled in, and he had his doubts that he could do the job. As he entered Mucky Hollow, he realized that he would still be a skinny white boy in the middle of nigger-town trying to fit in and run a chicken plant. He wished he had said no to his dad, but that didn't happen, and it was too late now. Besides, he wanted to show him he could do a good job.

He pulled into the old parking lot and smiled as he noticed the huddled group duplicating the ritual of the day before, adjusting their positions at the fire. He spotted Long Willy, for he was the tall one, and he was pleased that he had kept his word and made it to work. Not just because he was an employee, but more because he would be an ally, and Erik needed an ally to help him get started. He was mildly surprised, however, that Shake and Turner were not the only ones with him. The word must be out, reckoned Erik. The old auto shop was going to be a chicken place.

All of them watched him get out of the truck and saunter over to the fire.

"Good morning, Long Willy."

"Good mornin', Mr. Erik," was Willy's reply, as he smiled.

"Shake, Turner," Erik said as he nodded to each of them.

They looked at him with little expression and returned the nod, then stared into the fire. The two new ones didn't look up.

"That be our truck, Mr. Erik?" asked Willy.

"Yes, that be our truck, Long Willy."

They both continued to look at the truck, an old Studebaker three-ton. It was ragged looking, mostly red, with a large wooden stake-body; it supposedly came with a good engine.

"Well, sure be a nice one."

"My dad, Burt, bought it last week for the plant. I hope it does the job."

"Oh, it do it, I can tell."

Erik was impressed with Willy's confidence.

"Well, you ready to go, Long Willy? We're going to pick up some equipment; get this place running."

"Yes, sir, Mr. Erik, I be ready."

Long Willy then turned to the rest of the gang and said, "Me an' Mr. Erik have got no time to hang 'round the fire. We gots to get the plant running."

They all nodded in agreement. Long Willy had spoken, and the plant would get running.

The two of them left for the truck. Long Willy wore a bright woolen plaid shirt with his arm straps outside — wearing his work hand today, the steel pincher model — and Erik wore his faded blue jeans and a heavy Sears jacket. They climbed in, started the truck, and pulled out to the main road. As they passed the fire, Long Willy, white teeth shining through his broad smile, waved his steel hand to the gang. The gang waved back, and perhaps their thinking was similar to Erik's. ... What a pair ... a skinny white kid and a tall, forty-ish, one-armed Negro in an old, mostly red, Studebaker truck.

It was natural that the gang looked puzzled.

It was a busy week for Erik and Long Willy as they hauled in the equipment. The equipment wasn't new, and it wasn't clean. The kill trough with its funnels, the scalder, the chicken plucker — all were covered with various stages of dried feathers, blood, and chicken shit. Most of their time was spent cleaning the chicken shit. There was one exception however: The stainless gutting table was clean and shiny. Somebody had actually cleaned it.

"I think they give us the wrong one, Mr. Erik," Long Willy said as they placed it in the plant.

"I think so, Willy. Ain't no chicken shit."

And, as their eyes met, the smiles turned to chuckles, and they laughed. It was a good hearty laugh.

They made a good team. They worked hard, and the plant was taking shape. Long Willy was every bit the worker that Shake and Turner said he was. No, he was better than that. He did the work of two men, as they said, but they didn't mention his can-do attitude, his sense of humor, and his quick wit. Erik enjoyed the work with him.

Burt dropped in every two days or so to check on progress. Erik guessed that he was satisfied because he seemed to be in good humor when he was there. Sometimes he would kid with Long Willy, and Erik sensed that he was pleased with the progress they made.

Others dropped in also— the Mucky Hollow locals who were curious about the place. They all wanted to know if they were going to get chicken at a good price. Good price, meaning cheaper than any other place in town, of course.

Erik was pleased when his dad told him that he could sell wholesale to the Hollow locals. He cautioned Erik to make it selective, however, because the stores would be upset if they found out he was selling at the same wholesale price they had to pay. Erik thought it was worth the risk. Better relations would reduce theft and ease the tension.

Shake and Turner came into the plant each day, and Erik thought they were only interested in a warmer place to hang out, but on one of their visits, Shake said, "Mr. Erik you be hiring more?"

"Well, I think so Shake ... you be interested?"

"Yea, I be interested, Mr. Erik ... so would Turner."

"Well, it wouldn't be full-time, Shake, just not enough work."

"That be okay, part-time be better. You pay fifty cents?" Shake asked.

"Yep, we pay fifty cents ... can you gut chickens?" Erik asked.

"I do anything, Mr. Erik. Do it good," Shake said with confidence. "Now, Turner here, he don't do nothing but gut, and he be fast."

Erik looked at Turner, "You're fast, Turner?"

Turned nodded that he was fast.

"Okay, sounds good," said Erik. "Put you both on when we bring in a load. Fifty cents an hour, part-time."

"Thanks, that be good," responded Shake, "but Turner, he don't work for fifty cents ... that be right, Turner?" And Turned nodded.

"Well, what does he want?" Erik asked.

"He wants five cents a chicken," Shake said.

"You mean he'll gut for five cents a bird ... that's what you want, Turner?" asked Erik.

Turner nodded, and Shake said, "Yes."

Erik replied, "Well, sounds good to me. You're both on."

Turner spoke for the first time, "That be cash?"

"That be cash, Turner," replied Erik.

THE PLANT WAS READY, AND ERIK AND LONG WILLY WERE ON THEIR WAY TO THE Shenandoah Valley to pick up the first load. Ole Red — the new given name for the Studebaker — was loaded to capacity with empty chicken coops.

They made good speed down the narrow mountainous highways. Erik enjoyed driving Ole Red, but had some apprehension about the trip. It was the first live run, and he wanted it to be a success. Burt had briefed him carefully concerning the purchase and hauling of chickens. There was a lot to remember, but Erik was excited with the challenge.

It was a fresh, clean morning. The sun was bright, and the mood in the cab of Ole Red was good. Long Willy was freshly clothed with his wool plaid shirt and favorite suit pants. He had two new straps attached to his porcelain arm; it had been a rough couple of weeks. Handling that equipment was tough on the false arm. But one wouldn't notice that Long Willy had any problems. He sat back with his contagious smile, ready to converse with Erik on any subject so selected. His favorite, though, was Friday and Saturday nights in Mucky Hollow. He apparently had an endless source of stories and had already recounted some of them to Erik during their time together. Erik liked these stories; they were funny, and they were shocking to his young and inexperienced mind.

"Yep, Mr. Erik, when we gets back and the plant is running, I takes you over to the barber shop. You know, the one across the street in the Hollow."

"Long Willy, I don't get a haircut there."

"No ... no, Mr. Erik, I don't mean a haircut ... you looks fine. I mean pussy."

"Pussy?" Erik asked in half-disbelief.

"Yessir, pussy. Well, not just pussy, I mean black pussy."

"Pussy ... They sell pussy at the barber shop?" he asked, still a bit surprised.

"Yessir, black pussy, an shine (moonshine), and fried chicken ... we have a time there," he said through breaks in his laughter.

Erik was trying to digest all that he just heard. *There is so much to learn,* he thought as he smiled.

"You ever have some black, Mr. Erik?" asked Long Willy, still grinning.

"No, Long Willy ... don't think so."

"Well, we do it, some Friday."

Erik knew damn well he had never had black; he had only two pieces in his entire life. And both were white. And he wasn't really sure that either qualified as a piece. He certainly remembered the first. It took place in the back seat of his dad's car in the dead of winter. After a couple beers and three hours of heavy breathing, going through the no … yes … no … trauma, she finally agreed, and he scrambled to put it in. He wasn't sure, and she wasn't sure, if he ever got in, at least all the way. Made little difference though, he ejaculated, and she didn't say if she did or didn't, but he sincerely doubted that she did. Besides, he didn't know if girls could ejaculate. Regardless, it was an embarrassing first for Erik. And it wasn't over. It seems that the smell of sweated bodies mixed with the aroma of first love, or lay, can be a bit gamy. This heavy smell apparently mixed with the thick layer of steam on the inside of the car windows — and promptly froze. It remained frozen until his dad warmed the car up for work the next morning. Evidently it thawed out because Erik heard him call out to Rose, "What in hell has that kid of yours been doing with my car? … Smells like a damn whorehouse." Erik didn't know what a "damn whorehouse" smelled like.

The trip into the valley took around nine hours. It was dark when they arrived, so they couldn't do any chicken shopping until the next morning. Erik pulled up to a motel that had some sort of a rating and didn't look expensive or too dirty. He jumped out of the truck and stuck his head into the motel. He asked the night clerk if they had a double, and what did it cost?

"You want twins?" the night clerk said.

"Yes, sir, that would do it," Erik replied.

"Well, we're not busy tonight, can put you both up for three bucks."

"Thank you, we'll take it. Be right back; have to park the truck."

Erik parked the truck, and they grabbed their overnight bag and went to the lobby. He noticed that Long Willy had little to say. He was quiet.

They entered the lobby, and, before they reached the desk, the clerk called out to Erik, "Hey kid, you didn't tell me you were traveling with him. We don't sleep niggers here … and we don't sleep white trash who hangs with 'em …"

The words stunned Erik. It took a few seconds to collect himself. He was frightened, but anger overruled his fear. He looked at the clerk's red puffy face that housed a set of beady eyes and nervously replied, "Sir … I'm not white trash, and he is not a nigger. And yessir, we work together … and yessir, he's probably twice the man that your fat-ass will ever be!"

They stared at each other for a long moment. Erik could not recall ever being so angry … and ever so frightened. It was tense, and he didn't know what to expect. The clerk didn't move, but Erik had a gut feeling that time was working against him and Long Willy. He put his hand on Long Willy's shoulder and calmly said, "Long Willy, let's get the fuck out of here before we be dead."

And they made a speedy exit.

Some minutes passed as they drove down the road to no place special, just a spot to pull over and catch some sleep.

Erik was thinking, I've never talked to an adult like that. It bothered him, but, strangely enough, he felt that he would do it again in the same situation. Long Willy was the first to break the silence, "I'm sorry what I caused you, Mr. Erik … shoulda know better."

"You're sorry. Hell, it was my fault, Willy. I'm the one who should have checked. I caused you embarrassment, and I apologize."

The quiet returned, and, after a time, Erik heard what sounded like a chuckle.

"Anything wrong, Willy?"

"No, sir, Mr. Erik, don't know for sure, but you surprised him an' I think he be so mad he peed his pants. I seen some water!"

"Really? You saw some water … yellow water?"

"Don't know 'bout yeller," Long Willy answered as he shook his head and grinned.

"Well, I know he wasn't afraid of me; must have been afraid of you, Long Willy."

"Don't know," he said grinning, "Maybe he know, Mr. Burt."

"Yea, maybe," Erik replied, half seriously, "He sure makes me pee … and it's yeller."

They both laughed, and it was good that the tension had passed. They pulled over and had a decent night's sleep. As decent as you could have in a Studebaker cab.

CHAPTER EIGHTEEN

EARLY NEXT MORNING, THEY ARRIVED AT VALLEY POULTRY FARM. THE poultry house was impressive, a modern ten-story farm building. The top floor housed several thousand baby chicks, and they would move down one floor each week. They did this for nine weeks. If all went well, the chicks developed into three pound fryers in ten weeks and earned their way to the market.

Erik purchased twelve hundred fryers that were on the ground floor.

They loaded the fryers — about fifteen each — into the wooden coops, without incident. Erik was relieved. He had heard the stories of loading disasters and did his best to avoid one.

Apparently, chickens are so stupid and flighty that any sharp noise or sudden movement will cause panic. Not unlike the cattle stampedes you see in the movies. But there is a major difference; chickens don't have open fields to run in. They do their running inside, and all head for a corner of the room and pile onto each other. Sometimes five or six feet deep. Unfortunately, many are smothered almost immediately. The men loading had to leap into the pile and try to save those on the bottom by pulling them out from within. Eventually the chickens would settle down and cease the suicidal pileup. But, not without losses because the death toll could be sizeable, perhaps several hundred birds. And the dead had no commercial value because the meat turned red and was worthless as edible chicken. They generally ended up as fertilizer.

They loaded the crates onto the truck and secured them with rope. Then they put a large tarp over the entire load to protect the birds from the wind and chill. They were ready to head for Mucky Hollow.

The return trip was smooth, and they made good time. They stopped each couple of hours to check the load, and all looked well.

They pulled into the plant on schedule, around nine that night. Erik could see Shake and Turner waiting for them as he backed the truck into position for unloading. Erik had called them with an expected arrival, and he was pleased to see that they were on time.

"Long Willy, you and the guys can start unloading; get the birds out of the cold. I'll get the hot water going and will call Burt. Let him know we made it," Erik said as he lighted the fire for the scalder.

He called his dad at the packing house, "We got in okay, Dad … picked up twelve hundred nice ones. Just about finished with unloading."

"Did the birds make the trip in good shape?" Burt asked.

"Yessir, think so, don't know of any we lost." Erik replied.

"That's good. I was concerned. You start the kill, and I'll be down when I finish up."

Erik felt good … elated with the success of the trip. *By God, we pulled it off, Erik. The ole man can't jump my ass about this one.*

Long Willy called out, "Mister Erik, you better see dis!"

Erik was uneasy, "See what, Willy?" he said as he walked over to the truck.

"This tarp be torn in front."

"Oh, shit no," Erik said, as he climbed up the truck bed, "How in the hell could it be? We just checked it a couple hours ago."

"Don't know … but we gots some dead birds, Mister Erik," Willy said as he pulled back the tarp, "I can see a bunch."

"Fuck!" responded Erik, "I just told Dad we made it clean … and now this. Goddammit to hell, Willy, I think I've had the wiener on this one!"

With a sense of urgency, they rushed the unloading, checking each coop for dead, or almost dead birds. They salvaged some, but many exposed in the front coops didn't make it. Frustrated and discouraged, Erik counted one hundred and seventy-three dead birds. *God, this is going to be a fun time when Burt shows up. I can hardly wait.*

Erik didn't have to wait long. Burt arrived within minutes. Entering the plant, he saw Erik and Long Willy, "Understand you had a good trip?"

Long Willy answered first, "We did, till we gots here, Mister Burt."

Burt looked puzzled, and Erik said, "We lost some birds, Dad. The old tarp gave way …"

"You lost birds? You told me you didn't. So, what the hell's going on?"

"I thought we didn't lose any … but we did, almost two hundred of them,"

Erik said. He dreaded the response.

"You lost two hundred birds?" Burt yelled, "How in the hell could that happen? I know ... you were probably highballing the truck, just like you always do ... and lost your load. Jesus Christ, I should kick your ass!"

"No sir, I didn't ... it was an old tarp ... just came apart," replied Erik. He knew it was hopeless to try and explain when his dad was this fired-ass hot. His best out was to just shut the fuck up. And he did.

It didn't shut his dad up though, "Well that's a couple hundred dollars ... it's coming out of your pay, so you better get your ass humping. I want the birds finished tonight." And he hauled out of the plant.

Erik was tired and humiliated. *Why does he have to embarrass me like that in front of my crew? One of these days I will get the hell out of here. To where, I don't know ... or care.*

CHAPTER NINETEEN

ERIK HAD A GOOD CREW. THEY WERE FAST, ESPECIALLY TURNER. HE could gut thirty-five to forty birds an hour. Obviously, Turner had done this before, and Erik finally understood why he wanted to be paid by the bird. He could make two dollars or more per hour. The crew envied his speed — and pay day.

They had a good routine. Long Willy killed and scalded the birds; Erik picked them on the machine; Shake and Turner gutted and chilled them. Each person could fill in on any job if needed, but most worked their "specialty," as they called it.

They killed a thousand or so a week and worked long hours. Erik enjoyed working with the crew, particularly with Long Willy. He was captivated with Willy's ability to overcome his disability. He would take two or three birds out of the coop with his good hand, and place them head first into the funnels of the kill trough. Then he used his clamp hand to pull their heads down, then would cut them off with the knife in his good hand. When they finished bleeding into the trough, he grabbed them with the clamp and put them in the scalder. He swirled them around in the boiling water long enough to loosen the feathers. The timing in the water was critical, too much time would cook the skin and too little time made picking difficult. Long Willy seemed to have the knack. While scalding birds, Long Willy would take some ribbing from the crew, "Don't let dos birds bite your hand … da steel one," Turner would say.

Shake added, "Don't burn your hand, Long Willy … and watch that water, it'll rust you."

Ever so often Erik would hear Willy say, "Damn … that's hot!"

"What's wrong, Long Willy?" Erik asked over the noise of the picker.

"Burnt my hand, Mister Erik." He grinned with embarrassment.

"How could you burn your hand? It's made of steel," Erik said.

"Well, sometimes I gets in a hurry and forgets which hand I uses."

"That's kinda dumb ain't it, Long Willy?" Erik said.

"Yea, it be dumb," Long Willy answered. And they both laughed.

The chicken picker was a machine that turned a drum with many rubber-like fingers on it. The drum turned at high speed, and the fingers would strip the feathers off the scalded bird. Erik had the privilege of being the "chief chicken plucker," which he considered to be the worst job in the plant.

Attired in his long rubber apron and boots, he grabbed the bird by its feet and held it on the spinning drum. Hot wet feathers flew off one side of the bird; then he turned the bird over and repeated the process. There was a hood on top of the machine that was supposed to divert the mess to the floor, but Erik swore that it all landed on him. It wasn't the water and feathers that bothered him, it was the chicken shit. It flew everywhere, and a day on the picker left him covered with the stinking mess, some of which actually hit his apron, he conceded. But most splattered on his head and face. He couldn't believe how much chicken shit there was in a three-pound bird.

"Long Willy," he asked, one day, "You know how much chicken shit is in one of these chickens?"

"No sir … how much that be, Mister Erik?"

"Enough to fertilize two football fields … and still have enough for a chap stick," Erik said.

Long Willy laughed. Erik had told him the chap stick joke; the one where the guy with chapped lips goes to the pharmacist and asks for some relief. The pharmacist recommends chicken shit.

"Chicken shit for my chapped lips?" the guy asked in disbelief.

"No, not ordinary chicken shit," the pharmacist rebuts, "Just the white part of it."

"You mean the white part of chicken shit cures my chapped lips?" he asked in amazement.

"Nope, won't cure 'em, but it sure as hell keeps you from licking them," the pharmacist responds.

Long Willy liked that joke, and Erik stopped licking his lips.

After a month on the picker, Erik noticed that everything around him smelled like chicken shit and wet feathers. Then one evening after taking a shower, he realized that it was his body that produced the smell. He couldn't believe it. The smell of chicken shit came out of his pores — particularly when he sweat. And he was shocked when he passed gas. *The same smell of chicken shit. No wonder I can't get a date. Who would possibly date a guy that smells, sweats, and farts chicken shit and wet feathers?*

The next day he switched jobs. Shake became the head chicken plucker, and Erik became a gut man.

Shake said, "I don't care what I smells like ... 'cause my woman don't smells so good anyways."

Sometimes it was necessary to work nights, and the crew had no problem with this as long as it was not Friday or Saturday, their nights to "do it," as they said.

Erik paid them at three on Friday afternoons, and then they would start doing it. And do it, they did. The usual routine was to pick up their shine at the taxi stand, meander down the street, and gather in front of the store. The weekend party commenced.

One Friday payday, Long Willy said, "Mister Erik, why don't you come with us tonight and have some shine? ... It be a good time."

"Oh, I don't know, Willy, I'm kind of broke, and you know ... they might not like a white boy hanging around," Erik said.

"Ah, them mother-fuckers don't care ... they likes you ... you got the chickens," replied Long Willy, grinning as usual, " 'Sides, I'll get you some black pussy ... won't we, Shake?"

"Yea, we get you some," said Shake and Turner, "Good stuff that pussy is."

"Well ... I don't ... well, maybe," Erik replied. He wanted to join them, and he sure wanted to get laid, but he was afraid of the welcome ... or lack of one.

"It be fun, Mister Erik," Long Willy said. "Hey, you never been fucked until you gets fucked by a nigger." They all laughed, and Shake and Turner chimed in, "Yea, dem black asses take you apart, Mister Erik. ... They fuck you till your nose bleeds."

"Well, I'd like to have a nose bleed," said Erik.

"Tell you what, Mister Erik," Long Willy said, "You get some chickens and get some eggs ... then we takes them to the barbershop and we cooks 'em up, and we all fucks and eats."

"Yea, fucks an' eats ... and drinks shine," said Shake.

"Well okay, Willy," said Erik, "But I have to clean up ... and how many chickens?"

"No matter, six or eight ... don't have to be the good ones, they all eat good," replied Long Wllly, "And some eggs ... git the older ones."

"Okay, I'll meet you at the barber shop in a few hours. Have to finish here," Erik said. "Then you can show me all about the good stuff ... I be ready for a nose bleed."

They all laughed, and Erik's crew headed for the taxi stand. It was shine time.

Erik cleaned up and selected eight fryers and three dozen of the older eggs for the anticipated evening of good fucking and good eating. He had reservations, but he felt that he could rely on Long Willy to back him up. He had doubts about the others, but no doubts about Long Willy.

It was dark when Erik headed for the barbershop. He didn't see his crew in front, so he went directly to back of the shop.

Erik was surprised that the back of the barbershop was not really a part of the shop. It was a separate structure about the size of a large mobile home, maybe a doublewide, and it was made of wood, unpainted wood. It had a dirt yard with two old Buicks parked on it.

He was a little nervous when he went up the front stoop and knocked on the door. The door opened, and a colored lady stood there without showing any signs of greeting; she just stared at the white boy. Erik was uneasy. *I hope I didn't fuck-up ... I should have skipped the invite, but what the hell ... I've gone this far.*

Finally, he said, "Hi, I'm Erik ... ya know, the one with the chicken plant ..."

"Oh, you be the chicken-man," she said while breaking into a big smile, "You come in here and git warm. Long Willy say you might come by."

Erik had never seen her before, but she was friendly and her slight build with a prominent ass was kind of alluring. She was pleasant to look at, maybe in her early forties, and not real dark.

"Dey told me bout you. Dey say you be a nice man," she said as she looked at the large paper sack that Erik held.

"Oh, I'm sorry ma'am, almost forgot. Brought you some chicken and eggs," he said as he handed her the sack.

"Oh, that be a sweet man," she said, "I wondered what be in the poke ... dey call me, Flo ... Flo Florence."

"Long Willy ... Mister Erik's here," Flo said in a stronger voice, as she took the bag from Erik, "You get him some shine. I'm gonna fry up these birds ... yea, they gonna be good."

Erik anxiously looked about, then he spotted Long Willy and Shake on the couch at the end of the room.

"Hi, Mister Erik, glad you come," said Willy as he motioned him over to the couch.

It was a fairly large sitting room with faded throw carpets on the wooden floor. A small table lamp had a flower blossom shade that prevented most of the light from escaping. The light was sufficient, however, for Erik to see the tattered picture of the Sacred Heart of Jesus Christ framed on the wall. He tried to ignore it. *God, that's all I need. I'm trying to get laid ... and He's watching.* Erik sat on the couch and asked, "Where's Turner, thought he was gonna be with us?"

"Oh, he gone with some of the guys," replied Long Willy, "Thinks they need more shine. Here, Mister Erik, you take a shot of dis ... dis be good stuff." He handed Erik a glass with two or three inches of clear liquid in it.

"This good shine, Long Willy?" asked Erik as he tried to be cool. He only had shine once in his life, and that was not a pleasant experience.

"Yea, it be good," Long Willy laughed. "Gits you ready for the night."

"Well, thank you, sir," said Erik as he tipped the glass to Long Willy, "You going to join us, Shake?"

Erik noticed that Shake didn't answer; he couldn't; he was too damn drunk; he just stared into space.

"Looks like Shake is having a ball," Erik said, "Anything wrong?"

"Naw, Mister Erik, he gits like this ever Friday and Saturday. And Sunday if he gots money left," Long Willy said as he grinned. "He never stay awake to git laid ... buts I do, that's why dey calls me, Long Willy."

"I figured as much, Long Willy," replied Erik, returning the big grin.

Erik looked around the room. He saw two colored men sitting on the side of the room, one short, one tall; he didn't know them. He was surprised that he didn't see any girls, just Flo and another woman in the kitchen. He could hear them talking.

Two other rooms led off from the sitting room, but the doors were closed, and he couldn't see in. *This is quite a barbershop,* he thought as he listened to the radio spew its country music.

He tried to build his nerve to take a swig of the good stuff — the shine.

"Mister Erik, you not takin' a drink," said Long Willy, "I thought you likes it."

"I do. Yep, really do," Erik lied as he took a nice big swig of the clear, water-like stuff.

"Holy shit!" Erik said as he swallowed. It was similar to hot coals. *Christ, I'm a fire-eater ... have to keep it down.* The tears formed, then streamed down his cheeks.

"Yea, Long Willy, this is really good shit," he said as he tried to grin, "Good stuff ... the best."

Long Willy laughed; he could see Erik was having a bit of trouble.

"First one always a motherfucker, Mister Erik, you be okay when it settles."

Erik saw a man come out of the first closed door room and depart without comment. Soon after, a colored girl came out and went into the kitchen. She was a beautiful girl, slim, young, with a pretty smile. Erik's classmates called them "High Yellows." Yes, Erik surmised, she was definitely a High Yellow.

She came out of the kitchen and went over to the short man and took him into the same room. And closed the door. *So the two rooms are bedrooms, and that's where I'll get some black pussy.* He was becoming more enthusiastic after seeing the girl.

"Long Willy, that one of the girls you told me about?" Erik asked.

"Dat be her, Mister Erik, dat be Coleen," he said, "You likes her?"

"Damn, she's pretty, Long Willy, makes me get a hard-on," Erik replied, and they both laughed. Things were funnier to Erik, now that the shine stayed in his belly.

"Ya'll come on and git this chicken," Flo hollered from the kitchen. "And gravy ... and eggs that Mister Erik brung us. Come on now."

Erik, Long Willy, and the tall man headed for the kitchen. Shake didn't move. He continued to stare into space.

The food looked great and smelled even better. They loaded their plates and ate with gusto. Coleen and her short friend came out and joined in on the food. All were having a good time, and Erik felt more comfortable as the evening progressed.

While Erik was eating, he noticed the tall man take some chicken into the other room with the closed door. Erik wondered if the girl in there was as pretty as Coleen. *Really doesn't matter though ... I'm going to have Coleen.*

Two other men came in from outside. They announced that they could smell the chicken and stopped by for a good time. Erik guessed they were regulars because cf their warm reception. They seemed to know their way around. They spoke to Erik, and he returned the greeting; he had seen them over at the chicken plant.

Erik wondered what the next move was going to be, or when and where he was going to get laid. He was anxious, and it was getting late. Then, he noticed Coleen and the short guy get up and put their coats on. "Oh, shit," Erik said to Long Willy, "She's leaving with what's his face."

"It don't make no shit, Mister Erik," said Long Willy, "Amanda be prettier. She's in the other room, I think."

Erik was glad to hear that. The tall guy came out of the closed door room and left without a word.

Long Willy got up and went into the kitchen. He came out with Flo, and she said, "You ready now, Mister Erik ... you gonna visit one of the girls?"

"Yes, ma'am, I'm ready," Erik said with more enthusiasm than he felt, "I'm not sure what I do ... I mean pay ..."

"Oh, no, honey," Flo laughed, "It don't cost you nothin', you brought dos beautiful chickens. You visit Lucy, and she treat you right. You go in an' have a good time."

"All right, Flo, a good time I'm gonna have," Erik said as he departed for the room.

He closed the door behind him. The room was nearly dark. A low wattage bulb provided some light, but it took time for his eyes to focus. When they did, he was shocked. *Holy shit ... this is fucking awful.* He saw a colored woman stretched out on the bed with no sheets, just a filthy mattress. She was naked, laying on her back. She had a brief towel by her side. It used to be white, he guessed. The room smelled like mold, and she had wrinkles, and no tits of any size. A couple of chicken bones lay on the lamp table.

He turned to leave, but remembered, he had to be cool. *You handle this right.*

"Hi, honey, I be Lucy. What's yours?" she asked, in a low tired voice.

"Erik," he said, barely.

"Well, Erik, are you the last one, honey?" she asked.

"I don't know what you mean," he stammered, "I mean … there's a couple men out there …:

"Well, I seen 'em. You be last." She grinned, "I had a bunch today, but I don't come … always waits till last. I gets to come now … all over you, honey."

Erik saw her grin, and he thought he was going to throw up. He couldn't believe what he had just heard. And he lost the beautiful hard-on he brought in with him.

"Well, I'm … I'm not sure if I …" he said.

"It be okay, honey, lots of white boys can't do it with a colored girl … least not at first. I understands, just takes time," she said as she reached out for him.

Erik backed off, and he felt sad. Sad that he was there, and sadder that she was there. He wanted to be kind, but he wanted to be out of there.

He heard a commotion in the other room. The voices were raised, and one of them was Long Willy's. "Lucy, I've got to see what's going on. Thank you, and I'll be back," he half lied.

Erik came out into the sitting room, and Long Willy was standing face to face with the short man that had left earlier. Both were obviously bonafide drunk, the short one more so than Long Willy. They were arguing, and their voices got louder.

The other men left, except Shake. He continued to stare into space.

Flo came in and tried to calm things, but it didn't work.

"I can talk about any motherfucker I wants to," the short one yelled at Long Willy, "An' that white motherfucker ain't havin' my woman!"

"Nigger, he ain't fuckin' with your woman," Long Willy said, "I asked him over here, and your black ass can't do a goddamn thing."

Oh shit, he's talking about me.

Erik started to leave. At that moment the short one slammed into Long Willy and knocked him to the floor. Erik jumped in between them, but before he made contact, Long Willy was on his feet and went for his rival.

Erik had never seen Long Willy angry; he looked like one mean son-of-a-bitch with fire in his eyes. Long Willy shoved Erik aside with his good arm, and then using his false arm, made a full sweeping swing at the short Negro. It connected, and Erik could hear the crunch to the head, and he heard the snap of the arm. He saw blood spurt from above the ear. The short man dropped straight to the floor. And Erik saw Long Willy's arm fall off and hang by the tattered straps. Long Willy stood over him a moment. Erik could see more blood flow from the unconscious head. *This does not look good. … Christ, he may be dead. That blow would have stopped a goddamn truck.*

Long Willy looked at Erik and said, "We be getting out of this place, Mister Erik."

Erik nodded and headed for the door; Long Willy followed and said, "Sorry, Flo." Erik didn't hear if she responded.

Once outside, Long Willy seemed to calm down. They headed over toward the chicken plant. Long Willy's false arm dangled at his side, "Never did like that motherfucker, Mister Erik," he said, "But anyways, I best leave town for a bit. Gets my arm fixed and sees if he be dead."

"Yea, I think so, Long Willy," replied a nervous Erik, "You take some time off. It'll be okay … in a while."

"At least you got some good black pussy, Mister Erik," Long Willy said laughing, "Good, wasn't it?"

"Sure was, Willy … sure was good pussy."

CHAPTER TWENTY

LONG WILLY NEVER RETURNED TO WORK. ERIK WAS TOLD THAT HE WAS DOWN south with relatives. Erik tried to forget that scary night, but he missed Long Willy. The crew wasn't a fun crew with the new replacement. And he never heard a word about the short guy that Long Willy hit. *Must have lived.* And the job went on, and the work continued, but Erik had more important matters to think about. He wondered if he would ever get laid. He doubted it.

Several times a week, Erik delivered the processed poultry to the packinghouse. While there, he usually spent time talking to Paula, the "girl Friday" that worked in the main office. She was an attractive lady with a captivating personality, soft spoken and charming.

"Erik, she's not that beautiful," said one of the male employees. Erik discounted that statement because it was probably based on jealousy. But Erik thought she was gorgeous.

She was tall and slender, with long black hair and a set of brown, bedroom eyes. Her mouth was wide and sensuous, with a slight sexy gap in the front teeth. Her white skin was smooth and soft. *Yes ... sumptuous.*

She, however, was older than Erik, at least ten or fifteen years, so he didn't think of her as a potential date, just as a friend. But that didn't stop Erik's fantasizing when he was kidding around with her. She would ask him who he was going with ... and how's his sex life ... and who's next? Questions that left Erik slightly embarrassed. Regardless of the embarrassment, he welcomed the opportunity to be around her.

On occasions, she stood close and brushed up against him. It always startled him. He felt a rush of excitement from her touch and smell, always so female ... and delicious. *Someday, Erik, you are going to have someone like her.*

And then, he would realize how foolish he was, rather presumptuous — no, more like impossible.

It was Thursday afternoon when Erik made a delivery to the packing house. He had finished work at the chicken plant, and the crew was gone. It was a good day, he reflected, and he smiled when he realized that he didn't use the machine picker that morning. He should be relatively free of chicken shit. *That's good.*

He arrived at the plant, offloaded, and went into the office to handle the paper work ... and to see Paula. She was there, and friendly as always. *God, she's pretty.*

"Hi Erik, you have a good day with the chickens?" she asked, showing her perky smile.

"Sure did, Paula, just me and the chicken shit ... had a ball."

She laughed and said, "Oh, come on, Erik, it's not that bad, I think you smell like a real man ... kinda cute one."

"No ma'am, not that smell ... at least that's what the girls tell me, and you know how many dates I have ... just a real lady's man," Erik replied, jokingly.

"You mean no sweet thing has captured your beautiful, young body, Erik?" she asked in mock surprise.

"No ma'am, not that I remember. And believe me, I would remember."

"They just don't know what they're missing, Erik, you doll baby," she said as she playfully threw him a kiss.

A customer came in, and they broke off the bantering and took care of business. Erik was a little uncomfortable with the conversation, the kidding around. *Don't get out of line, Erik Larsen; she's a lady, and she's just being nice.*

She took care of the customer and returned within minutes.

"Erik, would you like to do something nice?" she asked more seriously.

"Yes ma'am, sure would," he replied.

"Let me fix you a dinner over at my place. Would you like that ... dinner with an older woman? I promise I'll be good," she said as she rolled her lovely brown eyes.

Erik lost his breath. *That did it ... this is not for real.* He wanted to be cool, to say something intelligent and grown-up, but all he could say was, "Yes, ma'am."

She noticed that Erik was practically in shock, so she said softly, "It will be fun, Erik … just talk, and a good steak. Think I could find a good steak around this place? Bet I could."

"Yes, ma'am, bet you could," he answered. *God, another beautiful answer … what a dummy, Erik, you are so smooth.*

"Then, I'll see you in a couple of hours, around seven … you know my place?" she said.

"Yes, ma'am," he said.

It was about seven when Erik arrived at Paula's apartment. It was dark, and he wasn't sure where you parked at her place, so he left the pickup down the street and walked a half block.

He had taken a double shower and zapped himself with an extra shot of aftershave, anything to smother the mark of his trade … chicken shit. And he spent at least an hour convincing himself it was a dinner with a friend and coworker, nothing more … He should not get his hopes up … that's all there is to it … dinner.

He was nervous when he rang the doorbell. The door opened and Paula stood there with a man's shirt on, nothing else, just a white dress shirt. Erik didn't hear Paula's greeting. All he could hear and see were legs. *Nice long legs clear up to her ass … no, clear up to her …*

"Erik, are you going to come in?" she asked.

"I'm sorry … yes ma'am," he said as he entered.

It was a cozy apartment, small, clean, and nothing fancy. *It made you feel at home,* Erik thought. The lighting was soft, and, for a moment, he felt comfortable.

"You sit on the couch, Erik, I'll get us a beer, then we'll eat … found some great steaks … surprised?"

"No ma'am," he said as he watched her depart for the kitchen.

He couldn't take his eyes off her legs. … *Damn, I better get a grip on things … start acting like a grown-up.*

She returned with two glasses of beer and sat down with her legs folded under her at the end of the couch. She didn't have panties on, and Erik thought he would have a seizure. Paula noticed his reaction and said, "I embarrass you … don't I Erik?"

"Oh, no … I'm not …" he replied. *Christ, what a lie that was.* He sensed that he was blushing.

"This is the first time, isn't it?" she said softly.

"No, no ... well, kind of ... the first, maybe," he managed to mumble. *Damn, I'm making an ass of myself. What it I fail? Maybe, I better get out of here ... no, that's not the answer. Get hold of yourself, Erik.*

"Erik, it will be all right. You just relax and be yourself. I'll take care of everything," she said as she scooted closer to him;

It was awkward, but Erik felt more at ease and gained confidence. "I'm sorry Paula. I guess maybe I haven't, really ... but God, I'd love to," he said, "Just ... you know ... it's a little different."

She looked at him with her soft eyes and said, "I know, Erik ... you come with me."

Erik followed her into the bedroom. She turned, and her shirt opened, exposing breasts and the small area of black hair between her long legs. Erik was numb. He was in heaven, his thoughts racing. *It's finally going to happen. ... I'm going to get laid by a beautiful lady.*

She took Erik's hand and led him to the side of the bed. She switched off the lamp and quietly unbuttoned his shirt. She pressed her firm white breasts to his chest. She unbuckled his belt and helped his clothing to the floor. Then Paula reached down and clasped his exposed penis, "God ... what a beautiful hard dick you have ... and so large," she whispered as she gently stroked it and pulled it against her soft legs. Erik had never heard a woman say "hard dick"; it was shamefully exciting, and it magnified all his desires. He could feel his knees buckle. *God, hang in there Erik ... oh God, don't come now.*

He heard their labored breath. He felt the surging ache. He clung to her body; he could smell the powder ... and lust.

Suddenly there was a noise. *Oh, Christ ... it can't be. Not now!* He heard it again, a noise from the kitchen. Erik and Paula both heard it. The moment was gone. "Someone is here," she whispered.

"Oh, shit," he said. Erik was damn near paralyzed with fear ... and frustration. She had told me she wasn't married. Who could it be?

"Erik, go over to the closet and be quiet, I'll take care of this. ... It'll be all right," she whispered.

In silence, Erik eased up his trousers, then short-stepped his way to the closet. He heard his own breathing. And his beautiful erection disappeared rapidly.

The bedroom door opened, but Erik couldn't see the figure. He heard Paula say, "I've got company."

There was more silence, then, "Damn … You should have told me," a man's voice said. Paula remained calm. After a pause, the man's voice continued with little emotion, "Well, I guess I'll see you later."

Erik could hear the departing footsteps.

The voice … that goddamn voice. He recognized the voice. It can't be, not that voice. But it was. It was Burt's voice … his father's. Burt was here, and he was going to bed with Paula. *My father, fucking around with other women.*

Erik was sick, and he needed to throw up; he heard the voice over and over. And Erik's mind wouldn't accept it. But, he knew it was his father's.

Paula turned the bed light on and said, "Erik, I'm sorry, I never dreamed … but he didn't see you …"

"See me … See me," Erik cried, "Hell, I don't care if he saw me … Shit, I saw him!" And Erik bolted out before she could see the tears.

It was black, and it was cold. Erik continued to walk. His thoughts were rambling and confused. *That son-of-a-bitch, fucking around on my mother … knocking me out of a great piece of ass … and he's too good to hug his kid … just beats the shit out of you. He makes my mother cry. Well, never again … never again you bastard. You goddamn phony bastard!*

CHAPTER TWENTY-ONE

ERIK MADE A SPECIAL EFFORT TO KEEP UP HIS ROUTINE. HE WANTED everything to appear normal. His father apparently didn't know that Erik was Paula's mystery guest, and there was no indication that his mother was aware of the incident. This pleased Erik, but he was troubled. He didn't want to be around his father, and he didn't want to forgive him. It was a dilemma, and he guessed that Burt would not accept his leaving the job, at least not without a damn good excuse. And he didn't have one that he could disclose, not without hurting his mother.

He thought about joining the military, but that wouldn't work because he wasn't old enough to join without parents' consent. Also, it was important to Erik that he finish high school. It was a big problem. He knew he had to leave, but he didn't know how to do it.

Then one morning he had the answer. It was all clear. He knew what he had to do. He would become a priest. A missionary priest serving South America.

Erik always tried to be a good Catholic. He clearly believed in religion and the necessity of moral law. A few months back he had attended a mission at the parish church, and it had left a memorable impression on him. The mission was a week long, in the evenings, and was given for the purpose of raising money and recruiting seminarians. The missionary priest, Father Davidson, belonged to the Order of the Most Precious Blood, commonly called the Sanguinists.

He was a dynamic young priest, well educated and charismatic. He explained the mission of the order: to save souls and enhance the native quality of life. The work was primarily in the jungles of South America. This appealed to Erik, and he had several meetings with Father Davidson to learn more about the school and priesthood. He was told that the minor seminary included high school and two years of college. You then went on to the major seminary for six years to earn your doctorate in theology and, if recommended, ordination to the priesthood.

"It is a good education, and it's all paid for by the order," " Father Davidson said. "And it's very strict," he added, "upon ordination you take the vow of poverty, and the vow of celibacy."

Erik decided that it wouldn't be any big deal to be broke; however, the celibacy part might be more than a nuisance. *But,* he rationalized, *I'm practically living a life of celibacy now, and, apparently, I'll never get laid.* He did, however, flinch a bit when Father Davidson told him that celibacy included abstention of any sexual thoughts or deeds, including boys' favorite pastime — masturbation.

Yes, Erik thought, that may be a real ball buster, but I can live with it.

He told his parents about the conversations with Father Davidson and that the order would accept him as a seminarian. He could go in as a senior in high school and then take eight years of college before ordination.

"And, it's free," Erik told them.

They both were shocked that Erik was considering such a vocation, but heartily agreed that they would be "very proud" to have a son as a priest. It was good news for Erik, and he made the decision to go for it. He would become a priest. A missionary priest in South America.

After making the decision, Burt asked Erik, "You're not doing this just because of me, are you?"

"No sir, it's not that …" he lied.

Within ten days, Erik arrived at Holy Orders Seminary in upper Pennsylvania. It was located out in "farm country" on several hundred acres of rolling farm land.

The main structure, a three-story building with a bell steeple, was constructed of old stone, and, with dignity, it towered over the smaller ones. The complex was set apart from the farmland by several acres of trees and grassland. It was a handsome site, impeccably clean, and the landscaping was postcard perfect. Erik sensed the tranquility and the stateliness.

Erik was greeted by Father Tom, the dean. A warm, pleasant individual in his early fifties, he led Erik to his office and proceeded with the orientation. "Erik, we want to officially welcome you to our home. We are most pleased to have you here, and I ensure you that we will do everything possible to assist you in your pursuit to serve God and humanity."

"Thank you, Father," Erik replied.

"I know there will be times that you will experience doubt and desperation. This is not uncommon, but please try to remember that we all, the faculty and students, are here to help each other obtain the most difficult and rewarding vocation on God's earth."

"I understand, Father, and thank you," replied Erik.

"We have no written rules and regulations here, Erik, but we certainly have them in effect. John Chambers, your classmate, is assigned as your student guide. He will teach you our routine. From this point, Erik, your life will change in ways that you've never imagined ... for the better, we hope," Father Tom said as he smiled warmly.

"May God bless you ... and good luck."

So began a year of change and challenge for Erik.

Erik was taken to the reception room where he awaited his student guide. Within minutes, a well-groomed young man appeared wearing a black cassock with a white collar.

At first, Erik thought that he was a priest, but then he noticed the collar had a vertical black stripe on the front of it.

"Hi, Erik, I'm John Chambers," he said as he offered a cordial handshake, "I'm your student guide for the next week or so, and I'm looking forward to it."

"Thank you, John, I'm glad to meet you," Erik responded, "I appreciate your help. I know I need it ... kind of a dummy."

John laughed, " 'Kind of a dummy' ... no way. Not with all you have done ... flying airplanes, loading coal, cutting meat, driving big trucks. Hey, the whole class is waiting to meet you."

"John, how did you know all of that?" Erik asked in amazement.

"Oh, we're pretty close here, Erik. Father Tom let us know that you were joining, and he gave us your background. We're happy that you're here. Now let's go meet your class. Most are on break in the rec room."

John and Erik went to the recreation room, and they joined the class. Erik was introduced around and was warmly accepted by his new classmates, some thirty of them. All wore black cassocks and polished black shoes. He was impressed with their friendliness and demeanor. They were all clean-cut young men who displayed genuine sincerity. Then, within minutes, all but John and Erik departed the rec room as if there was a silent signal.

"What's going on?" Erik asked, "Where does everybody go on cue?"

John laughed, "You'll get used to it, Erik. Our time is all scheduled, a tight schedule I might add."

"You mean everything on schedule?"

"That's right, Erik, everything. There's no wasted time here. I'll give you a rundown on the basics, then guide you through the next couple of days until you get the hang of it. It's not that bad."

"I appreciate that, John," Erik replied.

"Where do I start?" said John, half joking, "You can come into this rec room for twenty-five minutes, twice a day. You can have a cigarette if you smoke, providing you have signed permission from your parents. Do you smoke, Erik?"

"Well, yes, I do, but I don't have anything signed, John."

"No problem, you just write your folks, and I'm sure they'll take care of it."

"Can't we call? I don't want to wait a couple of weeks for a cigarette."

"Nope, we can't use the telephone, but you can write; in fact, you must write home once a week … and once a month to your parish priest. And you don't seal the envelopes because the proctor reads all the mail, incoming and outgoing."

"Damn, no cigarettes, and they read your mail," Erik said in almost disbelief.

"And we don't say 'damn,' Erik, not if you want to stay here," said John as he smiled.

Erik was embarrassed, "I'm sorry, John, didn't mean to say that. I'll have to watch myself."

"It's okay, we all had a hard time adjusting. … You're going to do just fine."

John proceeded to go over the rules and schedule with Erik. "A few of the rules," he said. He told Erik that the day begins at six in the morning and ends at ten at night. "You sleep, shower, shave, and attend mass before breakfast. Then on to classes until noon, then a half-hour meditation in the chapel, then break for lunch. You work your assigned job for two hours, then participate in sports for one hour, then back to class, dinner, evening chapel, and study hall until bedtime.

"And," John continued, "you must walk the circle, you know the circle pathway in front of the building? You walk that for fifteen minutes each evening with a classmate. But not the same classmate more than two times in a row. And you never walk with a junior classmate."

"Am I going too fast, Erik?" John asked, smiling.

Erik nodded that he wasn't, and John continued, "You cannot have money or jewelry, although you can have a cheap watch. Everything you wear has to be approved, all care packages, you know, cookies and things like that, have to be shared with the class. No candy, no alcohol, no special clothing, and no talking about girls or sex. No display of temper, no foul language, no fancy hair lotions or haircuts, no dirty jokes or connotations of such, and no discussion of homosexuality. No discussion of doubts about your vocation, except to your spiritual advisor. No sour face, no challenging of the teachings ... You can do that later in the major seminary, I'm told. No visitors, except on the third Sunday of the month, and only for three hours. Silent Sunday is every fourth Sunday, with no talking for twenty-four hours. No talking during meals on any day. Do not waste your food. Help classmates when needed. Show compassion and understanding. Accept all duties with cheerfulness and give your best performance. Accept all adversity as penitence to be offered to the honor and glory of God. And don't cheat, and don't whine or bitch ... Sorry about that Erik, didn't mean to say 'bitch.' "

Erik's mind was trying to keep up with all the do's and don'ts. He understood that they would be strict, but not to this degree. He was already having doubts about his decision. "Christ, is there anything that's not covered by rules?" asked Erik, and then he realized he said 'Christ.' "Sorry about that, John."

"Hey, don't worry about it, Erik. I know it sounds rough, but it really isn't. You'll fit right in. And besides, we get a vacation in the summer."

"I didn't know that," Erik said, "No one told me that we get the summer off."

"Oh, not the summer, Erik. We only get ten days off, during August, and then we're ready to hit if for another year. It goes by in a hurry. Your investiture, Christmas, Lent, Easter, and summer, all pass quickly."

"What investiture?" Erik asked, showing his ignorance.

"Your investiture ... you will be invested into the order as a seminarian ninety days from now, assuming you qualify and all that," John said. "Then you're eligible to wear your cassock, and 'voila' ... you're one of us."

"Well, that sounds great, John, and when do I start work?"

"Father Tom will talk to you soon. They generally start you off with a job that teaches you humility, but I don't know what he will do with you, being a senior and all … Also, classes will start Monday, and I'm sure he will talk to you before then."

Erik didn't respond verbally. He was trying to perceive his new way of life.

John glanced at his cheap watch and said calmly, "Welcome to Holy Orders, Erik, we have three minutes to make dinner … Your schedule has started."

CHAPTER TWENTY-TWO

TWO MONTHS INTO HIS RELIGIOUS TRAINING FOUND ERIK SHOVELING manure. It was a busy, exciting two months. His guide, John Chambers, hadn't exaggerated. His first job assignment from Father Tom was to clean out the holding barns for the wintering steers. Erik shoveled manure into the spreaders for days. A floor of manure six or seven feet deep was not unusual, and the ammonia fumes at times were unbearable. But Erik remembered John's advice and accepted all assignments with cheerful humility.

Father Tom praised Erik for his performance and told him that he was getting a new job assignment: a promotion so to speak. Erik was pleased; he imagined that he would be on one of the tractors, maybe even one of the big ones. However, the promotion entailed cleaning toilets and working in the laundry, sorting and washing skivvies for the students and priests. Not the nuns, they did their own. Erik had to smile when he thought how far he had come in life. *A few months ago, I was working with chicken shit ... now, I've climbed all the way to toilets, skivvies, and cow shit. Burt, would be proud of you, Erik ... really proud.*

Erik worked hard at his job and studies. His classes were rough, mainly because he was so far behind the other seniors. They all had good backgrounds in math, science, literature, and, in particular, the languages. They were in their fifth year of Latin, second year of German, and most had a year or two of Spanish. Erik had had a year or so of English, he guessed, but he tried not to be intimidated by their accomplishments. Besides, they were always giving him encouragement and praise in his struggle to catch up. Father Tom had decided that Erik could skip German because he needed the time for Latin. He then assigned him to Father Hartman, a retired priest, to study Latin three hours a day, six days a week.

Father Hartman, in his eighties, was a kindly gentleman with a great sense of humor. He wore an old hair piece that should have been discarded years ago, and his teeth didn't seem to fit properly, but his blue eyes were bright and alive. He had returned to the seminary to finish his remaining days in peace, and had volunteered to help Erik acquire a background in Latin. Erik's classmates kidded him on occasions, "Erik, are you sure Father Hartman is qualified to teach you Latin? He's only fluent in thirteen languages. I'd complain to Father Tom."

Erik found out later that he was not fluent in thirteen languages. It was closer to seventeen, Father Tom said.

Each morning after breakfast, they started the day with three hours of Latin. He was captivated with Father Hartman's knowledge and intelligence. As they spent time together, Erik became more impressed with his gentleness, his sincerity, and his love. He was the kindest person Erik knew, and the friendship was genuine. An odd friendship, however, a sixteen-year-old and an eighty-two-year-old priest.

On some days, Father Hartman became confused and went to the wrong classroom, but Erik would find him and lead him to safety. There were also days that he would be teaching Erik while speaking English, then suddenly slip into speaking Polish, or Chinese, or a combination of many. Erik would interrupt and tell him that he didn't understand because he wasn't speaking English, Father Hartman would then realize the mistake and begin laughing. A good hearty laugh at himself, during which his toupee would slide forward on his head, sometimes to the point of covering his eyes. Then he became more confused until Erik would slide it back into position.

"Erik," Father Hartman said, "if you ever get in a country and don't know their language ... just switch to Latin. That's what I do, and it always works. Remember that, son, just switch to Latin."

Erik replied, "I'll do that, Father, but I have to learn it first."

"Well, Erik, the best way to learn a language is on your mother's knee," he chuckled, "but you can't do that ... so I'm going to teach you."

The chuckle turned to laughter, and Erik had to readjust the toupee.

Erik learned later from Father Tom that Father Hartman was one of the few in the world who spoke Latin fluently. Many could write it, but few could speak it, he said.

It was a good relationship, and Erik did well. He learned much more than Latin from his loveable, devoted tutor.

CHAPTER TWENTY-THREE

DESPITE THE DIFFICULT SCHEDULE, THE DAYS WERE HAPPY ONES FOR ERIK. He loved his new life. He had never experienced such joy of learning, such joy of accomplishment, such inner peace.

He was invested into the order and was privileged to be selected for the choir to sing in the bass section. The choir received high acclaim throughout the state, and it was considered an honor by his classmates to be a member. So Erik proudly wore his new cassock and white collar. It was a great feeling to be accepted by his class and to be one of them.

In addition, his studies were going well, and he was learning to read. Father Mark, his English literature professor, realized that Erik's reading education was woefully inadequate, and Erik didn't disagree. He couldn't remember any books he had read, at least not since grade school.

Father Mark encouraged him to become more involved in the "love of books," as he called it. He would select a book for Erik and set a time some three or four days later to discuss it. They were simple books at first, but within a few weeks the classics were selected, and Erik discovered the thrill of good books. With Father Mark's encouragement he was soon reading a book a day, a goal that they both agreed upon.

Erik's confidence grew rapidly. The daily meditation provided an opportunity to read more difficult books of philosophy, such as the writings of Saint Thomas Aquinas and Saint Augustine. The scholastic itinerary didn't provide Bible courses or religious classes, per se, but it was a requirement to read the teachings of selected authors during meditation period. It made little difference if the students read a paragraph or the entire book, as long as they did their best to glean the author's message. They were told it was immaterial if they agreed or disagreed with the author's convictions, but they were encouraged to explore and analyze their doctrines.

When Erik first started classes, he had difficulties with the meditation period; it was his least favorite. It soon became his favorite period, probably because of Father Mark's insistence that he acquire a decent reading program. Although there was considerable material that Erik could not understand, he was fascinated with his own interpretation of the theories and beliefs of the learned philosophers.

Shortly after investiture, Father Tom conferred with Erik to discuss his progress. He told Erik that he was pleased with his academics, and he was even more pleased with his acceptance and handling of the less desirable work tasks. Erik assumed that "less desirable" referred to cleaning toilets and skivvies.

"I understand that you were a meat-cutter, Erik," Father Tom said. "Are you a good one?"

"Yes, Father, I've been told that I am," Erik said, trying to hide his excitement.

"Well, we've never worked a student in this position, but I'm told that Brother Tony could use some assistance. He has a heavy workload on the farm. I talked to the Monsignor, and he concurred that we should assign you as a meat-cutter, at least on a trial basis. Brother Tony is a good man, but a proud man, and we don't want to hurt his feelings. You understand, Erik?"

"Yes, sir, I do, and thank you, Father, I'll do you a good job."

"I know you will, son."

Erik was elated with his new job assignment. When he told his class the good news, they all congratulated him. "Finally, we'll have some good cuts of meat," they kidded.

Brother Tony was one of some twenty men who joined the order and became a brother instead of a priest. It was much easier to become a brother because they needed less education, and permanent vows were not required.

Most of the brothers were displaced persons from World War II, and they offered their work for room and board and a chance to serve God. Some worked with the seminarians in study hall, and some were in maintenance, but the vast majority worked on the farm in various capacities.

At first, when Erik worked with Brother Tony, it was a strained relationship. Perhaps, Brother Tony resented the assigned help, but once he realized Erik had meat-cutting skills, he seemed more friendly. He told Erik that he would much rather work outside with the animals than be cooped up in a building. So within the week, Brother Tony put Erik in charge of the meat-cutting.

As Erik became more involved, he gained more acceptance, more approval from his classmates. He found that he was not on the outside, but more in the center of activity, and he liked it.

Erik made many friendships, some closer than others, but formed no cliques. All had a great deal of respect for each other, and all were bonding as time passed. This was the intent of the order ... and it seemed to work.

One day in the rec room, Erik and five or six of his classmates were sitting around the table, talking about nothing in general. One of the group, Robert, a big good-looking seventeen-year-old and one of the most popular of the senior class, mentioned that he had a weird dream last night.

"Well, how weird was it, Robert?" Erik asked.

"Pretty weird, Erik," he replied, "I mean really weird. There I was ... naked ... in one of the stalls, sitting on the toilet ..." There was a pause; the group was silent.

"That was it ... sitting on a toilet?" a confused Erik responded, "Well, that is a weird dream, glad I don't have to dream like that."

Erik was uncomfortable, and he could sense the group felt the same way. He started to change the subject, but Robert continued, talking to no one in particular.

"And then, Brian ... you know that neat little freshman who sings soprano in the choir? He came into the stall. And he was naked. And he sat on my lap, and we talked, and I had my arm around his shoulder, and I wanted to hug him. Can you believe that? I wanted to just hug him ... he was so cute."

Holy shit, a stunned Erik thought. He looked at the rest of the group. They were in the same state of shock. No one said a thing, just glanced at each other in silence. Finally, one by one, they started to excuse themselves and left. Erik didn't know what to do or say. Robert was his closest friend. He was embarrassed for him. But he sensed that they were in a dangerous area of conversation. *God, why did he have to confess that; why confide to the class?*

"I have to go also, Robert," Erik said softly, "I'm sorry, but ... it's work time, and you know how they are if you're late."

Erik felt sick to his stomach.

The next day, Robert was not to be found. The class was told that he had a family emergency and was called home in the middle of the night. Erik had heard of such family emergencies a month ago. Two sophomores had those emergencies, and they also departed in the middle of the night.

CHAPTER TWENTY-FOUR

THE SUDDEN DEPARTURE OF ROBERT TROUBLED ERIK. HE WAS CONFUSED and saddened. He knew he had lost a close friend, but there was more to it. He was having doubts about his own feelings, his commitment, his vocation. He needed to talk, so he made a special visit to his spiritual advisor, Father O'Leary.

It was required that you meet once a month with your spiritual advisor, and Erik had done so, but he had never asked for a special visit to discuss a problem. Former meetings had gone well, and Erik had developed a deep respect for Father O'Leary. Erik trusted him; he enjoyed his upbeat attitude and his keen sense of humor.

When Erik arrived, Father O'Leary gave Erik a warm welcome, commenting on the beautiful steaks and roasts that Erik prepared for the cooks. He said that all of the priests and nuns were praising Erik for the good work.

"And what are we going to talk about tonight?" he asked.

"Well, Father, I've been concerned about Robert quitting ... or whatever happened, sir. I'm not real sure what I think."

"Would you like to go to confession, Erik?" asked Father O'Leary.

During one of his previous visits, Father O'Leary had told Erik that he would always offer an opportunity to have their discussions under the protection of confession, thereby ensuring their conversations could never be disclosed. Their words were protected by sacred oath.

"Yes, Father, I would like that," Erik said.

Father O'Leary put on his stole and biretta to hear confession. Erik kneeled, made the sign of the cross, and said, "Bless me, Father, for I have sinned, my last confession was a week ago."

"All right, Erik, let's sit, and have our talk," Father O'Leary said in a gentle tone.

"Thank you, Father," Erik replied while taking a seat across from his advisor. "I guess I don't understand what went on with Robert's incident, his departure or whatever, and I'm not sure exactly what's bothering me."

"Well, Erik, I can't discuss Robert's reason for leaving, but I can tell you why the departures are generally unannounced and at night. This is done to keep a departing student, either dismissed or one who lost his calling, from influencing his classmates in a negative manner. I think you understand what I'm talking about, Erik."

"Yes, Father, I think I do, but it's disturbing. How do I know I won't be the next one? You know, in the middle of the night?"

"We don't know that, Erik," Father said. "But we do know that God works in mysterious ways. Many are called, but few are chosen. And we have to believe this in the priesthood."

"But, how do I know if I'm chosen, Father?"

"You don't, Erik, at least not until you are chosen. You know … ordained," Father O'Leary said. "All we can do is continue praying for guidance and strength, pursue our calling, do the best we can, and God will answer. He will take care of us."

"I do that, Father, but sometimes … no, not sometimes, a lot of times, I begin to doubt my faith … doubt my calling."

"That's not unusual, Erik, we all experience it. Your classmates do … I do." Father O'Leary smiled, "The big boys call it the Devil … doing his work to plant seeds of doubt … to force you away from your vocation … a vocation he loathes. A vocation he is terrified of. Tremendous pressures are brought about. Look at Father Stowski and what he's been through."

Erik had heard the story of Father Stowski several times from his classmates. He had served mass for him, and his gnarled arm was always a reason for hushed discussion. The story went on that he would die on Good Friday, while saying mass. "Is that a true story, Father, he really lost his arm in the act of exorcism?"

"Yes, it's true, Erik," Father O'Leary said. "He was performing exorcism on a small child in Poland. No other priest would do it, and Father Stowski said he couldn't let the child continue to suffer. So he volunteered to be the exorcist and prayed for two days in preparation. Throughout the actual exorcism he said he could feel the presence of evil, the chill of the spirit. During the final act of the ritual, he raised his cross with his right arm in his attempt to cast out the evil. He said he could smell the pungent odor of sulfur … and see the suffering in the child. But in the struggle, he held his ground and his faith … and he sensed the exodus. Then, in agony, he watched in disbelief as his arm withered … to half of its original size. He never used the arm again."

"Wow, that's scary, Father," Erik said, "I guess I never thought about such power."

"Well, you know we Catholics don't dwell on the Devil … a lot of fire and brimstone … but we don't take it too lightly either. I know there is an evil force, or at least an absence of good, that provides us with our temptations."

"I guess he's working overtime on me." Erik smiled, with some resignation, "I don't seem to be doing too well."

"I know you are going through a difficult time … no, a damn tough time is a better way to put it. God gave us our sex drive, and sometimes I think he plays a cruel joke on us. And at times, I would like to kick him in the rear," he said as he smiled. "I'm just kidding, of course, but that's one big reason we keep you so busy. You know the old saying … 'An idle mind is the Devil's playground.' "

Erik was slightly shocked, not about the playground or kicking God in the rear, but that Father O'Leary would mention sex … and sense that he may have a problem with it.

Erik didn't know what to say. He was quiet, and then Father O'Leary broke the silence.

"Have you been masturbating, Erik?" he asked, "I mean since you've been here at the seminary?"

Erik blushed; he wished that he had put off the visit. "No, Father, I haven't," he said honestly, "but I know I'm going to. It's driving my crazy."

"Hey, Erik, I'm proud of you, sounds like you're doing a great job; many can't accomplish what you have," he responded. "Your faith is holding in there."

"Well, it doesn't feel like it, Father," Erik said while showing embarrassment, "I think I have a wet dream every night, and I feel bad in the morning … so darn guilty."

"Everybody has wet dreams here, Erik," Father said smiling, "That's not a big deal."

"Everybody?" asked a surprised Erik, "You mean it's not just me?"

"I mean every student, Erik, every night," Father replied. "At least if they're old enough, they do. Nothing to be ashamed of. God gave you the drive; it's not dirty."

Erik couldn't imagine two hundred thirty-five students having wet dreams every night, but he felt a little better about it.

"But I seem to have an erection all the time. Well, not all the time, but a lot of the time. Even at mass, and that's not right, Father," Erik said with real concern.

"Erik, you're seventeen years old," Father said calmly, "You're supposed to have an erection. Oh, you're not to dwell on it, impure thoughts and all. Just try to force the thoughts out of your mind. Say a little prayer.

"Don't you repeat this, Erik, but I'm sixty-three years old, and it still drives me crazy. Last month I sat on the train beside a nice-looking lady and tried to read my Breviary for the day. I read one page at least four times because her beautiful breasts kept getting in the way of my prayers. Thought I would have to shoot myself to get my mind off of her elegant body. But eventually I got over it."

"You did it through prayer, Father?" asked Erik in astonishment.

"No, she got off at the next station," Father O'Leary said laughing. "But I guess you could say my prayers were answered."

"I didn't know that priests had that much trouble, Father."

"Sure we do, Erik. We're human first, then priests. Hell, you've heard of a couple of popes whom the church would like to have had buried, early that is, preferably while they were alive. It gets tough," replied Father with a smile. "But you offer it up … some sacrifice is good for you."

Erik felt a bit more confident. Maybe I could tell him about the other evening, he thought. "You know, Father, I don't want to sound gross, but … well, maybe I shouldn't …" Erik stammered.

"Erik, son, there's not a thing a priest hasn't heard in confession," Father said with care. "If it bothers you, it's probably best to get it out."

"Well, I don't know if I can," he said, while blushing. "Well … it was the other night, I was in the stall on the toilet, just like Robert said his dream started. Well, I wasn't thinking of anything that I remember, but I had an erection, and I was trying my best to forget about it, not to touch it, and I thought I better get out of there in a hurry, before I did. Then it happened. A fly came buzzing through and landed on my penis. I could feel it, and it was a good feeling. It stayed there for a moment, and I felt my body tense. Then it started walking, and I was about to come. I'm sorry, Father, I meant to say ejaculate. And when it got up around the end, I was going half crazy … and I swatted it off. I think I'm some sort of a pervert or something, Father. Maybe a sex fiend."

Father O'Leary sat there fascinated. He had to restrain himself from laughing. No, he hadn't heard everything in confession; he just thought he had.

"No, you're not a pervert, Erik, that's a completely natural thing, happens all the time," he fibbed. "You're not the only one who was almost walked off by a fly." Then he realized what he had said, and he chuckled. "I don't mean to be flippant, Erik, I'm sorry, truly sorry. Yes, the Devil works in strange ways. But I want you to understand that all of this is very natural. I want you to believe that it's God's way of allowing temptation … maybe a little test or so. No, you're not a sex fiend, or a homo, or a pervert. You're one hell of a fine seminarian, and I'm proud of you."

"Thank you, Father," Erik said. He was relieved that he told him about the incident.

"Anything else, Erik?" Father asked.

"No, sir."

"Good, now you come back anytime. You don't have to wait until you're troubled. Now, for your penance, say one Our Father and three Hail Mary's … and give thanks to God for your opportunity to serve. Say a prayer for me. Now, your act of contrition."

CHAPTER TWENTY-FIVE

I
N THE FOLLOWING MONTH, ERIK FOUND A PEACE AND SECURITY THAT HE HAD never before experienced. His studies, his work, his faith, his friendships were all going well. Even his relationship with his dad had improved. Erik had forgiven his father, and that act of forgiveness released the guilt and resentment he harbored within. He was a happy seminarian.

Good Friday came and left. And Father Stowski didn't die as the rumor claimed he would. During mass, all student eyes followed him, waiting for the big event. God was going to take him sometime before the final blessing. And God didn't. Erik sensed that they were all mildly disappointed. *Maybe it was just our sick sense of humor.* He was told that they all respected the devoted, selfless old priest.

One afternoon in physics class, the teacher, Father Cochran, told Erik and another student, Philip, to remain after class. Erik had some concern, but he knew that he was a good student and that Philip was the best in the class. Erik had never met a better student than Phil, in any subject.

After class Father Cochran met with the two of them. "Do you remember the state exams in physics that the class took a couple of weeks ago?" he asked.

"Yes, Father," they both replied.

"Well, we got the results two days ago, and I was most pleased. Philip, you were first in the state, and Erik, you were fifth. Congratulations. That is quite an honor for both of you … and for the seminary. I'm proud of you," he said warmly, "and for that achievement, the University of Pennsylvania gives you both a four-year scholarship to major in physics."

"Thank you, Father," said Philip. Erik was still trying to grasp what the good Father had told them, so he remained silent.

"There's a small problem, however," Father continued, "apparently they question how two of the top ten students in the state could come from a small school such as ours. They didn't say so, but they implied that perhaps there may have been some cheating. I told them it was most unlikely, and now I pass it on to you."

Erik was confused. *Were they being accused of cheating?* He noticed that Phil was having the same problem. "Father, I didn't even know what the test was for," Erik said, "just a placement test … or something like that."

Phil nodded and said nothing. Father Cochran smiled at the two of them and said, "Well, I know there was no cheating. I was there during the test, remember?"

They both nodded.

"Well, the state is still a bit concerned, so they are sending two of their people over for your retest," Father said, "It will be a different test, and they should be here soon. That's all right for both of you?"

They both nodded and said, "Yes, Father."

Erik was disturbed. He knew he didn't cheat on the exam. And he couldn't imagine Phil doing such a thing. But someone thought they did, and that made Erik uncomfortable. It bothered him to be thought of as a cheat. They both went to the next class, and, shortly afterwards, Father Cochran arrived and requested that Erik and Phil be excused.

They accompanied him to his office and were introduced to the gentlemen from the state. Erik and Phil were warmly accepted, and the two gentlemen attempted to assure them that the retake had nothing to do with cheating. It was an administrative "goof" in the grading process, they called it.

Erik didn't believe them. He became apprehensive and uptight. *What if I don't do as well as before? Then, I'm known as a cheat. No way did I expect to be in the top ten, I could refuse the retake, say I'm not interested … but then they would really think I cheated.*

Erik wished he was home driving a truck … or killing hogs. But he wasn't, and he realized that he had to regain his cool and retake the test.

Father Cochran suggested two areas for the testing, and the gentlemen agreed. Each would take the exam in separate rooms with one of the state monitors.

Three stressful hours later, Erik completed the test. The gentleman thanked him and departed.

The next day in physics, Father Cochran announced to the class, "The State

Board of Education called me this morning, and we discussed two of our classmates, Phil and Erik."

Oh, God ... here it comes, he's going to say we cheated.

"It seems as though Phil had the best score in the state, on the Physics exam. He didn't miss a question — 100% correct. Congratulations Phil, that's quite an honor."

And the class clapped their hands in approval.

"Now, Erik," Father Cochran continued, "was in the top ten after the first test, but after retesting yesterday ... I have to announce ... he is now rated as ..."

And all eyes were on Erik, and he wished he had never heard of physics.

"Rated as number three ... well, tied for number three, in the state of Pennsylvania." Father Cochran said with a big smile, "Congratulations, Erik. Not bad for a hillbilly."

The class clapped in approval, and Erik experienced his first tears of joy.

CHAPTER TWENTY-SIX

IT WAS JUNE, AND THE SENIOR CLASS, INCLUDING ERIK, GRADUATED. IT WAS an impressive ceremony, and, after the congratulations, they took the day off for a class picnic. All had a grand time, reminiscing, recapping the past year, and making plans for the next one. Vacation would start soon, and most would spend their ten days at home.

Erik was apprehensive about the vacation. Certainly he wanted to see his folks, but he had doubts; he was leaving the safety of the seminary routine, and he didn't want to chance any run-ins with his father.

And he didn't know how he would be treated by his friends or how he would react to seeing real, live girls. Also, he was disturbed that he wouldn't be coming back to Holy Orders. They had to go on to Saint Joseph's College in Ohio. Erik had been told that it was better at St. Joe's because there was more freedom, more privileges. He wasn't sure he wanted more freedom or privileges. He was happy at Holy Orders, and he would miss the security of familiar surroundings.

Vacation time arrived, and Erik spent his first day home in more than eleven months. After a nervous start — such as the handshake with Burt — the reunion went well. Erik was particularly pleased that his father was trying to make things right. When the family seated for dinner, Burt said to Erik, "Father Erik, you sit over here by me."

Erik was taken aback, then glancing up to see his dad smiling, replied, "Well, thank you, sir, but you know I have a long way to go before you call me, Father."

They both laughed. "But you're going to make it, son" he said, warmly. "You will."

"Well, I sure hope so, Dad." And then he realized Burt had called him "son." It was a first.

"And besides, it will be nice to have a priest in the family," Burt said as he glanced up to the ceiling. "The way I have if figured, it would help me make it in up there. And you know I'll need help. You don't believe 'the big boss' would kick out a father of a real priest, do you?"

"No, I don't, Dad," Erik said, with a chuckle.

God, it was great to hear his father talk that way. The tension was gone. They had made up. And Erik could see the happiness in his mother's eyes. It was a good dinner. The best Erik ever remembered with his father at the table.

Erik's vacation routine started with daily mass at the parish church. He served as altar boy for Father Harris, and, after mass, they spent time discussing the vocation of priesthood and Erik's progress.

The first couple of days, Erik contacted some of his former guy classmates and joined them at the corner drugstore for cokes. Tommy Joe, Slim, and Eddy all welcomed Erik and made an attempt to show interest in his new lifestyle. But it didn't take long for Erik to realize how awkward "hanging out" became. The main topic of conversation was girls, and the word "fuck" was used all too casually. Who was fucking whom, and who was going to fuck whom, and who wanted to fuck whom — were the topics for the corner drugstore gatherings.

Erik was shocked. He realized how little time the group discussed any subject other than girls and girl parts ... such as legs, tits, and ass. Occasionally — once or twice — they mentioned personality or character. Erik felt isolated; he could not be part of the discussions mainly because he couldn't "do it" to whom, nor could he want to "do it" to whom. It was not a good environment, and he decided to spend more time alone, reading.

During one of his reading days, Burt dropped by the house and, seeing Erik settled into a book, said, "How come you're not out and about?"

"No reason, Dad. Just catching up on some study."

"Well, the guys at the plant were asking about you. They wondered why you haven't been by ... There's no problem is there?"

"No, no problem at all. Would like to see them."

"Well, I'm going out there now. Won't be for long. You want to come along?"

"Sure, sounds good, Dad."

As they were riding the fifteen minutes to the plant, Erik experienced many emotions. He wasn't quite honest with his father; he did want to see the crew, but he was reluctant because he didn't know how he would react if he ran into Paula. It would be difficult, he decided. *I'm the one who chose the priesthood, and I can't hide forever.*

And besides, she may not work there anymore. Dad hasn't mentioned her, and I'm not asking.

They arrived at the plant, and, upon entering the front section, Erik noticed the girl working in the office. It wasn't Paula, and he was relieved. After the introduction, Erik went back to the kill-floor. *That wasn't so bad. I really had some good times here, lots of fun times.*

He went through the big doors into the slaughter room and noticed the crew working hard, scrapping hogs.

"Hey, Jesse ... Cliff ... look who's here," Billy Bob yelled, "It's our good buddy, back from the jungles."

"Well, I'll be dammed, it's Erik," said Cliff. "Welcome back, son."

They all stopped the scrapping and shook hands with Erik. There was laughter and small talk. It was good to see the crew. Erik had missed them.

"Hey, Erik, you take that bull-dick cane to priest school with you?" Jesse asked.

"Heck yes, Jesse, you know I wouldn't go anywhere without my cane-dick," Erik said, "But sure had a tough time explaining what it was to the monsignor. Had to fudge a bit. Told him it was made of dried leather."

"Well, you know you can't lie, being a priest and all, Erik, God will git you," Billy Bob said. "You gotta tell 'em it was a real live dick. Yessir, an ole bull's dick."

"You're right, guys. I'll do that when I get back. Priests can't lie." They all had a good laugh, and Erik made his farewells, then departed the kill-floor.

As he passed through the big doors, he almost collided with another person. Erik excused himself, and then they both looked at each other. He was stunned when he recognized the person. It was a girl ... the girl was Paula. And she was all there — the long legs, the smooth white skin, the large brown eyes, the beautiful breasts. It was all Paula. *God, she is beautiful,* he thought as he recognized the smell of the perfume. *She's even prettier than before.*

"Erik," she cried as she hugged him, "It's so good to see you, God, we've missed you." She knowingly kissed him on the cheek, and Erik could barely stammer through a few words of greeting.

Why do I always make a fool of myself with her? I get so damn flustered. I know ... it's her bedroom eyes. He had to smile.

"Erik, I've got a big ole steak in the fridge, just waiting for you ... and me," she said while exposing her perky smile.

"Well, thank you, Paula ... but you know ... kinda ..."

"Oh, I know, sweetheart, didn't mean to flirt ... just hate it when the good-looking ones become priests," she said as she flipped her hair.

"But seriously, Erik, I am so darn proud of you. I'll be one of your first parishioners."

"Well, thank you ma'am, it would be my honor," he said lightly. *God, that's all I would need. Paula in my parish. Man, Father O'Leary was right, the ole Devil can sure play rough.*

Burt and Erik were on their way home, and Erik couldn't clear his mind. The guilt was overbearing. And all he could think of was a steak dinner, and taking Paula to bed, *and Dad's voice in the kitchen.*

He knew he had to force the Paula thoughts out of his life, and he prayed for the strength to go on with his calling. Apparently the prayers were answered, because three days later, he departed for the seminary at St. Joe's.

IT WAS GOOD TO BE BACK WITH HIS CLASSMATES. ERIK WONDERED IF ANY OF THEM had problems similar to his. He knew it remained a taboo subject, so talk about girls was avoided. Just a few inane platitudes were the summations of their ten days. They all seemed genuinely pleased to be back in the fold, back to the security of seminary life.

Classes started, and the heavy schedule became the norm. It was a welcome change for Erik. His doubts had subsided, and he quickly fell into the sheltered routine. He regained his confidence, and the fear of failure was fading into obscurity. He was again a happy young man.

Within the second month it was announced that the class would receive town privileges every other Saturday morning. Visitors were allowed, and you could go into the college town of Vinton, to shop, dine, or hang out until one o'clock that afternoon. Most of the class greeted the news with gratitude, but Erik was cautious. He would have preferred that things remain unchanged. He was uneasy, and he couldn't explain the reason for being so.

The town privilege day arrived, and some of Erik's classmates convinced him to go along for a couple of hours to mingle with the city folk. They walked the mile and a half into town, and Erik found it rather refreshing. It was fun being off the grounds.

They enjoyed the sights. And later they stopped at the corner drug for a milkshake (they were allowed to have three dollars pocket money). As they awaited their shakes, a pretty girl of college age came in and sat beside Erik. His body reacted immediately. The anxieties, the tenseness, were overtaking his faculties. *Stay calm,* he pleaded; *just ignore her.* He tried to remain impervious to her presence, but it was impossible. The perfume, the sweet smell of powdered skin kindled a terrible urge to touch and hold, to run off with her, to be part of her.

He saw her nipples press against her soft sweater; the young, small breasts that firmly held their place. She smiled, and Erik felt the pain of defeat rush through his body. The old demons of doubt were awesome. He had been kidding himself. The sexual feelings were not going away. If anything, they were worse. The wet dreams had become more intense, more vivid, and it was more difficult, almost impossible to shed the guilt. It was all so clear now, a blinding realization. No more pretending; he would not cheat his sacred vocation. He would accept his failure. He would not betray his God.

He turned away from the co-ed and faced his classmate next to him. "John," he said, "I can't handle it."

John was startled; he didn't smile, and he didn't answer; he looked frightened.

"I've had it, John. I've let everyone down ... myself, my dad ... and my God. I can't make it another day."

John recognized the intensity, the pain ... the pain that perhaps they all experienced at times throughout their sheltered lives. "You have to get to your spiritual advisor, Erik," he said, "You can't let this happen, you're too damn good. ... We all look up to you. ... You're going to make one of the best."

"God, I wish I could, John. God, I wish it didn't have to be like this."

"You can whip it, Erik, we all go through this ... you can do it. You have done it before."

Erik couldn't answer. He choked up. The pain of finality ... it was all too devastating.

The others were silent. They all stared at Erik. And Erik could feel his blush and his tears.

"I'm sorry guys ... I love you all, and God knows I'm going to miss you. I don't know what I'll do. God, I hate it. I can't go on ... Father O'Leary was right ... many are called ... few are chosen."

CHAPTER TWENTY-SEVEN

I T TOOK SEVEN WEEKS BEFORE ERIK WAS RELEASED FROM THE SEMINARY. The spiritual advisor did his best to help Erik make the proper decision. And, eventually, they both agreed that Erik was not chosen to be a priest. Father O'Leary told Erik that because of his sound character and morals, he would not have to depart in the middle of the night. He could bid farewell to his classmates. It was a sad day when he told them, "Goodbye, and good luck with your vocation." He would miss all of them.

Erik bused his way home, and told his folks he quit the seminary. His mother cried, and his father reacted with disgust. "I don't know why you had to quit," he said, "You had a chance to be something ... now you won't amount to a damn thing, will you?"

"Guess not, Dad," Erik replied with shame, "But I'll be out of the way. I'm joining the marines tomorrow, if they'll take me ... I want to go to Korea."

His mother cried a second time, and Burt, who looked surprised by the response, asked, "You're not joining because of me are you?"

"No, Dad, not because of you."

THE NEXT DAY, ERIK AND FORTY OTHER YOUNG MEN, MOSTLY DRAFTEES, WERE ON a bus that headed for South Carolina, the location of their first duty assignment. They were ordered to report to boot camp. Not the standard, humdrum, glad to have you aboard boot camp, but the Marine Corps' dreaded, notorious, and world-renowned, Parris Island Boot Camp. It was a day to remember.

It was a long trip. Throughout the afternoon and night, they traveled toward their new way of life. A bus filled with mixed emotions. The draftees appeared reluctant and concerned, Erik thought, but maybe they had good reason ... most remarked that they shouldn't be there. On the other hand, the volunteers (enlistees), such as Erik, displayed a reserved enthusiasm. You could feel the excitement and see the relief that most revealed.

For Erik, it was a meaningful time of liberation. He was conscious of his past failures, his attempts to please his father, but they seemed to lose significance now that he had a new start. *It's going to be great, and I'm doing something that he couldn't, or wouldn't, do … be a marine.*

Erik never knew the whole story about his father and the war. He did notice through the years, however, that his dad's relationship with his brothers had become distant, almost strained. His two brothers had earned Silver Stars in the army during WWII. Erik became more proud of them as he gained some years and had the opportunity to know them better. *They were good men, and I want to do as well, but I don't want to alienate my father. I'm sure things will work out, but it is good that I'm gone from the house … and from him.*

It was early morning when the silver Greyhound bus arrived at Parris Island and pulled to a stop aside a huge drill field. The door opened, and a voice entered; it was deep and loud as it screamed, "Now Hear This — All you shitheads get off this fucking bus now! Move it, Go! Go! Go!" A startled Erik and the other terrified sleepy recruits scurried to exit the bus. They rushed forward to the door and jammed the exit in their skirmish to be first out. With minor injuries, they eventually cleared the bus and swiftly moved to the asphalt drill field where they commenced milling around with the sand fleas in the hot, humid air. In their confusion they could hear the voice yell out repeatedly, "Get in line, you fucking idiots, I want three lines!" And the recruits, in ratty-looking civilian clothes, with bodies of assorted sizes, shapes, and colors, jockeyed about until they were in three lines.

At least a facsimile of three lines.

Standing in front of this rough formation was a lone marine. His fatigue uniform was crisply starched. His wide-brimmed campaign hat neatly brushed and blocked; his combat boots gleamed with reflected light; his sun bronzed skin announced, "I don't work behind a desk." He stood there, tall and erect, feet wide apart. He held his swagger stick and black gloves. He was "spit and polish."

He stared at the tattered formation. He paced a few steps, turned, and paced back to front and center. He was lean and hard, and he left no uncertainty that he was "the authority."

The voice ... he must be the voice. And I seriously doubt that the voice is here to chat about the good times.

"You·people listen up," the voice bellowed, "My name is Sergeant Bronson. I am your drill instructor. You will call me, Sir!" He looked at the formation for some moments. He made eye contact with most. A penetrating dark eye contact.

The silence was strange. It almost boomed. Taking a deep breath, he proceeded with a slow pace paralleling the front line. In tempo with his cadence, he struck his left palm with the swagger stick. With intensity, the voice continued: "You fucking people are nobodies. You are not marines. You are nothing. No, you are worse than nothing — you are worthless. You are an insignificant pile of unadulterated dog shit. A bunch of titty babies ... momma boys ... that is, if any of you ever had a momma that claimed you.

"You are a fucking mess, and my beloved commandant has ordered me to make marines out of the God-forsaken muddle. This is fucking impossible, but it is my mission. And I will not fail my mission. I will not fail my God, nor will I fail my beloved Marine Corps."

He paused as if to reflect on God and his beloved corps, then continued with his welcome aboard.

"You are nothing but a bunch of soft, pasty-white, pansy-ass queers ... useless as tits on a virgin ... breathing my air ... fucking up my space ... fucking up my world ... it's all you're good for. You are lower than snail shit ... that's right, snail shit ... and nothing is lower than snail shit ... but you are. I have to make you a marine, and God help me, I would rather suck a dead gook's dick than try to make marines out of this pile of shit. Do you people hear me?"

There was a spattering of "yessirs."

"I can't hear you," he screamed.

In unison, load and clear, they shouted, "YES, SIR."

"That's fucking better. Now my assistant DI,* Corporal Ferret, will be taking you to your Quonset huts, and, for the next fourteen weeks, you will be told when to eat, sleep, piss, and shit. You will be told how to do those things, and when, and how, to do other things. Little things, like shower and shave, and, from the looks and smell of you, it will be a new experience for most of you stinking clowns."

*DI: Drill Instructor

He stopped talking, looked around in disgust, and addressed Corporal Ferret, who stood in back of the formation.

"Corporal Ferret."

"Yessir."

"Get this fucking bunch out of here before I vomit on my beloved uniform."

"Yes, sir, Sergeant Bronson!"

And Corporal Ferret got the "fucking bunch" out of there before it ruined a "beloved uniform."

THE FOLLOWING FOURTEEN WEEKS AT PI WERE AWESOME WEEKS FOR ERIK. BUT because of his seminary time, with its strict and demanding schedule, he quickly adjusted to the rigors of boot camp. He enjoyed the challenge of the long days that started before sunrise and went into darkness. He felt his body grow and develop as he completed the tough physical workouts and the endless hours of marching on the drill field. He learned, and agreed with the need for unequivocal loyalty, unconditional discipline. That is not to say it was a snap. Not at all, it was crude, harsh, and rugged, but Erik had few problems. The worst being the degrading, foul language, and the acceptance of his shaved head, at least during the first few weeks. It rankled him when he first glanced in the mirror for the morning lathering of his face. It was demeaning, but he pretended it didn't matter.

He didn't like the toilet setup either, because it was embarrassing, an affront to human dignity, he concluded. There were no stalls, and some twenty-five toilets were lined in a row, maybe two feet apart. *Talk about togetherness ... naked togetherness on heads doing your daily ritual, your constitutional.* And most mornings, marines would line up to use the heads. They would stand in front and face the unfortunate individual sitting there. To encourage him to speed up the process they would say something like, "Come on man, you've been on long enough for Christ sakes." Then you would hear, "Man, I have to make formation, and I have to shit ... so let's cut if off and move your ass."

Maybe I'm being too sensitive ... it doesn't seem to bother the rest of them. Perhaps I'll do better in time.

And Corporal Ferret, the assistant DI, what an asshole ... what a little pompous piss-ant ... God, I would like to stomp the living shit out of the pint-sized mother. But Erik was not allowed to do that; he could only think about it. And, it shocked him that he could think that way, just out of the seminary. But he was sure that most of the platoon felt the same way.

Corporal Ferret was a little guy and probably made the minimum height-weight requirements, five-two or so, 110 pounds, wet. *Cocky little shit, even looked like his name ... a goddamn weasel.* Erik was sure it was his first time as a DI, and he couldn't understand how he made it.

ERIK'S BIG RUN-IN WITH CORPORAL FERRET CAME ABOUT SIX WEEKS INTO THE program. The platoon was in formation, standing at parade rest: eyes straight ahead, feet apart, and hands behind their back, rifles in stacked arms. They were a sharp-looking unit.

The platoon was on the drill field, in the hot sun, waiting for the arrival of Sergeant Bronson. Suddenly, two fighter aircraft appeared from the horizon and screamed overhead of the formation. They were low and fast ... *God, it was magnificent!*

Erik instinctively looked up, as did most of the platoon. Then he realized he had broken ranks. He immediately regrouped with eyes straight ahead. At that moment, Erik felt the stinging pain from a blow to the right side of his head. The ear went deaf, just a hum. He started to turn when he saw the dark swagger stick come from behind and slowly slide under his chin. He could barely hear the voice. It was Corporal Ferret's.

"Stand fast, Private Shithead. You like airplanes? Here, let me help you take a good look."

Erik felt Ferret's knee come up into the small of his back, and the agonizing pain of the stick being pulled against his throat, cutting into his wind pipe, forcing his head back. The pain filled his eyes with tear water, and air was in short supply; he gasped, he was near passing out. He dared not fight back; the risk was too great; he knew that he would be court-martialed for hitting a non-commissioned officer. He was in trouble, and he didn't know what to do, or how to react. He didn't see Sergeant Bronson come up to the formation, but he heard his stern voice snap, "Corporal Ferret!"

And the pressure released; the swagger stick dropped from the neck, and the knee fell away.

"Platoon, at ease!" commanded Sergeant Bronson, as he came up to Erik, "You all right, private?"

Erik tried to shout, "Yes, sir," but it came out softly, and so did the trickle of blood cut of his mouth.

"I think this one time we should get you over to sick bay … that was a bad fall you took, Larsen."

"Yes, sir," he replied quietly, the blood more evident, "but, sick bays are for candy-asses."

"Not in this case, Larsen, that fall was nasty … and I'll see to it that you don't have another. We'll have to be more careful, won't we?"

"Yes, sir … I will."

Erik was back on duty the next day. He hurt, and he couldn't speak, but there was no need to speak. And Corporal Ferret, the weasel, was not to be seen again. The incident was never mentioned, and Erik didn't take another fall.

The orders of the day continued. It was a no-nonsense way of life, no horseplay, and little laughter. Your time alone was brief, and you worked, played, and prayed as a unit — your platoon. If one of the unit decided he was above the rules, the platoon was taught to correct that individual. If the outfit had a thief, and you caught him stealing from one of the platoon, you were to bruise him up before you turned him over to Sergeant Bronson. He was very explicit on the matter, he said, "You bring me a thief, and, if he's walking, I'll give the platoon an extra twenty miles of duty. You better believe me on this. You carry him in here hurting; you beat the shit out of him. In fact, I don't give a goddamn if you beat him half-to-death. He's the worst; he steals from his buddies."

You did your own laundry with scrub brush and bucket. You marched to weekly church service, religion of choice, on Sundays. After service you wrote a letter to your mother, or to someone else in your family if you didn't have a mother. You learned to polish boots, to love your rifle, to caress it with Neat's foot oil and make it shine.

And you learned to shoot the rifle; shoot it straight, even at five hundred yards. You learned *The Guidebook for Marines,* page by page. You had school each day, perhaps two hours, sitting on your metal buckets, on the grass. You saw your body develop and harden from the marching and the obstacle courses.

And you learned to use lots of foul language, not from the *Guidebook,* but from the natural boot camp dialogue. Profanity was used in most conversational sentences. Erik was never proud of this usage, but it seemed to be the norm, and soon it became unnoticeable with the platoon.

You learned the Marine Corps' three-point method of teaching, that being:

1. The Corps tells you what they're going to teach you.
2. They teach you.
3. They tell you what they just taught you.

Teaching in the Marine Corps was geared to the weakest link in the platoon, and sometimes that was scary.

But Erik flourished; he was six feet one, 185 pounds of trim, no-fat body. He was tan and good-looking with blond hair and alert blue eyes. He believed in himself, or thought he did, maybe for the first time. He was tough physically and mentally. He was proud of the Corps, proud to be a marine.

Erik could now understand the philosophy of the Corps' boot camp. They destroyed you as an individual, made you believe … convinced you that you're nothing — yes, even lower than snail shit — and the shaved head encouraged this belief.

They treated all as equals, no favorites, and then they start the process of rebuilding your self-image, a step at a time. Each success as an individual, or unit, instilled pride and confidence, not in the old civilian "you," but the new "you," soon to be marine. The marine who would eventually be in combat and prove himself to be a part of the finest fighting men in the world. And many would die. But if you learned from your training, your discipline, your loyalty as a marine unit, you would have a good chance to stay alive. And almost as a reward for participating in this learning process, this rebuilding, they let your hair grow a trace longer for each stage of training. At the end of fourteen weeks, your head was covered with hair, short and crew cut, but not shaved.

THE MARINE CORPS ENCOURAGES ITS MEN TO REQUEST THEIR NEXT DUTY STATION. They want you to submit three choices in order of preference. If the request fits the needs of the service, you are assigned one of your choices. Erik's first choice was air control school, because he was ineligible to apply for flight training. *At least a career as an air controller will keep me in the aviation field.*

His second and third choices were both the same: infantry, and a trip to Korea. For some inexplicable reason, Erik was denied all three choices; he was sent to guard company at the New York Navy Yard. It was a disappointing set of orders, even though Sergeant Bronson told him it was considered "choice duty" by most of the regulars — those who were making a career out of the Corps.

The bid day arrived, graduation day, the day you officially became a "real marine." Boot camp was over, and Sergeant Bronson had done the impossible for his beloved commandant; he had turned a group of "worthless civilians" into a team of tough, proud marines.

At graduation, Sergeant Bronson shook Erik's hand and gave him an exceptional compliment, "You were one hell of a recruit ... and I congratulate you, Private Erik Larsen; you are now a marine and promoted to private first class."

"Thank you, sir. I had one hell of an example ... it was Sergeant Bronson, sir."

CHAPTER TWENTY-EIGHT

AT THE COMPLETION OF BOOT CAMP, ALL MARINES RECEIVED TEN DAYS of leave prior to reporting to their newly assigned duty station. Travel reservations were made for all graduates, and Parris Island provided transportation to the nearest bus station.

Erik arrived at the station with twenty-three other new marines to start their journey home to the mountains up north. It was a festive morning. All were happy to be out of boot camp and on their own. Their young bodies were hard and tanned, and they wore their new green uniforms with pride. *What a difference fourteen weeks can make ... no one would believe what we looked like when we started.* He smiled when he remembered that first day.

Sergeant Bronson was absolutely correct, what a shit group we were ... a bunch of feather merchants.

Fourteen weeks of mental and physical discipline produced the change. Sex, beer, liberty (club privileges), and visitors were all prohibited in boot camp. It required an adjustment for most recruits. Now they were marines, and they could do it all. The decision was theirs.

Spirits were high as they awaited the boarding call of the bus. "Hey guys, we have time for a beer," one of them said. "Maybe even a couple."

"Hell, yes, we do," chimed in another.

"Fuck yes," said another, "It's about time, we're not kids ya know."

"Got that right ... fucking 'A,' we're not."

There was a general nodding of heads in agreement, and they all set out to do what real marines do best ... they made their way to the bar.

It was a small bar adjoining the bus depot, and, upon entering, you rid your sunglasses to see that it was dark and run-down. It was a quiet bar with a fragrance of old stale beer. Seated on the end bar stools were two men in civilian clothes talking quietly with the barmaid, a plumpish gat in her thirties. The arrival of the "boots" didn't seem to surprise her. *She had probably seen many busloads.* But he did notice the facial expressions of the two men, probably older marines, with the look of, "oh shit, not another busload of idiot recruits."

"What will you youngsters have?" she asked. Her smile was pleasant, but resigned.

"Hey, we need some booze," said one of the Jersey boys, "I'll have a whisky, straight up."

"Yea, Mabel, how 'bout a Black Label?" one of the clowns said.

"Young man, my name is not Mabel," she replied, as she stared directly at the wise-ass, "You may call me, Anne."

"Right-on Annie with a pretty fanny," he replied, "Give me a ..."

"Listen, wise-off, I said it was Anne ... not Annie ... and I want to see your ID before I serve a drop of alcohol."

It went quiet. They were losing the festive atmosphere. "What do ya mean, ID? ... Hell, I'm a marine in uniform, and I'm plenty old for Christ sakes."

"Listen up, all of you," a loud, deep voice from the barstool said with authority, "You people have things to learn. ... You will call her, Anne ... and you will treat her with respect. And you will be eighteen to have a beer. You will be twenty-one for booze. And you better damn-well act like marines if you wear the uniform. Do I make myself clear?"

There was a rumbling of "yessirs." *Holy shit ... he's a real DI, in civvies.*

"Anne, may I have a beer? ... any kind will do," Erik said, "I would appreciate it."

"Coming right up, son" she said as she winked, "Any of you other marines care for a beer?"

"Oh, yes, ma'am," said most of the marines.

"Yes, please, Anne, that would be great," another said. And all were served their beers ... with a smile.

With the tension eased, Erik enjoyed a beer with his buddies. Conversation picked up during the second beer.

"Yea, that Sergeant Bronson ... what a lucky asshole he was," one of the louder ones said, "He's damn lucky I didn't kick the shit out of him."

"Yea," said another, a smaller one, "I was going to do the same thing. He is one lucky son-of-a-bitch. I'll tell you that."

"Yea, you got that right," another said, "That cocksucker was shaking in his boots."

Erik couldn't believe the crap he was hearing. He had to smile, although there was no doubt in his mind that Sergeant Bronson would kick the living shit out of each of them, one by one. And probably wouldn't have to shower. But they were all having a good time, drinking their beers and telling each other how tough they were.

A lady stuck her head into the bar and announced that the bus going north was ready to board, "So let's get with it, guys."

They all paid up and thanked Anne as if she was an old friend. The beer-time had been a fun time, and they departed to board the bus.

The driver put the duffle bags into the baggage compartment and climbed aboard. He took a long look at his new passengers. His look became irritable, and, with a light shake of his head, he took his seat behind the wheel.

He cranked up the diesel, and minutes later they traveled down the highway at 60 MPH. Erik noticed that the "beer-drinkers" were much more subdued now and not as festive as before. Then it happened, one of the tough new marines said, "Shit, I don't feel so good." Then he puked … all over himself and the bus. The stench spread rapidly, and then Erik heard, "I don't feel so good either." And that was enough for the bus driver. He braked the bus, pulled onto the shoulder, and swung open the main door. He stood up and turned toward the back of the bus. He was pissed.

"All right, that's it … all you 'combat vets' get out and grab some fresh air," he yelled. And all the combat vets got out as ordered. They milled around and breathed the good air … and they puked. Nine of the toughest puked all over the good earth. And one of the nine was Erik.

Fifteen minutes later they bused down the highway, with twenty-four celebrating marines … all sleeping.

ERIK ARRIVED IN SCANTSVILLE THE NEXT MORNING, AND HIS MOTHER PICKED HIM up at the bus station. She was delighted to see him looking so well. She said that his dad was working, and he was sorry he couldn't be there to meet him. She also said that Burt had left a panel truck for Erik to use during leave. Erik was pleased that he had such a warm welcome. He asked how both of them were, and how the business was going. Mom said that business was good, but they lost some help. "You remember Paula, don't you honey?" she said.

Recovering from the minor shock of his mother mentioning Paula's name, he said, "Sure do, Mom ... you know, we were not close or anything, but absolutely, yes, I knew her ... but not well." *What a stupid statement that was. Damn, get hold of yourself. ... This is your mother you're talking to.*

"Well, your dad said that she ran off with a meat salesman of some sort ... said he was going to miss her. She was a good worker, I guess."

"I bet he does miss her work, Mom," Erik said. *And God, that isn't all he's going to miss ... but damn, I was counting on her being here ... probably won't get laid on this leave.*

"Oh, Dad will find a replacement. ... It always works out," Erik said. "And how have you been feeling, Mom?"

"Oh, you know me, honey ... I'm always fine." Erik was glad he had changed the subject.

That afternoon, Erik saw his civilian buddies at the corner drug. It was good seeing them again. Tommy Joe, Slim, and Eddy. He was delighted that they were impressed with the uniform. They all commented on his physical change; they couldn't believe how good he looked. And they wanted to know if Parris Island was "really that tough?"

"Yep, it's so tough ... only the baddest of the bad, make it through. Yep, you have to be one mean-motha. You are damn lucky to be civilians," Erik said, with an exaggerated grin, "Even though I can't buddy with you anymore — top secrets, ya know." They all laughed, and Erik savored the limelight. He was onstage for ten minutes and told them all about the Corps. Then the talk switched to the important topic ... girls. And unlike his past vacation from the seminary, Erik joined in on the conversation, that being who was fucking whom ... and who wanted to fuck whom. It was fun ... talking "fuck."

Then, Eddy looked up and said, "Look who's coming in; it's Norma and Jennie Lee."

They all turned toward the girls, and Erik damn near panicked when he saw them.

"Hey, didn't you used to fuck her, Erik ... Jennie Lee?" said Slim.

Erik blushed, and said, "Well, you know ... kinda fooled around."

"Bullshit, fooled around, I heard you put it to her," Tommy Joe said.

"That's what I heard," chimed in Eddy, "You would horse-fuck her until she begged for mercy. ... Yep, until she cried Uncle." They laughed and looked at Erik. He smiled and winked. *God, if that were only true ... where do they get such garbage? Hell, she was the one in dad's car, my first ... the night the windows froze ... and not even sure I got it in. Jeeze, how embarrassing. Was never with her again.* The girls spotted them and started toward the booth. Erik wished he was somewhere else ... anywhere.

"Hi guys," said Norma with a cheerful smile, "Who's in the uniform?"

"Lord, it's Erik," said Jennie Lee, "Norma, it's Erik ..."

"It sure is. Wow, what a difference," Norma said. They leaned over and gave Erik a big hug, a "welcome back and good to see you" hug.

Erik felt more relaxed after the hero's welcome, and he found the courage to speak, "Here, sit down girls, we can squeeze you in, can't we guys?"

They made room for the girls, and Jennie Lee scooted in beside Erik. He could feel the warm reaction throughout his body. Norma chatted about their events of the day, and the guys joined in. Mostly talk, with little listening, and everyone had something nonessential to say. Then Jennie Lee said, "It's good to see you home, Erik."

"Well, thank you, Jennie, it's good to be with you," he said. He was proud that she spoke to him.

She touched his hand. "I hope I get to see you ... you know, I mean see you alone," she said in her sexiest voice. Erik was slightly staggered, no, stunned was more appropriate. *She made me an offer. I can't believe it, an offer to get laid ... maybe.*

"Well, thank you, Jennie ... God yes, I want to see you also ... you know, alone," he said while trying to maintain his cool. "Are you doing anything this evening? I can pick you up ... maybe a movie, or a drive, or something?"

"Oh, Erik, that's peachy ... just peachy keen," she said warmly. "We can go for a drive. You pick me up at the house ... my folk's house down in Creek Run. You can do that ... around seven?"

"Sure can, Jennie ... would love to."

"Good, I'll get you the address ... and see you then. You'll wear your uniform, won't you?"

"Oh yea. I'll have it on, Jennie."

She gave Erik the address, and he made his departure from the corner drug. *God, what a beautiful, flattering day. I can't wait until seven.*

Erik was punctual as he pulled up in front of the old, one-story, wooden house. It was rundown like the rest of Creek Run, but this evening it looked better than the other houses because pretty Jennie Lee was standing on the porch. *Damn, she's a picture, dressed in her light sweater, plaid skirt, bobby socks, and penny loafers.* She had a light kerchief around her neck, and her blond hair was pulled back and allowed to flow.

And I'm dressed in my uniform with a hard-on. He had to laugh. But he couldn't look away; she was just too cute and desirable.

She waved, ran to the panel truck, and they launched their date. She suggested that they go down by Thompson's Lake, listen to some music, and kind of — mess around. That was great news for Erik. He couldn't wait for the mess around part.

On the way to the lake she told him that she had a steady boyfriend, a coal miner named Daryl, but he was bear hunting on Rock Mountain and wouldn't be back until tomorrow. She said that she shouldn't be with Erik, but she wanted to see him again.

Erik wasn't pleased to hear about Daryl, but realized it was foolish to think that she wouldn't have a "steady."

They pulled up alongside the lake as the sky was turning nightfall-dark. They saw some figures building a fire, and Jennie commented, "Let's stay in the truck, Erik, they could be friends of Daryl ... and we don't want trouble."

By this time Erik was feeling a bit uncomfortable; it was just becoming too involved. *Maybe it's not worth the effort.*

She must have sensed the mood change and turned on the radio. She immediately snuggled into Erik's arms and gave him a long, lingering kiss. He forgot all about involvement ... and about talking. She was warm and powdery. She was tender and touchable; he couldn't keep his hands silent. They were sliding under the soft sweater, onto the softer breasts. He gently squeezed and nettled ... the sensations were fresh, intense. His desire and her response created new passions, a lust for life. Breathing turned into passionate gasps. She forced his hand off her breasts and guided it to her thighs. Erik moved quickly up the thighs and into that area of fantasies. There was an absence of panties, and he was surprised by the discovery; he became more aroused. The mystery was there for him to touch, to fondle, to enter. He felt the pressure building in his erection. It was almost painful, and he pleaded that he wouldn't come. She whispered, "Now, Erik ... now." Together, they struggled to the back of the van.

"God, I want you ... " Erik said, and they began to disrobe.

She grabbed his penis and said, "And I want you."

Their sweaty bodies were exposed. Erik scrambled to climb onto her ... but she evaded the attempt. "Erik, sweetheart," she said, "put your thing on. ... Hurry, I can't wait."

Erik was annoyed by the interruption, the change of spirit, "Thing on ... what thing on? We just took everything off," he said, then he realized how stupid he was; he had forgotten the rubber. "Oh shit, Jennie, I didn't bring one, I'm sorry. I just didn't realize."

"Oh, no, Erik ... Lord, how could you? You know I can't get pregnant. ... Oh darn, we'll just have to get one. We have to hurry though; they close at nine. ... We can make it." They untangled, dressed, and Erik cranked up the van and headed for the drugstore at Creek Run. He felt like a complete fool, a dumb kid who shouldn't be out alone. It was humiliating to be such a numb-nut.

They arrived at the drugstore, and Jennie said she would wait in the truck. Erik went in, and he guessed that they were about to close. He could see a middle-aged woman clerk with gray hair and eyeglasses putting stuff away at the counter. She smiled at Erik and asked what she could do for him.

Erik was nervous; he had never purchased a "thing" before, and never dreamed he would have to ask a lady. "Ma'am ... I need a rubber," he sputtered while blushing.

"A rubber what?" she asked.

Oh, Christ, she's puzzled ... this is going to be painful.

"You know ma'am ... not a rubber 'what' ... just a rubber. A plain rubber," he said. *Damn, why can't I think of another name; there's got to be one.*

She looked at him inquisitively. "A plain rubber?" she asked.

Another customer, a lady with a small child came in and waited at the counter.

"Doctor Ralston," the clerk called toward the pharmacy.

"Yes, Mrs. Stover," was the reply of the male voice.

"This young soldier wants a plain rubber. Do you know what he's talking about?" she asked.

"I don't know about a plain rubber, Mrs. Stover ... are you sure he doesn't mean a prophylactic?" the voice said.

She looked at Erik with puzzled indignation. "Do you mean a prophylactic?" she asked.

"Yes ma'am, I'm sorry. That's what I mean." *She just had to do this in front of a mother and child. I can't believe it. And she called me a soldier.*

She turned to the lady customer and handed her a small package, smiled, and took the money. Erik wished he was dead.

Mrs. Stover looked at Erik. She was obviously perturbed.

"What kind of prophylactic do you want?" she asked with an edge to her voice.

"I don't care ma'am ... any kind will do."

"Doctor Ralston, do we have different sizes of prophylactics?" she yelled toward the back.

Jesus ... I didn't ask about size ... Christ, now she's going to ask me to put my dick out on the counter ... to measure. And I'm not sure I could find it, after all this embarrassment.

"No, Mrs. Stover, just one size I think ... large," was the reply.

"Will a large do?" she said in a snip.

"Yes ma'am, any size, please," he said in surrender.

"How many large do you want?"

"Just one, ma'am."

"One ... only one?" she said, shaking her head.

"Yes ma'am, one."

She turned with one small package and handed it to Erik. "That will be twenty-nine cents," she said, squinting at him with disgust. "You know if you were married you wouldn't have to worry about the Devil's punishment ... that VD stuff. You wouldn't be sinning, and Jesus Christ the Lord would take care of you."

"Yes ma'am, I know. Thank you, ma'am."

That's all I need ... a sermon from a little ole, self-righteous lady, who's chewing my ass out because I'm horny ... and too stupid to bring a rubber. And another thing, she's so damn dumb she doesn't even know the difference between a soldier and a tough marine.

Erik went back to the panel truck. He had never been so devastated, not even when he was caught masturbating by his aunt, who, of course, promptly told his mother and dad.

IT WAS AFTER MIDNIGHT, AND ERIK WAS DRIVING HOME. *WHAT A NIGHT, NEVER before have I had a night like this. Thanks to Mrs. Stover, it took me thirty minutes to get hard enough to put that damn rubber on, then less than a minute to come after I put my dick into Jennie. God, how fucking embarrassing. Then the mess and the flinching with the yanked pubic hairs. Then the explanation and apologies to Jennie. Then the worry about Daryl returning early from his bear hunt, who probably went on the hunt with a switch, instead of a gun. Then the guilt trip, committing a mortal sin. Then confession time ... Christ, I'm not sure it was worth it.*

A little later down the road, he had to smile ... *but what a minute it was. Yes, that was one hell of a minute. It was damn well worth it.*

And ... it's going to get better ... two minutes next time. He had to laugh at that challenge. *Yep, life is great,* he thought, with a touch of arrogance ... *just fucking great!*

CHAPTER TWENTY-NINE

ERIK TRIED TO MAKE ANOTHER DATE WITH JENNIE LEE, BUT APPARENTLY Daryl the bear hunter had returned, and that put a skidding stop to Erik's one-time, momentous affair. It was a disappointment, but he reasoned that there would be other exciting girls in faraway places such as New York. Furthermore, he had been warned about the difficulties of keeping a relationship with the hometown girl. "It just doesn't work out," he was told. But regardless of all the good advice and his belief that there would be others, he couldn't get his mind off Jennie Lee — and the chance of furthering his sex education — that is, to get laid again.

He remembered driving home from their date when he noticed a tavern that looked active. Ira's Roadside Tavern was the name. Jennie Lee mentioned that she had a good time in Ira's, so Erik thought he would stop in. *It would be a chance to see her again, even though she will probably be with her bear hunter. But who knows, I may find another gal and do some dancing — and if lucky, get laid. And, if really lucky, find Jennie alone — and get laid.*

It was Saturday night, almost eight, when he pulled into the dirt parking lot. Maybe a dozen cars were in the lot, mostly half-old cars, looking even older in the dim light of a single bulb that hung from a skinny pole.

The tavern was made of wood, and it had a three-step porch with railings that served as a good place to lean on. He could see that the tavern used to be painted, maybe white, and the two blacked-out windows gave it a rundown, almost eerie appearance. But the country music that escaped from within was alive. He heard the fiddle and the cadence of the beat. It sounded like a good Saturday night crowd, and he hoped he would be welcome in his spiffy new uniform. *Mountain music is not all that bad.*

As he entered the tavern, he was slightly overwhelmed by the loudness of the band; he was startled by the smell of the heavy air laden with cigarette smoke, coal dust, and booze. The booze being mostly beer.

There was a four-piece country band in colorless clothing, plucking and picking away at high speed, with fiddle, banjo, guitar, and bass. It was happy music with cheerful colored lights dancing throughout the enclosure. They both helped to set the mood that seemed untroubled and carefree. Erik decided it was entertaining, and he made his way to the bar — a bar that ran the length of the bulkhead on the left side. On the other side of the room were ten or twelve wooden booths. Each would sit four or could squeeze in six. The dance area was in the center, made from the same old heavy board decking that was used throughout the room.

He spotted an empty bar stool and settled himself in for a cold one. He put his marine cover in front of him on the bar and motioned to the bartender. The bartender gave him one of those "Are you sure you should be in here?" looks, then yelled over the music, "What ya want?"

"I'll have a beer," Erik yelled back. The bartender promptly served him a longneck bottle of PBR.

Erik turned and made a quick scan of the room hoping to spot Jennie Lee. He was disappointed when he didn't see her. *Maybe later.*

And there was dancing, five or six couples of them, dancing as only mountain folk can. Several of the women wore flowered skirts, and all wore bright-colored flat shoes suitable for the old floor. The men, mainly miners, were much less colorful in their drab jeans, faded blue shirts, and their heavy steel-toed mining boots. Most wore an old ball cap tinted with shades of grease and coal dust. Typically, the miners were not smiling. When the music picked up and the beat became more pronounced, they would stomp the floor in sync with the rhythm. The dance floor would visibly sag with each stomp, and the coal dust would rise from the old floorboards and sparkle throughout the semi-breathable air. Erik was fascinated by the performance, and he smiled when he remembered the term "shit-kicking music." Now he understood the meaning.

The band finished the song and announced a fifteen-minute break. One of the girls, whom Erik had watched on the dance floor, was apparently returning from the restroom when they made eye contact. She altered her course and went over to Erik, "Hi, I'm Thelma," she said. "My brother is a marine, and I just love 'em."

"Well, thank you, Thelma, I'm Erik," he said, while trying not to be so obvious that he was staring at her large breasts, the two that were trying to break out of her sheer blouse.

She was a pretty girl, older than Erik, maybe thirty, a little on the generous side (big boned, Erik's mother would say), but tall with long blondish hair pulled back in a pony tail. Her big, blue eyes seemed to announce, "Hi, I'm Thelma ... let's fuck!"

"Well, Erik, how come you're not dancing? You should be, ya know ... being you're so cute and all ..."

"Oh, I'd like to Thelma, just don't have a partner," Erik said while starting to blush.

"You can have me," she said, excitedly, "or Edna, my friend ... She likes marines too." She pointed over at the booth where Edna and two rough-looking miners were sitting.

"Well, thank you, but you're with somebody," Erik said, while he glanced over at the booth. "I'm afraid your husband might not appreciate me dancing with his wife."

"Oh, don't be silly, them ain't our husbands; them just Vern and Lester ... wouldn't hurt a fly ... just good-fun guys."

Yea sure, ole Vern and Lester, wouldn't hurt a fly, but would kick the shit out of you and your coal truck if they had a notion to. I better cool this conversation while I still have all of my body parts ... connected.

"Well, I appreciate it, Thelma, and lord knows you're a pretty gal, but I wouldn't feel real good about it ... You know, the guys could get a mite upset." God, what an understatement that is, Erik thought. A mite upset, hell, they'd probably tear this place apart.

"Well, if you change your mind, you know where to find me," she said as she reached over and grabbed Erik's cover.

"It you're not going to dance with me, I'm going to wear your hat," she said in smiling defiance. Then she quickly turned, put the marine cover on, and playfully two-stepped across the dance floor.

He glanced at the booth, and he could feel the stares from Vern and Lester; Erik felt his heartbeat pick up speed. *This is not a good situation ... in fact this could be damn awful. I'll be lucky to get out of here with my hat ... and my ass.*

He turned back to the bar and ordered another beer. A beer to help him sort things out, he thought. *I could just get up and leave, but then I would be out of uniform. I need my cover. Or, I could go over, introduce myself, tell them I really like miners, and I have to run because I'm late for my date. Or, I could —*And then he saw his cover fall on the bar. It fell inches in front him. He turned and looked up at a tall, nasty-looking miner standing next to him. He was from Thelma's booth. "I think that be yor cap," he said without a smile, "and I don't cotton to no damn marine-boy fuckin' with my woman."

Erik stood up and said, "Sir, I wasn't fucking … I mean flirting with your woman. I'm sorry, I was just talk —" Erik felt the blow to the back of his head.

It isn't that painful, he thought, as he held onto the bar in an attempt to stay on his feet. The lights seemed to dim, and they lost their happy colors. Then, he could feel that he was being helped across the floor. The room was all fuzzy, but he thought he could see the door, and then he felt the cold night air. He was regaining his vision, and he could make out the parking lot; he was still standing, but someone was helping him to do so.

They reached the parking lot, and he felt stronger; he had most of his balance, and he could see the man in front of him, and he heard him say, "I said you ain't gonna fuck with my woman!"

And Erik didn't see the next blow either, the one that came straight into his face. The air became darker than the night really was, and he sank to his hands and knees. He wondered when the next train would come … and run over him. *I better get my shit together before this son-of-a-bitch kills me.*

Then he heard someone call from the direction of the porch, "Vern, hey Vern … don't hit him no more. Do you know who that is?"

"Hell no … why? Don't make a shit, he was fuckin' with Thelma … you seen him."

"Yea, I know … but you know who he is?"

"Fuck no … how in hell would I know?"

"Vern, that's Burt's boy … ya know, Burt up at the mine."

"Well, I'll be fucked, … This one's Burt's boy?"

"Yep, it's him all right, Burt calls him Erik."

"Well, I'll be goddamn. Are you Burt's boy?" Vern said as he brushed Erik off with his hands.

Erik was regaining his sight, and he stood without help. "Yea, I'm Burt's boy … at least I was this morning."

"If that don't beat nothin'," Vern said, "You come on back in, I'm gonna buy you a drink."

"Hey, we're both buying," another voice said (Lester had joined them). "Burt's boy is a friend of ours. ... Let's git on in and have one. We gots some good shine; it'll fix you up." And they helped Erik toward the tavern.

The very last thing I want to do is to go back into that shit-hole of Ira's and have a beer with good ole Vern and Lester. "Hey guys, I really appreciate it, but I've gotta get going ... you know, things I have to do ..."

"Shit no, good-buddy, we're gonna apologize, and you're gonna have one with us," Vern said.

Erik realized that it was pointless to pursue it any further; he knew he had to have a drink with his new buddies.

They entered the bar, and Vern called out, "Hey, Thelma, get us a cold, wet towel. Young Erik here, Burt's boy, kinda messed up ... and bring us some beer."

The wet towel cleaned most of the blood from the face and the back of the head, and the cold beer bottle felt good on the swelling. Burt's boy was going to live, but he had to wonder, again, if it was worth it. *Why can't I just get laid without all the bullshit? Oh, well ... right now my main purpose is to get the hell out of here.*

And after a painful drink or two, they allowed him to get the hell out of there. It was not a good night for Burt's boy.

CHAPTER THIRTY

ERIK CHECKED INTO THE MARINE BARRACKS AT NEW YORK NAVY YARD and was assigned to Guard Company, where he shared living quarters with a hundred and fifty other marines. The quarters consisted of two large rooms with shiny tile floors and rows of double bunks with locker boxes underneath. Each bunk had a stand-up locker against the bulkhead (wall). At the end of the barracks room was a large head containing the showers, sinks, and toilets. Erik was glad to see that the toilets were in stalls, and he was also impressed by the cleanliness. The entire complex was shipshape, and cleanup details were assigned to ensure that the barracks passed a rigid daily inspection.

Erik spent his first three days in training learning the standard operating procedures (SOP), which included such things as local uniform and dress codes, the rules of barracks living, work schedules, orders of the day, morning formations, liberty, and a multitude of do's and don'ts to assist you through a proper daily routine. Erik was fascinated with the structure, the organization of barracks life. He found that it was not difficult to comply with and agreed that most of the regulations were necessary to ensure order and control. He was pleased that common sense could be applied when in doubt of specific regulations.

It was the third morning aboard when Erik observed one of the common sense rules. It was new daylight when Erik returned from his shower. The barracks had awakened.

Five young marines, all six-footers with hard bellies — with the exception of one, he was six-four with a hard belly — approached the bunk across the aisle from Erik. It was Campo's bunk, and he was still in it. Apparently he ignored reveille — the wake-up call.

Campo had just arrived a month ago from boot camp, probably a class or two ahead of Erik. He had met him yesterday and guessed he was probably a fuck-up because he remained, or had been busted to, a private.

The hard-bellies arrived at Campo's bunk and immediately surrounded it. Their dress consisted of boxer shorts and skivvies shirts (T-shirts). The tall one did the talking. "Reveille time, Campo ... rise and shine ... beginning of a bright new day."

He shook the bunk; Campo sat up, sleepy eyed and startled. Erik noticed his black matted hair, his greasy skin, the stains on his skivvies, maybe urine. His sheets were not bright white, apparently they had skipped their turn at the laundry. The tall one continued talking.

"Campo, you stink. ... We think you smell like shit. ... Do you ever take a fucking shower?"

Campo looked at the group and, with alarm, replied, "Hell yes, I take showers. ... What the hell are you talking about? Fuck yes, I take showers."

Erik saw that Campo was frightened. Others in the barracks noticed the gathering, and most came closer to watch the proceedings.

"You know the rules, Campo," the tall one said. "You've been here long enough to know ... you don't come in and fuck up our barracks. This is our home, and, if you don't keep yourself clean, we'll do it for you."

"What the fuck you talking about? I keep clean ... clean as all you assholes ... hell, I shower," he said. Erik realized Campo was in trouble. He had heard of the G.I. shower, the scrub down, but had never seen it.

"Well, the barracks decided you smell like shit, and we're cleaning you up," the tall one said as he moved closer.

Campo leaped off the bunk; his eyes darted in fear; he was beginning to pale as he searched for an escape. The group closed in.

"No, goddammit, you're wrong. You fuckers ... I take showers. I've been busy, goddammit ... I'm going to bust your ass ——"

But he didn't bust anyone's ass. They grabbed him, all five grabbed him, and they dragged him to the showers. He kicked and cussed, but they had him restrained, and it was pointless to return any punches, or kicks. They arrived at the head with their unfortunate captive.

He pleaded, "Come on guys ... look, maybe I did skip one or two. Goddammit, I won't do it again. Come on guys ... Christ, a little break."

"You've had your break, asshole," the tall one replied. "You know the rules,

Campo, we talked about it before …"

They held him to the deck, and one of the group turned on a shower. Two heavy-duty scrub brushes and two bars of laundry lye soap lay beside him. Erik didn't know where they came from, but they were there.

They quickly stripped Campo of his skivvies. He was stark-ass naked. They flipped him on his back and held him down under the hot water. Two of them soaped up the heavy brushes. Then, as if on signal, they started on either side of Campo. The brushes dug into the skin; the old laundry soap did its job. Erik winced when he saw the brush marks on Campo's skin. The skin was turning red as he struggled to break free … he was obviously in pain and repeated, "Goddammit, I'll shower … give me a chance," but they continued to scrub. Erik cringed when they scrubbed his testicles and his penis.

The balls looked like they were scrubbed raw. They were steaming. *God, that must smart. And his dick, he won't be using that for some time, at least not for fucking. Maybe he can take a leak … if he's careful.*

It was over in five minutes. The hard-bellies put on fresh uniforms and departed for their daily routine. Campo sat up under the shower. Erik thought he could see Campo crying, but he was unsure because the flow of tears would have melded with the stream of shower water. It was quiet except fot the drone of the shower. Eventually Campo climbed to his feet and gingerly made it to his bunk. *Walking on egg shells,* Erik thought, as he could see much of the damaged skin, large sections of red rawness. Erik recognized that he was in pain. He felt sorry for him. *A bit harsh … but dammit, this is home. The tall marine was right. … No one fucks up your home.*

CHAPTER THIRTY-ONE

E RIK WAS ASSIGNED HIS FIRST GUARD DUTY. HIS GEAR ISSUE INCLUDED an M-I rifle with a bayonet, a .45 caliber pistol with holster, a night stick, a white cartridge belt, and a white helmet and red arm band with the letters MP (Military Police) on them. Erik was a sharp marine in his starched khakis and spit-polished shoes.

He was scheduled to go on duty that evening at 2000 hours (8:00 P.M.) until midnight, then again at 0600 hours (6:00 A.M.) the next morning. Between shifts, he bunked at the guard shack where the sergeant of the guard was desked. In addition to the fifteen or so bunks in the shack, there was a head with two showers, a coffee pot, a small reading room, and a holding cell. The cell was not large, maybe a ten-by-twelve-foot rectangle, eleven feet high. It was on the concrete deck in the middle of the bunkroom. A double bunk was the lone piece of equipment inside the cell. The steel frame of the cell was encased with heavy duty, chain link steel on the top and sides, and it had a door made of lightweight prison bars.

Erik was told that the holding cell was utilized as a temporary jail for military personnel who had been arrested for violating military law. Depending on the charge, they were incarcerated until they could be picked up and transported to the naval district brig or, in some cases, back to their units. But, most of the time, the cell was used to sober up a hell-raising GI who overboozed on his night of liberty. Occasionally one of the law enforcement agencies would bring in a military AWOL who was absent without leave or even a deserter who had been missing over thirty days.

Erik went to the guard shack and reported to Sergeant Tomkin, the sergeant of the guard assigned for the twenty-four-hour day. The ribbons on Sergeant Tomkin's uniform declared that he was a Korean combat vet who had been wounded. His military attire was impeccable. His dark probing eyes were much older than his twenty-two-year body. Combat had taken its toll. He was a no-nonsense type marine who depicted a stern, aloof personality. *He must have had a rough time over there,* Erik thought, like so many of the others he had met. The Korean veterans were different. They were much older, not in age, but older in life — and pain. His friends called him Little Tom, because of his stature, not his heart.

"PFC Erik Larsen, you're new here," Sergeant Tomkin said as he looked Erik over with a critical eye. "You do your job, and we'll have no problems. You're on post three tonight; you will be posted in forty-five minutes. Grab a bunk and be ready to go."

"Yessir," Erik replied.

He took his gear and went down a small passageway that led to the bunk room. The lighting was subdued, probably to allow sleep for those recently off duty. Erik was unsettled. He didn't expect the quiet, nor the absence of activity. The room was foreign, almost forbidding. He saw two or three marines sleeping, bunking out. The shadows were evident, but not distinct, almost hidden. It was disconcerting, and Erik couldn't identify the reason for his concern.

In silence, he made his way toward an empty lower bunk and stowed his gear. He turned to view the entire room when his eye caught a slight movement in the holding cell. When he focused on the cell, Erik was chilled; he could not accept what his visual sense told him. Less than twenty feet away a person was hanging by his neck. He was in a quiet struggle for life.

"Holy shit!" Erik said as he ran to the cage. He tried the cell door. It was locked. The man in trouble was young, maybe a year older than Erik. He was a pathetic-looking individual in clothing that had been slept in and puked on. He hung by a belt around his throat, and his arms were trying to pull himself up and out of the noose. The loop was too small, and he was unable to squeeze his head through. He was losing strength, and Erik was spell bound by the threatening sights and sounds. He heard a frail gurgling noise combined with heavy breathing. More gasp with clatter than breathing. His contorted face was colored in hues of blue, gray, and wine. The pleading eyes bulged twice their normal size. They begged for help.

My God, what am I doing? I have to get help. In near panic, he spun around and rushed down the passageway. He called out, "Sergeant Tomkin … sir, we've got a man hanging in the cell."

"What the hell you mean, hanging?" he said, as he looked up from the desk. "Yes, sir, hanging by the throat ... still alive though."

"Oh fuck ... goddamn bastard ... not on my watch, that son-of-a-bitch," he said as he hunted through the desk drawer. "Where in the hell are those keys? Goddamn asshole ... on my watch." He found the keys and walked toward the cell. Erik followed, and it appeared that Sergeant Tomkin was not to be hurried as he limped down the passageway. *The limp of the left leg explains the Purple Heart he is wearing.* Erik could see him shaking his head, as in disbelief, and he was talking to himself; it was inaudible.

They arrived at the cell, and Erik saw that the kid wasn't moving as before, just a slight quiver. His color had changed; his face was ashen, and Erik could smell him; the kid had urinated in his civilian trousers, and it formed a puddle on the concrete deck.

The scene was repulsive, a first for a frightened Erik. He watched as Sergeant Tomkin unlocked the door and shouted at the unfortunate, "Hey you ... you cock-sucker. You want to die? Go ahead, kill yourself ... you goddamn piece of shit." He grabbed the legs and spun the body around and tried to lift him out of the belt noose. There was no response. The legs were limp. Sergeant Tomkin looked up at the twisted face and, with a cutting voice, said, "You deserting son-of-a-bitch ... I get my ass blown off by a bunch of slant-eyed gooks while you remain state-side and fuck all the wives ..." He continued to stare at the figure for some time, then he spit into the urine puddle and turned to Erik.

"Where's your bayonet?"

"I'll get it, sir," he said as he ran over to the bunk and retrieved it from his gear. He rushed back and handed it to him. Sergeant Tomkin took the bayonet and with deliberation climbed up on the lower bunk, reached out, and cut the belt. The listless body fell in a heap into the pool of his own urine.

It was difficult for Erik to believe that he was dead. Sergeant Tomkin stood over the torso; he didn't touch him; he looked at him with utter disgust and delivered a solemn, bizarre eulogy. "I hope you're satisfied you worthless clown ... couldn't wait to do it on another watch, had to be mine ... well, you deserve it, cocksucker. You'll do well in a pine box."

After a moment, perhaps a reflective pause, he turned to Erik. "Larsen, you did all you could, now go call the OD and report this flap.* ... I'll try to revive

* OD: officer of the day

this asshole ... and then you have to be on post."

"Yessir." Erik departed and phoned the OD.

ERIK HEARD LATER THAT THE MAN IN THE NOOSE WAS SUCCESSFUL WITH THE SUICIDE; that he was a marine deserter who missed movement to Korea, and Sergeant Tomkin, along with another sergeant, was disciplined for not stripping him of his belt when he was put in the cell.

Sergeant Tomkin was now Corporal Tomkin. But his combat buddies didn't think less of Little Tom. To the contrary, they thought he should have been promoted.

And all deserters hanged by the neck ... until they gurgled.

CHAPTER THIRTY-TWO

GUARD DUTY WAS A BUSY ROUTINE. LONG HOURS AND LITTLE TIME FOR liberty were the norms. The company was shorthanded because most marines were in Korea doing their thing, taking their hits. Erik was disappointed, frustrated, because he wanted to be there to do what he thought he was trained to do … combat. But he was told he would serve a two-year tour at the navy yard, then ship out to Korea … if the shooting continued.

The adjustment to stateside military life was more difficult than he expected. It surprised him that he missed the security of boot camp, and even the security of the seminary. Both had offered a controlled environment that was totally structured. He found it difficult to cope with the new freedom and the transition into adulthood.

The learning process was taking place, and it provided Erik with meaningful information — some good, some not so good. He discovered that, if you were in uniform and had sufficient funds to buy a couple of drinks, you could get laid. And that was the good part, but it didn't happen that often because of the low pay for a PFC. But he liked the girls and knew that he had made the correct choice to leave the seminary.

Erik soon learned that wearing a uniform had its negative results also. He was surprised that some people (other than certain miners) didn't like marines, and, during his first few months, he witnessed many examples of the animosity from civilians, other branches of the service, and even his own unit.

The worst, however, was the continuous skirmish between sailors and marines. It seemed to Erik that they never got along, at least not at the bars. Perhaps it was because the Marine Corps was part of the Navy Department, and Erik was told that the Corps resented being the stepchild. But regardless of the reason, he soon found out that most marines considered the Navy to be a bunch of unkempt, undisciplined, long-haired clowns.

The two services seemed to foster a dog-cat relationship that had its own special jargon. "Dumb jarheads," "Hollywood gyrenes," or "sea-going bellhops" were select labels used by the sailors when referring to their marine brothers. Marines countered with their own tender names such as "Navy pukes," "Swabs," "Bell-bottoms," or "Squid."

Many times, when Erik and his buddies encountered sailors and booze was involved, there was an argument with the usual name-calling and, more often than not, a push and shove with the art of fisticuffs. It didn't take Erik long to experience his first scuffle with the Navy.

IT WAS HIS INITIAL LIBERTY INTO THE BIG CITY, AND HE REALIZED THAT HE WASN'T AS rugged as he thought he was. And certainly not as invincible as you were taught at Parris Island — that you were the toughest, meanest *hombre* in the territory.

On Saturday night Johnson and Erik went into a local New York bar for a beer. They noticed a few sailors, but the bar, even though rundown, looked friendly and quiet.

As they approached the bar stools, Erik heard a comment from the direction of the sailors.

"Well, looky here, a couple of Hollywood boots."

Erik and Johnson chose to ignore the remark; perhaps it was a one-shot comment, Erik thought. They took their seats and ordered a beer.

"Hey, don't you know this place is off-limits for you guys?" said one of the sailors.

Erik turned to Johnson and said seriously, "Hell, I didn't know that, did you?"

"Naw, they're just fucking with us; it isn't off-limits," Johnson said.

"Yea, that's right," said another sailor. "Owner said no more jarhead pussys in here; this is a straight bar, no gyrene fags," and they chuckled at their cleverness.

Erik couldn't ignore that blast. "That's not what we heard," he said. "The owner asked us to spend more time in here to protect you swabbies, like marines always do ... you know, when you're not on your toy boats.

"Hey, Erik," Johnson said, "you know squid don't call them boats ... that's an insult. They call them ships."

"By, God, you're right again, Johnson. Hell, I'm sorry, guys, I meant to say toy ships."

That must have hit the mark because a tall, lanky, ole salt sailor wearing a Korean service ribbon got up and half-staggered over to them. He stood there and glared at Erik, who by this time was on his feet sizing up his new opponent. *Shit, I can take him ... one solid punch and he falls down ... and goes boom.*

With confidence, Erik threw his best punch, one hundred ninety pounds of no-fat body punch, directly to the squid's chin. Then he waited momentarily for him to fall. Apparently the squid, the tall lanky one, had never heard how tough the marines were, because he didn't fall, and he sure as hell didn't go boom ... unless you count the boom that was made when he hit Erik, who did manage to fall.

The other two sailors jumped to their feet immediately and started toward Johnson, who fortunately kept his cool and said, "Hey guys, no problem, we were just kidding, and really, we were just leaving" ... and he whisked himself and Erik out of the off-limits bar.

It was quite an eye-opener for Erik — perhaps eye-closer would be more appropriate. One had swollen shut, the other was in the process. It was a lesson learned well, and he had a fresh, guarded respect for the other services, particularly if a big ole boy was in uniform playing his favorite sport — punching out marines. Erik became more tolerant of conflicting intraservice opinions. But he kept his sense of humor and, on occasions, his distance. *And what the hell ... no real damage done. Young bodies mend rapidly.*

ERIK WAS ON DUTY, MIDNIGHT TO 0400, GUARDING THE FENCE LINE PERIMETER ON the south side of the navy yard. It was probably 0100 when he reached the end of his post boundaries (the fence line running east and west). It was dark that night, moonless with clear, brisk air. All was quiet, and Erik was required to check in with the guard on post eight, which was the perimeter fence line running north and south. The fence paralleled a city street that intersected the main gate entrance.

The street was quiet, with just an occasional vehicle, and Erik could see three lonely street lights that offered some illumination, just enough light to produce mysterious shadows upon the street, fence, and vegetation. *It's eerie,* Erik thought, *always happening at this time of morning-night.*

At first he didn't see the guard, and Erik supposed that he was at the other end, some three hundred yards away. He turned to go back on his own post when he noticed an object, or person, up close to the fence on post eight. His curiosity was aroused, and he approached nearer to identify it. Within a few steps, he could see that it was a person standing with his face up against the fence. *Must be the guard ... but something isn't right.*

Erik called out, "Post eight ... All secure?"

There was no immediate answer, but Erik thought that he had heard him, because he saw him move. Then Erik saw other movement on the street side of the fence, directly in front of the guard. *Is it a dog? Is it alive? What the hell is it?*

He approached closer to the object, and then, somewhat surprised, he realized that it was a person, and Erik became even more confused because the person was getting up from the sidewalk. Once standing, the figure scurried on down the street. *What the hell is going on?* And Erik moved toward the guard.

The guard noticed his approach. "Post eight ... All secure," he shouted to Erik.

Then he quickly turned and moved on down the fence line.

Erik was puzzled, but he discarded the idea of any threat because the guard had given him an all secure. He didn't see any violations or trouble, so he resumed his post.

The next evening, Erik was off duty in the enlisted club, known as the slop chute, having a beer with three of the guard company. Two of the marines, Johnson and Gibbs, had been in the Corps a month or two longer than Erik, but the other one, Skinner, had several years in the Corps and had recently returned from Korea.

Skinner had been a corporal but lost his stripes because of disciplinary action involving some kind of a screw-up while overseas in combat. He was now a private and had to work some of the minor, less attractive posts. Erik had met Skinner, but the vet hardly acknowledged Erik's existence. He seemed to be more concerned about his forthcoming discharge date than he was about the present day.

Erik related the previous night's incident. "It was kind of strange," he said. "I came to the end of my post and noticed post eight standing up against the fence ... or I thought he was ... and when I called, I saw movement, and then I could see ... what looked like two figures. One outside, and one inside the fence. At first, I thought the one outside was a dog or something, and then I could see that it might be a person, maybe looking for something on the sidewalk. Then it stood up, and I recognized that it wasn't a dog. I guess the person saw me because he scooted on down the road. Then post eight checked in okay. It was weird man … really weird. What the hell was going on?"

Johnson and Gibbs looked at each other and grinned, then Johnson said to Erik, "You don't know what was going on?"

"No, not really … do you?"

"Have you ever had post eight before?" Gibbs said.

"No, haven't."

"Well, I have, and it gets kinda strange, ya know?" Gibbs said. "You get propositioned out there on the mid-shift. Don't you, Johnson?"

"Sure as fuck do," Johnson replied. "All the time."

"Holy shit," Erik said. "You mean these gals come up and want to get laid? Christ, I can hardly wait my turn."

"I didn't say laid," Johnson said as he grinned at Gibbs. "They give you a blow-job."

"Holy shit, a blow-job … Now I know I want my turn."

"Yep, they come up to you when it's dark and quiet, after midnight, and ask if they can give you a blow-job …"

"Holy shit," Erik said, "through the fence?"

"Yep, through the fence … you stick your dick through the fence, and they drop to their knees and go at it."

"Well, I'll be damned," said Erik, "through the fence … she goes at it, right on the street. That's amazing."

Johnson looked at Gibbs; they both grinned. "We didn't say 'she' drops to her knees, Erik. We said, 'he' drops to his knees."

"Yea, there's a slight difference," Johnson said. They both laughed.

Oh shit … how could I have been so stupid? Christ, they're talking about queers.

"Jeez guys, you must think I'm a dumb shit." Erik said while shaking his head and smiling. "I just thought it would be girls. But isn't that dangerous … ?"

"Well, I guess so … but I've never done it," said Gibbs, "But hell, it's tempting, sometimes they offer you money."

"Christ, guys," Erik said, "I don't mean dangerous as in VD. I mean dangerous as in court martial, ya know … dishonorable discharge for being a queer."

Skinner, who had been sitting quietly with them, slammed his beer bottle onto the table. It startled Erik and the others.

"What the hell you mean … being a queer?" Skinner yelled. His face was turning an angry red. "What the hell do you mean?"

Erik was taken aback at the intensity. "Hell, I don't know, Skinner, I'm just assuming …"

"Well, goddammit assuming what … assuming that I'm a queer? You fuck-head, are you calling me a queer?" Skinner shouted.

"No, I'm not calling anybody anything," Erik said. "Hell, I was just trying to find out what's going on. That's all Skinner, nothing more."

"Well, by God, I've had a lot of blow-jobs, and by God, I'm not a queer, and if anybody says so, I'll blow their ass off with my forty-five. … You can count on it."

Holy shit … I've really opened a can of worms with this one. "No, I'm not calling you a queer. … Hell, I'd like to have a blow-job; I just thought it had to be with a girl, you know … not a guy."

"Fuck no, it doesn't," he said. "If you get blown by a man it's all right … but if you suck dicks, you're nothing but a goddamn queer … and I don't suck dicks. You got that?"

Erik looked at the others, and they all nodded.

"Sounds good to me," Erik said.

"And I don't fuck them in the ass, and I don't take it in the ass. I just let them blow me, and that makes them the queer … not me. And I pity the son-of-a-bitch who calls me one. I hate queers." And he got up and stomped off without further exchange.

They looked at each other quietly for several moments.

"Christ … kind of stupid for bringing that up," Erik said, breaking the silence, "But, Jesus, I know the Marine Corps doesn't look at it that way."

The other two nodded in agreement.

"Who in hell was on post eight, mid-shift?" Erik asked.

"He was," Gibbs said, "Skinner."

No wonder I hit a nerve. So much for tonight's class on what constitutes a queer.

"Hey guys," Erik said. "Promise me one thing … beat the living shit out of me if I ever bring this subject up in front of Skinner."

They agreed ... and they all laughed.

CHAPTER THIRTY-THREE

A S TIME PASSED, ERIK BECAME MORE DISSATISFIED WITH HIS NEW CAREER as a marine guard. During the dark hours, you guarded the navy yard perimeter and the docks on the East River. That river you could identify by its foul odor. Ships in for repair or overhaul would be docked at the pier, and, in some instances, dry-docked. They were all unmanned, except for the civilian workers during the day. It was a standard joke among the guards to see who could formulate the best plan to steal a ship out of dry-dock.

"All we need is a big trailer," Erik said to Johnson.

"How big a trailer do we need, Erik?"

"Oh, I'd say about the length of a city block."

"Yea, that should do it," Johnson replied. "We'd have to have a decent truck to pull it, though."

"Definitely … one of those big mothas that goes 'spsst' when you hit the air brakes," Erik said. "Then we put the *Ticonderoga* on the trailer and yank her right out of there."*

"Yea, we can do it," Johnson said. "Then we sell it to one of those chili bean countries, and we're set for life. Get laid every night by some gorgeous señorita."

Actually they both knew that the real reason they guarded the ships was to act as fire watch. It was boring, lonely work at night, and Erik felt insignificant. His contribution was meaningless. *This is the pits, and I dreamed of being a fighter pilot. … Hell, I was better off picking chicken shit.*

During the daylight hours, the routine changed, and you would be assigned as gate guard to man the turnstiles and check the ID badges of the civilian workers. It was hectic in the morning rush hours as several thousand worker bees

* *Ticonderoga:* an aircraft carrier

jammed the gates to start work on time. It was on these gate posts that Erik realized why some of the civilians were not overly fond of their marine buddies. Regulations stated that you randomly check for contraband in packages, lunch boxes, and thermos bottles. The workers seemed to accept the necessity of such a search, but they didn't accept the way it was normally performed. And Erik agreed with the workers. Some of the guards would thrust their night sticks (a long billy-club) into the turnstile causing it to jam. This would bring the line to a startling halt, and the worker-bodies stacked up against one another. This always resulted in nasty looks and selected profanity.

Erik would not use his night-stick, but would ask the worker to stop and open his lunch box or package for a quick inspection. Lunch boxes were embarrassing enough, but it particularly bothered Erik when he asked them to remove the thermos cap, so he could smell the contents. Erik never smelled any nitro or other explosives, but, on occasions, he would smell a thermos of booze. Then the gate sergeant would come over and make a big production of pouring it out at the man's feet while a hundred workers stood in line watching. Not exactly promoting better military-civilian relationships. It was never poured at a woman's feet because the marines wouldn't stop the females unless they were pretty, and then only to get their phone numbers.

In spite of the negative aspect of being a stateside, non-combat, marine PFC, Erik strived to be the best in the unit. He took great pride in his uniform, which was always clean and starched with neatly pressed creases. In the heat of summer, it required three khaki uniforms a day. And the shoes, they were always spit-shined to a mirror finish. Erik knew he was a nobody, but he took some pride in being the best of the nobodies.

Your day of duty always commenced with a troop formation. It was called guard mount and served the purpose of roll-call, reading the plan of the day, and uniform inspection. At these times, there would be a marine officer in charge, usually a first lieutenant, sometimes a captain. Erik was deeply affected by their presence. He was visibly impressed with their professionalism, their décor, and the way they were treated by the enlisted staff. They manifested pride in being an officer, and Erik envied their status and would often visualize himself as being one. He had images of being respected, to command and lead, to be somebody, to be called Sir, instead of "hey you," or Larsen (enlisted men were rarely called by first names).

And there was another important reason to be an officer. You had to be an officer to be a fighter pilot, his special dream. At times his dream seemed beyond reach, and he would experience the futility of such an improbable goal. But he would not allow himself to become defeated by the negative thoughts, the road-blocks to success. He didn't have a reasonable explanation, but he knew within that somehow, someway, he would fulfill his dream. And he thanked God for bestowing such faith, and he prayed for the strength and courage to pursue.

Friday morning at guard mount, Erik observed another example of the indignities of being an enlisted man. The personnel inspection was over, and he passed with his usual high marks. Sergeant Rudley, the company's first sergeant, dismissed the formation and told them to fall in at the mess hall for short arm inspection. *Oh, God, not again. I just hate it. ... Christ, what an embarrassment..*

They formed in the mess hall; the company was in three lines.

"Company at ease," Sergeant Rudley ordered. "You all know the procedures, the Doc and I will inspect each of you for gonorrhea, you know ... the clap. I want a good firm milk-down of the penis, and if we don't think it's firm enough, the Doc will do it for you ... and I warn you, he doesn't like doing that."

They stepped in front of the first marine who dropped his trousers at the time. With his right hand, the marine milked his penis down with a single firm stroke, and there was no discharge of fluids.

"You're clean ... and dismissed," Sergeant Rudley said as he checked his name off the clipboard.

The next three checks were clean. The fourth, PFC Gomez, dropped his trousers and continued with the milk-down.

"That's not firm enough," the corpsman said. "Do it again, the proper way."

Gomez repeated the process with a firmer stroke, and, unfortunately, there was a secretion of white fluid.

"How long have you had that?" Rudley asked.

"Don't know, Top, wasn't there yesterday ... I just think it's a strain."

"Strain my ass," the first sergeant replied. "It's the fucking clap! ... Where did you pick it up, and who gave it to you?"

"Well, nobody, Top. I don't know where it came from."

"You damn well better remember," Rudley said, losing patience. "You don't get this shit from the toilet seat. You get if by fucking some bitch that has the clap."

Erik could see that Gomez was visibly shaken; he knew he could lose a stripe.

Top Sergeant Rudley looked up at the formation, "Listen up troops, Gomez here got the clap because he was too goddamn stupid to use a rubber, or too stupid to use a pro-kit. That will cost him a court martial. It's up to you ... you all know the procedures. You've seen the training films, and you've had your lectures. You know the rubbers and kits are free at the gate. Our beloved Commandant states that you can't be an effective fighting man when you're laid up with clap — or syphilis. So a word to the wise — you want your stripes, use a rubber." Gomez was standing there with his dick hanging out, waiting for Top to finish his lecture, his admonition.

"Gomez, get your ass over to the sick bay and get your shots. I'll see you later, and you better damn well have a name, or names, of those you've been fucking. We'll check them out, and, if infected, put 'em on the bulletin board before they contaminate the whole damn Marine Corps."

When it was Erik's turn to suffer the indignities of such a public examination, he had to muster all his courage to withstand the embarrassment. After passing the test, he silently resolved that the day would come when he wouldn't have to grab his dick in front of a formation. *I'll bet your ass the officers don't go through this disgrace.* He had to smile when he remembered what he had heard about officers and the clap.

Apparently, they don't get the clap. They catch a cold, a chest cold that requires penicillin shots. The story goes that a young officer goes to sick bay and tells the doctor that he thinks he has the clap. The Doc* says, "Lieutenant, you're an officer and gentleman of the United States Marine Corps, and officers don't catch such a disease ... so in the future, you say that you have a problem with sinuses ... or perhaps your elbow."

"Aye, sir, I can do that," the lieutenant responded.

"Now, what's your problem?"

"Well, Doc, it's my elbow."

"And what's wrong with your elbow, Lieutenant?"

"Well, sir, I can't pee through it."

* Doc: a navy corpsman

CHAPTER THIRTY-FOUR

THE KOREAN WAR (OFFICIALLY IT WAS CALLED A CONFLICT) WAS ESCALATING and producing more casualties, many of whom were young marines from the New York-Brooklyn area. Those that died from their wounds were designated KIA's (killed in action) and marine barracks was directed to provide partial military honors at the funeral if the marine's family so requested. The honor squad was referred to as the funeral detail, and these details consisted of six riflemen, a bugler, and a noncommissioned officer (NCO) in charge. They fired a three-round rifle salute, sounded taps, and presented the American flag to the surviving next of kin. These details became more numerous as casualties increased, and it was typical for Erik to be assigned funeral duty at least once a week.

Erik's first funeral was a traumatic experience. It was also his first encounter with a combat death and the family who lost their loved one to the war. The young marine, Angelo Fagan, was nineteen, Erik's age, and he paid his price for doing his duty, fighting a war he probably didn't understand, and died in the process. Erik saw the grief, and he saw the casket. It was a closed casket service as most combat funerals were. He was told this KIA, this Corporal Fagan, was hit by a mortar shell, probably a 60 MM. And he wondered if Angelo's body was in the casket. Or maybe just parts of him, along with sand bags to make up the weight difference. Erik had heard many horror stories from the returning vets about KIA's, body bags, and missing parts. He chastised himself for having such bizarre and inappropriate thoughts.

The priest at the grave finished his words over the casket, and then the NCO took the American flag, folded it, and presented it to a lady in black, who was seated on an old fold-up steel chair. She sobbed quietly when she accepted the flag and placed it on her lap without looking up.

A man from the funeral home hustled over to the casket that rested on a mechanical lowering device and initiated its slow decent into the cold ground. Upon command, Erik and the other five guardsmen raised their rifles and fired three times into the overcast sky. The noise was deafening as it shattered the calm of the cemetery air. And just as suddenly the silence returned.

The honor guard stood in formation at parade rest, and Erik could see that the casket had made little progress in its lingering descent. Then one of the pulleys began to squeak as it started to bind, and then it suddenly froze in place while the other three continued to turn. The frantic man stopped the other pulleys, but not until the casket was ready to slide out of the harness and fall end-first into the seven-foot-deep cavity. *What the hell is going on? Why all this crap in lowering the casket? I can't believe that some clown forgot to check out the gear. What an insensitive bastard.*

Then there was a gasp from the small gathering as the folded flag fell to the ground, and the woman in black cried out, "No … No … not my baby, not Angelo!" And she rushed to the edge and threw herself into the grave and landed atop the eschewed casket. She wept, pleaded, "You can't do this to my baby. … You can't hurt my boy. I won't let you hurt him anymore … no baby. Mamma's here, and they can't hurt you. … It's gonna be all right. Mamma's here with her baby …" And her cries turned into uncontrollable sobbing.

No one moved, for moments no one moved, and one could only hear the sounds from the grave. A state of shock had engulfed the site. The air was cold and gray. Erik thought he would pass out. He forced back the tears; he wanted to run. Others in the party began to cry as Angelo's father went over and knelt down beside the grave. He leaned forward and gently stroked his wife. Through his tears, he repeated softly, "It'll be okay, Mamma. It'll be okay. … God, is with him, Mamma …"

The half-hour ride back to the barracks was long and cheerless. Erik couldn't forget the scene, poor Mrs. Fagan. They finally got her up out of the grave. She was a heavy woman, and she had hurt herself. Erik was told that they took her to the hospital.

Mister Fagan gave each of the honor guard a five-dollar bill. He asked that they have a beer for Angelo because he loved the Corps and that's the way he would want it.

He looked at Erik and said, "Son, you are the same age as my boy. … God bless you ... and promise me that you will stay alive."

"I'm sorry about Angelo, sir ... I wish I had known him. And please tell Mrs. Fagan I'm sorry. And yes sir, I'm going to stay alive."

Erik was tormented with unanswered questions. *Why so young, and why was Angelo chosen, and why not me? Who determines, and on what basis ... and did he feel he was somebody before he died, and did he really care if he was somebody? And why do I feel so guilty sitting here in the states ... a nobody with a nothing job ... but alive, and not dead? None of it makes sense, but I know I should have been there, with Angelo and many others ... in combat.*

Erik and the others stopped and had a beer for Angelo, and for all of the Marine Corps KIA's in Korea.

THE FUNERAL DETAILS DIDN'T STOP, AND ERIK DIDN'T STOP PARTICIPATING. AND with each funeral, he became more determined to find release from guard company and transfer to the war.

Then one day, as if on cue, there was a Marine Corps memorandum from headquarters posted on the barrack's bulletin board. The memo stated that there was a need for additional aviators and that the requirements to become a naval aviation cadet had been lowered. Specifically, you no longer had to be a college graduate to qualify for the cadet program if you met certain criteria: sailors or marines under twenty-three years of age with a high school diploma; a GCT score (a form of IQ test) of 120 or above; acquire a passing grade on a two-year college equivalency test; successfully pass the aviation physical exam; and be recommended by your commanding officer. It also noted that the applicant's eyesight must not require any corrective lenses, and then it further stated that, upon successful completion of naval flight training (18 months), the cadet would be commissioned as an ensign or second lieutenant (depending on your service), and be designated as a naval aviator.

Erik could hardly contain his enthusiasm when he read the memo. He read it three times and decided it was for real. *Perhaps the break I've prayed for. A program that would enable me to become a Marine Corps officer and a fighter pilot ... and a combat vet.* It was a great day for Erik. He had the GCT

(136), the diploma, good health, and didn't wear glasses. It was up to him to pass the tests and receive a recommendation. *It can be done. Damn right it can be done.*

Within two weeks, Erik completed the required testing and, somewhat to his surprise, was told that Colonel Damen, his commanding officer (Erik had never met him), would recommend him for cadet aviation training.

It was a good feeling when Erik sent the required package to Marine Headquarters in Washington. Now he had the dreaded delay, the waiting period for the response. The days of thinking "maybe I did, but probably I didn't make it."

Thirty-seven days later (but who was counting?) the letter arrived from headquarters. Erik was excited, and yet, he was reluctant to see the decision. He imagined the worse, the villain doubts were closing in; he had lost his previous confidence, and he was miserable with uncertainty. Can I handle another failure, he questioned, will I cope with being at the bottom?

To hell with this kind of negative thinking. I've got as good a chance as anybody, maybe more.

He forced the debilitating thoughts from his mind and opened the letter. He read the first line: "This is to inform you that you were not selected to participate in the naval aviation cadet program."

Erik was numb with the pain of rejection. He stared at the words "not selected." Eventually he read the remainder of the letter and it caused more distress. He had passed all requirements, but one. He had failed the English grammar section of the college tests. He failed by two points. Then he became angry that he had let such an opportunity slip away, because he didn't prepare for the test. "Fuck ... I can't believe it," he said out loud to no one. He crumbled the letter and proceeded to do what most marines would do under the same circumstances. He headed for the slop-chute and had a beer.

It took a few days before Erik regained his confidence and his sense of humor. *Hell, if I had spent less time saying "fuck," and more time with proper grammar, I would be on my way to be a fearless fighter pilot.* He had to smile, even though it was feeble, then he signed up for a correspondence course with the MCI (Marine Corps Institute). Erik became a student of college English I.

CHAPTER THIRTY-FIVE

TWO WEEKS LATER, ERIK WAS ASSIGNED TO MESS DUTY FOR THIRTY DAYS. Mess duty was never considered a good deal, but all enlisted below the rank of corporal had to take their turn. Erik realized it was a necessary duty, so he was determined to make the best of it.

The days started early, 0500 in the mornings, and they didn't stop until 2100 at night. In spite of the long hours immersed in humbling work washing pots and pans and bussing tables, Erik enjoyed the break from guard duty. Feeding troops a good meal on clean tables was far more meaningful to Erik than guarding the aromatic East River.

It was on Erik's fourth day in the grease pits when Sergeant Stoops, the NCO in charge of mess men came up to him and said, "Hey, Ace, I'm putting you on the staff NCO's section tomorrow to replace Ace." (He called every mess man — all fourteen of them — Ace.)

And what a character ... a twelve-year veteran, around thirty, with a cook's hat and crew cut head. He wore a white tee shirt that strained to contain the first stage of a beer belly. A chain-smoker of Camels, he would yell out to the mess men throughout the chow hall, "Hey, Ace, get your ass moving ... and, Ace, get her cleaned up over here ... hustle troops, hustle." Erik understood why he was nicknamed "the pit boss."

"You wouldn't be upset if I pulled you off pots, would ya?"

"No, sir," Erik replied, "pots are not my bag."

"Yea, I know what ya mean. You'll enjoy the staff NCO's though. Do a good job, and they even leave you tips once in a while."

"I didn't know they left tips," Erik said, "that's a good deal."

"Just make sure their tables are set with plates, silverware, and cloth napkins. Then standby to get them ice tea or milk ... ya know, second helpings, desserts, anything they want. You just stay with them and act as their steward."

"Well, I appreciate it, sir. I'll do my best."

"I know you will, Ace ... and pick up a white cooks' jacket in the morning. Wear that over your skivvie shirt. That's your uniform ... and stay sharp. They are your bosses, ya know."

One would have thought that Erik had been promoted to colonel. He couldn't explain why, but he had good feelings about the rather trivial change of duties. He looked forward to his new assignment, working with the staff NCOs.

Two weeks passed, and Erik was not disappointed. He took pride in the new work and even purchased some napkin rings to dress up his tables. Apparently, the gesture was well accepted because he heard good comments about his work.

Erik strived to do his best, and he paid attention to the slightest detail. When he heard one of the staff complain about the warm temperature of the milk, he made it a policy to put the small milk cartons into the deep freezer prior to their meals. And then he came up with the idea of freezing a number of cartons solid, to be cut and used as ice cubes ... frozen milk cubes. They were an instant success, and soon Erik was known by all of the staff NCO's as Ace Larsen, the professional mess man. *How comical, a few weeks ago I had visions of being an Ace in a sleek jet ... at forty thousand feet. And now I'm an Ace in a piddly-ass chow hall. Burt would surely be proud.*

But the tips increased. In fact, they increased to the point that they were a dollar or two higher than his pay as a PFC (about seventy dollars a month). This was a welcome addition to Erik's income, and it enabled him to better pursue the meaningful things in a young marine's life ... like getting laid.

It was midmorning, and Erik had finished his setup for the noon meal. Sergeant Stoops yelled over to him, "Ace, you report to Gunny Sergeant Renzo in the butcher shop and help out for a couple of hours. He's shorthanded."

Erik was surprised. *How ironic, I'm going back into the butcher shop after joining the marines a year ago to get away from a damn butcher shop. Talk about full circle. ... This is real progress, Erik.*

He reported to Sergeant Renzo, who was busy on the cutting block working on a front quarter of beef. He was a sharp-looking marine, maybe thirty, but well proportioned with his 165-pound frame. Erik noticed the absence of the usual beer gut so common with cooks and bakers MOS's (Military Occupation Specialties). Sergeant Renzo introduced himself to Erik, and said that his assistant was transferred early and the shop needed help. "You can start by grinding that tray of beef," he said while pointing to the meat. "You ever use a grinder before?"

Erik had to smile, "Yes, sir, just a few hundred times."

Sergeant Renzo was a bit puzzled, "You're kidding of course?"

"Well, not really, sir, I kinda grew up in a packing house, my dad's place ... cut meat four or five years."

"Well I'll be damn," Sergeant Renzo said, "Helluva coincidence ... no one knew of this in the Corps?"

"Don't think so, sir. I've never told anyone in the service ... until now."

"Well, that could be a nice break for me," Sergeant Renzo said. "How much time you have remaining on mess duty?"

"Just ten days, sir."

"Damn, was hoping it was longer," Sergeant Renzo said, "but anyway, let's get on with the work."

Erik enjoyed his time in the butcher shop; it was good to work at a job where he felt productive and appreciated. But it had to be short-lived because he was scheduled for guard duty soon.

Sergeant Renzo came into the shop just prior to evening meal and said, "Erik, how would you like to stay on in the butcher shop?"

Erik was surprised, "You mean on mess duty, Sergeant Renzo?"

"No, hell no. I mean full-time duty as a meat-cutter."

"You mean no more guard duty?" he asked with even more surprise. "Just change my MOS like that, and become a meat-cutter ... I didn't know it could be done."

"Hell yes, it can be done; in fact it is done, if you want it. I've already told the mess sergeant about your good work. And he agreed ... told me he has approval from the executive officer, if you want to switch."

"Boy, that's kinda fast ..."

"Well, think about it; you haven't done so well promotion-wise in the guard; at least you can make corporal here. That's what the job rates, and you will have liberty every night, and your weekends will be mostly free. Most guard people would kill for it," he said.

Erik hadn't thought of the free time, liberty every night, no more sleeping in the guard shack ... and make corporal in a short time.

"I'll take the job, sir. And thank you, I'll do some good work."

"I'm glad to hear it. You start full-time in the morning."

It was difficult for Erik to realize that the change happened so quickly, but he was happy with his new assignment. He liked Gunny Renzo, and he enjoyed the shop.

THE BUTCHER SHOP WAS RELATIVELY SMALL, BUT ADEQUATE FOR THE JOB. IT WAS off to one side of the mess hall's large galley, and Erik guessed the shop was twenty feet long and maybe twelve feet wide. Two walk-in coolers, one for freezing, the other for cold storage, made up the starboard bulkhead. The port bulkhead, made of cement blocks, supported a stainless holding table, an electric band saw, and a grinder. There was a meat-cutting block in the center of the shop and a deep sink in the corner.

The shop entrance opened to the galley, and the door was made of chain link material that could be locked for security and still provide visibility. Opposite the entrance, at the other end of the shop, was a window that opened to one of the navy yard's old brick streets. It was a weird-looking window, tall and narrow, maybe shoulder width, made of two layers of frosted glass with chicken wire in between. *It's more of a small door than a window ... can't see through it, nor does it allow much daylight to pass through.*

On his second day as a full-time meat-cutter, he and Sergeant Renzo were cutting meat for the next day's menu when Erik heard two knocks on the window. Sergeant Renzo reacted with some irritation as he went over and cranked it open. He leaned outside and quietly talked to a person. Erik couldn't see who it was, but it sounded like a man's voice. Sergeant Renzo then went into the cooler and returned with a cardboard box, perhaps twice the size of a shoe box. He handed the person the package and then closed the window. He returned to the cutting block and continued his work. Moments lated he said to Erik, "That was a friend of mine — told him I would bring in some tools that he wanted to borrow. We exchange a lot of things ... ya know how friends are." Erik nodded in agreement, and they continued their work.

Twenty minutes later there was another knock on the window, and Sergeant Renzo repeated the process of cranking it open. He then went into the cooler and came out with another box. Erik was more curious this time, so he moved to get a better view of the visitor. *Christ, she's beautiful ... a real knockout.* He tried to hear what they were saying, but it was mostly inaudible. There was, however, a raised voice at intervals, and Erik sensed that there was some dissension in the conversation. The meeting ended, and Sergeant Renzo returned to the block. "That was my girl," he said without smiling.

"She was gorgeous," Erik said, "looks like a class act."

"Yea, she is. Wish I could afford her."

"She's expensive?" Erik asked.

"You got that right, especially for a gunny sergeant who's going through a separation."

"I didn't know you were married, Gunny," Erik said.

"Yea, five years ... my wife has the house, and I share a flat with a marine buddy. Wife and I did all right until the Korean tour."

"I guess war can be rough on a marriage," Erik said.

"Sure as hell can. ... You try to stay alive and be straight-arrow, but thirteen months is a long time."

"Yea, I can imagine."

The gunny never said any more that day about his marriage, and very little about his expensive girlfriend, but Erik sensed that he was under considerable pressure. He guessed that there was more to the story than he was going to hear.

That afternoon during work, Erik noticed that the gunny was fidgety, maybe apprehensive; he said he would leave early to take care of some business. Shortly after that, Erik heard another two raps on the window. *Christ, this must be Grand Central Station. ... What the hell is going on?*

The gunny cranked the window open and assumed his usual posture of leaning out to talk to the visitor. Erik could barely hear the subdued voices, but he definitely heard a man's voice, and it didn't sound friendly.

"What do you mean, today?" the gunny exclaimed. "You said next week!"

The other voice increased in volume, became more intense, and Erik was able to hear what was said.

"Listen asshole, I'm tired of fucking with you," the other voice said, "I gave you a break, and you're still trying to fuck me out of it; you pay up, or you'll pay the price, got that?"

"Look ... I don't have it now, but I will get it," the gunny said, "I thought you said Friday ... just a couple more days, and you have your money. Trust me, it was an honest mistake."

"Sure, honest my ass, but let me give you an honest reminder of what's going to happen if you can't pay on Friday."

Erik couldn't see what was going on, but it sounded like Gunny was in trouble, so Erik headed toward him. He heard a gasping sound, and then he saw Gunny jerk upright and turn away from the window. His hands were tucked under his apron.

"It's okay, Erik," Sergeant Renzo said, "just a little disagreement. You close that goddamn window; I have to get some stuff out of the cooler." He went into the cooler and closed the door.

Erik glanced out the window, but the person was gone. He tried to recap what happened as he cranked the window closed. *It all happened so fast, and I'm sure it was over money. And what the hell did happen?* Then he heard a thump-like noise from inside the cooler. Quickly, he jerked open the cooler door, and he was not prepared for the scene; Gunny Renzo was on one knee grasping his bloody left hand. Laying beside him was a beef loin that had been hanging on a meat hook.

"Holy shit, Gunny, you gonna be okay?" Erik asked. "What the hell happened?"

"Oh goddammit, you'll never believe it, Erik. I was taking the loin down when I slipped and caught my hand on the hook. ... Can you believe that shit?"

"Christ, that looks nasty," Erik said, "let me get you a towel to stop the bleeding ... think it went through the hand?"

"Yea, think it did."

"Well, hang on a second ..." And Erik scurried out and picked up a fresh clean towel, then hustled back to the cooler. He wrapped it tightly around the Gunny's hand and then helped him out to the shop where he took a seat on one of the crates against the bulkhead.

"Gunny, why don't you take a breather while I get the mess sergeant, and we'll get you over to sick bay."

Erik saw the mess sergeant, Master Sergeant Mario, over by his office, and he called out, "We've had an accident, sir ... Gunny Renzo, needs help!"

Sergeant Mario turned without a word and headed toward the butcher shop. "What happened, Jim?" he said when he saw the gunny.

"Oh, just fucked up, Mario ... I'll be all right with some stitches or something."

"Can you walk?"

"Hell, yes, I can walk." And they departed for sick bay. Sergeant Mario told Erik to remain on the job.

After they departed, Erik went into the cooler and looked at the meat hook. It was covered with fresh blood.

Master Sergeant Mario came by the shop the next morning and told Erik that Gunny Renzo would be okay, but would be on sick leave for thirty days. The meat hook had penetrated through the hand and screwed up a bone or two.

"Did you see what happened, Larsen?" he asked.

"No, sir, not really ... some kind of an argument — or words, I should say. It wasn't loud, but I did hear a man's voice; then the talk ended suddenly when I headed over towards the window. I didn't see the man when I looked out. He was gone. And I didn't see any blood before Gunny went into the cooler ... his hands were kind of hidden, though. Then I went into the meat cooler, where I saw the meat hook, and it was covered with blood."

"Kind of strange," Sergeant Mario said, "but I'll get the story ... Well, the main thing is that he's going to be all right. Now we have to get down to business; can you handle this while he's away?"

"Yes, sir, from what I've seen it should be no problem. A couple of extra nights maybe, but no big deal."

"Good, I'll get you some help when you need it. ... Now, we have to get together for next week's menu planning; meet at my office at 1300, any problems?"

"No, sir, I will be there."

Erik entered Master Sergeant Mario's óffice at 1300. The chief cook, the baker, and Sergeant Stoops, the pit boss, were also there. Sergeant Mario told them that Erik would sit in for Gunny Renzo because of his accident. He immediately got down to business and went over the next week's menu. He came to the meat requirements and said to Erik, "You see any problems, Larsen?"

"No, sir, but I have a suggestion."

"All right, shoot."

"Well, I've seen some waste of good cuts, sir, you know, top round for hamburger that goes into SOS and things like that.* We should use front quarter and save the better cuts to make into minute steaks for steak and eggs at breakfast. At least a couple times a week. Gunny Renzo said we get four hindquarters a week, and that's more than enough for steak-night and breakfast steaks."

Sergeant Mario didn't reply; he looked at Erik … and then, all looked at Erik. He wished he had kept his mouth shut. *Now I've pissed the boss off. I'm nothing but a damn know-it-all.*

Sergeant Mario finally said, "What do you mean by four hindquarters?"

"Well, sir, that's what I was told."

"Hell, you get six hindquarters a week … I do the ordering," he said.

Erik was surprised. He knew Gunny had told him four … *Where in hell were they?* But he figured he may as well go for broke. "Well, I'm sorry, sir, I was misinformed, but if we get six, I know I could put out steak and eggs every morning. Could almost guarantee it, sir."

The others looked at each other as if they were thinking, "What the hell is going on, and who's this young shit?"

Then Sergeant Mario said, "Okay, Larsen, try it for Wednesday, and we'll take it from there. Don't fuck up Thursday steak-night, though. I'm counting on you, Erik."

Christ, can you believe it? He called me Erik.

Wednesday came and breakfast was a success, as were all the meals the next two weeks. The troops loved the option of steak and eggs for breakfast, and he heard decent feedback about Thursday nights. "The best steaks ever," he was told on occasions.

Erik was working at night when Master Sergeant Mario came in with two of the guard company officers, a First Lieutenant Jones and a Captain

---

* SOS: creamed beef on toast called "shit on the shingle"

Pierce. Erik recognized them from guard mount inspections, and he was somewhat concerned that they were visiting the shop at night.

Sergeant Mario looked serious when he said, "Larsen, you know these gentlemen; they are going to ask a few questions. They know you haven't been here long, so answer the best you can."

Erik damn near had a seizure. *What could they possibly want?*

The captain did the talking, "We hear that you're doing a good job here, Larsen, or I should say, Erik, it is Erik isn't it?"

"Yes, sir."

"Well, Erik, we want to know more about the policy here at the butcher shop. Inventory, security, things like that. Now, have you ever seen anything go out of here that wasn't used in the galley?"

"No, sir."

"So, to your knowledge, everything out of here is used for the troops."

"Yes, sir."

"Well, Erik, how do we account for the fact that we seem to have more beef available since you arrived," Captain Pierce asked as he smiled. "You haven't been donating to the Corps, have you?"

"No, sir," Erik said. "I don't know, sir ... maybe I'm getting more usage out of the cuts, or better estimates, but not that much ... you know, I'm sure Sergeant Renzo was doing a good job."

"We're sure he was also, but you think closely. Nothing goes out of here unaccounted for ... like packages, boxes?"

Oh shit ... the window. "Well, sir, I was just thinking of meat ... but I did see a couple of boxes go out of here through that window."

The three glanced at each other, and the captain asked more seriously, "And who did that?"

"Gunny Renzo, sir, the first couple days we worked together before his accident. He passed a box to his friend outside the window. ... He said it was a box of tools from home. Funny though, he kept the box in the cooler. The other box went to his girlfriend; he said he had cut her a steak ... I forgot about that. Said they allowed him a steak or two if the meat was going bad."

"Who were 'they'?"

"Don't know, sir, he never said, and I didn't think any more about it."

"Did he ever offer you any steaks?"

"Yes, sir, but I told him no thanks because I didn't have a place, or a girl." *What a stupid answer that was.* But it was the truth. The visit was not going well.

"Then you haven't accepted anything out of here?"

"No, sir, I … oh damn. Yes, sir, I have … I'm sorry, sir, didn't mean to cuss. And, yes sir, he gave me a stick of pepperoni … and I took it."

Erik watched them look at each other again. *Christ, I'm dead. How in the hell could I be so fucking dumb?*

"And what did you do with it, Larsen … sell it?"

"Oh, no, sir, we ate it."

"Who's we?"

"I took it to the slop chute, and whoever was off guard duty. We ate it, sir … with a beer."

"So you and the troops had some pepperoni that Gunny Renzo gave you?"

"Yes, sir, I'm sorry. I never thought about it as stealing or anything. … I guess it was … wasn't it, sir?"

Captain Pierce looked straight at Erik and said, "No, it wasn't, son. He was your boss, and he was a staff NCO, a gunny sergeant, and you are a young PFC. As far as we're concerned you are a damn good marine, doing one helluva job. Keep up the good work. … And another thing Erik, you are not further involved in this investigation. Thank you for your integrity."

A MONTH LATER, ERIK WAS BUSY IN THE SHOP, CUTTING MEAT. HE NEVER SAW Gunny Renzo again. *Kind of sad … court-martialed, and found guilty of selling the stolen meat.* He was awarded a bad conduct discharge.

Master Sergeant Mario was transferred somewhere, but Erik heard that he wasn't court-martialed. He only received an unsatisfactory fitness report.

And he never heard a word about the accident … or the loan shark. And the weird-looking window, Erik had to smile when he turned and looked at it. *It will be a cold day in hell before I ever crank you open.* They had welded it shut.

CHAPTER THIRTY-SIX

A NEW MESS SERGEANT CHECKED IN FOR DUTY, AND ERIK WAS SUDDENLY transferred back to guard company. He never received a satisfactory explanation. Guard was undermanned and needed him," they said. He suspected that the transfer was related to the package out the window incidents. The transfer was a shock to Erik, and he was most discouraged, almost despondent.

It was a difficult time, back on guard and still a stateside PFC, *about as low as you can be,* he thought. He had his doubts that he would ever amount to a damn thing. *Maybe Burt was right, seems as though everything I try ... turns to shit.*

He was afraid he was losing his faith, his love of God, his belief that things always work out for the best. But he knew within that he couldn't give up, regardless of how tempting. It was a struggle in the seminary, and it was a struggle outside. He had to do better, and he doubled his efforts to regain his fervency, zeal, and his zest for life. Erik summed it up; I want to be a better person, and, with the help of God and hard work, I will be.

Erik had just completed another exciting four-hour watch guarding the East River. *I must be doing one hell of a job,* he thought as he smiled; *no one stole the river. It's still there in all its stinking glory. But it's better than post eight with our queer buddies on the fence line — on their knees. And then arguing the moral and legal implications with my good friend, Private Skinner.* Erik had to laugh when he thought of their previous conversation.

The sergeant of the guard came up and said, "Larsen, you are scheduled tomorrow morning to take a test over at the center. Transportation departs the shack at 0700."

"Yes, sir, do you know what kind of test?"

"No, they didn't tell me, but it's written, and others are going ... Perhaps it's your corporal's test." Erik had passed the test before, but it didn't seem to make a difference because the promotions went to the returning combat vets. And Erik had to agree; he thought they deserved it. It was just an unfortunate situation for Erik and others in the same position. Promotion would have to wait.

The next morning Erik and fifteen other enlisted took the tests. And they were not all promotion tests, at least his wasn't. It was an education test of some sort, covering math, English, physics, and science. The only part he felt really comfortable with was English because he had just completed the college correspondence course.

Three weeks and many uneventful guard duties later, Erik was ordered to report to the commanding officer, Colonel Damen. The order to report was not good news to Erik. Nobody goes to the Old Man and comes out in better shape. *Christ, why didn't I join the French Foreign Legion? I know why, because I can't speak French. Oh well, what can they do to me? Probably make me a PFC and send me to guard company.*

He reported to the adjutant, "Sir, PFC Larsen reporting to see the Commanding Officer as ordered, sir."

"Colonel Damen will see you now," the adjutant said, a chief warrant officer. "You proceed directly front and center, three feet from the colonel's desk, stand at attention, and report. You may go in now ... and Larsen, good luck."

Why did he say "good luck?" Erik wondered. I must be in more trouble than I imagined.

Erik entered the CO's office, and he was jarred by the formality, the professional décor of the room. It was a well lit, carpeted office with Colonel Damen sitting behind a large oak desk framed by two seven-foot flags on staffs. The American flag was on his starboard; the Marine Corps flag with streamers stood on the port side. Large photographs of Harry S. Truman, the president of the United States, and General Shoup, the commandant of the Marine Corps, hung behind the desk on either side of a huge globe and anchor that shouted, Semper Fidelis. Erik almost forgot to report to Colonel Damen, the one individual who had more control over his life than any person he knew. And that included Burt, his father.

He snapped to attention, front and center, and reported professionally.

Colonel Damen looked up, removed his shaded glasses, and said, "Stand at ease, Larsen."

Erik stood at parade rest because he was unable to be "at ease" in front of the colonel. *His command presence is awesome* ...The Colonel was a formidable figure with his blue steel eyes, tanned body, and six rows of colorful ribbons, that included a navy cross and two purple hearts. Erik heard he was one helluva combat marine, and he had to agree because he sure as shit looked like one.

"You're out of the butcher shop and on guard duty?" he asked.

"Yes, sir."

"Good. I imagine that you were surprised with the orders, but I made the change ... Do you know why?"

"No, sir, but I thought maybe it had to do with the incident, the meat shortage incident," Erik said, displaying some nervousness.

"Well, the situation did call for a clean house, but that's not why I pulled you out of there."

"Yes, sir," Erik replied while trying to control the multitude of negative thoughts.

"Every year or so, the Commandant initiates a small program for a limited number of enlisted men to become Marine Corps officers. There is such a screening program now, and I took the liberty of recommending you for the course. I assume this is satisfactory with you?"

Erik couldn't speak; he was in a state of minor shock. He could only hear the words, "Marine Corps officer."

"Larsen, are you with me?" the colonel said as he was smiling. "Did you hear what I said?"

"Yes, sir," Erik said quietly, still in a state of bewilderment.

"Well, I must say you made an impression with the Staff NCO's, as well as with a couple of my officers; they all recommended you. You must be doing damn fine work, and I commend you for it."

"Thank you, sir," Erik said. He smiled when he thought about the frozen milk and the morning steak and eggs.

"And I put you back in guard, so we could change your MOS back to infantry ... I won't recommend a cook and baker MOS to become an officer," he said as he grinned.

"I'm just too much front line, I guess."

"Well thank you, sir," Erik repeated, "I appreciate it, sir."

"Good luck, Erik," the colonel said as he stood up, "Oh, by the way, your orders arrived this morning. You have been accepted and will report to Quantico for the Officer's Candidate Screening Course. You start in ten days. Congratulations, Erik ... and don't let the Old Man down."

"No, sir," he stammered.

Holy shit, Erik thought, as he was leaving the office. *Is this for real? It has to be; it's from the Old Man himself. Christ, can it possibly be?*

The adjutant met Erik at the colonel's door, "Congratulations Erik, you should be very proud. It's not an easy course to get into, less than a hundred out of the entire Marine Corps. That's over two hundred thousand troops. And we know you can do it."

"Thank you, Gunner. I just haven't grasped it all. It's just so damn amazing."

Erik made his way to the guard shack, and he wasn't sure his feet were touching the pavement. He didn't care.

As he entered the shack, he heard a voice call out, "Attention on deck ... officer aboard."

"Erik snapped to attention, as did the three staff NCO's inside. They were all looking at Erik without breaking ranks, and, finally, Gunny Sergeant Ormond said, "That's officer candidate Erik Larsen aboard."

Erik realized what they had done, and he couldn't stop blushing. With the finest military demeanor he could muster, he turned and said, "At ease, gentlemen, I'm just passing through."

CHAPTER THIRTY-SEVEN

HE TEN DAYS PASSED, AND ERIK CHECKED INTO MARINE CORPS SCHOOLS at Quantico, Virginia. He thought that it was probably the best ten days he had ever experienced. After his meeting with Colonel Damen, he was promptly relieved from the river fence line posts, and put on the elite Admiral's gate. The staff NCO's shook his hand in congratulations, and the lowly enlisted, like himself, buddied up to him. And even the Korean vets gave him attention. And there was his mom, Rose, who upon hearing the news on the phone, cried out with joy, and his dad, Burt who said, "That's good, now you can get your meat-cutting job back, and maybe do something right."

"No, I don't think so, Dad," Erik replied. "Marine officers don't do that kind of work." *That man is never going to be proud of me, but what the hell ... I haven't made it yet, anyway.*

IT WAS A BEAUTIFUL SUNDAY AFTERNOON, AND ALL OF THE NEW OFFICER CANDIDATES were assembled on the athletic field, awaiting the first encounter with their instructors and the welcome-aboard speech.

Three sharply dressed marine officers, a major and two captains, arrived and took charge of the gathering. The major did the speaking. "Gentlemen, may I have your attention?" he announced. "Please fall in, three ranks, and stand at rest."

God, I'm going to enjoy this. He didn't scream, and he didn't call us fuck-heads.

They all joined ranks, and the major continued, "Welcome aboard, marines. My name is Van Arsdale, Major Van Arsdale. My two assistants with me are Captain Mitchell and Captain Winford. They are your monitors, and you will probably celebrate the day when you last see them — at least in this course.

That day is thirty days away, the day that half of this formation, thirty-two of you, will walk off the stage as second lieutenants in the United States Marine Corps. Who that will be is your decision." Major Van Arsdale ceased talking for a moment, probably to let the words "your decision" sink in.

"During this course," he continued, "you will not wear any rank insignia, except a pair of silver lettered OCSC pins, on your collars. You will not be addressed as Sarge, Gunny, Ace, or shitheads. It will be Sir or Candidate. You will not be debased with profanity, nor will you be ridiculed; this is not a boot camp, although, because of the focus on the physical aspect, you may think so at times. You are here because somebody thought you were outstanding marines with the potential of becoming an officer. Many of you are decorated combat veterans, in World War II, in Korea, some in both. I commend you for your sacrifices. The younger candidates may not have had their opportunity to serve in combat, but their day will come. If you choose not to complete this screening course or are unable to do so because of any circumstance, you will not be considered a failure; you will not be degraded, and you will not be humiliated. You will be reassigned duty of your choice, as one of the Corps' best. Are there any questions so far?"

The candidates looked and remained quite. Major Van Arsdale continued, "Do not think of this as a school. We do not teach you. That will come later for the fortunate in Officer's Basic School. Our mission is to evaluate you, then select the upper fifty percent to be commissioned. You will be graded on your professionalism, your present and potential abilities, your leadership qualities. You are here for one purpose, one purpose only, and that purpose is to show us ... no, prove to us, that you have the desire, the loyalty, the professionalism to be a marine corps officer. It's that simple. We provide you with the opportunity to succeed, and we provide the same opportunity to fail. It is your determination." He turned to his assistants and said, "Captain Mitchell, Captain Winford, you will lead our candidates through their welcome-aboard warm-up."

"Aye, sir," they responded as they snapped to and saluted.

"Gentlemen," Captain Mitchell said, "half of you will line up across the field with me. The rest with Captain Winford. We are going to do one-hundred-yard sprints. We will set the pace, and we will sprint until we, your monitors, tire ... or think you've had enough, whichever comes first." The two officers grinned at each other. Some candidates smiled, others had the thousand-yard stare.

Captain Winford added, "Gentlemen, do not let the fact that Captain Mitchell was a long runner alternate for the 1948 World Olympics intimidate your performance."

"But that was four years ago, Wins," Captain Mitchell said while laughing. "And gentlemen, don't let the fact that Captain Winford was there with me … not as a long-runner, but just a sprinter … intimidate your performance either." They laughed again, and most candidates smiled; some began to pale.

"Any questions?" Captain Mitchell asked as he looked over his newcomers.

"Sir, what if we can't do all of the sprints, sir?" asked one of the older, deep-voiced veterans.

"Oh yes," Captain Mitchell replied, "I neglected to tell you … we don't care how many you run, but we do care how you run them. You complete the sprints with us, or you run until you regurgitate, it counts the same. Or you decide not to run and that doesn't count the same; you decide not to run and you choose to fail the program."

Erik looked at the other candidates, and they seemed to be in the same state of semi-shock that he was.

"Gentlemen, we are not here to break you. We are here to evaluate your desire and your potential to be an officer," said Captain Winford in a serious tone. "That means we have to have a measure of sorts, and today you are measured on whether you quit, complete, pass out, or puke."

"Or any combinations of the above," added Captain Mitchell as he grinned. "We will now commence our sprints."

Erik lined up abeam Captain Mitchell, and he noticed the painted red cross on the military field ambulance that took position on the edge of the grass. *Things are getting serious now … never, ever forget what you're here for, Erik. This will be your only chance.*

THREE WEEKS PASSED, AND THE COURSE WAS DRAWING TO A CLOSE. ERIK WAS still a candidate; he was lucky; many had dropped because of various reasons. Only forty-two candidates remained, and the final field exercise would claim a few more. The exercise that was supposed to separate the winners from the weak and the infirmed would take place the next two days. The winners would be the ones to wear a set of new gold bars.

He smiled when he reflected on that first day, the afternoon of the warm-up sprints. It was a fitting day in that it set the tempo for the remainder of the course. He and many others threw-up that day, and a few of the older candidates were still doing it.

Each day (except Sundays) the grueling routine started at daylight and ended in the hours of darkness. The physical training included obstacle courses, field trips, forced marches, hand-to-hand combat, swimming relays, and morning exercises to loosen the body up (in case you were still alive).

The normal routine also included a daily two-hour period of problem solving in the field. The course had preplanned situations that required teamwork and a logical thought process to find reasonable solutions. These course problems were situations such as deep river and ravine crossings, scaling of cliffs and other high barriers, transporting the wounded, construction of makeshift weapons, survival, and enemy evasion. The ground rules, necessary assumptions, and the equipment (or lack of) were issued for each situation.

Erik and the other candidates were divided into four-or-five-man teams that were assigned a problem. A time limit was set fot the teams to physically demonstrate the solution. The team personnel were changed daily without a designated leader, and they were encouraged to vocally express their thought processes during the search for a proper resolution. The monitors would silently observe this process, and grade each member on their participation. They were specifically graded on their rationale, logic, physical ability, cooperation and leadership. Erik enjoyed the challenge of these exercises, and even though shy at first, he felt confident that he would be recognized for his participation.

And there was some weapons training — just a half-day on the pistol range — because, traditionally, officers carried pistols. One young candidate asked, "Why carry pistols when they were so inaccurate, compared to rifles? Wouldn't they be useless in combat?"

Captain Winford laughed, then he said, "I agree somewhat, but you carry one for shooting your horse … or yourself … if either of you breaks a leg."

In your spare time, you were encouraged to read and study the *Officer's Code of Conduct.* The code that definitively sets the minimum standards expected and required of all Marine Corps commissioned officers. Basically, the code reads that you are an officer and gentleman, by act of Congress, and you will act like one, morally and professionally, or you will be replaced by one that will. "No big deal," Major Van Arsdale said, "It's just your job and career, if caught screwing up."

Erik was impressed with the code. It covered every conceivable facet of commissioned officers' behavior. Major Van Arsdale summed it up by saying, "You can do nothing that would bring discredit to your uniform, your country, your God. And that covers a lot of ground when you think about it." he said. "Things like loyalty, honor, and duty are taken for granted, but the code covers much more, such as guidelines that will enable you to become a professional. Terms such as intoxication, adultery, morals, command presence, dignity, discipline, respect, integrity, leadership, décor, propriety, protocol, gambling, etiquette, esteem, demeanor, courage, reserve, intelligence, modesty, moderation, decisiveness, compassion, scruples, physical appearance, polish, and poise are just a few that you will deal with during your entire career."

"And I haven't even touched upon the behavior of wives, girlfriends, and children who are your responsibility as well, not to mention delinquent debts, unkempt lawns, and dirty vehicles ... should I go on?" he asked as he smiled. "You will learn all of this in basic school ... it's not that tough. Just be above reproach as an officer, a gentleman, a husband, bachelor, father, neighbor, and citizen ... and ..." He smiled again, shook his head, and departed.

Holy Christ ... what kind of life is left? I may never get laid.

Later that day, during a break, Erik was talking to some of his classmates about the major and his summary of the code. One of the old-timers, still aboard as a candidate, Gunny Sims, told the group that he had an old friend who was commissioned, and this friend gave him his summarized example of the code — his transition from enlisted, as he put it.

"Yep, he gave me some key words of wisdom," Gunny Sims said. "Neat things like, don't holler 'fuck' at the bar; don't urinate in the punch bowl; don't pass gas in dress whites; don't throw up at the general's reception, and don't bring as your guest, a stripper who gives nickel blow-jobs and free fucks; and don't ask the General's wife to show us your tits; don't spear the hors' d'oeuvres with your dress sword; and don't use improper calling cards such as, 'Have dick, will travel.' And do not moon the commanding officer's children, and you don't hang around school zones attired in nothing but a poncho. And, when invited to the White House for a state dinner, don't goose the first lady with your swagger stick, and … don't wipe your ass on the drapes. And never, never, ever … start your favorite joke with, 'Mister President, did you hear the one about these two Chinese cocksuckers?"

CHAPTER THIRTY-EIGHT

THE BUS WAS FILLED WITH CANDIDATES. FILLED WITH DIRTY, GRIMY, exhausted candidates. It was midday when they completed their last field exercise, and they were too depleted to cheer.

Erik and the others had started the twenty-mile forced march with full field packs yesterday morning before daylight. They set up camp that evening in the wooded hills of Virginia, and, almost immediately after the last shelter was secured in the darkness, the camp came under attack by cherry bombs. They are large heavy-duty firecrackers that are used to simulate incoming mortar fire. The explosions were numerous and irritating to the ears; the intense flashes of light caused temporary night blindness, confusion, and disorientation. Captain Winford or Captain Mitchell would run through the site yelling, "Incoming, incoming ... move out troops ... break camp, move out, and follow me!"

Erik set up camp three or four times that night (he couldn't remember), and each time they would receive more incoming and break camp and race through the dark underbrush again. Much of their personal equipment was strewn throughout the area, and the damage from the tree branches, thorns, and vines left a visible mark on each marine. The exposed skin of the face, hands, and neck were blotched with a combination of scratches, cuts, mud, and dried blood that they had accumulated throughout the night. They were a disheartened, listless group of candidates. And they were silent, as Erik was, because they were all too weary to make conversation.

In the morning they had rendezvoused in a designated zone some fifteen to twenty miles from home barracks. When they approached the cleared zone, Erik could see Major Van Arsdale in his jeep parked by a Marine Corps bus and a field ambulance. *God that bus looks good ... it will be a blessing to give these sore feet and this tired body some relief. May even catch a little shut-eye on the way in. Thank, God, it's over ... and I didn't drop out as some did.*

"I know it has been a rough thirty-hours," the Major announced, "and I commend each of you that made it. I had intended to provide bus transportation to the barracks, but, unfortunately, it's mechanical, and mechanical things break. I apologize, but we have no alternative but to march back. Captain Winford will set the pace, and you should cover the seventeen miles in less than five hours. And remember, as always, the field ambulance will follow to assist any stragglers or dropouts. Also, my jeep is available for any that would rather return with me. Good luck, *Semper Fi* … and move them out Captain Winford."

"Aye, sir." And the troops reacted with a spattering of moans and "fucks."

"Fall in-trail, and let's move out … I'll take the point," Captain Winford ordered. And the unhappy troops formed and slogged off down the road at a decent pace. Erik noticed one candidate get into the jeep; he didn't recognize who it was. Poor bastard, he was so close to making it. *Thank God, it wasn't me,* he thought, as he grinned. *No fucking way will I give up. … They're not going to break me. I'll die first. And the way it's going, I may have to.*

They were on the road an hour while the sun bore down, taking its toll. Erik saw two candidates drop to the side, apparently finished. *Christ that's sad. I'm on your side, God … please be on mine.*

And the file moved on with only the sounds of leather boots hitting the dirt road. They rounded a bend, and there it was in all of its Marine Corps color. A bus was waiting, with its engine running. Captain Mitchell stepped out and announced, "Gentlemen, the field exercise is over. Please board your transportation, and we will proceed to home plate. I caution you to remain awake. … Do not let your buddy sleep. Upon arrival, you will remain seated until called." *Why do they care if we are awake?*

When the bus arrived, the candidates remained seated as directed. A staff sergeant appeared at the bus door and stated, "Candidate Baker, will you follow me, sir?"

Erik watched Baker follow the sergeant to a small white building aside the barracks. Baker entered, and the staff sergeant returned. Within minutes, he repeated the process with another name.

Erik fought sleep in the hot, humid bus. He was reminded of his first stinking locker room the day he started his football career. He had to smile. *God, I hope I do better today than I did then … so long ago, and now …* "Candidate

Larsen," the voice said, "please follow me, sir."

Erik followed the staff sergeant to the white building, and he saw another candidate come out. The candidate was pale, teary-eyed. *What the hell is going on?* Erik was frightened, confused.

He entered the building and was startled to see all three monitors seated in the small room. *How could they have had time to get here for this?* he wondered.

Major Van Arsdale was behind a desk, and he was in full dress "A" uniform. Captain Winford was on his starboard, dressed in a white tennis outfit and sitting on a fold-up steel chair. Captain Mitchell was on the port side, suited in athletic warm-ups, and he was also seated on a steel chair.

"Candidate Larsen, thank you for coming in," the major said. "I'm sorry you had to wait so long."

"There was no problem, sir," Erik replied.

"Please sit down, and we will begin your evaluation."

The word evaluation shook Erik; he hadn't realized that the end was so near. It startled him to come down to the last phase.

He took the chair that was in front of the desk. The bulkhead behind the chair was no more than six feet away, and Erik felt crowded. *Perhaps I'm just tired,* he reasoned.

"What do you think of our course, Larsen?" the major asked.

"It was tough, sir, but I enjoyed the course."

Thump ... went the ball as it slammed into the bulkhead above Erik's head.

Christ, he's throwing a goddamn ball. I can't believe it, Captain Winford is throwing a tennis ball.

Thump ... it went again, this time closer to his head.

"Well, that's good ... Now, how do you think you did with the course?"

Thump ... the ball bounced off the bulkhead and back to Captain Winford. *Damn that ball!*

"Well, sir, you know better than I do ... but I hope I did well. No, not only hope ... but I think I did well."

Thump ...

"How would you rate your monitors?"

Thump ... Christ, what a loaded questio ... I'm sitting here with them, and

I'd like to shove that goddamn ball up a monitor's ass.

"I thought Captains Winford and Mitchell did a great job, sir ... two fine officers ... never asked you to do what they couldn't."

Thump ...

"Does that ball bother you, Larsen?" the major asked. He looked concerned.

Thump ... Erik was getting a little pissed. *Don't lose it, Erik ... just hang in there.*

"No, sir, it's rather annoying. But nothing I can't cope with."

Thump ...

"That's good," the major replied. "Now, Candidate Larsen, why do you suppose you failed the course?"

Failed the course ... that can't be ... not this close and lose it. Not my dream ... oh shit no! It can't be over!

Thump ... the ball almost hit him.

Erik had to pull himself together. "Sir ... I don't think I failed the course ... I did everything asked, and I did it well, sometimes better. I'm shocked. I can't believe I didn't make it."

Thump ... went the fucking ball, and Erik was almost in tears. It was difficult to breathe.

Major Van Arsdale turned to Captain Mitchell, who was looking at some papers on his clipboard. "Captain Mitchell ... Larsen says that he did a good job with this course. What does your record show?"

Thump ... went the ball ... and Erik didn't hear it.

"Sir, my records show ... here it is, sir."

The ball came straight at Erik's head, and he abruptly raised his left hand and made a dead-on catch. *Fuck that ball, and the horse it came in on.*

Major Van Arsdale looked at the record, "Oh, yes, I must have been thinking of the other Larsen (Erik didn't know another Larsen). This is Erik ... is that correct, Captain Mitchell?"

"Yessir, this is Erik Larsen."

"Well, it says right here on this paper that Erik Larsen is ... well, I'll be darn ... recommended to be selected as a second lieutenant in the United States Marine Corps. Congratulations Erik!"

Erik was dazed. Five minutes ago, he thought he failed ... now, all he was aware of were the words, "commissioned as a second lieutenant."

It took a moment to reply, "Thank you, sirs ... I don't know how to ..."

The three officers stood up to shake hands, and when Erik extended his hand to do so, he realized he had the ball in it. *God, how stupid I am. They must think I'm a complete dumb-ass.*

He glanced up at Captain Winford who smiled, and then winked at Erik. He handed him the ball. And then Major Van Arsdale shook his hand, "Erik, you did a good job. ... Thirty-five of them didn't, but you passed the course," he said as he smiled at Captain Winford. "You passed our little stress test."

"Thank you, sir," Erik repeated, "I appreciate all the help, sirs."

"Congratulations, Erik," the major said, "or, I should say, congratulations, Lieutenant Larsen. Well ... not really until Sunday."

I can't believe all this beautiful news. Thank you, God, thank you.

Erik looked at Captain Winford, and they both smiled. He handed Erik the ball, and after a moment's hesitation, Erik yelled, "Yes!" as he hurled the ball against the other bulkhead. *God, I love this fucking ball.*

CHAPTER THIRTY-NINE

O N SUNDAY MORNING, ERIK STEPPED ONTO THE STAGE, AND MAJOR General Martin, the first marine general Erik had ever seen, pinned on the gold bars, then shook his hand. At twenty years and two months, Erik became the youngest officer in the United States Marine Corps. He had beaten the minimum age requirements by two months.

Erik felt ten feel tall when he left the ceremony and received his first salute from an enlisted man. Traditionally, Erik called him back, and said, "Thank you, Sarge. That was my first salute," and then Erik gave him a silver dollar.

Erik called his folks and told them the good news. His mother was overjoyed and said that she always knew that Erik would make it. Then she put Burt on the phone.

"Well, I put the bars on today, Dad. I'm now Lieutenant Larsen," Erik said. It was difficult to conceal his pride.

"Well, I'm glad. I know you must feel good about it … more money, isn't it?"

"Yes, sir, sure is. Four or five times as much," Erik said.

"I was talking to Frank the other day, you know, Frank Lewis the fish broker out of Boston?"

"Yes, sir, I remember him," Erik said.

"Well, he has a son who's a staff sergeant in the marines … and Frank said that it was really an honor to be a marine officer, and I should be very proud of you. He says very few are chosen, and the fact that you don't have a college degree makes it even more difficult. Must have been pretty rough to get."

"It was kind of rough, Dad, but you have to be lucky also."

"Well, that's what I figured … probably more luck than anything. Well, you be sure to work hard and try to stick with it for a change."

"I will, Dad ... you bet I will." Erik had to smile.

Can you believe him? He still isn't proud. But you know what, Erik? You did it without him, and you're damn proud of it ... and he can't take it away.

Then, Erik thought of his mom, and her love and support. Then how his dad worked so hard to feed the house, his family ... and did it. *But, he is screwing around on Mom ... or, he was.*

ERIK'S BASIC SCHOOL CLASS COMMENCED WITHIN A FEW DAYS OF HIS COMMISSION, so there was no chance to take leave for a home town visit to show off his bars.

It was a small class of only fifty officers. Thirty or so from Erik's screening course and the remainder from college graduates participating in the NROTC (Naval Reserve Officers Training Corps) program.

The school was six months in length, and Erik was proud to be included in an officers class of second lieutenant students. It had it's drawbacks, however, because of his lack of education. At times, he had a terrible feeling of inferiority, since most of them were college graduates, and those that didn't have a degree had much more enlisted time in the Corps. The majority had been SNCO's (Staff Non-Commissioned Officers), and that was considered a mark of distinction. Erik's previous experience and his earlier rank of PFC were the lowest in this group of former marines. It was a difficult transition for him, but one that he had to accomplish if he was to be a successful fighter pilot. He knew it would take maximum effort to make the grade (and yes, get the breaks too).

Maybe I don't have it yet, but I will have it. Each day, Erik repeated this thought — *I will have it.*

The instructors (SNCO's and officers) were experienced and effective. They knew that you were capable of learning the many subjects considered necessary. And more important, reasoned Erik, they treated you like officers and gentlemen. *Yes, and I like it. What a difference.*

After a month had passed, Erik received a strange letter from Headquarters, Marine Corps. Addressed to PFC Erik Larsen, it read: "Congratulations. You have been promoted to the rank of corporal in the United States Marine Corps."

Erik was in minor shock. He had to laugh. *Can you believe it? After all those months as a PFC, and couldn't make a promotion ... Now I'm a second lieutenant, and they offer me a reduction to corporal ... Should probably grab it ... yea, sure.*

He took the letter up to personnel in admin, so that they could send a correction to headquarters. He thought it important because some poor clown was denied a promotion (they only make so many) to corporal. He was met by a first Lieutenant Jebs who said, "What can we do for you, Larsen?"

Immediately, Erik disliked him. He was unkempt, short, with little or no command bearing, and, more important, he called Erik by his last name. The first to do so since Erik was commissioned. Also, he didn't wear any Korean or other foreign campaign ribbons, therefore he was non-combat, Erik presumed.

"Well, sir," Erik said, "I received this letter from headquarters, and they stated that I was promoted to the rank of corporal. Kind of funny. Don't you think?"

"And what am I supposed to do?" he asked curtly.

"I don't know, sir. I thought that headquarters should be notified so that they don't waste a promotion ... that's all."

"Then you should notify them," Lt. Jebs said as he turned and disappeared into an office.

What an asshole ... he even looks like that clown at Parris Island, the assistant DI, Corporal Ferret, or something like that. It was Erik's first distasteful encounter with a marine officer. But it was a good lesson for Erik. *No, they're not all gods ... there are some real shitheads. At least, one.* He later found out that Lt. Jebs was a reserve call-up, a passed-over captain, and a non-combat marine.

Basic school was okay, Erik decided, but he looked forward to graduation day. Classes inside were generally a grind, however, he did enjoy the outside class work, such as field tactics. During these exercises, they were assigned various leadership billets for a designated time period. One day as battalion commander, and the next day you could be a squad leader. It gave each student a sample of the different billets and their responsibilities. It was interesting work, Erik concluded, but the real excitement came at the combat range. There, they fired most of the heavier weapons such as the machine guns, flame throwers, mortars (60 and 80 MM), howitzers (105MM) and the 3.5-inch rocket launchers (commonly called bazookas). And all of the weapons fascinated Erik. He loved the firepower. *What a far cry from the seminary. I was going to save lives as a priest, and now I'm learning to blow their asses off. Not sure I'll ever figure it out.*

Erik had to laugh when he thought of his day to fire the 3.5 rocket launcher. It was a close call. He was teamed with Lt. Dick Boswell, and they were to fire two rounds apiece. Both were fired from the shoulder, while kneeling, at one of the tank hulls located downrange. Dick fired the first two rounds with good results. One near miss and one direct hit. It was Erik's turn, and he was one enthused gunner when he lined up the sights to kill the old tank. Just as he was squeezing the trigger to fire the rocket, he was startled by a cry of, "Hold on, Lieutenant," and then running footsteps, and almost instantly, someone grabbed his arm and pulled. Erik reacted with a tug backwards as he turned toward the intruder … and then he heard that unmistakable sound … "Swoosh" … the rocket fired. Erik had fired the rocket … and it didn't head for the tank.

"Holy shit!" Erik yelled.

"Look at that son-of-a-bitch go!" yelled Dick as they stared in awe at the rocket as it arched toward Main-side, Quantico. *I'm dead. They'll have my ass for this.*

The person that had jerked Erik's arm was Captain Tabor, the range officer for the day, and he witnessed the entire event with Dick and Erik. The flabbergasted threesome stood there in passing silence. Capt. Tabor was the first to speak. "Sorry about that, Lieutenant Larsen. I thought I saw something wrong with the launcher … not loaded properly. But, obviously it was. Christ, I shouldn't have tugged your arm. I know better … don't know what happened."

Erik scarcely heard him. He was too captivated with the episode that took place. A small (but dangerous) warhead had raced toward the heart of Quantico. Toward Marine Corps Schools. Toward the barracks. Toward the general's office. *Lord, only knows … it could be anywhere in that area.* The seriousness of the incident overwhelmed Erik's thoughts. He was crushed.

"Think I killed someone, Captain?" he asked in humiliation.

"No, I doubt it," Captain Tabor said, "fortunately we have a large buffer zone around the range … don't think a 3.5 can carry beyond it. Thank God."

"Well, sir, I don't know quite what happened. I know it was my fault … should have handled it differently."

"No, it wasn't your fault, Lieutenant. I'm the one that caused it ... screwed up," the captain said. "Hell, I pulled on you ... right when you were aiming downrange." Again, the three stood in silence, maybe to ponder the situation. Erik's mind was jammed with a multitude of thoughts. All negative. *How could I have been so damn stupid? So fucking dumb?*

Then, Captain Tabor said to Erik and Dick, "As a matter of fact ... let's not say anything ... and if you both agree ... I'll handle it. No use making a fuss if nothing happened ... you know?"

"Yes, sir. No use making a fuss," Erik said as he attempted to breathe normally. And Dick nodded that he agreed with them.

Later, Erik heard a few of his fellow students talking about the stray round at the combat range, but it didn't seem to be a matter of concern. No repercussions, or so it seemed at that time.

Erik was truly impressed. The incident never became an issue. Apparently the buffer zone did the job. And apparently, Captain Tabor did his part to downplay the episode.

Erik, you have to be one lucky person.

WHAT A STRANGE TELEPHONE CALL. AT FIRST ERIK WAS RATHER excited, then he became discouraged. It was Jennie Lee who had called.

"Erik, honey, I'm so sorry I didn't call earlier," she said, in her sexiest voice. "But, I wanted to congratulate you. Heard that you were an officer now ... doing just great."

"Well, thank you, ma'am," he said as he regained his composure. "It's really sweet of you to call." Erik was overjoyed to hear her voice. It brought back the memories, both real and imagined, of the wondrous powdery smells, the touch and taste of her smooth skin, and her cute, perky way.

He had dated other girls on occasion, but actually there was very little time to get involved. It was a tight schedule, and, with all the screw-ups that Erik seemed to generate, he thought he'd better give his *all* to the task at hand. That is, to become a fighter pilot. Then, there would be time for pretty girls.

After the social amenities, and Erik's partial recovery, he said, "Sure would love to see you, Jennie ... but what about Daryl, you know the bear hunter?"

She laughed at that remark. "Oh, I forgot you called him that. Well, Daddy wants me to marry the bear hunter, but I'm not sure if I'm ready to … you know, marry him. I don't think you heard, but Daryl joined the army, and now he's on his way to Korea. I'm kind of glad … not about Korea … but it gives me some time to straighten things out."

Damn, she's free to date … but he's going to Korea. And Erik remembered what they had learned in their code of conduct class. "Well, Jennie, I'm glad you held off on the marriage because I think we could hit it off … but the Korean thing, it can be a real problem. It hurts to say this, but it's a matter of honor with the Marine Corps. You don't date another man's girl while that man is serving in combat. Just not fair … you understand, don't you?"

There was a pause in their conversation, and Erik realized that he had probably acted prematurely when he brought the subject up.

"Well, I guess so," she replied in an uncertain tone, "but I just told you that we may be breaking up … and we're not married or anything."

Erik was hesitant to answer, "I know, sweetheart, but as much as I want to … I can't take the chance. They'd ship my buns to the North Pole … after the court-martial, of course. But, things could work out. You know, after a breakup, or something." *Way to go, Erik. What do you mean "or something?" … gets his ass blown off? You better get a grip, Erik.*

The phone call was not going well. So, they both said a pleasant, "Glad you called and take care of yourself." And it was over.

Christ, what a crock. That joker has to go to Korea. I'll never get to see her.

THE FINAL DAYS OF BASIC SCHOOL ARRIVED. THE STUDENTS THAT REQUESTED flight training had taken their flight physicals and written tests. Ten officers had applied for such, and seven of them passed the demanding requirements. Erik was a lucky one. He passed. *Another plateau… Just a few more to go.*

Erik never questioned why he chose the marines instead of another military service. It was an automatic choice for him. Perhaps it was a way of proving to his father that he could do it. Or perhaps, it was a way to prove to himself that he could do it — to be one of the best. For years he remembered, quite vividly, the day a marine corsair flew over Scantsville and made several passes overhead a house. Probably the house of the pilot's girlfriend, he would imagine.

What a glorious performance. Then to add support for the Corps, Erik had the thrill of seeing the movie, *Flying Leathernecks*. That did it for him. From the time he watched John Wayne airborne in his fighter, there was never a question as to "which service?" Apparently it was just a matter of time when he grew up. Seminary, or no seminary.

Orders to their next duty station arrived. It was an exciting day for all the officer-students. They would graduate and depart basic school within the next two days. Erik and several of his classmates arrived at admin to pick up their orders. First Lt. Jebs passed them out separately, and, when he came to Erik's, he said, "Oh, Larsen, I see you're going to naval flight training ... you're going to be a pilot. Well, that's good, because I don't think you would have made a decent ground officer."

That statement caught Erik by surprise. He knew that it was uncalled for ... He had good grades in basic school.

"Well, maybe not, Lieutenant, but I am going to be one hell of a pilot ... and I *will* serve in combat. And become a real marine."

It must have been a good comeback because Jebs glared at Erik, then went to his office. *Can you believe this clown? Christ, he never lets up.*

Erik hoped he had not overstepped his bounds with his reply to boy wonder, the non-combat who was passed over for promotion. But Erik was glad he had the chance to needle him. It felt good. *Anyway, who cares ... the only item of importance today is the receipt of my orders to flight school.* He had heard that he had been selected for flight training, but this made it official. He was proud, elated, to have made another hurdle.

Later, Erik talked with the other classmates selected for pilot training. They concluded that most grunts (ground officers) resented marine aviators because they received flight pay. "Hell, Erik, they all hate the extra pay we'll get. ... They think grunts are the only ones worth a damn ... and all pay should be equal," said one of the lucky ones. They all agreed. They also agreed that they had more important things to do than worry about the grunts' position on flight pay ... like success as a student aviator and earning their wings of gold.

CHAPTER FORTY

I T WAS ERIK'S FIRST DAY TO FLY IN THE NAVAL AIR TRAINING COMMAND. THE preflight ground school was completed, and now the day had arrived. The day he dreamed of. In a few hours, he would take his first hop in an SNJ trainer.

The home of the Naval Air Command in Pensacola was tough for Erik ... he always seemed to be a day behind in classwork. He reasoned that it took many hours of midnight study to offset his lack of college education. And rightfully so, for there was much to learn in a short time span of six weeks. The basics of principles of flight, power plants, navigation, meteorology, FAA regulations, and many other subject classes that went on during the year's tour, such as celestial navigation, Morse code, and water survival, had to be acquired. There was a good side, however, because most of his flight class was made up of naval and marine cadets who had to take military ground training, such as drill, code of conduct, and military regulations, in addition to all the aviation subjects. Erik, as an ex-enlisted and a Basic School graduate, had completed far more ground training than required, and, therefore, his schedule was not quite as hectic.

But today, ground school classes were not foremost in Erik's thoughts. He was scheduled to fly. And it was difficult to contain his enthusiasm. All the struggle and hard work would soon pay off. *Yes, the ole West Virginia boy done good.*

Attired in his new flight suit, wearing new flight boots, and holding his fresh helmet and gloves, he arrived at flight operations to get his aircraft assignment for the first flight in the syllabus ... somewhat of an orientation flight. "Yessir, I'm Lt. Larsen, scheduled for the 1400 launch," he said to the duty officer who stood behind the counter. "Where do I find my flight instructor, sir?"

"Oh, that's Captain Cahill ... had to go topside. Said he would meet you out at the plane. You go ahead with your preflight, and he'll be there soon as he can. This is your first, right?"

"Yessir, it's my first, and I sure hope I don't screw up."

"Oh, you'll do fine ... everyone's a bit nervous on their first few hops. But you have a good instructor, Korean vet and all ... tough marine, flew Corsairs ... but you'll do all right.* Good luck, Larsen."

"Thank you, sir, will do my best."

Erik walked out on the flight line to find his bird, number 47. *There she is, ... Lord, it looks huge.* He checked the front cockpit and proceeded with the remainder of the preflight inspection. As he closed the left wing fuel cap, Captain Cahill came up and introduced himself.

"Hi, I'm Cahill ... you Larsen?"

"Yessir, that's me. Glad to meet you, sir," he said to the captain. Erik had expected his crew cut instructor to be taller. *Shorter than I ... and his red face doesn't smile much either. And he doesn't seem to be too happy with his job ... maybe, the combat took its toll.*

"You get the preflight done? ... All fueled ... ready to go?"

"Yessir, all fueled and ready to go. Looks good," Erik replied.

"OK, get your ass strapped in, and we'll get out of here. It's damn hot today." Erik and his instructor strapped in. Erik was in the front cockpit, and within moments a navy line crewman came up to the plane and yelled to Captian Cahill, "You ready to crank, sir?"

"Roger, contact," he yelled, and then, before the starter was engaged to turn the prop ... Erik heard his instructor yell, from the back, "Holy shit ... what the hell's going on? ... Larsen!

Erik was startled when he heard his name. It sounded like trouble, and instantly he looked up from the instrument panel ... and he couldn't believe it. A fuel truck had pulled up in front of the plane. For a fleeting moment Erik thought, *this is impossible ... they have made a mistake.* Then a sailor leaped out of the truck and commenced to refuel Erik's aircraft.

Christ, I'm dead.

"Larsen, you asshole; what the goddamn hell is going on? ... Didn't you tell me you checked the fuel? You trying to bust my ass? ... What an idiot ..."

* Corsairs: F4U's

Then, Captain Cahill promptly climbed out of the back seat, looked up at the terrified Erik, and said, "That's it for today, dummy."

And apparently in disgust, Captain Cahill departed for operations.

Erik was damn near paralyzed with fear ... and shame. *Well, I guess that's the end of that ... what could have happened? I know I checked them ... the fuel tanks. Oh Christ.*

It was a long walk back to operations. *God, how embarrassing ... my whole damn career, shot. Shit ... did it again.* Erik was devastated.

As he walked into ops, he saw his instructor and the duty officer talking.

"Goddamnit, Evans, I'm giving him a down for an unsatisfactory flight ... That clown Larsen is not ready to fly," Cahill said.

"But we don't give downs at this stage. It's his first flight, for Christ's sake ... and you didn't even fly him."

"Well, the dumb shit didn't even check the fuel."

Evidently the duty officer had enough of the conversation. His voice was stronger as he said, "Listen, Cahill, you were supposed to be out there with him. It's a goddamn orientation flight, and you expect it to be a fuckin' solo or something. We're not accepting a down. ... Now you take Larsen back out and fly ... And if you don't, you can see the Old Man, and that's fine with me. Now that's the last word."

And Cahill stomped off. Apparently he chose to see the Old Man.

*Jeeze they were hot. Thank God, the duty officer was a high*er ranking navy lieutenant commander and could talk to him like that.

The duty officer turned to Erik and said with a half smile, "Hey, don't let this do you in. ... It's just a screw-up, and it's not that bad. You probably forgot to put your finger into the fuel itself ... otherwise, the reflection makes it look full. Happens all the time."

"That's it," Erik said with some eagerness, "You're right, sir. I remember now ... I didn't touch the fuel ... like we were taught in ground school. That's what happened because it looked full."

"Well, you're not the first student to forget ... and trust me, you won't be the last," the duty officer said. "Now, we don't have another instructor available for this afternoon, so you'll be scheduled again tomorrow. I'm sure you'll do fine."

God, I hope so, Erik thought ... still feeling like the dumb-ass of the century.

THE NIGHT WAS LONGER THAN MOST ... WITH DREAMS OF FUEL TRUCKS AND NAVY linemen that jumped out and refueled your bird. *Yes, true nightmares ... and now my class will hear ... what a klutz.*

Erik reported to ground school that next morning. He dreaded to see his classmates, but maybe they didn't hear about it, he wished.

"Hey, guys, it's Erik, the screw-up," Beau said as he kidded, "Good to have you aboard, Ace." Beau was a big, blustery, fun-loving, Southern boy who was liked by all. It was not a surprise to Erik that he was kind of a natural class leader.

"Yea," J.J. chimed in, another Southern big boy who partnered with Beau, "we heard you set an indoor record ... first hop, first down, and never started the engine."

"And gets a new instructor," Beau added.

Christ, how could they have heard so soon? Jeeze I'm dead.

"Well, guys ... I wanted the best ... not some prop jockey, like Captain Cahill," Erik said. "It was a rough decision, but had to do it because I rated a real jet pilot." Then, seriously, he added, "Hey, guys, I screwed up big time, but we're all kidding of course ... Captain Cahill didn't turn me down, did he?"

"Don't know about that," Beau said, "but we did hear that the Old Man chewed Cahill a new ass, and then things really got bad because Cahill told him a few things ... and *voilà* — they haul Captain Cahill off to the funny farm. You know, the rubber bungalow."

"You're shitting me," Erik said, "He really did all that?"

"Yep, guess he mouthed off to the Admiral also," J.J. said, "We only got part of the word ... but sure it happened."

"Holy Christ, can't believe it. Captain Cahill must have snapped," Erik said, "too much Korea, maybe ... now I really feel bad."

Then the ground school instructor came through the door. "Take your seats, gentlemen," he said, "we have work to do."

Erik reported to flight ops that afternoon for his rescheduled hop. He was not quite as perky as the day before, but functional. He saw his student name on the flight board, but it was not listed with Cahill as instructor. The name was Anderson. *Well, damn, I guess the guys were right ... I've really done it this time.*

"Are you Lieutenant Larsen?" the voice asked from behind.

Erik turned and said, "Yessir, I am. ... Are you Captain Anderson, sir?"

"Yes, Erik, that's me, and I was assigned to be your instructor. You had some trouble yesterday ... right?" he said as he smiled.

"Yessir, I did. I really blew it, and I'm not sure what's next ... wish I could start over."

"Erik, remember one thing," Captain Anderson said, "you wouldn't be here if they thought you would flunk out. ... It was a nothing screwup. Now, lets go out and have the best damn time known to man ... well almost."

"Thank you, sir," Erik replied.

And they did!

CHAPTER FORTY-ONE

LORD, IT WAS HECTIC, YES, DEMANDING AND HECTIC. GROUND SCHOOL, FLY-ING, and study seemed to be the order of the day. Erik had never experienced such competition, such pressure, such rivalry to succeed.

Most of the students wanted to be fighter pilots, but, unfortunately, only ten percent of the graduates from basic flight training would be so assigned ... the remainder went on to multi-engine transports or helicopters. So, that primarily explained the added incentive to excel. Results from the competition were the determining factor.

All of the flight phases were demanding. The basic training phases included instruments, formation, gunnery, bombing, aerobatics, cross-countries, and, the toughest of all, qualifying on the airfcraft carrier. And most phases included day and night flights.

And Erik treasured it all. *What a change from my screwed-up almost first flight. Thank God for Captain Anderson and his professionalism ... and patience.*

In spite of the competition, Erik's class had become tight — not from booze, (there was little or no drinking) — tight, because they were colleagues of the same calling. Their missions were consistent, that is, to capture the gold wings and fly. It was natural that many friendships developed and some would be permanent. Erik was no exception.

And there was little time for Jennie Lee and other pretty girls ... just too busy for honest romance. *That will come later ... letters and random dates will have to do for now.*

When the infamous day arrived, you could feel the excitement, the desire, the dread ... all of the mixed emotions that were present. The orders of Erik's

234 • Ralph Sorensen

class were out. The transfers to their advanced duty station were promulgated. And where you go determines what you fly. Those selected for multi-engines or hellos would go to Corpus Christi. The lucky few who were selected for fighter/attack jets would transfer to Chase Field, in Beeville, Texas. *Yes, this is the day of reckoning.*

Beau arrived at the bulletin board first, and, onstage, he was reading the list out loud when Erik joined the eager group. "Jacobs, Johnson, and Slick to Corpus. Sorry guys," he said. "Kramer, to Corpus. Larsen, that's you, Erik ... Chase Field. Hey, guys, the first hop screw-up made it. ... Way to go, Ace. We all three made it, you, J.J., and me. We'll have a ball."

Beau went on with the list, and Erik didn't hear, or care, at the moment. He was dazed by the ecstatic words ... Chase Field. *There is a God ... and I thank you. Only one more hurdle ... and I will have made it.*

Erik departed his classmates ... he was flying high at forty thousand feet ... and still on the ground.

CHASE FIELD LOOKED LIKE MANY OTHER NAVAL FIELDS, BUT IT WASN'T. NO WAY. At least not to Erik. It was the home for advanced training, and when the jets came over to break for landing, he nearly had a minor seizure. *Christ, they're beautiful. One day ... soon.*

The first stages of advanced had gone well for Erik and most of his class. For the past couple of months, they flew the North American T-28s. They were the first class to fly the new aircraft, and it was an exciting bird, even though it was propeller drive. Factory fresh and powerful, the naval version had a 1450 hp radial engine with a three-bladed prop. The aircraft's performance was often discussed by the class (hangar talk, it is called) during breaks, or especially at night after flight operations.

"Can you believe this bird? God, it's great," Beau said.

"Well, I hear the Air Force bought the smaller version. Can you imagine that? It's just 725 hp with a two-bladed prop, I think ... hear it's a real dog," Erik replied.

"Yea, that's what I heard," Beau said, "about time we get a plane better than those clowns."

"Bet I could take 'em in one turn," J.J. said. "Yep, have their ass in any dogfight. Big time." The three laughed. J.J. was always talking about tearing up someone's ass in a dogfight. *He was fun to be around.*

The students were still considered boots by the real pilots, the instructors, but already, Erik could sense a change during those past months ... a change in the students' personalities. They were more boastful as they gained experience. The interservice rivalry was more noticeable. They became more aggressive each day. More confident ... more inflated. And Erik was no exception, he was as cocky as the rest of them, maybe more so. Their flight instructors had to caution them on occasions. "Let's not get too salty," they said, "you can bust your ass in a blink of an eye." *Yes, but it's always the other guy. Not us.*

Erik appreciated advanced training even more so than he did basic. The T-28 was designed with a tricycle gear and was therefore much safer (and easier) to handle on the ground than the old tail wheel models. You didn't have to "S"-turn to see in front of your aircraft during taxi, and it also didn't have the tendency to ground-loop during landing touchdown and rollout (such as the SNJ did). In addition, because they were newly engineered, they were much less frustrating to fly. Everybody agreed that they were a pleasure to pilot.

Another factor that made advanced training more enjoyable was the attitude of the instructors. *They seemed to be more at ease than the basic flight instructors, and more accomplished. And they have more spirit. They seem to enjoy their work, while taking pride in their accomplishments.*

It was not a dull syllabus; however, to the contrary, it was exciting. Formation, instruments, gunnery, bombing, air-to-air tactics, and, of course, the granddaddy of them all, aircraft carrier qualifications made up your routine. It was your day at the office. *And you get paid for this. Can you believe it?*

In spite of all their good hops, their satisfaction of accomplishment, they had, on occasions, their thrills of near-misses and other screw-ups that resulted in minor (sometimes major) ass chewing. But only two in Erik's class dropped out or washed out of the program. Erik didn't know them well, but had seen them often at ground school. They were naval cadets, and, apparently, they couldn't make the grade, so the training command washed them out. It was a good lesson for Erik and the others. To be so close to your goal, and yet, a couple of screw-ups, and you're out. The lesson provided added incentive to work harder. And Erik increased his efforts to be the best of the lot. And for good reason because he understood that the most demanding stage of the syllabus was coming up, soon … like, tomorrow. *Yes, tomorrow, we take on the ultimate, the jets … the jet fighters. That's what it's all about. Don't screw up, Ace.*

TOO MUCH HAS HAPPENED, ERIK THOUGHT WHILE HE WAITED IN THE READY ROOM for his instructor. It would be Erik's first jet flight briefing. And his head was swirling from all that had to be retained. In their new syllabus, they had completed ten straight days of intensive ground school. Study, study, and more study. Jet engines and their performance, hydraulic systems, fuel and boost pumps, oxygen systems, airborne fuel dump, ejection procedures, speed brakes, false starts, hot starts, fire warning lights, and high-altitude flight physiology became household subjects within the class. They had completed the high-altitude pressure chamber and the ejection seat trainers. All new and exciting. You learned that fuel flow and state (quantity) were major concerns of jet flying. As opposed to prop flying (they burned far less, but more expensive fuel) it was critical that you monitored your fuel state constantly. "You'll get the picture," the instructors would say. "You don't deal in a matter of hours. You deal in a matter of minutes. Twelve minutes before flame-out, not twelve or six hours before you run out of fuel. It'll come … it'll be second nature." Erik wasn't so sure of that.

"Hi, I'm Captain Holiday, Skip Holiday," the instructor said, "You are Erik. Right?"

"Yes, sir," Erik said as he stood up and shook hands with the tall Skip Holiday. "Glad to meet you, sir."

They took their seats and Skip said, "This is your first jet hop … and you're here. Bet there was a time or two that you doubted that you would be?"

Erik was a bit puzzled. He didn't respond immediately. *Damn, why did he say that?*

"Well, I did have kind of a shaky start, sir," he said with some embarrassment. "But that was a long time ago. I was hoping no one in advanced had heard of it."

"Don't blame you," Skip said with a wide grin, "but it's our job to know what's going on. We all had a big laugh when we heard that some poor clown got a down on his orientation flight in primary. And then, I'm assigned to Erik

Larsen, and reviewing his jacket, I find him to be that poor clown. God, can you believe that?"*

"I'm sorry, sir. It wasn't a good day." *Jeeze, I'm dead again. Maybe, Dad was right.*

"No ... I thought it was funny, Erik. Hell, you're one of two, at this stage, that's never had a down. Bet you didn't know that?"

"No, sir. Didn't know that." Erik felt much better. He really liked his new instructor ... now.

"Well, I'm going to cover a few things, and when the briefing is over, you will fly the machine, and I'll talk you through it. Okay?"

"Okay, sir." Erik was so anxious he hardly heard the briefing.

They completed their preflight check and were strapping into the T-33. Erik took the front cockpit of the two-place Lockheed tandem jet. It looked like a stretch version of the F-80, one of the United States's first in the field of jet aviation. Erik didn't attempt to hide his enthusiasm. He was fascinated with the layout of the cockpit. It was compact but filled with a horde of switches, dials, instruments, lights, and levers. *This is a long way from Harry and the J-3 Cub.* Then he had to smile when he remembered those days of five years ago ... and Major Belford, his idol, until he decided that Erik didn't show the proper appreciation. *I wonder what happened to him ... the gay blade? The bastard. Get back to work, Erik, it's a big day.*

Actually, this was not Erik's first time in the T-33 because you had to pass a blindfold cockpit test before your first hop. He had spent several hours in the bird memorizing (by feel, not sight) the location of every switch and dial in the cockpit. But that requirement didn't diminish his fascination. And the knowledge amplified his confidence and ability to handle the bird well.

"Okay, Erik, you can start her up as soon as you're comfortable," the soft-spoken instructor said over the intercom.

"Roger, sir, will crank her up," Erik replied. Then he signaled the plane captain and made a smooth start. *Christ, this is beautiful. No prop. No blustery noise from the big reciprocating engine. The smell of smoke and fumes was minimal ... and in the back of the plane, not the front.*

---

* jacket: critique and grades

"Okay, Erik, that's good. Now, take us out as briefed. I'll follow you through."

Erik climbed to thirty-five thousand feet and proceeded with his maneuvers of glides, turns, rolls, and stall recoveries. *It is awesome. It's like a sleek silver bullet. And I'm part of it.*

Captain Chip demonstrated a four-G turn, and Erik felt his G-suit inflate and put additional pressures on his stomach and leg sections. You react by bearing down and tensing these muscles, and this helps retain the blood supply in the upper part of the body. Otherwise, the blood tries to pool in the lower legs and feet because of the increased gravity pull. And it's difficult to think straight if all your blood is in your feet or your ass, he remembered the instructor say.

"Okay, Erik, let's go and shoot a couple of touch and goes (landings to take-offs, without stopping the aircraft), and then we will call it a day."

They set up for landing at one of the practice fields, and the instructor demonstrated the first touch and go.

"Okay, you have it, Erik. Give me a couple, and we're on the way home. You're doing great."

Erik took control of the bird and made his first touch and go by the book. It was a good one — and he was proud.

On the next one, Erik allowed the bird to touch down slightly nose-wheel first, and they bounced into the air. Maybe twenty feet of so. Erik was embarrassed, but *no problem,* he thought. *I'll just correct, and let it touch down again. It's just a bounce, and I've had those before.*

He must have overcorrected because it came down nose-wheel first and bounced a second time. It careened into the air some fifty to a hundred feet ... and the aircraft was dangerously slow. The situation had turned into a can of worms, and Erik knew it. *Christ, you're in trouble now, Ace.* It was not good ... the aircraft was almost stalled ... and Erik was slow to add power.

At that instant he felt the throttle tear from his grip and move forward, fire-walled to full power, and at the same time he heard, "I've got it."

"Roger, you've got it, sir" he replied while releasing the stick. He sat there motionless while the aircraft arched toward the runway. *This is going to be the big one ... I hope we don't splatter. Just one big hairy bounce.*

They were sinking fast, and Erik thought that his screw-up may kill them both (they were too low to eject). *Damn, you've done it this time, Erik. Didn't even get my wings.*

He pictured the fireball he had seen in a training film, where some poor clown porpoised into the runway. It was not a pretty sight. At that instant, he felt the thrust take hold ... and as if by a miracle ... the craft touched down gently on its main gear ... and within seconds regained takeoff speed, and became airborne.

"Now, that's how you handle *that* situation, Erik," the calm voice said over the intercom. "You've got the bird."

"Roger, I have it, sir," Erik replied as he tried to regain his composure. *Jeeze, I can't believe he pulled that off. Lord, you have a lot to learn, Ace.*

"That's what we call a porpoise, Erik. I was going to show you one, but you did it for us. If there's one thing you can do in a T-33 ... it is bust your ass in a porpoise. You touch down nose gear first, and you're going to porpoise ... the oscillations get larger as you overcorrect, and then you're dead — Katie buys the farm. Remember, how we handled it here — and I think you will. Get the power on. Don't be afraid to use it, then keep your flying speed and attitude. Not altitude, but attitude of the aircraft."

Erik made two more landings. They were smooth and professional — in spite of his nervous state-of-mind. *No, Erik, you're not going to porpoise again.*

"Okay, Erik, let's go home. That was a solid hop, and you learned a lot. Just keep up the good work."

Can you imagine an instructor like him? Christ, he has the balls of a high diver. What a guy. What a pro.

CHAPTER FORTY-TWO

THEY FINISHED THE T-33 SYLLABUS, AND THEN MOVED INTO THE PANTHER F9F-2. It was a single seat navy and marine fighter made by Grumman. Panthers were flying in Korea, so it was Erik's first in an aircraft that was operational in present day combat. It was difficult for Erik to express his feelings.

They would graduate within a month. Get their wings. Only twenty hops to go. For thirteen months (seventeen months for the cadets) in the training command, he struggled to make the grade ... to be the best ... to stay alive. To graduate and wear the wings. To be a Marine Corps fighter pilot. *I can't believe it's this close.*

On "campus," as the class called it, those flying the jets were the big boys. Even the instructors seemed to display more respect toward them. *It's an awesome feeling ... from the wannabe football star with electrical tape around his cleats to a fighter pilot in a few years.* Erik had to grin when he thought of that.

The jet flight line was separated from the T-28 line at Chase Field. The jet pilots had their own hangar and ready room. Erik always got a kick out of the big wooden sign in the hangar. It simply stated: Jet flying is hours of *shear* boredom — broken by moments of stark terror. He had to smile each time he saw it. He remembered the porpoise landing on his first jet flight ... and the smooth response of Captain Holiday. *And, I thought that sign was meant for combat flying only. No way.*

Erik and his instructor were preflighting their F9's for a section flight with two aircraft when a flight of two Panthers came over the field at high speed to break for landing. Erik always watched the break maneuver when he could. Today was no exception as he observed the lead aircraft break left (roll ninety degrees left then pull through level). The second bird broke left after a two-second interval and rolled to the ninety-degree position, hesitated momentarily, ...

then continued to roll another twenty to thirty degrees with the nose falling ... and then knife straight into the ground. The muffled explosion shook the earth. Then simultaneously, a tremendous fireball climbed to the sky. Perhaps a thousand feet or so ... and the smoke drifted with the cross wind.

There was no ejection that Erik had seen. It was all finished ... the break for landing was completed in seconds ... and Erik remained motionless. He didn't talk; he didn't move; he didn't cry. He stared at the spot of impact. The crater in the field. The fireball was gone and only a small fire lingered, but he couldn't feel the heat or smell the fumes. *The air is colder.*

The wails of the fire truck shattered the silence as the crash crew raced to the scene. Their flashing lights left chilling patterns that imprinted Erik's mind, even in the daylight hours. Then he suddenly realized that his classmates were the only students flying the F9's. *Oh, Christ ... please, not one of our class.* But he knew the chances were slim that it would be an instructor.

Erik was startled when Captain Holiday said, "Let's get back to the ready room. Find out what we can."

They arrived within moments, and already there were several of Erik's classmates standing around in a somber state. He spotted Beau. Erik was glad to see him alive.

"Not so good, Beau ... bad day," Erik said. "Do we know who it was, yet?"

"Yea, we do, Ace. It was J.J. ... He bought the farm. Poor bastard. Christ, I feel terrible."

Erik was stunned. All he could think of was *why?* And why him?

"I'm sorry, Beau. We all loved J.J. ... What the hell happened? Christ, I saw them come in to the break ... looked good ... and then J.J. augers in and buys the farm. Christ, I don't know," Erik said. "I wish there was something we could do."

"I do too," Beau replied as he put his hand on Erik's shoulder. They both were shaken ... and near tears. It was their first real loss. *It wasn't all play toys.* The duty officer came in and asked, "Did anyone see the accident?"

Erik replied that he saw the break. Yes, he saw the accident.

"Was there anything unusual ... with the break?"

"No, sir, don't think so," Erik replied. Then he thought for a moment and said, "Wait a minute, there was something different. Now, that I think of it, sir, there was. When J.J. started his break, I noticed smoke, or something like it,

242 • Ralph Sorensen

coming from the top of the fuselage. It wasn't much ... I thought it was just a streamer or something. It was just a wisp ... a light spray."

"Was it just aft of the cockpit?" he asked with some concern.

"Yes, sir. It was. Just a foot or so aft. Out of the top, I think."

"Damn, I was afraid of that." the duty officer said, "It has to be the hydraulic boost pump. Must have failed right at the break. Poor guy didn't have a chance ... too low to eject, and a bad angle anyway. Would have fired himself into the ground."

"Listen up, all of you students," he continued, "I know he was a good friend ... a good student. I'm sorry as hell. But you youngsters still have some weeks to go ... and you may come up against this again ... only it will be one of you. Jets are a new ball game with all kinds of new problems. High-pressure hydraulics is just one of them. You blow the boost pump's hydraulic line during break ... or anywhere close to the ground ... and you're in deep trouble. You may buy the farm. And we don't want to lose you. We can buy more planes ... but you're tough to replace."

It was a sobering thought. Erik and the others remained silent for some time. Then the duty officer continued, "I said that J.J. didn't have a chance. Well, that's not quite true. It if was the boost pump, and you catch it early enough, you can override it with your mechanical linkage. Remember, it takes fifty to a hundred pounds of pressure, and you can't baby it. Throw your ass into that stick and make the bird respond. And don't let that nose get down, or you *have* bought the farm. Remember those rudder pedals. You stomp on the top one with all you've got, and the nose will come up if you're close to ninety degrees of roll. I know you don't have the experience yet. And poor J.J. didn't. But we have to stay on top of it, or we won't get the experience. We all do. Your instructors, me ... all of you. You've heard it before ... and now again. You give these birds some slack ... and they'll jump up and bust your ass."

"Make the bird respond." Probably the most impressive words I've heard. And J.J. is dead ... He didn't make the bird respond. And who's next?

CHAPTER FORTY-THREE

LIGHTS DURING THE FINAL THREE WEEKS WENT WELL. NO ACCIDENTS. AT least no big ones, just minor incidents such as a few blown tires. But the students kept their aircraft on the runway and avoided serious damage. Erik was lucky. He experienced some hydroplaning, but he didn't blow a tire. He was learning.

The flying was over and they would graduate in five days. J.J.'s death had put a damper on the final weeks. His crash was not easy to accept. He was seriously missed, but Erik could feel a resurgence of class pride and spirit. Again, they were all becoming hot fighter jocks (to hear them tell it), and they were certainly a brassy bunch of boots. And that included Erik. *Maybe we have a right to be … for awhile, anyway.*

The last days were set aside for administrative purposes. Cadets had to get new officer uniforms (they were promoted to second lieutenant or ensign when they received their wings), and all had to get their orders, pack, and arrange transportation to their next duty station.

Erik called home that evening to let the folks know that he was alive and well … and would soon be a fighter pilot. His mother answered the phone. Erik was glad to hear her voice.

"Well, wanted to call and let you know that I made it, Mom. Put the wings on Sunday morning," he said.

"Oh, I think that's great, honey, but I never had any doubts. … I knew you would do it. Congratulations, sweetheart."

"Well, there were times when I had my doubts … but that's over the dam. And I thank you for hanging in there … couldn't have done it without you."

"Oh, silly, you know you could've … but what a nice thing to say."

"And speaking of support, or non-support, I should say … where is Dad?" Erik asked with some humor.

"Oh ... You know he loves you, honey. But, anyway, he doesn't get home much. You know ... work and all."

Her words startled Erik. "What do you mean he doesn't get home much? Not at nights?"

"No, not often. It's been a couple of weeks. Not sure what's going on ..."

That bastard. "Well, Mom, you know he always did get carried away with his work. It's just a stage ... I'm sure. It'll work out." *That son-of-a-bitch.*

"Well, that's kind of what I hope ...," she said, her voice trailing.

Erik sensed that she may be in tears. It tore him apart. "Mom, it's going to be okay," he said, "You know how he works all the time. Lord, I've seen him sleep in the chair at the plant. And that's not unusual. It's probably no more than that." He hoped it wasn't a lie.

"Well, that's what I thought too. He does work hard," she replied in a more positive tone.

Erik felt more relieved. "Mom, I heard that our orders are in, and I'm going to a fighter group at El Toro MCAS. That's in California ... and if you want, I'll send you a ticket for a visit. Would you like that?"

"Oh, I would love that," she replied. "I feel better already, ... I've never been to California. Yes, that would be fun."

"Alright, we'll plan on it. I'll call you soon and let you know," he said.

"Okay, honey, I'll talk to you then ... Oh, almost forgot. I met Jennie Lee last week ... up at the store. What a lovely girl. She asked about you ... said she wanted to call you, if that would be all right. Asked me to tell you that she didn't go with Daryl anymore. ... I don't know him, but he had a court martial, or something. Anyway, he's out of the army, and they split."

"Hey, that's great, Mom. Makes my day. So you really liked her?" he said.

"Yes, I do ... she's just lovely. I didn't know you dated her."

"Just a couple of times, Mom. Had a few things to work out, so it didn't go much further. But maybe it can now," he said.

How could I ever forget Mrs. Stover asking me, "What's a rubber? And what size did I want?" What a night.

Then, Erik was rather ashamed of himself. *I'm all excited about Jennie Lee, while poor Mom is trying to cope with a rough marriage. I best wind it up.*

"Well, Mom, I have to report to admin. You take care ... will call next week. Thanks, and love you." *Christ, what a call. So good. So bad. Maybe I'll send two airline tickets.*

That night, the night before graduation, was difficult for Erik. He didn't celebrate with his classmates because he wanted to be alone. The talk with his mom had affected him more than he realized. As he gained maturity and confidence in flight training, he started to believe (more than hope) that things would work out between his father and himself. Now, the news that Dad was staying away from home was most disturbing. It was the pits. Erik was not ready to accept it.

What the hell is going on, Dad? And what about, Mom? You can't just pick up and leave after twenty-some years of marriage. And, dammit, you should be here for my graduation. You were always there for my failures ... why not now? Too jealous? Too insecure? Too afraid that we may shake hands, even hug in forgiveness ... and I would know that you understood what it took to get here. Afraid that you would realize your son's pain and tears, his anger, his sense of failure, his loneliness ... and his desperation to be a success. Yes, Dad, you would have been proud of your son. You would have cared!

Then, Erik was shamed. He realized that he was angry ... and feeling sorry for himself. And he was glad that no one saw him ... he was alone.

Erik was in his dress-whites uniform the next morning. The differences with his father didn't seem as important now. *Last night must have been a tremendous release. I've made it, and, if I feel sorry for anyone, it's Dad. Sure not for myself. No way ... I'm just too damn happy. Yes, Dad, I'm in my element now.*

The Admiral pinned the wings on Second Lieutenant Larsen. His Wings of Gold. *This has to be the best moment of my entire twenty-one years. Yes, the klutz from West Virginia, ole Banana Head, made it. Thank you, God.*

Then, he sent two messages by Western Union. One home, the other to the packing house.

The first read:

246 • **Ralph Sorensen**

> Dear Mom,
>
> Yes, few *are* chosen, and thanks to you (and Dad),
> I'm one of them.
>
> Love,
> Erik

*And Burt, here is the second message: a little card from your son, Erik —
you know — the one who quits? The one who made lieutenant in the United
States Marine Corps? The jet fighter pilot?*

> Dear Dad,
>
> Fuck you ...

EPILOGUE

Gabe healed properly and got out of the mines. He found a good job in heavy equipment.

The short man that Long Willy Washington hit with his false arm recovered. But, he didn't return to the back of the barbershop.

Also, Long Willy never returned to Mucky Hollow.

Erik never saw Paula again. But wished he had.

Scantsville High School has a sign that reads: "No bull-dick canes allowed on premises."

Burt ran off with another woman. And he divorced Rose.

Erik was a respected jet fighter pilot at El Toro, MCAS, California.

Rose and Jennie Lee visited El Toro. All had a great time. Including Erik.

Erik ceased to think of himself as a failure ... just an occasional screw-up.

**For more on the future of Erik and his humorous
and heartrending episodes, read the forthcoming sequel,**

Absurdities of War